The

Rise

of a

Necromancer

Rosie Scott

 This is a work of fiction. The names, characters, locales, and events are pure invention, and all incidents come from the author's imagination alone.

Cover art by Nikita Drizhenko.
Map design by Rosie Scott.

Dedication

To my two favorite dudes. For your support, your love, and your willingness to brainstorm with me to make this book as awesome as it can be. I am grateful to share my life and imagination with you.

I dedicate Kenady's character to all the tormentors of my youth who were determined to drive me to suicide with their cruelty and came dangerously close to success. Kenady is the culmination of all of you. May either humanity or justice find you.

Most importantly, to all those readers affected by mental traumas caused by the cruelty of others, may this story give you hope for a brighter future. Just remember: *the best form of revenge is success.*

Other Books by Rosie Scott:

Dystopian

The New World series:

The Resistance

The Betrayal

The Acquisition

The Insurrection

The Calamity

Fantasy

The Six Elements series:

Fire

Earth

Water

Air

Life

Death

The Six Elements Origins:

Rise of a Necromancer

For More Information:

Publisher's Website:
www.amazon.com/author/rosiescott

Author Blog:
www.rosiescottbooks.wordpress.com/

Business Inquiry Contact:
rosiescottbooks@gmail.com

Alderi - Casually referred to as *dark elves*. Blue, purple, or blackish in color with black eyes. A brutal and crude race suited to the underground and sly dealings.

Alteration magic - A school of magic dealing in the altering of material objects. Used for practical purposes and for battle support. Includes spells like telekinesis, detect life, and shape shifting.

Amora - The goddess of love.

Ancients - An ancient race of beings that not much is known about. Possibly based only in myth.

Arrayis - The world, consisting of all continents and oceans.

Bjorn Berg - A general of the Seran Army and a member of Sirius Sera's court.

Cel Mountains - A mountain range between the Seran Forest and the forests of Celendar, containing the dwarven city of Brognel and the secluded Whispermere.

Celdic - Casually referred to as *wood elves.* A peace-seeking race not prone to battle. Most have light complexions and stand slightly taller than humans. Most reside in the tree city of Celendar.

Celendar - One of Chairel's four major cities, made of nothing but trees that date back to the time of the Ancients. The pearl-white bark of these trees is found nowhere else on Arrayis, and the trees rival the nearby Cel Mountains.

Cerin Heliot - Dual caster of death and life magic. Half-breed of Icilic and human blood.

Chairel - A rich country known for its four major cities of Sera, Comercio, Celendar, and Narangar. A land of forests, grasslands, and mountains. Known for its strict magical law system.

Dark Star - The season of winter. 90 days in length. Last season of the year.

Dual Caster - A mage capable of wielding two elements.

Elemental magic - Sometimes referred to as destruction magic. Deals in the elements of fire, earth, water, air, life, and death.

Gods - An race of creatures said to have been created by the Ancients. The source of most of the religions on Arrayis. While many claim they actually once existed as tangible beings, none have been heard from in hundreds of years.
Golden Era - An era spanning 5782 years before the current Mortal Era, said to be a time of discovery, including the forming of most major nations of Arrayis. An era of which little is known for sure, given the mix of myth and history passed through the generations.
Glacia - A continent that also serves as its own country, home to the Icilic elves, at the northern most point of Arrayis.
Half-breed - A person who carries the blood of two separate races and contains traits from both.
High Star - The season of summer. 90 days in length. Second season of the year.
Human - The weakest of the mortal races, and the most common race to populate Chairel.
Icilic - Casually referred to as *snow elves.* The oldest lineage of elves in all of Arrayis, known for their magical abilities and disdain for other races. Extreme isolationists.
Illusion magic - A school of magic dealing in the creation of illusions for entertainment or nefarious purposes. Includes spells such as charm, frenzy, or invisibility.
Kai Sera - Wielder of the six elements. Adopted daughter of Sirius Sera.
Kenady Urien - A peer and tormentor of Cerin Heliot's at the Seran University of Magic. Comes from a wealthy and influential family. Dual caster of earth and life magic.
Kilgorian Law - Named after its discoverer, Arturian Kilgor, it is a scientific law which states a mage's magic energy is pulled from reserves in a natural order: environment, weather, self.
Leeching High - A term to describe the heightened state of awareness and strength necromancers can achieve by leeching the life force of foes. Usually takes six harvested lives to trigger, though injuries/race/size

can affect the amount of life force available from one foe. The high only fades once the energy is expended through magic use or fatigue from physical exertion or time.

Moons - Another word for *seasons*, as in, there are four moons in a year. Sometimes used as a method to describe the passing of time.

Mortal Era - The current era, directly following the Golden Era, said to belong to the mortal races of Arrayis given the disappearance of the immortal races such as the Ancients and the gods. Any dates referred to in *The Six Elements* are of the Mortal Era, unless otherwise specified.

Nahara - A poorer country known for its giant beasts and vast deserts. Just south of Chairel.

Necromancy - Another term for death magic, and the only element that is banned across Chairel. Deals in the reanimation of the dead, the leeching of energy from life, and the decomposition or plague of living forms.

New Moon - The season of spring. 90 days in length. First season of the year.

Orders of the Mages - The name that encompasses all of Sera's mage armies, broken down into different Orders.

Queen Edrys - The ruler of Chairel. Has a regent in each of the four major cities. Resides in Comercio.

Red Moon - The season of autumn. 90 days in length. Third season of the year.

Sera - A rich, mostly human city that was built on the edge of a mountain. Attracts tourists and seekers of magic services. Home to The Twelve, and the famous Orders of the Mages. Ruled by Sirius Sera, who also serves as headmaster to the Seran University.

Seran University - The only place in Chairel that officially teaches magic and grants magic licenses to prospective mages.

Servis Ocean - The ocean which separates the continents of Arrayis.

Sirius Sera - Headmaster of the Seran University and regent of Sera. Wielder of air and life magic.

Terran Sera - Biological son of Sirius Sera, and heir to the Seran throne. Wielder of earth magic.

The Twelve - A prestigious arm of the Seran Army, consisting of twelve of its highest ranked soldiers, utilized for reconnaissance missions and to serve justice in the name of Sirius Sera. Each is awarded her or his own griffon mount.

Valerius the Undying - A rogue necromancer that serves as Chairel's justification for the prohibition of necromancy. Though he was human, he lived from 5592 G.E. to 267 M.E. (457 years) by feeding off the life force of the living.

Life

Givara le life - Heal

Sheel a phisica - Shield for physical damage

Sheel a mana - Shield for energy damage (ward)

Death

Enflic le plague - Inflict plague

Corpa te risa - Raise corpse (singular)

Corpa te risa a multipla - Raise corpses (area of effect)

Absort la mana del life - Leech (translates to "absorb energy from life")

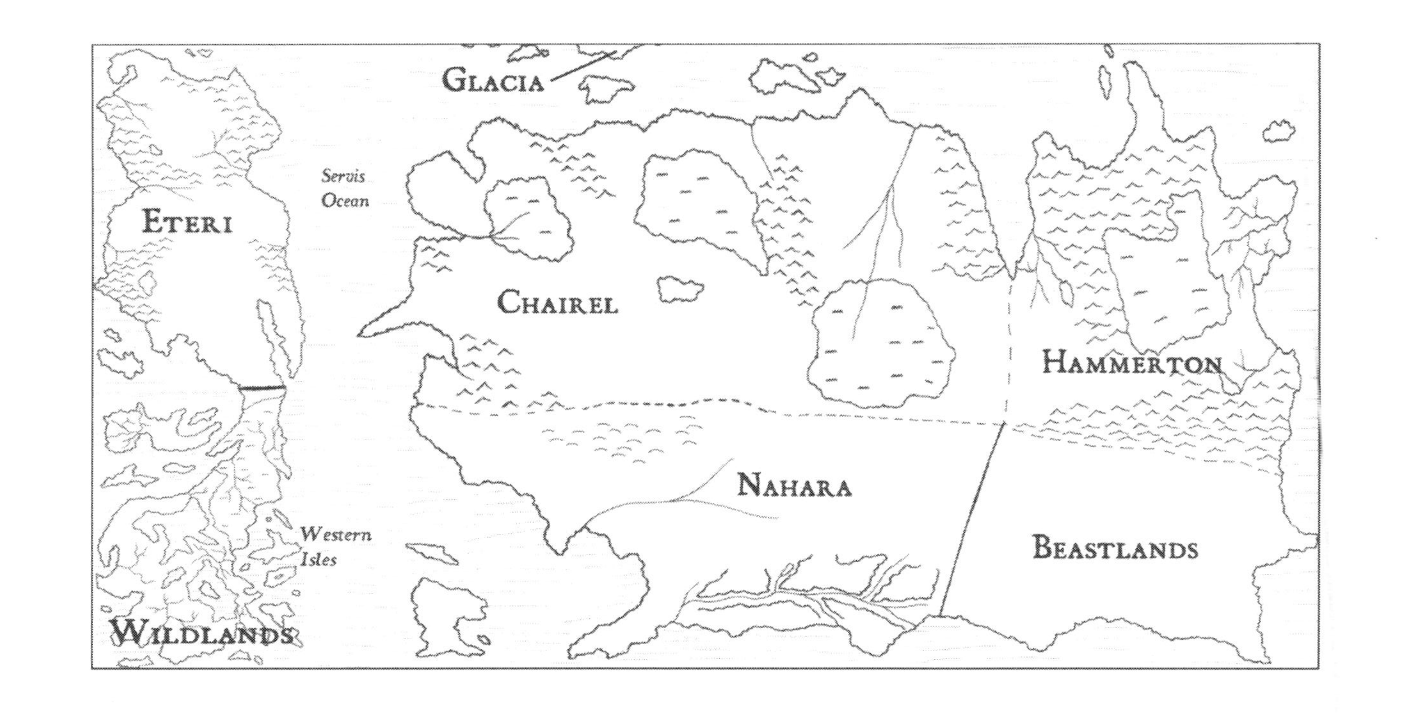
Glacia
Servis
Ocean
Eteri
Chairel
Hammerton
Nahara
Western
Isles
Beastlands
Wildlands

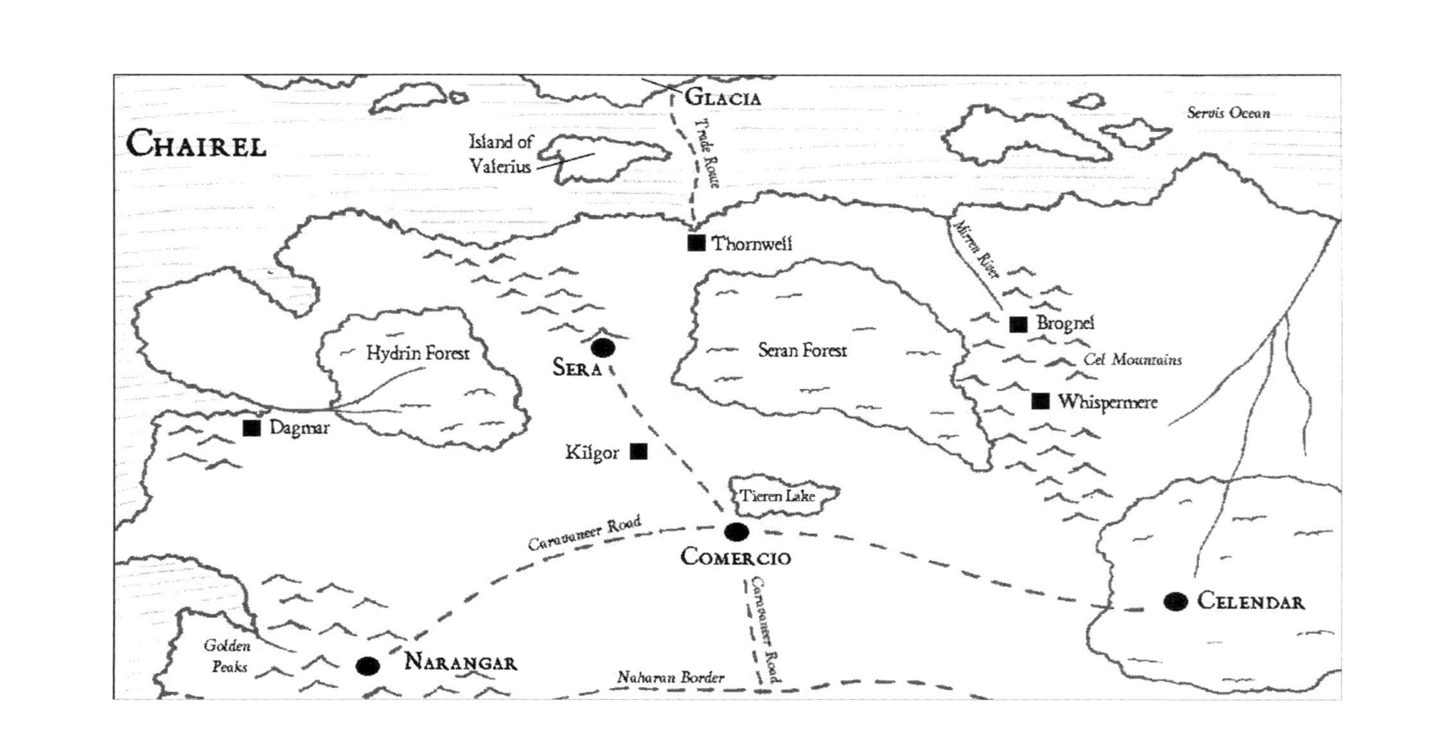
Chairel
Glacia
Trade Route
Island of Valerius
Servis Ocean
Thornwell
Mirren River
Brognel
Cel Mountains
Whispermere
Hydrin Forest
Seran Forest
Sera
Dagmar
Kilgor
Tieren Lake
Caravaneer Road
Comercio
Caravaneer Road
Celendar
Golden Peaks
Narangar
Naharan Border

One

14th of New Moon, 407

The ever-expansive waters rolled toward the northern coast of Chairel, rocking our small fishing boat and persuading it to inch closer to the town of Thornwell. The murmur of my hometown was a constant buzz far to the left, but the water had my attention as I waited for nibbles on the hooked bait of my fishing rod. A cool breeze blew over my mother and me, picking up our black locks and coaxing them along its current. Despite the chill, neither of us wore more than simple tunics and slacks. My mother's Icilic blood ensured I would forever have a higher resistance to cold weather. But while I was merely comfortable in such weather, she glistened with sweat on the other bench. Unlike me, she was full-blooded. Even mild conditions were hot for her.

"We should come back out in the evening," I commented, gazing out over the calm ocean waters to the north. "Few fish are biting now."

My mother's full lips pulled up on one side in an admiring smile, and she teased, "You're a natural fisher, Cerin. It's like you've done this all your life."

I raised an eyebrow and replied, "I have. *You* taught me."

She chuckled, rested her fishing pole against the side of the boat, and leaned down to pull off her clunky leather boots. Once her feet were free, she wiggled her toes in the open air to cool them off. "I know. It just makes things hard on me, is all. I needed an excuse to bring you out here to talk to you, so I lured you in with the prospect of fishing."

"Like a fish to bait," I mused dryly.

My mother laughed joyously. Her black hair swept back from her face, exposing her glistening pale skin to the direct sunlight until it was transparent. For a moment, every vein beneath her skin was visible before she pulled her hair protectively back into place. "Regardless, you know the ways of the ocean. Your persistence in arguing that it's a terrible time for fishing proves you're already an expert. I can't rely on such lies to get you alone."

"Why do you need lies to get me alone at all?" I questioned. I worked on pulling the fishing line out of the water and looping it back to the tip of the rod.

My mother silently watched me work. Then, "There are things I have told you never to reveal or speak of to others." My gaze moved up to meet hers in realization. The silver eyes that matched mine went somber as she added, "I think it's time you learned why."

I said nothing. I waited for her to continue as I put the fishing rod beside me in the boat. Another breeze blew inland from the open ocean, picking up my long hair and convincing it to flee the heat of my neck.

"You know the story of how I met your father," my mother continued, bringing her fishing rod back in the boat to give her eyes something else to focus on. "But that's where all this secrecy starts, so I think it's necessary to tell you again. This time, I'll leave nothing out."

"You came from Glacia," I said, more as a test of the statement's truthfulness than anything else. Glacia was both a country and a continent of solid ice that sat far to the north of all other countries on Arrayis. In Glacia, the Icilic elves reigned. Little was known of the country outside of those who lived there, for the so-called snow elves were extreme isolationists. My mother was the only Icilic elf I'd ever seen outside of those who came to the shores of Thornwell on trading ships, and even then I'd been shooed inside like even their presence was dangerous.

"I did," my mother affirmed, peering off to the north as if she'd be able to see the giant glacier. "Glacia is beautiful, Cerin. It is a land of ice and snow, but its people are as cold as the land." Her eyes swept back to mine. "Your grandfather is rich. He is a merchant who handles the imports and exports in southern Glacia. He raised me in the business. As you know, I met your father when he came to the coast to trade. He wasn't allowed on shore in Glacia. They allow none other than the Icilic on shore."

I frowned. "Why?"

My mother met my gaze. "The Icilic are the oldest lineage of elves, Cerin. They are proud of this. Over the millennia, it has made them arrogant and uncaring. They don't like to associate with the other races for fear of diluting their blood. If Glacia had access to metal reserves and other such necessities, I doubt they would rely on the other races for anything. Regardless, I saw Lucius a few times over the years. He made it a point to come to my dock because he knew I would be in charge of handling his cargo. We found each other exotic. Your father—he was forbidden. Falling in love with a human was never an option for my people. Everyone assumed I viewed him with as much disgust as they did, so they trusted me to enter his ship alone." She sighed and looked off over the ocean again. "I became pregnant with you while I lived in Glacia. I'd never been more scared in my life."

"Was the pregnancy hard?" I asked, trying to understand.

She chuckled lightly and reached over to pat my knee. "Bless your naïve heart. I wish I could keep you in the dark forever, Cerin, so you would never have to learn just how cruel the world truly is." She sighed and leaned back again. "I love you more than anything else in the world."

"I love you, too."

"I want you to know that most of all before I tell you this: I felt a need to terminate the pregnancy. When I found out I was pregnant, I wanted you so badly. But I knew having you would give you a death sentence." She exhaled heavily and announced, "The Icilic want you dead, Cerin, and they will kill you on sight."

My heart sunk. "I've never met an Icilic other than you."

"I know," my mother conceded, her face contorted with pain as she reached out and brushed through my hair with her fingertips. "It doesn't matter. They must cleanse impurities in the bloodline. Having you was selfish. But once I carried you in my belly, I couldn't terminate. I loved your father, and I *wanted* this. I wanted a life with him. I wanted to raise you. Such a life was impossible in Glacia. As soon as I told your father I was pregnant, we formed a plan of escape. I left everything behind. My career, my family, my home. I told no one where I was headed. I hid on Lucius's ship until he came back here to Thornwell. Taught your father everything I knew about fishing because he needed to change jobs for his own safety. But the life of a fisher is less prestigious than that of a trader, Cerin. Our lives are hard compared to many, and that is because of the changes we had to make to keep you safe. Your father and I try to give you the best life we can." She frowned, and her fingers moved from my long hair to my jaw. "You know that, right? We would endure every hardship just to keep you happy and safe."

"I don't want you enduring any hardships for me," I replied.

"We do it because we have to," she said.

"You left without telling the others where you were going or why," I pointed out. "We should be free of them here. Don't let their bigotry affect us in Chairel."

"My father is rich and well-known in Glacia," she replied. "When I went missing, there were no doubt rumors and theories. There have been questions thrown around at the docks about me from Glacia's traders. They search for me, Cerin, and the Icilic bigotry is relentless. If they find out I fled with a human and diluted the bloodline by having you, our lives will be in danger."

"They would *murder* to keep the bloodline pure?"

"Absolutely," my mother said with no hesitation. "They hunt down and kill every Icilic half-breed they see or hear about. It doesn't matter to them how it happened. It doesn't matter if the person is minding their own business. They will kill you on sight simply for being a half-breed, and they won't hesitate to kill me for going against the law of my people. *This* is why I taught you to go inside when Icilic traders come here. *This* is why I told you to only consider yourself human. Let no one know you are an Icilic half-breed, Cerin. People chatter. Information spreads." She reached out to graze a finger over the rounded upper arc of my ear. "Many consider human ears on an elven half-breed to be a sign of inferiority, but when you came out of my womb with human ears, I considered it a miracle. Your ears cannot give away your identity. Your paleness is unique among humans. Some may mention it to you. You may avert the question or even lie, but never admit it comes from your blood." She hesitated and added, "When you are out in public, it may be best to cover up. By hiding your skin in shadow, its paleness will be less noticeable."

I couldn't help but feel hurt by that prospect. "You expect me to live forever hiding who I am?"

My mother noticed the pain in my voice, and her expression fell into one of sadness and regret. "If it would keep you from harm, I have to suggest it. I would never expect you to live in any particular way, Cerin. They imposed such a thing on me and I rejected it. But know that if you refuse to *hide,* you must be prepared to *fight.*"

I nodded shakily and sighed. "Okay. Who will train me?"

My mother chuckled lightly. "Let's hold off on that for now, son. There's a reason I'm bringing all of this up now. Some in Thornwell already know about your origins."

"You told *me* not to tell anyone," I pointed out, noting the inconsistency.

"I told no one, if that's what you're hinting at," she replied, her tone lightly teasing despite the heavy subject. "I was noticeably pregnant when I first came here. You popped out not long afterward, looking just as much like Lucius as you resemble me. People put two and two together, Cerin. We said nothing. We didn't *have* to." She nodded toward Thornwell. Under the early afternoon sun, people in thin clothing traversed well-worn dirt and grass streets between small wood cabins. A few of my father's fishing friends prepared a boat to take out for an evening catch. All were human; while dwarven and Celdic traders sometimes stopped by Thornwell to trade, my mother was the only Icilic to live outside of Glacia as far as we knew. "These people aren't looking for trouble. They like us because we take care of ourselves and cause no trouble. But Thornwell is a small town, and we're *all* poor here. No one's looking for trouble because they can't *afford* it. Outside of Thornwell, give no one your trust unless they earn it."

"I'm not planning on leaving."

"Aren't you?" My mother smiled at me and grabbed the two oars lying by her bare feet. "Let's go home, son. I have a surprise for you."

I smirked as she rowed us back to shore. "Your surprises aren't the best, mother. Being told I have a target on my head didn't brighten my day."

"That was necessary for you to know before I gave you the *good* surprise," she said as an excuse.

I waved when I glimpsed my father enthusiastically greeting us from the coast near our small home. Though he looked just as poor as the rest of us with his worn clothing, calloused fingers, and smudges of dirt on exposed skin, he was still a handsome sight. He kept his black hair as long as mine, and it swept by his upper neck just beneath a sharp jawline. He was tall for a human at just an inch under six feet. My mother was the same height, but she was short for an elf. Elves tended to be tall and thin while the short height of humans was only second to dwarves. My father often teased my mother about how if she had been any taller, he wouldn't have fallen in love with her. It was a lie, of course; my parents adored one another, but it was rare to see men with women taller than themselves.

As our small boat reached the shore, my father reached out to grab it and tug it up onto land.

"Well, aren't you the gentleman?" my mother teased. In response, my father held out a hand to help her out of the boat. My mother promptly ignored it and climbed out herself, taking bundles of fishing gear with her.

My father glanced around at our belongings. "Get back out there," he jested dryly. "You didn't catch anything."

"Wasn't anything to *catch,"* I replied, grabbing the small box of bait I'd taken out with us. Inside was a mound of moist earth and wiggling worms from our garden. As I buried the worms back in the shaded dirt and rinsed my hands in a nearby bucket of water, I overheard my parents talking as my mother situated our boat on the hangers she'd installed on the other side of our tiny cabin.

"How'd it go?" my father asked.

"Oh, you know," my mother replied vaguely. "As expected. I spent most of the time talking and he spoke five words here and there. He gets his quietude from you, you know."

"Ah. Blame *me,"* my father jested lightly.

"I *will.* It drives me crazy sometimes. I can never tell what's going on in that mind of his. I've become an expert at judging facial expressions."

My father chuckled in response. "Just ask him outright, Celena. He's always honest with you. Just takes a little prodding to open up, is all."

Quietly, I circled the house to enter it. My parents stopped conversing as they watched me enter the cabin and close the door behind me. Their murmuring picked up again once I was inside, but I could no longer ascertain their conversation. It amused me that they thought their prior conversation had gone unnoticed. Sometimes the best part of being quiet is that eavesdropping gets easier. People oddly don't expect one to hear noise if they rarely make it.

Our tiny cottage was dark and filled with shadows until I brushed back the drapes and lit an oil lamp with a match before setting it back on the kitchen table. Its heat leaked into the vicinity, so I opened the window facing the ocean, allowing the scent of its salt and the coolness of its breezes to come through. Movement in the northern Servis caught my eye. A trading vessel cut through the calm ocean waters. Instead of the green sails of Chairel ships or the blue sails of the neighboring country of Hammerton, someone made this ship's sails out of the tanned hide of mammals. They decorated the ship's bow with the cranium and horns of a creature. Such things were signs of Glacia's ships. Now that I knew more about my connection to them, my eyes bored into the side of the vessel as it came to dock. The squeak of the front door finally got me to break my glare, and I plopped down in a chair at the kitchen table.

My father smiled warmly at me as he walked in and tossed a small box on the table. "Got something for you."

I leaned forward and pulled the box toward me. As soon as I lifted its lid, the welcoming aroma of fresh tea leaves hit my nose. "Thank you. Did you trade for these?"

"Of course," he replied. "Nadiya told me today that she has a section of her garden dedicated to your favorite tea. So I told her I catch her favorite fish just to trade for it." He chuckled. "Oh, and Ela asked about you."

I thought of our neighbor Nadiya's fair-haired daughter and asked, *"Why?"*

As my father laughed at my perplexity, my mother sighed. "Let him be clueless, Lucius," she mused. "If he gets into any trouble at all, it won't be over girls. They'd have to be hardheaded and persistent just to get *through* to him."

"I'm eleven," I protested dryly. "Don't *even* start."

My father laughed again at my dry humor and collapsed heavily in the chair opposite me. "What's wrong with Ela?"

"Nothing's *wrong* with her," I replied vaguely.

"Lucius," my mother warned, glaring at him.

"I'm *curious,* Celena," he replied with a smile. "My son is growing into a man. I want a glimpse into the type he'll become."

"He's eleven," came her retort, repeating my own words.

"That number means nothing," my father argued. "His voice already changed." Turning his attention back to me, he prodded, "Ela's been batting her eyelashes at you for almost a year. Every time I visit that family I have to tell her how you're doing, even if nothing ever changes."

"That's...weird," I decided.

Even my mother chuckled at that. "What's weird about it?" she inquired, sitting on their bed across the open floor to take off her boots.

"Why wouldn't she ask me herself?"

My mother raised an eyebrow as she exchanged glances with my father. "Some girls lack in confidence, Cerin," she replied after a moment.

"Then there's your answer." My eyes met my father's. "There's nothing wrong with being fragile, but fragile people don't catch my attention."

"You're wrong, Celena," my father said, leaning back in his chair and clasping his hands behind his head. "He *will* get into trouble because of girls. He's after the *fiery* types."

My mother chuckled before it evolved into a worried sigh. "Gods, Lucius, don't make this harder than it has to be."

Father sobered. "Sorry. I'm just having good fun, is all." His fingers tapped a random tune on the wooden table as we waited for my mother to join us. When she did, she brought over her lute and an envelope. The envelope had a broken red wax seal on its flap. She set the envelope on the table so its label faced downward and then sat in the chair next to my father.

Mother bit her lip as she stared at me a moment. "How do you feel about what you learned today?"

"Overwhelmed." After my parents exchanged glances, I thought of their earlier conversation about my lack of words and added, "I don't know what more you want me to say. There are people who want me dead for things outside my control. I don't want to hide in Thornwell forever, but I mentioned learning to fight, and you told me to wait."

"Remember when we talked about your options for the future?" my father asked, glancing up at me as he drew invisible designs on the table. "You said magic interested you."

“Many are interested in learning magic,” I replied. “Few get to.” Magic was a commodity in Chairel, only taught at the Seran University of Magic to the west for exorbitant amounts of gold. Only the rich could afford an education there, and the rarity of magic and corresponding services ensured that educated mages only became richer. My mother often told me that given my pale skin and black hair, I would likely learn one of the elements of air, life, or death. Because Chairel and its neighboring countries banned death magic, necromancy wasn't an option for me. But there were other elements and the lesser schools of alteration and illusion. Because the Icilic were a magical race, I was likely magically literate. None of that mattered if we couldn't afford a Seran education. And from where I sat, I could see the entirety of our house and all our belongings. We weren't swimming in gold.

My mother played a few notes on her lute before picking up the envelope and tossing it over the table at me. I frowned, but I picked it up and turned it around. The return address immediately caught my eye.

Seran University of Magic
Office of Sirius Sera
100 University Court

The tune my mother played on her lute picked up its pace in excitement. I opened the flap of the envelope and pulled out the letter.

Celena I'lluminah:

The Seran University of Magic has received your application and fees for your son, Cerin Heliot, and has considered its merits. We are pleased to inform you that Cerin passes the entry requirements, and we believe he would be a good fit for our magic program. To enroll Cerin in the 407-408 school year, please send 10,000 gold pieces and the enclosed entry form with a trusted messenger. Alternatively, you may send the gold with Cerin when he travels to Sera for the oncoming school year. Dormitories open on the 1st of Red Moon. (The Seran University may not be held responsible for any lost, stolen, or misplaced dues, nor is the entity required to take in children sent to Sera without entry fees.)

The 10,000 gold includes the two-year pre-magic programs and dormitory fees. We will send a second bill in New Moon 409 to collect for the first two years of magic training. Please see enclosed list of elements and corresponding fees so you may financially prepare. Life magic training automatically includes surgeon's classes unless you opt out (at an additional 25,000 gold per year). If your son is a dual caster, fees will increase according to both elements. If you'd like to opt out of particular schools of magic or education for dual elements due to financial concerns or otherwise, we will send forms to this address giving you these options.

Thank you for your application. We look forward to receiving Cerin's entry fees and welcoming him here in Red Moon.

Sirius Sera

I folded the letter and put it back in the envelope without a word. The lute's playful tune slowed before all went silent. My mother's hopeful face faded. “Aren't you happy?” she questioned.

“We can't *afford* this,” I protested. “It's ten thousand gold for *pre*-magic training. That's more gold than I ever expect to see in my lifetime, and all just to line their pockets. That's gold out the window before I learn a *single* spell.”

“You are pale, son,” my father spoke up, nodding toward my bare forearms that glistened in the flickering glow of the oil lamp. “You are a fantastic candidate for life magic. And you know life mages are the richest of all. It may cost us dearly now, but it will set you for life.”

My heart ached at the hopeful, desperate tone with which he'd said it. “Did you *see* how much they charge for surgeon's training? Even if I learn life magic, it will render you both destitute before I make any of that gold back. And that's *if* I learn it.” I flipped a hand out to call attention to where their marital bed was on the opposite wall of my own. Our house was essentially a one-room shack. “We're *already* destitute. I will fish for my gold. I enjoy it and I do it well. I couldn't enjoy learning magic if I had to think about you two here at home struggling.”

“What do you feel toward the Icilic, Cerin?” my mother asked. It was a seemingly random question, but she asked it with purpose as she lightly fingered the polished wood of her lute. “Especially now that you know the truth of their culture?”

“Anger,” I said. *“That's* what I feel.”

“So...” she trailed off and met my eyes again. “How would you feel if you could learn magic using *their* gold? What if those who want you dead had to pay for you to train in magic and better your life when they only want to end it?”

I was quiet for a few moments. “How is that possible?”

"I told you your Icilic grandfather is rich, Cerin," my mother replied. "He taught me everything there was to know about his business, including its finances. He's as racist against the humans as any Icilic. When I left, I relieved him of some of his endless gold to help support the grandson he'd never see." A mischievous smile brightened her pale features. "The Icilic are naturals with life and death magic. The chances of you learning life is high. We *are* destitute. But if you become a healer, you could change that. We wouldn't have to live in Thornwell. We could live somewhere far away from the northern coast where the Icilic still search for me. It might not even matter by then if you tell others your true nature because you could afford to hire mercenaries to guard you."

"You've thought this through," I murmured.

"We would never force you to do anything you don't want to do," she replied. "I've kept the gold safe all these years hoping magic would interest you. You said it *did*, so I hope you're not angry with me for setting all of this up without asking you. I wanted to surprise you. I have set nothing in stone yet. If you're interested, I'll send the gold with you when you go. Otherwise, we can forget all about this and put it behind us."

My parents were so excited for me that I felt the energy of it in the air. The only qualm about the plan I'd had was rendered nonexistent. I'd never considered learning magic because the option never felt obtainable. Now that it was, I jumped at the chance.

A smile of excitement lifted my lips, and my mother's face brightened as she clapped with glee, anticipating my next words. "I guess I'll be going to Sera."

Two

A full moon after agreeing to train in Sera came the day to leave Thornwell. I felt jittery with nerves even though I wouldn't see the famous city of magic for two-thirds of a season, for that was how long it would take to get there. My parents couldn't come with, for they planned on overworking themselves to save up additional gold while I was away. If I proved to be a natural with life magic as they surmised, my education would be the most expensive of all. As rich as my Icilic grandfather was, my mother hadn't stolen all his gold, and what she had taken wasn't limitless. As I watched them rush around our tiny home ensuring I had everything packed to leave with the waiting trading caravan, I felt a rush of gratefulness rise in my chest.

"Thank you," I said. Like all the words lucky enough to escape my lips, they were low and traveled over the rough edge that had belonged to my voice ever since it changed from a boy's to a man's.

My mother stopped searching through a cabinet and glanced back. "Did you say something?"

"I said thank you," I repeated, looking away when her silver eyes humbled with realization. "For setting all this up. For using this gold for my education instead of just buying a bigger house."

"Oh, *Cerin,*" my mother blurted, hurrying over and grabbing me in a tight embrace. Her hair exuded the fresh saltwater of the ocean even though she hadn't yet been in her boat today. "You're welcome." She turned her face and kissed me noisily on the cheek. "I love you more than the world. I'm so anxious that you're leaving us because I'll miss you like crazy."

She pulled back and held me at arm's length. "But I'm also so happy that you'll get to experience things I never have. Sera is a magnificent city, Cerin. You will write and tell me all about it."

"You'd better write and tell us about *everything,"* my father piped up from the kitchen table, where he piled folded clothing back into a satchel after checking its contents. "If all goes well, you'll be away for years. We don't want to miss it even if we can't be there. Successes, failures, friends..."

"Girls," my mother added with a smile since father avoided saying it.

"You shouldn't be looking," I teased my father. "You have the best one right here."

Father laughed at my quip and walked over to grab me in a hug. "I sure do. I'll miss you out on those waters, son, but what you'll be learning is much more exciting. *That's* why you have to write us. Bundle up all the letters and send them once a season."

"I gave you two coin purses," my mother cut in from over his shoulder as he finally separated from me. "One is spending money if you need it. Use that to send the letters with a messenger. In the other purse is your tuition. *Don't lose it."*

"Losing it was the *first* thing I planned on doing."

My mother smirked and reached over to ruffle my hair. "Every once in a while you loosen up and show a little bit of that sarcasm you get from your father, and I'm not sure if I want to be overjoyed or strangle you."

"You haven't strangled *me* yet," my father mused, picking up the bag of my belongings from the table and carrying it over to us. "I don't know why you'd suddenly take it out on our poor boy."

I smiled at their bickering. "I'll miss you both."

"You sure will," my mother teased, shaking my shoulder lovingly and kissing me on the cheek again as she led us toward the door. "We're the only people you actually *speak* to, and even then we don't hear enough out of you." She opened the door and led my father and me outside until the heat of High Star bombarded us. She added, "Remember: *talk,* Cerin. Open up to people. Make friends. It'll make the next few years easier on you."

"I'll try," I begrudgingly agreed.

We walked together over dirt roads that stunk of gutted fish and to the grassy hill that inclined to the plains north of the Seran Forest. Just over the crest of waving grasses, the heads of two horses came into view before the rest of their bodies and the wagon they pulled. A dwarven woman held the reins, sitting on the wagon while chewing the end of a blade of grass. Long blonde hair hung over one shoulder in a side braid, and hazel eyes looked over my mother with intrigue. They then moved to my father and settled on me.

"Ah," the trader mused with realization. "Gettin' him far away from the northern coast, aye? Smart idea, that."

"That's one benefit," my mother replied, walking straight up to the side of the wagon and lowering her voice. *"Please* don't talk about his identity on the road. If something were to—"

The dwarf held up one stout hand. "Don't ya worry yerself. I get the need for secrecy." She motioned to my mother and me and added, "I'm from Hallmar, originally. We had an escapee of your kind there. Wasn't long 'til they found 'im gutted in the streets."

"Half-breed?" my father questioned.

"Nah. Full-blooded," the trader replied. "But he had the *chance* to make a half-breed. He was sniffin' around some dwarven woman, ya see."

My father frowned and glanced at my mother with a mixture of love and concern.

"I'd think about gettin' out of Thornwell if I were you," the dwarf continued, speaking to my mother. "I won't claim to know yer story, but they have ways of findin' who they're lookin' for."

"We're trying," my mother replied. "One step at a time."

"Aye," the trader agreed with a quick nod.

"Well," my mother breathed, grabbing my shoulders and facing me. Anxiety and hope filled her silver eyes. "This is it."

The reality of my situation settled in then. "This is the last time I'll see you in years."

"No," my father interrupted, looking pained by that idea. "The university has breaks every High Star. We'll find a way. We'll travel to Sera or arrange for a trading caravan to bring you back."

My parents shared a glance. Though they didn't say it, my father's hopeful ideas of visitation were more fantasy than reality. Traveling was expensive, and my education already took every bit of gold they had. I suddenly felt the fear of disappointing them, for any failure in future studies could ruin them.

"Write," my mother pleaded, her eyes gaining an edge of panic.

"I will," I promised. As my father hugged me one last time, I overheard my mother's pleas to the trader.

"Cerin's so quiet you might forget he's there," she rambled. "If he gets sick or needs something, he might not even ask you. Please make sure he has everything he needs—"

"Celena." My father separated from me and held a hand out to stop her as I climbed in the back of the trader's wagon. "Our son is quiet, not incapable. We wouldn't send him off if we couldn't trust him on his own." He turned back to meet my eyes as I settled on a small crate of goods. "Growth comes through hardship, son. Never forget that. You've lived a relatively peaceful life here; adjusting to studying magic in Sera might be shocking at first. But it's the ability to *overcome* that makes a man a *man."*

My father's words echoed in my head as the wagon finally lurched forward from its long-standing wait. My parents stood together on the grasses, calling out words of love and reminders until I could hear them no more. When we were far enough that they appeared only as tiny dots in the distance, my mother turned toward my father and shook as he embraced her.

"Yer lucky, kid," the trader mused over the rumbling of the creaky wagon wheels. "Yer still young enough to have parents, and those who *love* ya, at that."

I gazed over her head to the land beyond. Nothing but rolling grasslands stretched toward the cerulean horizon. I'd heard they built Sera on the side of a mountain, and because it was a rich city, I assumed it was magnificent. But I saw no evidence of mountains yet.

The trader went on after she realized I would give no response. "My pa was a good man. Loved me in his own way, like. Worked all the time, though. My ma picked fights with 'im every chance she got. He was always bruised and bloodied. Never hit her back. I never understood that, even as a kid. I sure wanted to hit her back. Stop her yappin' tongue. Anyway, one day she picked a fight with someone stronger than her. She used her fists; the other guy pulled a blade. Ain't no yappin' anymore."

I frowned and said, "I'm sorry."

She chuckled. "I ain't. She got what was comin'. I'm sorrier for what happened to my pa. He worked construction, ya see. Was always down in the Hall of the Dead expandin' it. We never talked about what happened to my ma. Probably because we were both just relieved she was gone and felt bad for thinkin' it. Well, one day he goes to work and never comes back."

"What happened?"

"All that diggin' pestered the minotaur. Ya know what minotaurs are?"

"No."

"Creatures that live underground in tunnels and mines. Attracted to the mazes of dwarven underground architecture, ya see. Ain't nobody see 'em go in or out. They're just *there.* A single minotaur killed over seventy men before they finally killed it. My pa became a statistic." She reached a hand up and snapped her fingers. "Just like that. That's the day I found out that nobody cares about nobody, kid. I was orphaned in a single day. Ain't no time to mourn or get shit together. Ya have to pick up and keep going. They expected me to take over paying taxes and rent. I'd been trainin' in blacksmithin' for years, but all that came to a halt. I wasn't makin' no money trainin'. So I had to give up my dreams. That's why I became a trader, ya see. Always on the move. Don't have no rent to pay if I ain't got a home."

After I said nothing, she laughed dryly. "Don't mean to depress ya, kid. Just know how lucky ya are. The real world don't stop to help ya. Parents are supposed to bring their kids up right, but havin' parents who *care* is rare enough. Havin' parents who care *and* bring up their kids right is even rarer. Those are usually the ones who don't make it very far."

"With what?"

"Life, kid. Good people die young. To make it in a cruel world, ya have to become its match."

"You've made it this far."

The dwarf laughed boisterously as if I'd made a joke. "I'm not sure if I should take that to mean I look old or kind," she mused. "Aye, I've made it this far, kid. And I ain't no saint. If I was, I'd have been dead in a Griswald back alley fourteen years ago, and they'd *still* be cleanin' up my giblets."

I decided not to ask her about that story since my imagination did a fantastic job of filling in the blanks, giving me some form of amusement as our wagon etched a path to the west.

As the weeks passed in our trek, the land changed. Our path angled slowly from west to southwest, and the ocean's purr faded and disappeared as the Seran Peaks rose from the horizon like white and gray incisors. The closer we traveled to Sera, the more travelers and traders we ran across. There was no road between the famous city of magic and Thornwell, but a worn path of folded grasses and the sporadic pile of horse manure marked the journeys of all who came before us. At night, a slight glow exuded from the southernmost mountain of the nearing range, reaching its fingers into the starry skies like beacons directing all to Sera. Even before we could ascertain any detail of the famous city it boasted its magnificence.

The cry of a bird of prey woke me from my slumber just a fortnight away from the 1st of Red Moon, and I stirred and pulled myself up as the wagon rumbled along.

"Ah, ya heard that, did ya?" the trader asked, before pointing far ahead in the skies. "Ya ever see a griffon?"

"No." Above the gray mirage of Sera's stone architecture, a handful of moving dots ascended into the sky. Only when they flew over the city and came west could I see any detail. Long bodies bulkier than horses swept through the skies with the help of a wingspan of sixteen feet. The sun glistened off the opalescent hues of feathers that trailed down elongated necks and softened into the thick fur of torsos. Four muscular limbs curled up beneath their bellies to cut down on air resistance as they swooped over the plains and headed toward the Seran Forest in the east. Each griffon was paired with a rider in prestigious green and black armor. Though two griffon riders looked our direction, they found little of interest and continued on their way.

"Those were the Twelve," the dwarf informed me. "A fancy-smancy military unit of Sera's, ya see."

"There were only four."

The trader chortled. "Aye. They rarely send more than a handful at a time. Depends on the level of the threat or job. They act as messengers and a reconnaissance unit for the Seran Army. Damn good fighters, too. Travel across the land quickly, can see farther than a cavalry unit, and the griffons fight just as much as the soldiers."

"What are they doing now?" I asked, following their movements until they disappeared.

"Don't know. They're headed east. Maybe there's trouble in the forest or maybe they're deliverin' a message to Brognel or Celendar. They could be lookin' for an escapee. Sirius Sera sends the Twelve out to kill his most-wanted criminals."

"Kill? Not capture?"

"Aye," she replied with a huff. "Ain't no second chances in Sera, kid. Ya abide by the rules or don't plan on livin' there at all. Sirius Sera rules with an iron fist here. He ain't popular with most but he's both the regent of Sera *and* the headmaster of the university. Popularity don't matter when yer royalty and the odds are stacked in yer favor."

"I've heard Sera is a beautiful city and that people find it marvelous," I commented. It seemed to contradict what the trader told me.

"Aye. From the outside lookin' in, it's great. Don't start diggin' too deep and you'll be fine."

Sera conquered the entire southern face of the last mountain in the range, its stone buildings glowing in the direct sunlight in tiers that unfolded from the peak in ever-widening clumps of dwarven-inspired architecture. The city's walls arced out from the mountain's base in a gigantic circle, keeping us from entering the city in the east until our wagon traveled around to a massive gate. Farms and orchards stretched over the plains just outside its wall, crops brightening up the southern grasslands in spots of color. A wide dirt road etched forth between the farms from the south, crowded with trade caravans and traveling mercenaries.

"Caravaneer Road," the dwarf told me, pointing south to where the path faded in the distance. "The busiest road in the world, they say. It marks the middle of Chairel like a cross, ya see, connecting all major cities. If yer from Chairel, ya travel it. If ya wanna go to Hammerton in the east or Nahara down south, ya travel it. Road goes right through the capital of Comercio and by the great Tieren Lake."

"Have you traveled it to all cities?" I asked her curiously.

"To all other than Celendar," she replied. "I ain't allowed in Celendar. The Celds are real protective of their forest and don't like to let none in other than themselves."

"Which city was your favorite?"

She chuckled. "Narangar without any doubt, kid. Looks dwarven, sounds dwarven, *smells* dwarven. It's just as much of a wonder as Sera, but it ain't as pretentious." She lifted the reins to point at the open gate we traveled toward as the murmur of the inner city escaped it. "Our paths will separate soon. I gotta go take this cargo down the street to the northeast a ways. You'll be going up the hill."

My eyes traveled over the seemingly never-ending tiers of the mountain. "How far?"

"*All* the way, kid. Ya see that building that sprawls over the mountaintop with all the pointy towers?"

I glanced up at the highest section of the city. Just below a blanket of hanging clouds that protectively hid the snowy mountain peak from view, the entire top level of Sera was one building. It stretched its greedy fingers in every direction, dominating the peak from wall to wall with long hallways and towers of solid stone that bullied the lowest clouds into submission. Lights glowed from stained glass windows in the towers, and soldiers walked along the surrounding walls.

"I wonder how big it truly is if it looks gigantic from here," I mused softly, in awe by it.

"It *is* gigantic," the trader replied. "That's the Seran University of Magic, kid. *That's* where yer going. Yer lucky, ya know. Even most who live in Sera never see it up close, 'cause they can't afford to even speak its name." She snorted and spit over the side of the wagon.

I continued to stare at the wondrous building as the wagon stopped just inside the massive gate of Sera. The hot weather cooled considerably when the wall's shadow overtook us, and I took solace in the break from the heat as the trader exchanged information about her goods with a guard near the gate.

"Where's *he* going?" the guard asked, bringing my attention back to their conversation. The human stared at me in confusion after comparing my appearance to the dwarf.

"The university," she replied, glancing back at me. "Time to get out, kid."

"Oh. Sorry," I murmured, standing from my seat and grabbing my bags.

"Make sure ya have everything," the trader continued, turning as far as she could to look through the things in the back of her wagon. "Bags, tuition, yer *shoes...*"

I hopped out of the wagon and carried my things to the front. The trader smiled at me from her seat. "I was only bringin' ya here for the gold, but havin' ya along wasn't nearly as annoying as I thought it'd be. I normally can't stand kids, but you ain't so bad."

Baffled, I only replied, “Thanks?”

The dwarf chortled and saluted casually with one hand as she urged her horses forward again. “Good luck in Sera!”

The guard looked over me and my bags and nodded toward the upper mountain. “Keep taking this main road up the mountain. There's a wall separating the university courtyard from the merchant's sector. The university's doors are gigantic. Can't miss them.” He noted my perplexed and awed face and added, “If you *do* need help, ask any soldier or employee in the courtyard. They'll help you find your way.”

“Thank you.”

He nodded once and turned back to the gate.

Sera bustled with life and activity. Crowds of tourists flooded through cobblestone streets, many carrying bags of goods or whole turkey legs they bought off of street vendors. Chairel was a melting pot of races and cultures, and Sera made this evident. Celds who decided not to live in their great forest to the southeast walked along the streets with pale skin and fair hair and eyes, many of them sporting rings on their fingers indicative of magic use. Dwarves traveled in groups that exuded the scents of raw metals, ale, and body odor, many of them dressed for work or battle. One dwarf's sheathed ax was still crusted with dried blood and ripped tissue, proving he'd seen battle recently but had been too lazy to clean his blade. The rest of the populace was human, and many seemed to live and work here.

Sera separated its populace by classes via its architecture, for the widest lower tiers of the city were poor and working class. They prettied the areas nearest the main roads for passing tourists, but a simple glance down a side street proved that architecture and people degraded quickly from there. Men and women missing teeth handled shady dealings at street corners and in shadows, and suspicious looking children hung around trader's stalls, waiting for the opportunity to pickpocket or grab forgotten merchandise.

Farther up were the tourist and merchant's sectors. The roads closest to the main avenues were filled to the brim with stores and entertainment options. Illusionists collected gold from awed tourists as they put on magic shows, while posters announcing upcoming plays and their locations were situated on walls and lamp posts. Laughter and arguments resounded out of the open doors of nearby taverns where the rowdiest crowds already drank even before the sun hit the midpoint of the sky. Standing tall over the multi-story shops and inns were expensive homes and apartment buildings for the city's affluent. Humans in expensive attire drank tea while looking over the city on their balconies without a care in the world.

The wall surrounding the university courtyard loomed just ahead. It had a gate, but it was kept open for now and no guards stood at its entrance. It wasn't necessary, for the entire courtyard was full of soldiers and employees. The grunts and playful banter of sparring warriors echoed out from the right before I even passed the wall. Though Sera was a city of magic, it clearly employed more than just mages in its armies.

I stumbled forward abruptly as someone pushed past my shoulder, and one of my bags fell out of my grasp and spilled its contents over the cobblestone.

"*Excuse* me," a kid my age announced, glancing back with a raised eyebrow and disgusted expression. The boy next to him laughed cruelly as they continued on their way.

My nostrils flared with humiliation, but I said nothing. I crouched down and gathered my things, piling them back into the satchel. My eye caught on a tiny box that had fallen out of a folded garment of clothing, and I picked it up and turned it over to find my mother's handwriting on an attached note.

Cerin—don't open until Sera. Happy twelfth birthday since we'll miss it. We love you!

My chest congested with longing. I slowly opened the box, finding another note and a simple silver band.

You can't become a mage without wearing rings! You'll likely collect more over the years, but here is your first. Your father picked it out, so it's not too fancy. Hope you love it anyway. Don't forget to write!

My birthday wasn't until the 73rd of Red Moon, so the idea that my parents had thought so far ahead and planned this just made me miss them more. I pulled the ring out of its holder and tried it on each digit until it finally fit on my left pointer finger. I closed the box with the note inside and put it in the bag before I stood up once more and headed into the courtyard.

A training yard stretched out to my right where warriors sparred with wooden weapons. To the left, employees tended to lush gardens that surrounded a wooden platform. On the platform was a machine I'd never seen before, made of wood, steel, and rope. It had three holes in a piece of wood near its base, and a sharpened steel blade attached to a rope, its acute edge facing the base. Given the red stains in the machine's wood and its platform, I assumed the machine was a guillotine. I thought back to the trader's words about Sirius Sera's treatment of criminals and looked away.

"Ya need any help?"

The voice boomed out from the right. A human of bulky stature but with an aura of friendliness took a few steps forward from a building beside the training yard. It surprised me that he was human, for it sounded like he'd picked up a slight accent and certain dialect from the dwarves. His prestigious armor gave away the fact that he was of some importance here. Warm hazel eyes peered at me underneath copper-red hair that shone with grease from a long day of physical labor. Chaotic facial hair grew from his face to his upper neck like he never found the time to tame it.

"I, uh..." I trailed off. A flash of red pulled my attention behind him. Standing against the wooden pillar of an overhang was a svelte human girl my age. The brightest red hair I'd ever seen flowed wildly over her shoulders and to her mid-back, shimmering in shades of orange and gold in the direct sunlight like the flames of fire. Piercing metallic gold eyes met mine from between high cheekbones and a sharp brow bone. She said nothing, but she didn't have to. The strong bone structure of her face and her confident stance reeked of self-assurance and intelligence, and I felt dumbfounded by the sudden rush of nerves and attraction that rolled through me.

Dear gods. I understood it, now. The glances of desire and attraction my parents shared. I suddenly understood what that was like.

"Magic," I blurted, the word a hiccup on my rough voice.

The friendly man burst into laughter, and the girl behind him looked away to hide an amused smile. "Yep, we got that here! I can tell you're nervous, so follow me." He nodded back toward the girl at the forge. "I'll be back in a minute, Kai."

"I'm not going anywhere," she called back teasingly, her voice robust with an edge of huskiness.

Kai. A shiver rolled down my spine at her unique voice. Everything—*everything* about her was unique. Even those golden eyes. I'd never seen such metallic—

"The university is huge," the man leading me interrupted my thoughts, waving a big hand toward the sprawling building. "The good thing is that it also serves as Sera's castle, so ya won't have to get acquainted with *all* of it. It'll all come in time. I'm Bjorn, by the way." He smiled warmly at me just before leading me into the shadow that fell before two gigantic doors.

"Are you a mage?" I asked.

Bjorn chuckled. "Nah. Never learned any magic. Never cared to. I lead armies with a sword and shield, friend. Getting a lil' *old* for it so sometimes I creak when I shouldn't, but it happens to the best of us." He grabbed the large carved handle of the door and grunted as he pulled it open.

The entrance hall of the Seran University of Magic was gigantic and open, spanning over five-stories with polished wooden floors that reflected movement and inhabitants, mirroring everything so it seemed even larger. Stone walls and wooden furniture lit in an orange glow from the firelight of chandeliers and perched candelabras. The hall also seemed to serve as a gathering room, for benches around its walls were filled to the brim with people of all races, including darkercomplected humans who wore clothing meant for the harsh deserts of Nahara to the south. Many appeared sick and impatient. Perhaps they were here to apply for healthcare from Sera's mages and had waited for a while.

"Sirius!" Bjorn called. I recognized the name of the headmaster and regent and stood up straighter to give a good first impression. A man hurrying down the left hallway skidded to a stop and glanced back at Bjorn with annoyance. When he said nothing, Bjorn added, "New student here."

Sirius was silent for the moment. Compared to Bjorn, Sera's regent seemed puny and weak. Sirius had a head of dark hair that thinned over his cranium, and wrinkles marred his face from overusing the muscles needed to scowl. Cold gray eyes overlooked me as Bjorn led me over to him. Despite his appearance, I couldn't help but feel intimidated with each step I took to him.

I held out a hand as we neared, prepared to introduce myself despite the pounding of my heart.

"*Why* would you bother me with this?" Sirius demanded, his voice barely over a hiss. He ignored my outstretched hand, so I pulled it back.

"I apologize. I don't normally bring in students, but he looked lost," Bjorn defended himself.

"So why start today?" Sirius retorted. "Every year, the new students *somehow* make it to the right places without your help. No need to start now and make *my* day harder than it has to be."

Bjorn said nothing, but a thick exhale blew through his nostrils in a whistle.

Sirius glanced at me. "I assume you've already paid your tuition."

"No, I have it with me," I replied, digging through my most protected satchel for the coin purse.

"He needs to go see Regina to pay his tuition," Sirius told Bjorn as I dug through my satchel. "What's the date today?"

"The 87th of High Star," Bjorn replied.

"Then make sure he pays his tuition *and* the costs of three days of additional boarding." Sirius glanced at the coin purse I brought out and finished with irritation, "He's three days early. Boarding costs are only covered starting on the 1st of Red Moon."

Sirius turned without another word and stalked down the hallway, a royal green cloak fanning out behind him as he went. A sick feeling twisted my gut. I'd already ruined my chances of making a good impression on the headmaster here, but I had no idea how I could have handled it better.

"Where is Regina?" I asked, clutching my coin purse close to my chest.

"I'll take ya to her," Bjorn replied, his offer friendly despite the irritation that lined his voice. When he turned to lead me through the entrance hall to the right hallway, I rushed to grab my second coin purse.

"Do you know how much three days of boarding costs?" I asked, hoping to the gods I had enough.

Bjorn cursed under his breath before he said, "I have no idea, but it doesn't matter. It doesn't cost this school anything for you having the decency to come here on time. The dormitories are already prepared. You won't have to pay an extra coin."

I pondered his words a moment. “If Regina asks, should I—”

“She won't,” Bjorn assured me. “Allow me to be the first to apologize for Sirius's cold greeting, my boy. He ain't easy to get along with. The rest of us work together to put up with him. That man could roll around *naked* in all the coin he makes. He won't miss three days of boarding.” He huffed dryly as if still angry at the earlier confrontation.

I tried to make myself feel better by imagining that Bjorn's words of Sirius were literal. I smirked at the idea of the regent having an odd and intimate fascination with gold before I put the second coin purse safely back in my satchel.

“I didn't miss that smirk, boy,” Bjorn commented with a smile. “Whenever Sirius is particularly moody I like to think of such ridiculous things to humiliate 'im in my head. Makes me feel better.” He patted me on the back as if to encourage me past Sirius's harsh greeting. “Welcome to Sera.”

Three

23rd of New Moon, 410

Mother/Father:

Almost three years has passed, and yet little has changed. The university claims to have two years of pre-magic training, but we have yet to learn our elements this far in our third year. It's coming up, so they tell us. In a fortnight, we'll have our final class of the year where our predispositions to the elements are tested. Only then will we know how much the next years of schooling will cost us, right when we're in the middle of our second term. How convenient for them.

Forgive me if I sound bitter. It is hard being in Sera. The kids here are awful with few exceptions. They make fun of me for both my quietude and my appearance. The most common rumor is that I'm sick and on my deathbed because they claim I'm as pale as a corpse. I let them think this. Out of six elements, Sera only refuses to acknowledge death. This absurd overblown fear of necromancy will hopefully make my "corpse-like" appearance more intimidating. It works sometimes. Some kids have this irrational fear of me because I look intimidating and do not speak. People fear what they don't understand.

The one bright light through all the darkness is that same girl I've written about before: Kai. I have seen her around several times, but usually at a distance. I think she might work at the forge outside because she is often out there with Bjorn if I pass to go to the inner city. Or maybe she's his daughter. Regardless, my hope that she trains as a mage here doesn't seem to be the case because she is in none of my classes. I find her interesting and beautiful and want to learn more about her, but we are never in the same place long enough to speak. The most we've ever said to each other is "hello" and once she directed me to the library when I wandered around lost. I spend most of my time there now. Partly because I have no friends and read instead, and partly because Kai's immediate knowledge of its location makes me hope I'll run across her there.

I hope father enjoys these rambles about Kai I'm saving up in these letters because losing my mind over a girl I barely know just makes me feel pathetic. Is this what it was like with you two?

I hope all is well and peaceful in Thornwell. I will send this next packet of letters with a messenger later this year, I promise. I like to wait until Red Moon since all the hot weather festivities and chaos is over then and the prices of messengers go down.

Love,
Cerin

I folded up the letter and added it to the pile I'd saved up on my desk. Standing from my chair, I grabbed the aluminum key to my dorm door and hurried through the tiny room to leave, locking it behind me. Other students only treated me with disdain, so I didn't put it past them to break in and steal my things.

The university hallways were thick with stuffy heat even though most windows were open to let them air out.

Nonetheless, I pulled the hood of my black shirt over my head, hiding most of my face in shadow. The shirt was one of the few things I'd bought for myself using the spending money my parents gave me. I'd once scoffed at my mother's suggestion to hide my appearance, but I found safety and peace in slipping by my tormentors unnoticed.

I was taller than most students here. My final growth spurt the year before stretched me to an even six feet, probably due to my half-elven blood. Had I been full-blooded Icilic, my height alone could have called attention to me in such a crowd. Thankfully, some humans reached this height as well, and I had no expectation of growing more. My father's human blood was a benefit to my secrecy in more ways than one.

A group of students loitered in the intersection of hallways up ahead, led by a particularly loathsome bully named Kenady Urien. Kenady was in some of my classes, and no matter how successful I was at keeping quiet and alone, he always called attention to me just to humiliate me in front of others. Kenady was loud, obnoxious, and boasted frequently; everyone had heard repeatedly that his parents were rich, for his mother was a healer and his father a prestigious trader. At our impressionable age few peers found this distasteful and instead befriended Kenady for a chance to visit his family's expensive mansion in the upper tier of Sera. Kenady figured out I was poor by virtue of my worn clothing and lack of name recognition in Sera, and he often used this wealth difference between us as a reason to torment me. He'd barraged me with questions asking how long I had left at the university before I'd leave due to a lack of funds, and once he'd even humiliated me by suggesting I exchanged degrading sexual favors for admission. I'd never said a word to the bastard. The last thing I needed was to be reprimanded for lashing back at a student whose parents likely had connections with university higher-ups.

As I approached the intersection where Kenady and his friends chatted and joked, I kept my face angled down in my hood's shadow in an effort to pass them without incident. It wasn't meant to be; Kenady glanced up as I neared. Though the hood hid my face, my clunky buckled black boots announced my arrival like a harsh song of clonking materials and jingling gear.

"Agh!" Kenady screeched, feigning terror and rushing away with his hands on the sides of his face. "The university is *haunted!"* His friends burst into laughter at the scene as he scrambled around the intersection, calling everyone's attention to me. "There are ghosts! *Ghosts!"* Kenady stopped his nonsense and grinned cruelly. "Oh, *wait.* It's just destitute *Cerin."* He pointed off to the center of the university. "The graveyard is just out that door and down the street if you're trying to get home."

As the others snickered, a booming female voice demanded the attention of all. "The *prestigious* Seran University of Magic sure has gone downhill in recent years." I glanced over to see a fiery mane of hair that framed metallic gold eyes. My heart skipped a beat as I realized it was Kai, and the air grew thick and energetic as she came to stand beside me. She glared at the still-laughing kids and crossed her arms over her chest. "They're letting in *riffraff* now."

Kenady retorted, "Oh, fuck *you,* snooty bitch. Don't stick your nose into places it doesn't belong."

"Based on your conduct, I think *you* are the one who doesn't belong here," Kai replied evenly. "How unfortunate.

Your parents can afford to give you a good education, but their gold can't buy you brains, can it?"

Kenady's nostrils flared as he prepared a retort, but he thought twice and backed up a step in retreat. He glared at me for a moment before motioning to his friends. "Come on. Nothing interesting to look at here."

I watched them walk away with a mixture of pride and intrigue. Kai's mere presence was intimidating, but I'd always thought it was because of my attraction to her. Her courage demanded attention and respect from even the worst tormentors.

"Cerin." A pleasurable shiver traveled down my spine as I heard my name on her husky voice. Kai's unyielding golden eyes were already on mine when I dared to look. She smiled warmly at me from her shorter stature and reached out her right hand as if we were two professionals. "Now I know your name after almost three years of wondering."

My heart picked up its pace as I took her hand for a quick shake. Even holding her hand for a moment was enough to fry my brain.

"I'm Kai," she offered when I said nothing.

"I know," I replied, internally grimacing at the awkward response.

Intelligent golden eyes flicked down the hallway and back to me. "Why do you let them treat you like that?"

I hesitated, caught off-guard by the blunt question. "If I argued with them every time they insulted me, I'd have no energy left for learning."

One red eyebrow raised as if my response impressed her. "So this happens often."

"All day, everyday," I replied. Working up the courage to say more, I added, "You saw the way Kenady acted. I needn't say a thing for him to prove he's an idiot."

Kai chuckled, and the uninhibited cheerfulness of it nearly washed all my nerves away. I felt overly proud of myself for making her laugh. "Kenady is one of those kids who *needs* a family name to hide behind," she said with sympathy. "If he weren't rich, no one would like him. It's a wonder his mother didn't glimpse that ugly face sliding out of the womb and push him right back in." I couldn't help but laugh low at her jest, and Kai seemed happily surprised to have amused me. "Anyway, I admire your patience," she went on, "but I certainly don't share it. If I were expected to grin and bear it every time I was insulted or wronged I'd explode in a million pieces."

"That would make quite the mess in these well-decorated hallways," I jested dryly.

Kai laughed again. "Then I'll hold off on it. I like your dark wit."

My mind grasped onto that compliment to remember it forever. "Thank you."

"We have the same class together soon," Kai went on, to which my heart picked up its pace. "With professor Beatrice Ply. Learning our elements." She motioned to her hair. "I'll probably learn fire. The appearances of mages rarely lie. Are you hoping to learn any element in particular? Obviously, we can't tame nature's biases, but one can always hope."

Her incessant curiosity intrigued me. "I'm really hoping to learn life magic," I told her. "The riches of being a healer would allow me to move my family out of poverty."

Kai's expression softened. "Oh? Where do you come from?"

"Thornwell. It's a fishing village to the northeast of here."

"It sounds familiar," she replied. Kai's eyes betrayed questions she didn't dare ask. She likely wondered how I could afford to be here if my family was poor.

"You don't think I'll learn life magic," I finally surmised when she'd said nothing else.

"What? *Oh,* no." Kai huffed with amusement. "Forgive me. My mind wandered. You *do* look like a good candidate for the healer's division." She added with a dramatized lowered voice and mischievous smile, "Either that or the dreaded element we *shall not name."*

I smirked at her teasing. Most in Sera regarded the simple name of the death element with fear as if saying *necromancy* was enough to die from it. Kai's light-hearted mention of it was refreshing. It seemed there was little she feared at all.

"Kai, for the love of the *gods."* Sirius Sera approached the intersection with a younger man by his side. The young man appeared to be in his early twenties, with long brown hair and green eyes. The multiple rings on his fingers indicated he was already a mage. A green cloak swept by the back of his royal armor. I assumed he was Terran Sera, Sirius's son and the heir to the Seran throne.

Sirius glared with distaste and irritation at Kai as he came to an abrupt stop just feet away. Beside him, Terran looked over Kai with a much softer gaze, though he was quiet.

Kai said nothing. Sirius's approach stole the cheerfulness from her face and demeanor, and her confident stance faltered.

"Does standing around chatting help your studies?" Sirius inquired pointedly.

"No, father," Kai replied softly. I felt faint as I connected puzzle pieces in my head. Throughout all my time at the Seran University, I'd never once considered Kai was royalty. She and Sirius looked nothing alike, and every time I'd seen Kai she'd either been traveling through the hallways or spending time with Bjorn. Clearly, Sirius's first heir was his only concern.

"Then why the hell are you doing it?" Sirius stared unblinking at Kai as she averted her gaze. "You expect me to consider you for my armies when you can't prove you're worthy to serve in them?"

Kai silently watched the floor. Terran noted his sister's discomfort and fidgeted on his feet until he broke the silence. "Father, the diplomats are waiting."

Sirius turned and left the intersection without another word, and Terran kept his pace beside him, looking over his shoulder once to check on Kai as they left.

Kai appeared embarrassed that I saw the exchange, and she offered weakly, "I apologize."

I swallowed hard at the desolation that exuded from the same voice that had just been so confident and happy. "There's nothing to apologize for." She smiled softly, and the need to keep her happy grew in my chest until it felt congested. "Perhaps you'd like company," I offered, my face heating.

"I..." Kai trailed off, looking down the hallway with a forlorn expression. "I appreciate the offer. I think it's best if I get studying done." She took a hesitant step to the hallway leading to the entrance hall and added, "I'll see you in class."

I watched as Kai shambled out of sight exuding depression. It was such a drastic change from her earlier demeanor that hatred for her father grew within me, but I was helpless to do anything about it.

The Seran University's gigantic library opened around me minutes later in mazes of bookshelves, puffs of parchment dust, and cascades of sunlight which flowed through clear windows above the tallest bookshelves. The librarian glanced up at my arrival but said nothing. My presence here was nothing new. Books could fill the holes of perpetual loneliness I often felt by distracting me with historical accounts of Chairel's most infamous necromancers.

Necromancy had intrigued me ever since my mother suggested years ago I might be predisposed to learning it. During my time at the Seran University, my interest in death magic only grew. Chairel's military was the mightiest on Arrayis, yet their coveted city of magic dared not speak of the most powerful element. Simple curiosity evolved into obsession over this oddity. Chairel's greatest military failures over the millennia were when they'd lost scores of men to a single necromancer. No matter their strategy, no matter their resources, necromancy time and time again proved to be the strongest magical force on Arrayis.

I wandered through the back aisles of the library where the sun held its rays back from shadowed corners. I'd read most of the books which would interest me in the earlier aisles. All of them said the same thing: necromancy was too brutal and sordid for civilized modern warfare. Stories of necromancers using the plague, empowering themselves with the life force of their foes, and raising the dead intimidated most, but they intrigued me.

A crate of books caught my eye, for it blocked my path to browse the last few shelves of the back aisle. I wandered over and glanced inside. A piece of parchment sat loosely over a pile of books that stated: *Donated D.S. 409. Check, sort, and file.*

I moved the parchment to the side, taking books out and flipping through them for anything of interest. There were books about military tactics, alchemy, cooking, a few fables, and...

My pale fingertips grazed over the dark leather cover of a thick book near the bottom of the pile, leaving smudges in a thin layer of dust. An artistic rendition of a hand etched in its center. On first glance, it appeared inconspicuous. However, I couldn't help but imagine that the artist drew the hand to look like it raised out of the earth. I flipped through the pages, and a musty smell hit my nostrils as I scanned the text for key words.

...elemental school of magic...Kilgorian Law...magical warfare...

A few blank pages followed. I frowned, thinking the book was incomplete. Then, a new section of text began.

...harvest energy...leeching high...secrecy...corpses...

I stilled abruptly and glanced behind me for witnesses, my heart thudding against my ribcage like a warning. The library was just as quiet and void of visitors as earlier, but I couldn't take the chance. Simply *looking* at necromantic paraphernalia was a crime, and that was what I held if this text had spells. My hands grasped desperately to the book as if it had already become my lifeline and someone would take it from me.

I quickly grabbed another three books from the pile, stuck the necromantic book between them, and walked carefully out of the aisle to the nearest study desk.

After putting the books on the desk and sitting down, I only breathed hard and stared at them for sometime. In the back of my mind, I understood all too well that I would delve into dangerous and irreversible territory. It didn't *matter* that I felt Chairel's ban on necromancy was ridiculous; it was illegal, and they had never budged on this view. Furthering my innocent obsession with death magic by learning it would turn me into a criminal overnight.

If they find out. The subconscious thought floated in and out of my ponderings with a mischievous wink.

Magic was finicky. The Seran professors already taught us that one cannot help their elemental predispositions. Either you can learn an element or you cannot, and that choice isn't up to you. They told us to prepare for the inevitable possibility that many students would leave the university disappointed when we were tested for magical literacy soon. Some would learn an element. More would learn the lesser magics. Few would learn two elements to become the ever-coveted dual casters. Learning three or more elements was an impossibility. Some would learn no magic at all after spending a fortune on pre-magic schooling. But *none* would learn death, and only because the university refused to teach it.

Inwardly, I reasoned this meant it would be a miracle if I learned death magic to begin with. And even if I *did,* that didn't affect my ability to learn a second element or none at all. Nature had long ago decided that for me as Kai hinted at earlier.

Whether I learned necromancy or not, no one had to be the wiser.

I kept still and silent for a few seconds, listening for movement behind me. Only when I felt it was safe did I separate the necromantic book from the others and open it.

Whoever had put this book together had thought intelligently about how to hide its importance. They filled the first and last one hundred pages with generic magical information about things we'd already learned in school. It broke down the Kilgorian Law, which was the scientific method every battlemage had to learn before being able to wield magic, for it detailed how mages must use energy reserves so they are not a danger to anyone else. It listed the various energy sources for mages: residual energy of movement, body heat, weather, and your own life force. It went on and on about this rudimentary level of magical understanding before it cut to a few dozen blank pages.

Then, a wealth of necromantic information was at my fingertips. The text scrawled across the page as if whoever had written it wanted to disguise their own handwriting. Death magic spells were written one at a time, followed by the detailed explanation of their pronunciation and handling.

Inflict plague. Raise singular corpse. Raise multiple corpses. Leech life. Weaken immunity.

Five spells. I took my time reading and rereading each one, sounding it out under my breath and memorizing it. We hadn't yet learned how to summon spells in school, but it was common knowledge that the simple mispronunciation of a word could cause a spell to kill its caster with a misfire. Every time I was sure I had it right, I double and triple-checked.

I summoned nothing. I just studied and studied until the library went dark with nightfall, leaving only the soft muted firelight of strategically placed candelabras. It became so late even the librarian left, for when I passed the middle aisle to put the book back in its crate with the others, the front desk was empty.

After dumping the book and hiding it beneath a few others, I hurried around the end of the aisle, jittery with nerves as I stalked toward the door. I'd managed to learn five necromantic spells with no witnesses, though it still remained to be seen whether I could wield them. A mixture of euphoria and fear consumed me for doing something forbidden, and then the intense emotion ripped away as my eyes caught on a cascade of fiery red hair.

I stopped and stared. In this darkness, all I could see was within the circular glow of an oil lamp. The light directed my eyes to the hair that fell over the edge of another desk like someone slept on it. From this angle, I couldn't tell if it was Kai. She'd said earlier she needed to study, but then she'd gone in the opposite direction of the library.

I took a step toward her, then another. "Kai...?" I winced at my voice, for its natural roughness sounded ever more intimidating in the dark, particularly while I tentatively approached a sleeping girl.

She didn't move. I walked ever closer, and the pungent smell of alcohol suddenly hit me like a wall. I stopped again, this time in shock. The girl sleeping at the desk surely looked like Kai. She was svelte and fair-skinned, and the ear that seemed lost in the mane of fiery hair was human. But like me, Kai was fourteen. Even if she wanted alcohol, it should have been hard for her to obtain.

I reached out to the face covered in red hair, though I hesitated and said again, "Kai." When she still didn't move, I gently brushed the hair back from her face. I swallowed hard with indecision and sadness when I realized it truly was her.

The unwanted second heir to the throne of Sera had passed out drunk and now slept over an open book. A stack of others she must have been interested in sat nearby: *Siege Tactics Volume III: 4001-5782 G.E., The Celendar Annexation: A History, The Military Trials and Triumphs Against Valerius the Undying.* All three books related to military tactics; between that and Sirius's words earlier that Kai strove to fight in his army, I began to understand she had a fascination with warfare. Most interesting to me was the third book about Valerius the Undying, for it was one I'd read myself. Valerius was the most infamous necromancer in Chairel's history, for he was human and lived over four hundred years by harvesting the life force of others through leeching to empower himself. The Chairel Army finally cornered him on an island to the north and burned him alive. Without that success, it was possible Valerius would have grown to be immortal.

I wondered whether Kai's interest in the subject came from fear or intrigue, but for now, my main concern was getting her safe. Kai had either entered the library after the librarian's work shift unnoticed, or she passed out here so often they said nothing of it.

"Kai," I said once more, shaking her shoulder.

"Mm?" It was barely a moan. She reached up, scratched once at her temple, and laid her arm on the desk.

"You have to..." I trailed off, fighting for words. I was the worst possible person to help someone drunk get home because I had little social experience in general, but Kai had no one else. Feeling utterly incompetent, I murmured, "You fell asleep in the library, Kai. It's nighttime. You have to go home."

"I'm home," Kai mumbled low, hardly coherent. "I live here."

That made sense given she was royalty, but the university was so gigantic I wouldn't know where to take her. "Okay," I murmured. "If I help you walk, will you take me there?"

"Who are you?" she asked. One golden eye opened, found me, and stared dully.

"Cerin," I replied, preparing to recall our earlier conversation to her so she could remember who I was.

"Cerin," Kai repeated, and her lips formed a lazy smile. "My only friend."

That statement put another damper on an already depressing situation. "You barely know me," I replied, frowning sadly at her.

"But I *want* to know you," Kai mumbled, reaching out to touch my arm. When she failed to make up the gap between us, she stopped trying and laid her arm back on the desk. Kai sighed heavily and proclaimed, "You're sweet. Intresting." She frowned and tried again. "Intrepsing. *Shit*. Intrespassing."

"Interesting?" I suggested.

"That," she agreed with another lazy smile.

"Let me take you home, Kai," I repeated. "You're in the library."

"Okay," she mumbled. "I trust you."

I barely knew this girl, yet I experienced heartbreak for the first time as I helped her stand. Kai laid her head heavily against my arm as I led her out of the library and down emptying hallways, trying my best not to care about the glares sent our way.

At one point, Kai tapped on my arm with an impatient finger, and I looked down at her shorter stature.

“Cerin,” she murmured, her glassy golden eyes looking over my face. “You're beautiful, Cerin.”

My breath caught in the back of my throat at the shock of hearing it. After years of being bullied for my looks, hearing such a compliment from the most gorgeous girl I'd ever seen was surreal. Then reality crashed back over me, reminding me that alcohol did the talking.

“Thank you,” I said, the words sounding defeated to my ears. Kai squeezed my arm in response though she said nothing.

Kai's drunken directions sent us to the right area, but even she seemed confused about the endless hallways and doors of the royal section of the university. We wandered around for a few minutes before boot steps on polished floors echoed through the hall we'd come from.

Terran Sera passed the corner of the wall and came to a stop when he saw us. His own eyes were glassy with a buzz, and he exuded roasted herbs like he'd just come from a rowdy tavern. He seemed to vaguely recognize me from earlier in the day, but his main concern was Kai. I stiffened just before he spoke, expecting cruelty to match his father's.

“Where was she this time?” Terran asked, his voice rough with drink as he scrounged around a pocket with one hand until he pulled out a brass key.

"The library," I replied. "Sleeping on a desk."

"Did you bring her ale?"

"No."

"Do you know where she got it?"

"No," I repeated.

Terran sighed and walked over. He gently took Kai's right arm with one hand and lifted her face with the other. "Come, sister. It's time for bed."

Kai shimmied out of my grasp and went to her brother, collapsing against him like she'd just done with me. I tried to swallow my sadness before I turned away.

"Hey."

I glanced back at Terran's voice. He balanced Kai with one arm as he prepared the key with his other hand. "Thank you for taking the time to bring her here."

Where were you? I wanted to ask. *Does your father not understand what he's doing to his daughter?*

I couldn't ask those questions because I had no power here. I didn't have the right to question royalty. I simply nodded once and turned away in silence.

Four

I stared at the corpse, and it stared right back with an expression of indifference.

Leaning my shoulder against the doorframe of my dormitory closest while staring into it, I marveled at my luck. After learning necromantic spells a week ago, I'd been impatient to try summoning them to see if I could. The problem? There was no way I *could* test them without hurting or killing a fellow student. As much as the *idea* of giving Kenady the plague and laughing at his misfortune pleased me, that wasn't an option if I planned on keeping this a secret.

Now, I'd finally gotten tired of the stench wafting out of the closet I never used and checked it out to see the culprit. A dead rat curled up in the back right corner, its sharp incisors bared in eternal torment. Its beady black eyes open but cloudy. A chunk taken out of one velvety round ear. Whether it was from the gnawing of insects or an injury it'd sustained during its life, I didn't know.

I reached out with a boot, tapping the corpse until it moved with the pressure. Even its long scaly tail made no bendable movement, for it had long ago went stiff with rigor mortis. I pondered over whether the age of a corpse could affect its usability in battle with death magic.

"Only one way to find out," I mused to myself, collapsing on the floor with a huff and the jingling of boot buckles. I had a while to try summoning a spell before the first class I shared with Kai, anyway. I'd abruptly woken up early because another student banged his fist on my door and ran like the ever charming and intelligently evolved creature he was. So far, finding the rat corpse in my closet was the best luck I'd had in Sera.

That wasn't the *best* endorsement for the famous city of magic, but it was the only one *I* could personally give.

Keeping my voice low, I repeatedly sounded out the spell to raise a singular corpse. Saying a spell wouldn't summon it. Combining my university education with what I'd read in the necromantic book, I knew that to summon a spell, one had to say it *or* think it and harness the energy from the environment into your focus of one hand or the other. That was easier said than done, and I couldn't know how noisy or chaotic summoning would be. But with an opportunity like this literally staring me in the face as this unfortunate rat was, my unceasing curiosity convinced me to risk it.

Finally, with my heart raging in my chest, I made a point of acknowledging the sources of energy in my room. My body heat rose from exposed flesh. The flame of the candle in the sconce on the nearby wall exuded heat as it waved while fighting the breeze that blew in my tiny open window. I hoped that was enough energy to summon one spell. I put all my focus into my right hand until the skin furrowed between my eyebrows.

"Corpa te risa."

I'd expected nothing but failure, so when a black foggy energy slowly materialized over my palm, the resulting shock I felt broke my focus until it disappeared, unintentionally dispelled. I stared at my hand like it belonged to someone else.

I am a necromancer. It was a simple thought, but the weight of its meaning made it so much more profound. I was still and silent, my mind moving a mile per minute. For some reason, I thought of how the full-blooded Icilics would want me dead for my racial impurity before I related it to my ability to wield death magic. Perhaps my mind connected the two because in both situations someone would want me dead for something harmless.

I took a deep breath and repeated, *"Corpa te risa."*

As if I watched the air itself turn into energy, black misty swirls materialized over my palm again, but this time I didn't break my focus. The energy developed in a circular shape as if tracing the edges of an invisible ball I held, but as more collected, it filled out until a swirling black fog hovered over my hand. I moved my fingers slowly, and the energy near the bottom edge of the magical barrier moved away from the motion, though it didn't break the spell.

Staring at the rat corpse, I recalled the directions for the spell from the book. The singular raise corpse spell was summoned differently from that to raise multiple corpses. For this spell, I didn't have to touch the dead body, but I had to direct the energy to it.

With my gaze unflinching, I pushed my arm forward and willed the energy to the rat. It hissed softly like the release of a breath as it funneled outward into the corpse, and my heart pounded so hard that its noise screamed in my ears as the blackness absorbed into flesh and fur.

I pulled my hand away and leaned back as if that would keep me safe from the spell's effects. For a moment, nothing happened. Then, the rat blinked, its cold eyelids gliding over cloudy ruined eyes. It rolled onto its stomach, and its tiny nails scratched softly against the wooden floor as it picked itself up to a stand.

I stared at the corpse, and it stared right back with an expression of expectation. Formerly bared teeth were hidden once more in a closed mouth, and the undead rat curled its tail to sit by its side. It lifted its snout and sniffed like it still had senses, and its tiny torso expanded and fell like it breathed.

I can control it. I racked my mind for the instructions of the book like I worried the rat had a limited waiting period before it would get bored and leave. *Will it.* I remembered those words specifically because they used the same phrase to describe how to summon a spell to begin with.

Will it to what? I glanced over at the other end of the long closet and wished for the rat to relocate itself. Immediately, the rodent shuffled away and out of sight behind the double door of the storage area. I wished it to come back and it did.

This was the most fascinating thing I'd ever witnessed. I felt a surge of pride, for not only had I taught myself how to pronounce and summon a spell correctly with no professor looking over my shoulder, but after three years of living amongst a pretentious and cruel populace of peers, I finally had *control* over something. It didn't matter that none of the others would know. I didn't care that this had to remain a secret.

It was a secret worth having.

I laid my hand on the ground, palm up, and the undead rat waddled over and climbed into my hand like a loyal pet. It turned around to once again meet my eyes in expectation. It looked like a pet, yet *I* was its consciousness. That knowledge was tremendously empowering. Fascination and awe overtook my mind for so long that when I finally realized just how filthy it was to hold a corpse, I abruptly jerked my hand away until the rat fell off. It scrambled around on the floor for a moment before righting itself and standing back up. Though I'd been rough with it, it only stared at me with expectation like before.

"I'm sorry," I murmured. The rat's expression didn't change.

The dull murmur of a waking city filtered through the open window, reminding me that I needed to go to class. It would be the first time I'd see Kai since taking her home, and I wanted to make sure she was okay. Kai was not only the one friendly peer I'd met, she also gave me a sense of hope. I often compared how attracted to her I felt to the relationship between my parents, and ever since her kind drunken words to me I hoped I could have such a bond with someone. For now, I stayed in denial about the flaws with such an idea. I didn't think about how Kai was royalty, or how her royal father loathed the same illegal magic I'd just delved into. I didn't think about how I'd have to keep this from her forever and how hard it would be to keep secrets from someone I wanted to spill my soul to.

I waved my hand past the rat corpse's face, putting my focus into dispelling it. The fuzzy body slumped to the floor, once more going stiff as the death magic ceased its helpful control of cold bones and ligaments. Before I left my room for class, I rinsed my hands in the bucket of wash water near the door and cleaned them with the university provided soap.

The bucket of water sat just outside my dorm a moment later, and no one was the wiser about what I'd used it for. I fought to keep back a smile of pride and accomplishment as I navigated the university's sprawling hallways to class.

Many students went quiet as I walked through the door. A few snickered. Some ignored me. Others threw insults. I ignored them all, searching for fiery hair. When I didn't find Kai,

I swallowed my disappointment and picked a seat at an empty table farthest back in the room, hoping to avoid the others entirely. My worry for Kai was so prevalent that I didn't even think about how it was likely I would learn no elements today. Dual casters were extraordinarily rare, after all, and I'd already learned death.

Hushed voices sounded outside the doorway, and I paid little attention until a flash of red drew my gaze to Kai. The other students quieted again as she walked through the classroom, though they regarded her with a distance. While they hated me, they seemed to *fear* her.

I glanced away, feigning interest in the next table over even though Kai headed my way. I didn't want to *expect* she'd come over to me, but it felt like my life depended on her doing so.

"Cerin," Kai greeted, her voice bright and robust again. One cream-colored hand adorned with silver rings of various designs held onto the back of the chair opposite me. I finally allowed myself to look at her, and she instantly smiled. "Is this seat taken?"

"Literally no one wants it," I replied, my response drier than I wished it to be.

"I do," Kai retorted lightly, setting two books on the desk before tugging out the chair and plopping into it. She promptly went about pulling the books apart and putting an inkwell and quill on the table that she must've kept in her pocket. Kai had such a confident way of doing things and carrying herself that I absolutely adored. I wasn't sure how she managed it after the hell her father put her through.

"How..." I trailed off, my face heating when my voice broke with hesitation. When Kai glanced up, I tapped on the table and watched the movement of my fingers as if it were the most interesting thing in the world. "How are you?" I blurted, the words sounding forced and rushed.

Kai chuckled and unscrewed her inkwell. "I'm well, thanks. How are you?"

Her bright tone confused me. It was as if she had no recollection of the last week's events. "Never been better."

She smiled with amusement at my sarcasm and said, "Good."

"I really meant..." I trailed off and huffed, frustrated with my inability to speak frankly. As sad as it was to see Kai succumb to alcohol, her drunken vulnerability had made it easier to speak to her. "Do you remember last week?"

"When we saw each other in the hallway?" she asked, tilting her head. "Of *course* I remember."

"I saw you in the library that night," I said hesitantly.

Her expression faded, but only a little. "Oh? Forgive me. I didn't see you. You should have said something."

I sensed nothing but honesty from her tone, so I replied, "I didn't want to bother you. You were sleeping."

Kai chuckled and looked away. "Father says study, so I study. But sometimes it's a bit much. You didn't come near me, did you?"

To say *no* would have been a lie, so I said nothing. I didn't like the idea of lying to her.

Kai's eyes suddenly widened. "That sounded crass. I apologize! I meant it in a self-deprecating way." She hesitated. "I snore sometimes."

It was a white lie. She wanted to make sure I hadn't noticed her drunkenness. Wishing to save her from embarrassment, I replied, "I didn't hear you snore."

"Thank the *gods,"* Kai jested, and I smiled.

"Your father seems nice," I commented dryly.

Kai snorted so loud with sudden laughter that other kids in the room glanced back with annoyance. Despite her show of amusement, turmoil flashed through her mesmerizing eyes. "Then that *wasn't* you last week in the hallway because you surely haven't met him."

"I get my penchant for sarcasm from *my* father," I told her. "Forgive me. Having a father as useless as yours is no laughing matter. I'm sorry for the way he treats you."

Kai sobered, and we shared a gaze that I broke away from first. "He treats most like that," she finally replied. "I am no exception." There was a long pause. "Once I learn my element, I'll train hard and rise to be the best battlemage in the Seran Army. Then he'll have no *choice* but to love me." When I glanced back at her, she smiled as if it were a joke, but the humor weakened with a semblance of truth.

I wagged a finger back toward the rest of the classroom. "Why do they fear you?"

Kai smirked and raised an eyebrow. "Because I'm *terrifying."* After I chuckled, she added, "The same reason none of them befriend me, I suppose. I'm royalty. They either think I'll go running off to tattle to my father or I'll get preferential treatment."

"Then *they* clearly haven't met your father."

Kai shrugged and turned her attention to her pile of supplies. "The luckiest among us haven't."

Scrambling footsteps preceded the entrance of our late and frazzled professor. Beatrice Ply hurried to the front counter and plopped down a stack of books until they collapsed in a messy pile. A bird's nest of copper-red hair piled on top of her head, and she'd attempted and failed at taming it with a few terribly placed hair pins.

"Good morning, everyone," Kai whispered across the table from me. "Sorry I'm late."

Ms. Ply glanced up at the class until her apologetic eyes found Kai. "Good morning, everyone. Sorry I'm late."

I smirked as Kai grinned at me with her victory. She'd clearly had this professor before. It seemed the students weren't the only ones who watched themselves around her due to her relation to Sirius.

"We'll waste no time this morning," Ms. Ply began, not flinching when one of her many books fell off the counter and to the floor with a loud bang. "It's about time you learned your elements. Now, your earlier classes should have gone over with you about how many mages resemble the elements they wield in one way or another. Using what we know of these similarities, I will separate you all into groups based on which elements you are most likely to learn. We will test each of you multiple times to ensure we discover any dual casters. Some of you will learn elements right away. If you *don't,* please don't fret. You may learn a different element or one of the lesser schools of magic. If any of you have forms opting out of elements or schools of magic, please pass them forward now."

Rustling echoed through the room as a few students passed up the forms. Ms. Ply looked through the forms and compared their requests to their appearances. When she finally separated us into groups, those were the students she started with.

Sometime later, five groups of students stood in clumps in the classroom. *Fire. Earth. Water. Air. Life.* Ms. Ply placed Kai in the *fire* group due to her hair, but she stood alone. No other student had such fiery hair, and while the professor said those with red irises often could learn fire magic, such eyes were rare in humans, and most students in our class were humans. On the far side of the classroom, I stood in the *life* group. As I'd expected, Ms. Ply selected me for my paleness.

Ms. Ply walked up to Kai first. Though the professor guided her on how to summon a spell, Kai's natural confidence made it seem like she was already an expert.

Kai practiced saying the simple fire spell given to her multiple times before Ms. Ply instructed her on how to summon it. After repeating it one final time, Kai's full lips curved in a relieved grin behind the hovering flames over her palm.

"Gods, it's hot," the student nearest to her in the *earth* group said, flinching back.

"It's *fire,"* Ms. Ply replied matter-of-factly. "Don't forget: though you are summoning magic today, the elements are *very* real. If they weren't, we couldn't use them in warfare." She turned her attention back to Kai. "Do me a favor, Kai. Stand with the potential *air* summoners. If you're a dual caster, I think your fair complexion makes the most sense with air."

After Kai dispelled the magic and did as asked, Ms. Ply continued testing students one group at a time. Kai's victory was the great start to a lackluster day, for only half of the hopeful earth summoners were successful. Much to my dismay, one of the successful earth mages was Kenady, and the boastful grin plastered on his face pleaded for the rude interruption of a fist. Ms. Ply ordered Kenady over to the life group next due to his cool gray eyes to test him for a second element, and I stepped to the side as he walked over to be as far from him as possible. Ms. Ply shuffled most who failed to learn an element to other groups to check for other predispositions. Others were left behind, disappointment and utter heartbreak lining their features as they were left with only the potential to learn the lesser magics.

When Ms. Ply tested the *air* students, Kai was successful once again. Ms. Ply clapped with happiness and announced, “A dual caster, everyone!” The others weren't as amused, and jealousy darkened already distant faces. I glimpsed Kenady mocking Kai silently as another student withheld laughter. I suddenly wished my eyes were blades, for the glare I gave Kenady then could have committed murder.

“Life is the most coveted element,” Ms. Ply reminded everyone, coming to stand before me for my test. “Many go on to make riches in healthcare or become the most sought after soldiers, but it is the rarest element of all.”

“Isn't it a little ironic to try teaching life magic to a corpse?” Kenady quipped nearby. A few students snickered.

Ms. Ply glanced at him and scolded, “Kenady, *please.* Cerin was quiet when you learned your element.”

“Because he can't speak with a rotted trachea,” Kenady retorted, “and he'd be hard-pressed coming up with the gold to buy a new one off the black market.”

Ms. Ply only stared at him with distaste. Kenady smirked in response. All the professors Kenady and I shared let him speak over them due to his wealthy lineage. He knew this and tested their limits all the time. Thankfully, there was one other student in the classroom who knew she could get away with the same.

"Larynx," Kai announced.

Kenady frowned with irritation and retorted, "What?"

"You don't speak with a *trachea,*" Kai explained, and by the tone of her voice I could tell she mentally added the word *idiot* to her correction. "If you're wanting to learn life magic, you might want to pick up an interest in anatomy."

Kenady stiffened and spat back, "If you want to be taken seriously as an heir, maybe lay off the *bottle.*"

Kai's eyes dulled with humiliation as the other students snickered, and she went quiet. The red tinges of anger in my vision overcame me. I caught Kenady's attention and said, "Give your parents that advice so they don't make the same mistake twice."

"Oh, *look,*" Kenady blurted, his voice elevated with anger. "A filthy fucking *peasant* with a hard-on for royalty. Where have we heard *that* story before?"

"Students!" Ms. Ply exclaimed, exasperated. "Do I need to get the headmaster in here to oversee this? This should be a *joyous* day for many of you. If you can't get along, at *least* be quiet."

I rolled my neck to the side, and the resulting crack of my vertebrae cut through the classroom's silence. Ms. Ply finally sighed and refocused on me. "All right, Cerin. You're up first. I want you to put a hand around my wrist and recite the spell *givara le life.*"

I wrapped my fingers around her arm as she asked, feeling Kenady's glare. It seemed he wanted me to fail just as badly as I wanted to cast the plague and see him gurgle on his own pus. *"Givara le life."*

I internally pleaded for it to work. It was extremely unlikely; dual casters were so rare. But if I didn't learn another element or school of magic, I'd have to leave Sera. And I wanted to stay despite its faults to see where this budding friendship with Kai led and to make my parents proud. I couldn't make a living as a necromancer, after all.

With my hand on the professor's arm, I couldn't see or feel any energy. As if suddenly near a campfire, her skin warmed beneath mine, however. Ms. Ply grinned and nodded with happiness.

"Congratulations, Cerin," she said. A wave of relief washed over me until I audibly exhaled like I'd held my breath for years. Ms. Ply glanced back toward the rest of the class and announced, "We have ourselves a healer!"

Only one student shared in her happiness. Kai smiled warmly at me from the *air* group and gave a thumbs up in silent support.

Ms. Ply moved on to the others in the *life* group. When one student failed at casting the spell, the professor sent him to another group and focused on Kenady. When she announced he cast the spell perfectly, I couldn't help but feel an overwhelming surge of annoyance.

"What a class the gods blessed me with!" Ms. Ply exclaimed. "We have two dual casters and a healer."

Ms. Ply walked away to test the others for the lesser schools of magic. In my peripheral vision, Kenady turned to leer at me.

"Being a healer might teach your poor ass what gold *looks* like," he hissed, "but you'll forever be in the *lowest* ranks of the army. When I'm on the field claiming victories as a dual caster, you'll be stuck all alone in the medical tents with the corpses of soldiers you failed to save. That'll be fitting for you, but wouldn't it be a *shame?"*

"If you ever come back from battle mortally wounded," I began in a rough murmur, "I might conveniently find I have as little knowledge of anatomy as you do. My face could be the last thing you see before Arrayis is mercifully relieved of your filth." I turned my head ever so slightly and gave him an intimidating stare. "Wouldn't *that* be a shame?"

Kenady glared back at me, but there was a smidgen of confusion behind his gray eyes like he hadn't expected me to defend myself. "You'd do well to remember who you're talking to," he growled under his breath.

I held our stare and replied, "Ditto."

Kenady laughed low like he found me pathetic, but he said nothing else. He wandered over to the *air* group to be among peers who accepted his nonsense without question. I could tell I'd intimidated him, even just a bit.

Two dual casters and a healer, Ms. Ply had announced. Kai could wield fire and air, and Kenady learned earth and life. Unbeknownst to the others, this class had *three* dual casters, and my abilities of wielding both of the rarest elements transcended most. Despite Sera's awful introduction and my obnoxious peers, my patience with it all rewarded me with success after success. For the first time in my life, I felt truly lucky.

Five

The rat rocked back on its haunches and lifted its front end into the air, sniffing toward me as if sensing the food I held in my hand. Over the past few days, the corpse had further decomposed. Its internal acids and oils leaked out onto my closet floor until it was little more than a husk of dried flesh over knobs of bone. As it waited to see what I had, it gazed at me with the hollowed stare of only one eye. The other had been missing for two days now. I wasn't an expert in rodent anatomy, so I didn't know if it decomposed or served as a snack to other vermin.

I kept the sickly sweet stench of decomposition at bay by keeping my window cracked at all times even if I left. My room was situated on the university's fourth floor, so getting caught by someone who smelled it or glanced in from the outside would only happen if one of the Twelve griffon riders ascended nearby. That was unlikely. I hadn't seen the Twelve utilized since I'd first entered Sera with the dwarven trader almost three years ago. They were used more often than that, of course, but it clearly was a rare event to witness their take-off.

The aroma of death bothered me at first. Not because it disgusted me, but because it bewildered me. One expects death to smell as rank as its subject matter, but I found it smelled oddly sweet before degrading into a mix of various gasses. The ever-evolving stench of decomposition fascinated me because I sought to understand the anatomical processes behind it all. It seemed an interest in necromancy spurred intrigue in other matters.

My parents had often teased me in Thornwell that I needed to find something of interest other than fishing. I hadn't written to them about my discovery of necromancy; while I knew in my heart they wouldn't disown me for delving into the forbidden, I couldn't trust giving them such information other than in person. During my time in Sera, my parents hadn't visited once. They'd expressed a deep desire to in their letters, but it was financially infeasible. Now that I'd learned life magic, the strain on them to save more gold for life magic *and* surgical training was harsh. They wouldn't know about my life magic abilities until late this year, for I wouldn't send my letters out until Red Moon and it would take a season for someone to deliver them. It had been over a year since I'd received any mail from them, so I assumed they were busy with work. I hoped that the good news of my magical abilities *and* my budding friendship with Kai would make them happy.

I sat down on the floor before the rat. It sniffed toward a broken piece of cracker in my hand. I'd saved it from dinner the night before because I wanted to see how the undead treated food.

"Do you *smell* that?" I asked, watching its reaction to my hand. It still stood on its haunches as if wanting to reach up toward my hand. As I brought the food down, its gaze followed the movement. I tossed the cracker on the ground before it, and the rat didn't notice. It still eyed my hand.

"Ah. You're following my focus," I murmured. I moved my gaze to the piece of cracker, willing the rat to follow my lead. It did so, sniffing at the food before grasping at it with cold hands. It lifted the cracker, but its decomposing fingers lost their grip. The food dropped. It picked it up again, eager to do my bidding.

"What do you plan to do with that cracker, little guy?" I inquired, twisting my lips to the side as I pondered. "You won't eat it. *That* makes sense. I know you would *fight,* but..." I stared at the cracker. "With *that?*"

The rat twitched its nose. The movement dislodged a remaining whisker from degrading flesh, and it fell to the floor.

I glanced over to the pair of boots that sat near my door. I leaned back to grab one. I put the boot between the rat and me and projected a feeling of hostility onto it.

The rat lurched forward with a sputtering hiss, grasping onto the toe of the shoe before spreading its razor-sharp incisors. The sudden reaction caught me off-guard, and I grabbed the boot to save it. The corpse's grasp was so tight onto its target that it came with, its shriveled body hanging from the shoe until I shook it.

Crack! The rat landed on its side, the weight of its body landing on one leg and breaking the bone. I quickly realized my mistake and simply pulled my focus away from the boot. Even when I set the shoe down, the rat didn't bother it. Slowly coming to an understanding, I directed the rat to grab the cracker. When it did, I once more viewed the boot as an enemy. In seconds, the rat smashed the cracker to bits against the toe of the shoe until I willed it to stop.

"We're teaching each other many things, you and me," I murmured, setting the boot back. "You've learned today that crackers don't make good weapons. But *I've* learned that you thirst for battle regardless. If I tell you to use something as a weapon, you'll do it."

The rat put all four feet on the ground and sniffed the floor. It waddled over when I willed it to, and I reached out, attempting to heal its broken leg with life magic. When nothing happened, I understood why. Dead bodies could not heal. But could I *shield* them?

"Sheel a phisica," I recited. When an egg-shaped life magic shield surrounded the tiny corpse, I smiled. "So you're just like any other soldier," I told the rat, who appeared as interested to hear that as anything else. "The only difference is that you lack a working brain."

I glanced up at the window when I noticed the soft periwinkle glow of morning cast across the opposite wall. I directed the rat to return to the closet before I dispelled it. The corpse fell in the same corner it died in, and I secured the door before leaving for class.

Nothing about this class was supposed to be special. As I sat in my usual seat in the back of the classroom and waited for Kai to arrive, I had no idea that history would be made this day and set off a series of events that would drastically change the world and the way it viewed magic.

Murmuring sounded outside the door again as Terran dropped Kai off for class. As usual, I said nothing and averted my eyes as she walked in. Her continued insistence on seeking friendship with me baffled me. Kai was confident, beautiful, and talented, yet she sought to befriend the worst outcast in the university. I fully expected her to realize her terrible judgment and stop seeking me out.

Kai glanced at the other students who whispered and gossiped at her arrival, noticing their jealousy and distaste. A rush of sympathy flowed through me. I *wasn't* the only outcast here. Despite our drastically different upbringings, Kai felt just as isolated as I did.

She set down her books and supplies across from my pile of magical notes and went about preparing her inkwell and quill. I averted my eyes to the nearby window, feigning interest in slow-moving clouds.

Whoosh!

A gust of wind blew through all my notes. They separated and swirled through the air, ruining any semblance of the order I'd carefully kept them in. The scattering of the parchment over polished floors drew the attention of the class while the culprit and his friend burst into laughter one table over.

I set my jaw and left my seat to gather the papers. Anger heated my head as I tried to keep them in order, but I gave up after a few seconds and grabbed them randomly just to escape the glares of my peers.

"Your powers aren't to be used so needlessly," Kai hissed at the air mage. After her chair screeched back, she joined me, squatting over the floor and rushing to pick up the papers nearest her.

"Or what, girly?" the bully sneered back. "You gonna tell daddy and get me sent back to Kilgor?"

"*No,* I'll tell Ms. Ply about this so she makes it known you're not taking your studies seriously." Kai glanced around to ensure all papers were gathered and handed the stack to me.

"Thanks," I murmured, my voice almost breaking. I inwardly cursed at my awkwardness.

I put an arm protectively over my notes once I had them on the table again, but Kai and I didn't speak until Ms. Ply came in, late and disheveled as usual. She wasted little time in starting the lessons of the day.

"Does anyone know what would happen if you were to say a spell incorrectly?" Ms. Ply questioned. "Suppose you said, *givara les fiers?* Or even, *creatius le life?"*

Kai raised her hand, but she'd been called on earlier, so the professor pointed to another.

"Nothing," said the student. "Nothing would happen."

"Correct. To give fire is an incorrect statement as is create life. Even in necromancy, the spells are not stated as you *creating* life because you are not. You are using energy to reanimate the dead. Even if you have a corpse standing before you, it is not living, because it cannot. It is only existing and acting upon your will because you are commanding the energy animating it. Does this make sense?" A few students nodded as I pondered that prospect. Ms. Ply went on, "Now would be a good time to remind you all that if you see any student—or anyone, for that matter—using necromancy, please report it to your nearest professor or guard. Necromancers are enemies of Chairel and are often put to death."

Put to death. The same people surrounding me would see me dead for an innocent interest. I marveled at that as Ms. Ply gave us an assignment to practice creating spells using words of the language we already knew.

"Cerin," Kai spoke up, as the professor walked around the classroom to check up on the progress of the others. "Have you ever tried to wield another element?"

I stiffened, a pang of panic slicing through me. I connected Ms. Ply's warning about necromancers to Kai's sudden question and slowly looked up to meet her gaze, keeping mine as neutral as possible. "Why would I do that? I'm no dual caster like you."

Kai noticed my distance but forged ahead anyway. “How would you know if you've never tried?”

Was it possible Kai had stopped by my dormitory and noticed the smell? I'd tried so hard to keep it at bay, and I no longer noticed it. But perhaps I was used to it. If Kai somehow knew I practiced necromancy in secrecy, wouldn't her tone of voice betray more than simple curiosity?

“Are you saying I have?” I asked, my voice colder than I would have liked it to be.

Kai frowned. “No. I'm sorry. I meant nothing by it.” She glanced down at her spell books and went on, “I just wonder what would happen if you tried, you know? Once you have designated elements, you're not supposed to branch out. But what if you did?”

Perhaps it was her incessant curiosity, nothing more. My heart calmed its racing and I replied, “I've heard nothing happens. You can attempt a spell of a different element, but it doesn't work. If you're a dual caster, anyway.” I thought of how easy it had been for me to learn *life* after *death*. “If you only cast one element and casting another works, well...I guess that's how you find out you're a dual caster.”

Kai relaxed and smiled. “Yeah, I guess so.”

There was that beautiful smile again. Wishing to keep it there, I pushed my spell book across the table toward her. “Do you want to try it? Let's see what happens.”

“Oh, so I get to be the guinea pig?” she teased.

I smirked. “I doubt it'll hurt you. It's life magic, after all.”

Kai flipped through a few pages until she found the first spell. “How will I know if it's working?”

"You'll feel a warmth," I replied. "Put your hand to your skin, and you'll feel warmth from your hand and tingling from what it's touching."

"Okay." Kai put her right hand on her left arm and recited the simple spell. After a moment, she glanced up in shock. "It's working."

I stared at her in disbelief. Surely, this was another joke of hers. No mage in the history of Arrayis had ever learned more than two elements. "It can't be," I murmured. "You already know fire and air."

Kai abruptly reached across the table and grabbed my hand. I stiffened at her sudden touch as she repeated the spell. My hand tingled with warmth from the magic mere seconds later, and I jerked away like she was dangerous.

"That's impossible," I whispered, rubbing my hand.

"Then how am I doing it?" Kai asked, metallic eyes open wide.

I said nothing. Perhaps Kai had failed at wielding air. I'd seen her wield fire, but air was hard to *see.* Ms. Ply checked each air mage for accuracy, but maybe she'd gotten something wrong.

The professor came to our table a moment later to ask about our progress. Kai interrupted the question to ask, "Why can I wield life?"

Ms. Ply frowned and stared back at her before chuckling softly. "You can't, Kai. You wield fire and air."

"I just used Cerin's spell," Kai protested, motioning at my spell book.

Ms. Ply glanced over at the book. "Kai...it is impossible to wield more than two elements. You know this."

Kai grabbed the professor's arm and recited the life spell once more. Ms. Ply jerked back and rambled, "I saw you wield fire and air yesterday."

"I know," Kai acknowledged. "I've done both. And I just wielded life."

Ms. Ply hesitated before stuttering, "Then—then do this for me. Lift your palm like you will wield simple fire." As Kai did as instructed, the professor went on, "Now repeat after me. *Creatius la agua.*"

Moments later, water collected over Kai's palm much like death energy had siphoned into mine not long ago. The whole class went silent with awe as we watched.

"Dispel it!" Ms. Ply exclaimed, and Kai broke the spell. The water splashed to the classroom floor. Baffled, the professor asked for her to repeat an earth spell. When the energy above Kai's palm consolidated into a ball of swirling dirt and minerals, Ms. Ply pointed at the student closest to the door. "You," she blurted in a frightened, hushed tone. "Get the headmaster. *Now!*"

The girl scrambled out of her seat and hurried from the room. The class was eerily quiet as we waited for Sirius's arrival. Even Ms. Ply was at a loss for words. If Kai could truly wield all elements, she was a historical anomaly.

Sirius walked in with a close entourage minutes later. I recognized Bjorn and Terran, but the others were strangers. Kai looked hopeful as Ms. Ply relayed the situation to her father. Perhaps Kai felt her rarity would make him find merit in her.

Kai was tested once more for all five legal elements, and she succeeded with each one in front of her father. Sirius said nothing the entire time, though Terran and Bjorn seemed concerned.

"Kai is human," Bjorn murmured to Sirius. "Wielding *two* elements is hard enough on the body. Even if she *can* wield them all..." he trailed off and met Kai's gaze. His own exuded love for her.

"I don't care, Bjorn," Kai said desperately. "You *know* I was born for warfare. If I can wield all elements—"

"You were born for warfare, sister," Terran conceded, "but if you wield all elements, you will *die* by warfare."

Kai went silent, but she breathed hard with both desperation and discovery.

Sirius spoke at last. "This makes her the greatest asset of war that exists." Beside him, Bjorn grimaced at the regent's cold detached tone, but Kai seemed hopeful that she'd finally won her father's favor. "Unfortunately, that means *nothing* when such power is granted to the inept."

Kai's hopeful face fell, and mine heated with anger. A few students giggled at the open insult.

"Good *gods,* Sirius—" Bjorn protested with distaste.

Sirius held up a hand to quiet him. "End classes for today," he announced. "The university will go on holiday until further notice. We will put Kai through extensive testing." The regent pivoted on his heel and stalked toward the door.

"Should..." Kai slowly stood as her chair squeaked over the polished floor, watching her father's back as he left. "Father, should I come with you?"

Sirius didn't glance back as he hesitated near the door. "No. I have things to attend to. I'll send someone to fetch you. Terran, come with me. Bjorn, don't you have things to do?"

"Nothing that's more important than this," Bjorn retorted, standing across the table at Kai's side.

Sirius finally turned back, his face shadowed with irritation. "We have five hundred new recruits who need weapons and armor—"

"And they'll *get* their damn weapons and armor," Bjorn interrupted, his normally friendly eyes sharp with anger. "I'll work overnight if I have to."

"Kai won't be going with you," Sirius retorted.

"Don't concern yourself with Kai," Bjorn spat. "You have things to attend to, as you said. *Attend* to them."

Sirius's glare turned colder at his general's combativeness. "Did I *not* say class was dismissed? What are all of you still *doing* here?" All the students scrambled to gather their things and hurry out of the classroom. I was the last out. Just as I passed by the open doorway, Sirius hissed behind me, "Bjorn, I want you to see me in my office first thing tomorrow morning. Expect a dock in pay."

For the second time in my life, I felt the overwhelming desire to kill someone.

*

Classes resumed days after the discovery of Kai's immense skill, but the anomaly herself didn't return. Kenady and the others picked up their incessant bullying with me as their only target, but I paid them no mind. I compared my situation to that of the heir and felt nothing but sympathy for her. My family came from poverty, but at least I had parents who loved me. I could not imagine struggling with alcoholism at fourteen because I couldn't measure up to my father's impossible expectations.

Kai finally came back to class a fortnight after the discovery, but she said little and exuded depression. Dark circles marred the skin beneath her stunning golden eyes, and when she plopped down in her seat, the resulting breeze smelled of alcohol.

I'd given up all hope of speaking with her until class was dismissed. I took longer than normal to gather my things, hoping she would say something or I'd find the courage to.

“Cerin.” Kai's voice cracked. She was the last student in a chair like she never planned on leaving. Her golden eyes were on my stack of belongings as she asked, “Can I speak to you?”

My eyes suddenly burned. The desperate turmoil so thickly entwined with her voice leaked out and affected me. “Of course,” I agreed immediately.

“I apologize if you had plans, but...” Kai trailed off and stared blankly at the wall. “I have no one to talk to.”

It was the second time I'd experience heartbreak. “You have me,” I offered.

She nodded shakily and glanced up, managing a smile. “Thank you.”

Kai led me through the university's western royal halls until we exited a door onto Sera's highest wall. My breath caught at the view. From here, the city descended the mountain in waves of polished stone and crowds of tourists, and the expansive plains south of Sera shimmered with a light breeze. The Seran Forest was a good distance to the east, but we could see it from this height as a smudge of deep green near the horizon.

The view became even better after Kai led me inside a watchtower between two sections of the wall that stretched up toward the lowest clouds. A few Seran guards noted our presence with curiosity, but they said nothing when they recognized Kai. As horribly as her father treated her, it seemed her royal position granted her some benefits. I wondered if her status made it easier to get alcohol for her habit.

Kai and I stood on the top floor of the keep, looking out over her father's lands. She was quiet for sometime before turning to the north and pointing. I followed her finger until I saw the faintest glimmer of the rolling Servis Ocean.

"You can see the ocean from here," Kai murmured. "I thought you'd appreciate that since you came from Thornwell. Do you miss home?"

I couldn't believe Kai remembered me telling her that. Her interest in me was far greater than I ever gave her credit for. "I miss Thornwell," I admitted. "I miss waking up to the smell of salt and I miss fishing with my parents. But Sera has its merits." As I said it, my eyes traveled longingly over the waves of her fiery hair. When she turned to meet my gaze, I looked away.

"Do your parents love you?" she asked.

An ache clenched my heart. "Yes."

"Good."

I thought of a million things to say before I decided on, "You are an anomaly, Kai."

"Yes," she agreed softly, staring unceasingly at the ocean. "It is a death sentence."

I swallowed hard. "Why?"

"You are a mage, Cerin. You know the Kilgorian Law. Once all environmental energy reserves run out, you use your own life force to summon magic. Dual casters live shorter lives than those who wield a single element, and mages live shorter lives than non-mages. I am human. I already have a puny lifespan of what, eighty years? If I'm *lucky?"* Kai laughed humorlessly, but she continued staring at the ocean. "Because I can wield all elements, I might as well prepare my eulogy *now."*

I hadn't thought of that aspect before. My personal focus on death magic meant I no longer feared the health detriments of wielding magic because necromantic leeching could reverse its effects. Kai's fear for her lifespan stuck out to me like a problem that needed solving.

"You said..." I trailed off, working up the courage. As unfazed as Kai seemed by the idea of necromancy in the past, it was still a risky subject to broach. "You wield *all* elements."

"Yes."

"Including death?"

Kai hesitated. "I have the *ability* to, yes. But don't think that means I am a necromancer. Death magic is banned. My father has a distinct hatred for all who wield it. Necromancers aren't given a trial. They're simply executed."

"Then how do you know you can wield it?" I inquired.

Kai glanced over at me with hesitation. "I don't really wish to say."

"Okay," I murmured. After another burst of courage, I blurted, "If your father legalized necromancy, you could wield it freely. Leeching would *lengthen* your lifespan."

Kai was quiet for so long that I glanced over to check on her. A million different thoughts and ideas ran through her eyes. Hope welled in my chest, for she seemed to latch onto the idea. Given her usual open-mindedness, it felt safe to talk about with her.

Finally, her eyes dulled again. “My father would *rather* me die young than relax his laws,” she murmured. “In a way, I should consider this new development a relief. I have no life here. I thirst for warfare, but using my abilities will kill me and I have no other skills. Father reminds me of this every chance he gets.” Kai huffed humorlessly. “I *love* irony. I am the first mage to have access to the six elements, yet I can't wield them without killing myself. It's like fate is trying to convince me to finally commit suicide because my father's prodding hasn't worked.”

“You *have* things to live for,” I protested, alarmed by her talk of suicide. “As awful as life can get, there are *always* ways forward.”

“Can you see the future?” Kai questioned, leaning her head on her arms over the battlement and staring at me.

“No.”

“Then how do you know?”

My mind scrambled for words. “Because the strongest people persevere,” I replied, “and every time I'm around you without your father, you exude strength and confidence. You carry yourself with such intelligence and self-assurance that people everywhere *notice* and are intimidated, Kai. I *can't* see the future. I *don't* know where you'll go or what you'll do. But regardless, I *do* know that you'll be great at it.”

Kai sobered at my compliments, but she didn't pull her gaze away. “For years I hoped I could prove this to my father by rising to be the best battlemage in his army,” she murmured. “The best form of revenge is success.”

“There are many roads to that success,” I pointed out.

She sighed. "Yes." Kai stood up once more, pulling her hair to the opposite shoulder until her slender neck teased me with glimpses of its beauty. "You are easy to talk to, Cerin. Now that I know what it's like to have a friend, I don't want to lose you."

A dull ache spread through my gut. Kai had called me her only friend before, but this time she wasn't drunk.

"You are very blunt," I replied.

Kai chuckled softly and smiled mischievously at me. "Does that bother you?"

"No. I find it refreshing and appealing." When her smile brightened, I felt a surge of attraction and blurted, "Your father's an idiot."

Kai laughed and said, "See, *this* is why I like you. You bombard me with compliments and my father with insults." She leaned on the battlement with her forearms again. "I will tell you something few people know since we're friends. Sirius is not my biological father."

No wonder they looked nothing alike. "Where are your parents?"

"I don't know," Kai replied. "I was dropped off here as an infant like they knew I would have magical skill. That's why Sirius took me in. Terran and I have thrown theories around over the years about my heritage, but we've figured nothing out. Whenever I go to the inner city, I keep a lookout for golden eyes like I'll actually find my parents close by. I've never seen eyes like mine on anyone else. Terran says the same, and he's been to other settlements."

"I'd never seen golden eyes before yours, either," I admitted softly.

"Then I suppose I can cross Thornwell off the list of places to look," she replied with a smile.

"If you find your biological parents, perhaps you could understand why you have the powers you do," I suggested.

"You are just full of ideas," Kai teased

"I'm trying to help you."

"I know." Kai's bright smile faded into one of appreciation. "Thank you." After a quiet moment, she added hesitantly, "I felt drawn to you, Cerin, ever since you came here three years ago. I recognized the loneliness surrounding you because I feel it every day. The closer we get, the more I want to know about you and share things with you." Her cheeks reddened as she realized just how much she'd revealed to me before she concluded, "I just want you to know that you can talk to me. Like you understand my troubles despite having your own, I want to know about and help you with yours."

That was the exact moment I fell in love with Kai Sera. The logical side of my brain protested it would ruin me, for she would die young because her royal father refused to consider the merits of necromancy; yet here I was, a necromancer who fell dangerously and hopelessly in love with her. It wasn't meant to be, but my heart spit curses at fate and loved her anyway.

Even so, I did not dare tell her my secrets of practicing necromancy. If Kai was destined to die young, I didn't want her to die viewing me as an enemy. After knowing nothing but loneliness, I wished for the only friend I'd ever had to live out her short life thinking of me fondly.

Six

79th of Dark Star, 410

Cerin—

Meet me in the library come nightfall on the eve of the new year if you have no other plans. I apologize for being so busy with all my classes, but I'd like to make it up to you. The stars are most beautiful while viewing them from the northeastern wall. I want to celebrate the new year with you and take you out for a night on the town. Most shops and restaurants are open all night for the holiday. We'll stay out as late as possible if you can keep awake for it!

I hope to see you there. If you don't show, I'll understand. But I'll miss you.

-Kai

I read and reread the note Kai slipped to me in the hallway earlier that day, a nervous anticipation in my chest. I still had no friends other than her, and we didn't see each other as often as I would have liked. Kai was overwhelmed with classes, for Sirius insisted on training her in all five legal elements despite the probable fatal ramifications. I shared no classes with her anymore, and the only times we saw one another were when we'd run across each other in the library. It seemed Kai came there whenever she had a spare moment. I liked to believe it was because I was often there.

I read Kai's note again just to convince myself it was real. The new year wouldn't come for another eleven days, yet just the prospect of spending it with her turned me into a nervous wreck. Even though we'd been friends for nearly a year, Kai still didn't know I pined for her. A mixture of youthful cowardice and fear of her succumbing to an early death kept me reserved in her presence. Internally, however, I felt insane with loneliness. I had so many secrets I wanted to share with her, some of which I'd *never* be able to. I tried to feel better about it by reminding myself that no matter the secrets between us, I had Kai's attention. I may have been an outcast subject to scorn by most Serans, but when holding this note that she'd addressed to *me,* I felt like the luckiest person in the world.

Tap. Tap. Tap-tap. Tap.

The rat skeleton shuffled around the floor of my room, each tiny step making soft music as bone tapped on wood. It pulled me out of my pensive trance, and I folded up Kai's note and put it in my trouser pocket for safe-keeping. Over half a year after first discovering the rat corpse in my closet, all flesh and tissue had dissipated and left nothing but bone. I'd long ago tested every magical curiosity I had with and on the creature. I couldn't leech from my minions, for the dead didn't generate energy like the living. I couldn't heal them. But I could shield them, and my thoughts could affect them in battle.

I revived the rat repeatedly because despite knowing otherwise, it felt like having a pet. When it fell too late to see in the library, I'd revive the rat and play with it. It could retrieve thrown objects and do little dances, and sometimes I allowed it to roam my room freely while I studied. Corpses couldn't speak, but they made better company than most of my peers.

A low murmur sounded out behind me, but when I glanced at my door, nothing happened. I waited a few moments in case a student tried to scare me by banging on the door as a prank, but the noise never came.

I left the rat to its freedom and stood, pulling out a pack of matches from the top drawer of my desk and lighting the lamps in the room one at a time. Circles of firelight flickered over stone walls, making up for the ever-darkening evening skies.

Crr-ching!

I frowned and glanced toward the door at the unmistakable ring of a key in a lock. It was likely one of the other rooms, for the loud locking mechanisms could echo in these stone halls—

My heart skipped a beat as my door opened, its widening arc chased by infiltrating light from the outside hallway. A professor I recognized but couldn't name peered in without any warning, the key to my door in his hand. Behind him in the hallway stood Kenady and one of his mindless sidekicks. Kenady glared at me with a cruel look of satisfaction that claimed proud responsibility for my current ails and inevitable exile. He'd clearly reported me. Based on the whispering I'd heard at my door I assumed he and his friend saw something through my keyhole or a crack that was just a little *too* wide. Panic seized my chest. Excuses and plans came to mind, but I froze and did nothing.

The professor's eyes found me, then traveled over my bed to the floor. Remembering I'd left the rat animated, my eyes widened as I searched for it. The small skeleton waddled over to the corner within the professor's view and sat down with a tiny *clink* of bone on wood.

I dispelled the necromancy without a word, and the rat's bones collapsed into a disorganized pile. That ended up being the catalyst to a series of unfortunate events.

The professor stumbled back out of the room like he'd witnessed a murder. *"Students!"* he commanded, turning to Kenady and his friend in the hallway. "Get to your rooms and *lock the door.* Do *not* come out until morning." Turning to a passing employee who appeared curious by the ruckus, he added, "*Get the headmaster!*"

Death magic is banned. My father has a distinct hatred for all who wield it. Necromancers aren't given a trial. They're simply executed. Kai's words floated into the forefront of my mind as I tried to decide what to do, giving me advice and wisdom. She knew her father better than any of us, for she often suffered on his account. I could not reason with the unreasonable.

So I ran. I was fully dressed, and the only thing I could think of to grab was the tiny stack of letters to my parents from the desk. I shoved them into a trouser pocket with Kai's note and left the rest of my gold, books, and belongings, rushing out of the room as the professor screamed after me.

The jingling of my boot buckles echoed off stone walls as I pushed aside university employees and hopped down sections of steps at a time, my mind set on the giant front doors which would be my redemption. Calls for guards to stop me came from multiple voices and directions. Pounding boot steps to match the ferocity of my own multiplied as the group of my pursuers grew.

I will not die here. It repeated in my head like a chant, like thinking it would make it true. I thought of Thornwell and my parents, and I told myself I refused to die until I saw them again.

The multi-story front doors of the university were just ahead, but my pursuers were gaining. My tall height gave me a naturally longer gait, but I wasn't physically fit. Spending time in a classroom for years practicing magic wasn't ideal for gaining muscle.

The Seran University's entrance hall had a giant fireplace that many gathered around to wait for the disappointment of finding out they couldn't afford its services. We were amid the coldest season of Dark Star, so many waited beside it now soaking up its heat. But fires required constant oxygen flow, and as the long, emerald green drape hanging over a nearby window waved into the hall from a cold outdoor breeze, I realized how they fueled it. Instead of rushing to the heavy doors to flee, I abruptly dodged left, shoving the curtain to the side and hopping up onto the windowsill.

The casement window was longer than it was wide, but my half-Icilic blood kept me thin. I turned to the side and pushed between the glass and frame, sucking in my stomach as I pleaded for it to work.

Pfft! With a final jerk to the outside, the window frame rubbed harshly against my forearm, leaving a friction burn but letting me free. I fell from the window and to the cobblestone below. The epidermis of my right forearm peeled from the burn, revealing the pinker layer beneath. I waited to heal it, scrambling up on the stone before the nearby guards could understand why the hell a thin pale student climbed out of a window without being dressed for the weather.

Just after passing the wall separating the university's courtyard from the middle tier of Sera, the giant doors creaked behind me before a hoarse male voice called, *"By order of Sirius Sera! Stop or you will be executed!"*

You'll execute me regardless. I kept running, my lungs scorching holes in my sides as evening passersby backed out of my way, startled by my frantic pace while they tried to figure out my crime.

"Prepare the Orders of the Mages!" It was a cry on another voice far behind me. *"A necromancer's on the loose!"*

The crowds I pushed through gasped and dispersed at the dreaded word, pulling back from the street like the air around me was toxic. Slams of doors reverberated off stone as people retreated inside. The main street descended ever downward, the smooth cobblestone glistening silver in the moonlight of the encroaching night. Each step I took was closer to safety.

Shik!

The ground rushed up with a rude greeting, and my forehead hit stone. The resulting headache was so biting that I only realized someone had shot me when I turned to the side and the shaft of an arrow stuck out of my right calf. A handful of soldiers jogged down the street from the university, and the one with the bow raised it again.

Sheel a phisica. I thrust a hand out, life magic glowing over the palm.

Zwip.

A glimmering transparent white egg-shaped magical force surrounded me, and when the second arrow meant for my eye zipped near, it bounced off harmlessly and rolled into a nearby crack between stone. The soldiers hesitated as they noticed the life magic, so I pulled out the arrow, hissing under my breath at the stinging pain as I healed the wound. As the white magic sunk past broken flesh and into muscle, slowly melding it back into place, the soldiers voiced their confusion.

"We have the wrong kid," one protested.

Another called, *"What* was the crime? We thought you said *necromancy!"*

"It *is* necromancy, you *idiot! Stop him!"*

"He's a healer!" came the retort.

"He's also a necromancer!" another screamed, enraged.

It was hard for them to believe. Life was the rarest element, and death was rare due to its illegality. Thus, such a dual caster had never knowingly existed before in Chairel. Necromancers had to learn their magic through illicit means, so rarely did they visit the city which would execute them without trial, let alone attend its university to learn a second element. And life mages required heaps of gold to go through training here; with potential to be among the elite, why dally with the forbidden?

With the arrow wound healed, I stood back up. The life shield still glowed around me as I took off toward the lower city once more, taking advantage of the bafflement of my pursuers. Shouts and orders rattled through the air behind me, but other than two more arrows that bounced off my shield, the soldiers couldn't catch up.

I didn't stop until I passed the eastern gate of Sera and collapsed in the long grasses between the intimidating city wall and the nearest farm pasture. Each breath ran tiny knives along my lungs until it felt too painful to breathe, but my needy body forced me through the trauma. I couldn't afford to stop, but every muscle in my body ached and thousands of thoughts barraged my mind.

From this point forward, I would forever be a criminal. Everything I'd ever worked toward—a life magic license and the subsequent surgeon's license, getting my parents out of poverty, a possible relationship with Kai—was ruined. I felt nauseated as I imagined how my parents would react when they found out I'd wrecked any chance of giving them a better life. After all their worries, encouragements, and gold, I couldn't even give them that.

And what now? My parents wouldn't disown me for learning necromancy, but the secret was out. What would we do when we couldn't afford to move far away from Chairel's laws? Where would we go?

"By the order of Sirius Sera, lift up your hands." The booming voice echoed off the nearby wall and back to my ears. I laughed dryly with exasperation. I couldn't even stop to *breathe* without them catching me. Maybe fate was as thirsty for my death as it was for Kai's.

"By the order of Sirius Sera, *lift up your hands,"* came the command again, more demanding.

"For *what?"* I asked, standing up and turning around. Sixteen soldiers approached me carefully along the exterior of the near pasture fence, all tentatively holding weapons or summoned spells. I would have gawked at the idea of facing sixteen at once if I felt there could be any positive outcome to this at all.

"You are under arrest," the middle-aged human at the front stated, his eyes watching my hands for spells as he took small cautious steps toward me. A steel shield protected his upper torso while his right hand gripped a short sword. "Your charge is necromancy."

"What incentive do you give necromancers to come with you for arrest?" I retorted. Despite my argument, it was an honest question. *"Either way,* Sirius will execute me."

It must have been a good argument because as the soldiers came forward, they gave no answer. One had hair as red as Kai's and held fire in one hand. Because I'd only given myself a magical guard to withstand physical attacks, I prepared a ward to reject offensive magic.

Sheel a mana.

Zwip.

Giving myself a second protection convinced them that I wouldn't come peacefully. Under the pale moonlight of a briskly cold night, sixteen soldiers charged me.

I scrambled back over long waving grasses, refreshing my physical shield when another barrage of arrows clashed into it. My mind frantically searched through options, unused to having to think so quickly in a fight.

Absort la mana del life. Death magic pulled the energy straight out of the surrounding breeze and collected in my palm as a dark swirling ball. I thrust my hand out toward the first soldier's chest, and the foggy magic stretched between us in a funnel. As soon as it hit him, a deep crackling sizzled and popped in the air between us like bubbling oils on a skillet. The black magic became murkier and darker as it siphoned his life force from his chest and sucked it back to me. His energy didn't collect in my hand; instead, it sunk into my palm and its collection of veins, traveling through my bloodstream to my heart. My veins protruded under my pale fresh, becoming more pronounced as they carried their harvest.

"Leave me be!" I screamed at them, my rough voice hoarser with desperation over the sizzling of my magic. I continued backing away defensively, and even though the man just before me slowly fatigued with my leeching, he pursued. *"I am no threat to you! I don't want to kill you! Leave me be!"*

The soldiers said nothing. They only attacked. As life force collected through the death magic and settled into my core, I realized that while it fatigued the man, it strengthened me. My body's earlier heaving protests from my flight were little more than vaguely quickened breaths. Instead of shredding my ribs like earlier, my heart now arrogantly goaded me to give it a challenge.

Fff! Fff!

Two fireballs hissed as they rampaged toward me, trailing wisps of smoke that left hazes over patches of the starry night sky. The first hit my ward and dissipated as it was rejected. The second missed me entirely, and the orange flash lighting up the nearby pasture fence proved the flames hit the long grasses and spread to my left. One soldier screamed obscenities and built water magic in her palms, rushing over to put the fire out before it could risk the land.

As the others focused on the fire, the man before me slowed. His eyes dropped to the funnel still crackling between us. While he'd hacked away at my life shield, I'd only regenerated it with the life force I collected from him. Now, he stopped trying. He dropped his sword, and then the magic between us stopped crackling. I frowned with confusion until I realized the noise ceased because the spell had no life left to harvest.

I backed up a step as he fell toward me and collapsed in a lump over his sword. I stared at his body in a state of shock. It was the first time I'd ever taken a life, and it jolted me as I took so many things into perspective. A series of random panicked thoughts flew through my head in a ramble.

I just killed someone. One season after turning fifteen, I killed someone. He lived over forty years just to die like this. All because I raised a rat from the dead. All because of curiosity. I asked them to leave me be. If they'd left me be, this wouldn't have happened. Will I be able to tell my parents? What would Kai think? I just killed someone. And it was so...

I stared at my hand. I still felt the other man's life force empowering it.

...easy.

"Murderer!" The water mage hesitated from putting out the fire and pointed at me as I stood over the corpse, still holding up my hand and studying its power.

Corpa te risa. Using the life force of their comrade, I built a new spell. Once the black magic formed in my hand, I sent it into the fallen corpse.

The pursuing soldiers slowed as the man flinched. The corpse lifted on its forearms, groaning incoherently as if I'd woken it from a long comfortable nap. It pulled itself to a stand. Like it had its own consciousness, it eyed the sword it dropped only moments ago and leaned down to grab it.

"Oh, *gods!"* one soldier wailed, her body shaking with shuddering sobs as an undead former friend rushed toward her with a sword and hollowed gaze.

"Abigail!" another soldier shouted toward the sobbing woman. *"Keep it together!"*

The corpse paid no mind to their bickering. With my focus on Abigail because she sobbed and caused a scene, it headed to her first. It hobbled with a purpose, swinging its sword through the air when it was close enough. Silver glimmered in an arc toward Abigail's throat before her sobs cut short. Blood spurted up like a fountain from the severed arteries surrounding her spinal cord, splattering over the previously unmarred corpse and another soldier who rushed forward to Abigail's defense a moment too late. The zombie soon fell to the ground from a quick decapitation by the defender, and its head rolled until the open eyes stared directly into Abigail's, blood spewing out of the throat into a weighty puddle over the grasses. Body heat rose like smoke from the blood into the frigid cold air.

Dear gods. My eyes stuck to the blood puddle that only grew as the mutilated parts of two separate bodies audibly gushed. A single spell had caused this. It was one thing to take a life by simply weakening the body with leeching. It was *another* thing entirely to see such gore while I was still in a state of shock.

Crrk!

A water mage's ice shard crashed into my ward and broke apart into glowing whitish-blue pieces, leaving the magical protection flickering with weakness. I regenerated the guard and managed, *"No one else* has to die. *Please* stay back and leave me be." My voice trembled with the echoes of trauma from what I'd witnessed. It felt like I'd fallen into a dream-state and would wake up at any moment. For now, I didn't want to fight anymore. I wanted to be still and think about all of this for a long time. Possibly forever.

"Fuck you, murderer!" the fire mage screeched. She unsheathed a sword with a metallic *shing,* and as she held it still, her other hand swept over the blade, imbuing the steel with flames.

A shaky breath of resignation shuddered through my lips and spewed into the night as wisps of smoke. I summoned another spell.

Corpa te risa a multipla.

Just as the necromantic book specified, I thrust this spell toward my boots. Black magic clouded out around them in a circle like thick mist with a slight hiss. In seconds, clouds of energy pulled together into dozens of dark tendrils. As if the magic itself lived, the cirri slithered off in multiple directions. One headed for Abigail's body and disappeared. Another absorbed into the decapitated body that fought for me earlier. The others sunk into the ground as if they'd found nothing.

I reached out with both hands, leeching from two pursuers at once with separate funnels. In my peripheral vision, the two decapitated heads rolled over the grasses toward their respective bodies seemingly on their own. As soon as broken bloodied flesh met, the corpses rose to fight. Blood still leaked from the location of their decapitations, their mutilated parts only kept together via black magic.

The earth trembled. The two soldiers before me swung weapons and threw magic at my shields until they fatigued and dropped dead, their life force depleted from my leeching. Their cooling bodies shook as the land beneath them rumbled protests.

Pop!

As the grasses exploded amidst a spray of cold dirt nearby, it wasn't just the soldiers who hesitated to see the ruckus. I heaved with adrenaline as I realized the tendrils that sunk into the ground hadn't fizzled out. From a patch of land near the pasture I'd tried to leave far behind me by continually retreating, multiple skeletal cattle launched themselves out of a shallow grave. Grimy hooves gripped the ground and churned dirt like butter as they pulled the rest of the bodies from the earth's greedy grasp to heed my call. These cattle had been dead for a while, for even the most recent corpse only had slivers of old leather hanging from non-existent joints. I assumed someone slaughtered them at the nearby farm and put them in a mass grave. Now, they stampeded toward our fight, thirsty instead to be the slaughterers.

Foggy black magic linked the bovine skeletons together in place of ligaments. As they galloped toward the panicking soldiers who looked to dodge the stampede, Sera's city wall flashed in pieces between moving bone.

Instead of me versus sixteen soldiers, it was now me, six skeletal cattle, and four recent human corpses against twelve remaining foes. Necromancy had always intrigued me, but seeing its power in action was mesmerizing. Unlike most magics or weapons that fatigued wielders over time, my power only grew.

With a sound reminiscent of smashing a large fruit mercilessly against stone, the first skeletal cow bashed its cranium into the fire mage's chest. The woman flew back in a spin from the charge's momentum and crashed to the ground with the crunch of bone. Her flaming sword escaped her grasp and spread its fire to the long grasses nearby. The leather armor covering the mage's chest bloated and creaked with internal hemorrhaging, and after a few wheezy breaths, she went still.

I continued backing away from the scene and shouted again, *"Leave me be* and I will dispel them!"

Clunk!

The breath forcefully escaped my lungs from the rapid emergence of stone beneath my boots. I fell off the rock pillar to the ground, and my shield flickered out from the force. The earth mage who'd summoned the obstruction stalked up to me, building a metal blade in his palm.

I didn't regenerate my shield right away. I only sat there, overwhelmed and pondering over whether it would be best just to let them kill me. A harmless interest in necromancy had rapidly devolved into multiple casualties, and all because they wouldn't reason with me. Why even try?

The earth mage eyed the growing metal until he was satisfied with its size. Since I sat back on the grass with no protections from a physical hit, my pale throat was vulnerable and beckoned to him in the moonlight. I only stared at my killer with a confused mixture of resignation and defiance, waiting for death and hoping for it to be quick.

Then, it was raining. In the frigid night air of Dark Star, heavy hot droplets rained over me and the surrounding grasses as the skeleton of a bull impaled the earth mage with one horn through the temple. With a hollowed beastly cry, the bull threw its victim into the air, releasing the body from the horn until it spun surrounded by an ever-widening arc of blood, shattered bone, and brain matter. My traumatized breaths were all I could hear as I realized I was covered in the aftermath. A sliver of the man's gray brain sat on my pale arm in a steaming lump, and one dislodged green eye stared at me from beside my boot.

I swallowed down nausea and scrambled back over the grasses, desperate to separate myself from a fight that only grew bloodier. Ahead, cattle rampaged through the soldiers as weapons and the elements were thrown back at them, and though one skeleton collapsed into a heap of bones, the dead had the upper hand. Unlike me *and* my foes, morale didn't affect my corpses. They didn't care about the gore and destruction. When a corpse ally fell, they didn't panic or lose their focus. They simply fought, protecting me and destroying those who would wish me harm until they were either defeated or dispelled.

I regenerated my shield and stood, so shaky on my feet that I nearly fell back to the ground. I didn't want to fight anymore. Watching the battle ahead with a distant gaze, I realized I didn't have to. One by one, the soldiers were either gored by cattle or defeated by former friends. In the chaos of the stampede, they hadn't been able to focus on fighting me.

As heavy breaths echoed in my ears, the remaining bovine and human corpses walked back to me like loyal pets and loitered around like we met for a demented family gathering. We were all covered in blood. I noticed the blood streaming down the bull's horns and remembered how this skeleton had been the one to save my life even though I'd given up.

"Thank you," I murmured, my shaking voice making it incoherent.

Internally, I understood talking to corpses was pathetic. But right now, I had no one else.

Screams echoed out from Sera's gate, where soldiers and civilians rushed to look outside the city at the ruckus. The fire from the mage's earlier spell still raged over the grasses, lighting up the gory battlefield as if helping the city find the culprit.

I waved my hand quickly in the air, and the corpses collapsed. Bones fell without rhyme or reason, and the decapitated heads separated once more from severed spinal cords. I backed away from the scene a few more steps before spinning to rush toward the asylum of the Seran Forest, my thoughts the only things racing faster than my heart.

Seven

The first few days in the Seran Forest were a mish-mash of crazed traumatic rambles, frenzied shivering, and blank stares at falling snow and hanging icicles. The Icilic blood running through my veins made the frigid cold bearable, but I was not immune to the inexorable consequences of severe weather. I didn't sleep or stop moving for a few days, desperate to keep my heart rate up and body warm.

The Seran Forest was a coniferous mix of burly pines, evergreens, and thick mosses that gave off bursts of color through the glimmering icy dew of cold mornings. I ate little other than twilby and gotton berries, for they were the only plants I recognized. Gotton berries were a popular snack at the Seran University for the raw energy boosts they gave to studying mages. As I ate them now, I marveled at my new circumstances.

The face of the first man I'd killed haunted me. The look of confusion he'd had when staring down at the last of his life force stuck with me like a taunt.

Why wouldn't he retreat? My mind kept going back to that. Then the other side of my brain played devil's advocate and ask, *why wouldn't you?*

I didn't want to die. I have things to live for. I thought back to how I'd pleaded with Kai to look forward to something. Yet, I'd nearly given up during the fight because continuing it only meant more death. Why would Kai follow my advice when I didn't follow it myself?

Kai deserves to live. You don't. I frowned against the subjective musings as a painful ache of self-loathing sliced through me. I heard her words to me, over and over, about how I was her only friend and she didn't want to lose me. By now, surely Kai knew what happened. She would know of my secrets and my crimes. Not only had I ruined any chance of forming an everlasting bond with the one person I'd ever connected with, she would die lonely while viewing me with the same disdain I felt for myself.

Depression overtook me. On the eve of the new year, I read Kai's note repeatedly under a sliver of moonlight that shone through the needled canopy and sparkled off fallen snow. As my eyes stuck to Kai's bubbly handwriting, it reminded me that this hopefulness was no longer my reality. Eleven days ago, I'd longed for friendship and a decent future. Even in the best-case scenario where Kai didn't know of my crimes, at the very least she'd spend tonight thinking I rejected her. Guilt devastated me; not only did I think about Kai dying young and friendless, I felt like a murderer. Seeing my parents again and hearing their advice was the only solace I looked forward to.

The frigid season of Dark Star melded into the budding first season of 411. The weather warmed with the advent of New Moon, though the shadows of trees and their pine needle adornments kept the temperature comfortable even on the hottest days.

I felt awful. I smelled awful. My already thin form weakened with undernourishment and melancholia, and the clothes hanging off my frame exuded the stench of sweat and death, for the fabric still bore stains from the soldier whose head exploded. When light rains trickled through the canopies, I tried scrubbing myself and my clothes as clean as I could, but the half-hearted attempts did little without soap.

I traveled ever northward while my companions of traumatic introspection and depression evolved into denial and apathy. The Seran Forest was expansive, stretching from just east of Sera all the way to the Cel Mountains where it hugged the base of the range's midsection. Thornwell wasn't far from its northwestern border. While I could travel to Thornwell without entering the forest at all, I liked staying hidden beneath the canopies. I recalled the initial trip to Sera with the dwarven trader and how she'd said Sirius sent the Twelve after escaped criminals. Every time the canopies parted to allow me to glimpse the skies, I searched for griffons.

It was the 3rd of High Star, 411 when I took the first step out of the Seran Forest's safe embrace and onto the rolling plains between it and Thornwell. The incessant heat strangled me with its thickness, and my pale skin gleamed with pouring sweat. Nonetheless, I trudged forward, my eyes on the collection of worn shacks that blurred in the heat haze of the distance. The need to see my parents and be reminded that there were people left who cared for me clogged my chest like blocked arteries.

They'll know what to do. They'll accept me no matter what. They love me.

Fate took notice of my sudden optimism and concluded it liked me better when I suffered misfortune. Over the buildings of Thornwell, three griffons of various shades ascended into the air from a standstill, each carrying a soldier dressed in prestigious green and black armor. Even from this distance, I could hear the winds stirred up by their wings.

It had been an hour since leaving the forest, but I spun and hurried to the south. If members of the Twelve were in Thornwell, they clearly searched for me. There was no other reason for them to *come* to Thornwell.

A foreboding lump lodged in my throat when I was only halfway back to the forest. Far to my right over the shimmering waves of grass, the shadows of three griffon riders drew ever nearer.

FWOOSH. FWOOSH. FWOOSH. FWOOSH.

Though my eyes stuck to the safety of the nearing shadowed forest, I came to a sudden stop. Running was no use. It hadn't worked with the Seran soldiers, and it wouldn't work here. I couldn't run forever.

I turned and looked to the skies. Three Twelve members hovered far above me to the north, their griffon's wings manipulating the air so masterfully that the grasses below danced to their flapping tune. One rider carried a bow. Another held a great spear with a single blade. The third only stared at a piece of unrolled parchment before his eyes flicked up to me in comparison. Perhaps Sirius already had sketches of me prepared to put on death warrants. Possibly after getting someone I once trusted to provide my appearance details. Possibly his own daughter.

I blanked out that upsetting thought and decided not to waste any time. *Nothing* would stop me from going to Thornwell and seeing my parents today.

Let's get this over with.

As two balls of black magic grew under the palms I splayed toward the earth, the Twelve realized they'd found who they were looking for. The man rolled the order back up and put it in a leather bag that hung by the side of his saddle, and while the archer grabbed an arrow, the third prepared his spear and kicked his griffon into action.

A blanket of black energy spread across the sweltering grasses like an out of season frozen fog. As the magic searched for nearby corpses and assembled into tendrils, I quickly switched to life magic to give myself protections against weapons and magic.

Two arrows bounced off the magical barrier before the archer hesitated, choosing to waste no more until the shield was gone. As the earth shook beneath my boots and prepared to offer me an army, I backed over the grasses toward the forest, my eyes on the rapidly approaching spear that pointed at my chest past the elongated neck of a swooping griffon.

Shing!

The spear hit my shield with such force that it threw me back within it. I spun with the momentum and landed in a lump feet away. I inhaled sharply once I realized the oxygen fled my lungs and tried to reorient myself.

Shik!

I cursed in a yelp as something sliced by my temple, splitting the soft skin. Blood trickled down my cheek like a lost tear. Only then did I realize that landing so hard from the spear hit broke my life shield, and now the archer targeted me again. I'd assumed only offensive weapon hits could weaken the guard, but sheer force damaged it as well.

It seemed the Seran University's curriculum couldn't fully prepare me for the realities of true battle. *Every* fight was a learning experience.

Zwip. A new shield surrounded me, but I couldn't afford to stay on the defensive. Though the blue skies above morphed into a concoction of moody grays over the Servis Ocean in the north, the inevitable coastal storm was not yet here. Thus, energy reserves were low. The dreadfully hot and windless day was the worst time for a magic battle; given the Twelve's reliance on weapons, they knew this as well as I did.

But I knew necromancy. If I could only convince my foes to come close enough, I could harvest energy straight from their bodies.

Pop! Pop-pop! Pop!

Bursts of dirt, clay, and broken blades of grass erupted over the field like we'd unintentionally stumbled across caches of underground dwarven explosives. Humanoid skeletal hands clutched the earth's crest to pull bodies out of dormancy. The still-decomposing skeleton of a deer lifted out of the grasses from its side. A shriveled eyeball that had rested snugly in its socket fell out in a clump once the skeleton rose, turning its hollow gaze to the skies and pawing at the grasses with an impatient hoof.

This far from the forest, there weren't many cadavers. Civilians would have been found and put to rest, and if wildlife died here, their corpses were likely torn apart and carried off in hunks of separated meat. My new minions were nonetheless a curious mixture. Three humanoid corpses with abnormally large yellowed bottom incisors gathered around me, two carrying weapons and one missing both a weapon *and* an arm. I figured these had once been orcs; the brawny warmongers were native to the woods and mountains of Chairel and Hammerton. Only once had I glimpsed one after a mercenary party stopped by Thornwell to trade years back and burned the imposing body near the village. The orc skeletons stood at seven to eight feet tall, and I assumed they would be my best soldiers by the intimidation factor alone.

The rest of the carcasses were wildlife. The deer was missing a few of its ribs, but it didn't need them. A tiny squirrel skeleton twitched its long bony tail and chattered its bare incisors rapidly with impatience near my left boot. Oddly, the remains of a fish flopped around uselessly near one of the orcs. Since we weren't on the coast and the skeleton was incomplete, it hinted at being the remnants of a hastily eaten last meal.

I dispelled the fish, and the tiny bones lost themselves between waving grasses. I kept the rest like a loyal guard beside me as I continually backed toward the woodland. Most of the benefits the griffons had against me revolved around their reliance on the open sky. I needed them to land to harvest their energy.

The archer reloaded her bow expeditiously, shooting off arrows at the largest orc skeleton beside me. The first few bounced off bone, but when I gave my minion a life shield, the archer rewarded me with a glare of irritation.

The spearman set his sights on charging me once more since it worked so well the first time. The brown and white spotted griffon beneath him screeched as it fluttered in the skies, and the rider patted its neck in reassurance before positioning his spear like a lance. After a quick kick from rider to mount, the duo swooped in a death rush toward me from above.

The skeletons surrounding me hissed in gusts of hollow air, determined to spill blood to protect their master. The spearman paid little attention to them, intending to bypass them all for me. But I was their eyes and ears; as I backed toward the forest as if to retreat, my mind formed a desperate plan and willed my corpses to put it in action.

Two orc corpses left my side and spread forth like the prongs of a fork eager to capture a chunk of meat. The determination on my foe's face grew, for the departure of the corpses left me exposed.

The griffon's legs tucked under its belly as it swooped so close to the grasses they released a whistle to accompany their dance. When the mount was close enough to me that I could smell the soldier's body odor, I directed the orc corpses inward like two sides of a clamp.

One skeletal hand swiped through the air and grabbed the extended spear as it passed. Though the corpse's grip was strong, the griffon's momentum was greater; it carried the skeleton along for a few feet before the soldier released his weapon from the excess pressure and weight. The orc skeleton stumbled away from the area, one hand gripping the weapon it'd been buried with while the other held the Twelve's spear like coveted treasure.

At the same time and on the other side of the griffon, the second orc corpse swung its ax into the oncoming wing at the location of its radius.

Snap!

The griffon's exterior radial bone snapped in two beneath a cascade of blood spray as the beast screeched with sudden agony and lost its balance. As I hurried to the side to avoid its crash landing, the second orc skeleton collapsed in a pile of bones, forced to dispel due to the blow back of its own hit.

Screams of rage from the man's two companions still in the skies echoed in my ears as I hurried after the fallen griffon. Its rider tumbled over the saddle and onto the grasses, but I passed him. I figured the griffon was more likely to be a threat since the man dropped his spear, so I sought to weaken the beast first.

The griffon came to an abrupt stop at the end of a smear of broken earth from its landing. Crackling sizzled through the air as I leeched from the wounded mount with two funnels before it could regain its composure. Once my veins protruded with energized life force, I finally had the energy to cast more spells. The power would come from my own life, but that didn't faze me since it did so at the same time I empowered it with more.

Panicked whines echoed harshly off the trees along the northern Seran Forest as the bird of prey struggled to stand after breaking a leg in its fall. Still leeching with one hand, I raised the collapsed orc skeleton with the other. Seconds later, the bones sang like the rods of a wooden wind chime as they collected together to rise again. I directed my minions from afar. The orc that hadn't had a weapon grabbed the one-handed ax with its only arm. The skeleton that had once wielded the ax hobbled over to grab the Twelve's fallen spear with two hands. Now, *both* skeletons had weapons they could use, but such a strategy had required my intelligent input.

The soldier picked himself off the ground favoring his arm. He noticed the skeleton wielding his spear, and his eyes flashed with panic. As the orc corpses surrounded him, the griffon beside me screeched with new pain, drawing my attention back to the beast.

Blood spurted over glistening feathers from a severed artery. While I'd harvested the griffon's life force, the tiny squirrel minion had climbed it and gnashed through the flesh at the back of its neck. Just in front of the saddle was a messy pile of broken feathers and frayed tendon. Tiny rodent bones were newly painted in blood as it gnawed at the beast with gusto. The injured griffon finally slumped with death from a combination of magic and mayhem. Clearly griffons had more life force to harvest than men; not only had it taken me longer to kill, but I felt jittery with excess energy.

I raised the griffon from the dead and set my sights on its rider. Though he'd lost his spear, he now defended himself with a short sword against two orc corpses after defeating the third. The ax from earlier looked lost in a pile of the fallen bones. I headed there, raising the skeleton again before looking to protect the others with new shields.

Click. Click-click.

I spun, coming face to face with the looming beak of a griffon. The other two Twelve members had landed and dismounted their animals, forcing me to contend with four foes rather than two. I summoned two leeching funnels to double my efforts of stealing its life, only switching elements to regenerate my defenses with the beast's own life force. As I contended with the griffon, I checked on the orc corpses, for they surely should have killed their target by now.

The spearman still had his sword out and fought off the orc corpses, deflecting each swing. The orc skeleton with the spear swung it at its old wielder's side with the flat of its blade toward his armor.

Thunk.

No wonder they're not getting anywhere, I mused to myself. As the griffon before me slowed its pecks at my shield with fatigue, I directed the corpse with the spear to thrust with it rather than swing.

Shing!

The Twelve member abruptly stilled, impaled through the gut with his own spear. Its blade glistened with blood and bile where it poked through beside his spine, and the man coughed up blood. While he still stood, another skeleton decapitated him with an ax, for the impalement hadn't killed him quickly enough. Happy with their success, the corpses bounded off to contend with the other soldiers.

That was when all my senses sharpened.

Perhaps it happened gradually and I only just noticed it, but suddenly, it was as if I saw the world as someone else. As the griffon slumped with death before me, its life force still trembled in my veins like electricity. The energy hitched a ride with my circulatory system to each of my senses, heightening their awareness and power. As my heart pumped ferociously like I was suddenly a much larger beast, I heard it clearly. I *heard* the Twelve archer's arrow scraping by the others in her quiver as she retrieved it even though she was on the outskirts of battle, trying to aid her remaining comrade. I *heard* the happy tweeting of birds far from our battle in the forest. The bitter stench of stomach bile suddenly overwhelmed me, but the corpse it leaked from wasn't close by. Every color in the world was more robust —the yellow-green of waving grasses, the periwinkle of progressively moody skies, the red of spilled blood.

Momentarily confused by my newly bolstered senses, I summoned the spell necessary to recruit the fallen Twelve member to my side. As soon as the energy escaped me and collected in my palm, my senses returned to normal. Intrigued, I eyed my palm and dispelled the death magic, allowing the energy to return to me. The extra power was mine once more.

Is this the power of leeching? I flexed my hand as if the motion would give me an answer. The necromancy book had mentioned leeching *rages* or *highs* that could affect a mage once their body was so overwhelmed with life force it affected the mind, but I didn't feel like I was in a rage. I only felt...*smarter*. Quicker. Able to react better due to a higher awareness.

Unwilling to let this new power go, I left the corpse lying on the ground for now and instead planned on leeching more. As the Twelve archer scrambled back toward the forest chased by a ramming skeletal deer and rabid squirrel, the three orc corpses surrounded the final griffon. As for the other Twelve soldier...

Shing!

I stumbled forward within my shield, the magical force field flickering with weakness from a powerful swing behind me. I regenerated the protection and spun. My senses returned to normal with the expense of energy, but at least I was safe.

The third Twelve soldier wielded a longsword, determined to cut through my guards and get to me as quickly as possible. I stretched both arms toward him, siphoning his life force with two funnels. Alarm passed through his eyes as he felt my magic drain him. With a grunt, he lifted the sword a second time.

Aided by additional leeching, my senses sharpened again. But this time, as I fed my greedy veins with even more, something in my subconscious snapped.

"Aggh!" The hoarse scream was so omnipotent in magnitude I hardly recognized it was mine. I stumbled over my feet, my brain throbbing against the smooth internal walls of my skull as if it rapidly expanded. An uncontrollable excitement

combined with a lust for blood and power in my soul until it felt I would burst into trembling giblets. A hum of surplus strength and a deep desire for carnage fueled me. Now this...*this* was a leeching high.

The Twelve soldier finished his swing, but my sharpened senses alerted me to its speed and arc. I evaded the blade and violently kicked a clunky boot into the hands that held its handle.

Crack!

The two-handed weapon dropped as three of the foe's fingers broke and swelled with my kick, darkening with bruising as he gawked at me with bewilderment. His eyes betrayed thoughts he dared not speak. Though I stood taller than him, I was much thinner and had nearly non-existent muscles. Yet, a single kick disabled him. He seemed to connect my rush of power with my earlier scream, and he panicked as he tried to figure out what it was and how to combat it.

I leeched from the Twelve soldier relentlessly as he backed over the grasses toward the forest. Though his right hand was broken, he carried a side weapon, and he reached across his waist with his left to grab it. He swiped and thrust the sword at my safeguard, weakening it. I only paused from leeching long enough to refresh the protection with the energy of his stolen life force, and his eyes flashed with resignation.

Proud and arrogant thoughts flooded my head as I pursued him, fueled by the influx of excess power.

You should have left me be. I will end you.

In the back of my mind, I understood these thoughts were uncharacteristic of me. But I didn't care, for the leeching high took control and left my consciousness floating in the ether to watch the actions of my emboldened body.

The swipes of the Twelve's blade slowed before it fell to the ground. Its wielder quickly followed, depleted of life. I turned away from the corpse. I wanted more power, but I only had one enemy left to harvest it from.

The orc corpses had butchered the final griffon on the grasses that fell in the shadow of the nearby Seran Forest. The Twelve archer was the last foe left, and she panicked as her eyes scanned over the casualties on the battlefield. She'd slain the deer and squirrel skeletons simply by using the force of her arrow shots, and only two orc corpses were left. Even still, her only side weapon was a dagger, and she couldn't go up against the rest of us with that.

The woman spun toward the woodland and ran. The corpses followed suit, their bones clacking off one another with the pressure of their footfalls as they passed the forest border and ran through brushing foliage. Intent on keeping my leeching high, I rushed after them all, only skidding to a stop to seize the fallen spear from a heap of loose bones.

I wasn't sure what I would be able to *do* with the spear. I'd never wielded one before, but my newfound power and corresponding audacity seemed to assume I could use it.

The soldier's alarmed and exhausted breaths echoed hoarsely off surrounding pines as she desperately sought retreat. The vitality of her comrades throbbed in my veins as I pursued her over fallen logs and blankets of brush, barely breaking a sweat. I passed my corpses on the way. When I was close enough to the woman I reached out to leech from her, and the crackling of harvesting life force reverberated through the forest.

She spun in panic, realizing running would get her nowhere. She dropped the bow and snatched her dagger, backing away from me as I stalked after her. The soldier heaved and wheezed as she swung her dagger at my shield. Behind her and to my left was the bare trunk of a dying tree that shed its needles and most of its branches. I sidestepped to the right, directing her there in her retreat.

Moments later, her back hit the trunk, and her eyes widened in realization. I dispelled the leeching funnel and gripped the spear with both hands, using the power of excess life force to plunge it forward at her gut.

Shink.

An exhale escaped her lips, born from fatigue but weakening with the slight sob of pain. She desperately grabbed at the handle that stuck out of her navel as the split leather armor leaked a concoction of abdominal fluids. She didn't have the strength to remove the spear since it impaled through her and to the tree. The skin between her eyebrows creased with a mixture of intimidation and confusion as she watched me leech her remaining life. When she finally died, her last breath was one of relief.

I lifted both hands and stared at them in disbelief. They were just as pale and thin as they'd always been. The source of such strength was life force, and I had no other foes. I panicked as I realized that eventually this strength would leave me.

You are normally weak. To stay strong, you need more.

I glared into the forest as the veteran's corpse leaked blood in a puddle beside me. The two orc skeletons finally caught up and peered at me with hollow gazes. I dismissed them, and they collapsed in a mixed pile at the hanging soldier's feet.

My enhanced hearing picked up on the tweets of birds and the chattering of animals, and my leeching high grew hungrier.

More, it reminded me. *More.*

Thornwell didn't seem so important to me at the moment. I headed into the Seran Forest, on the prowl for power.

Eight

The woodland animals were weak, but they weren't stupid. As I hunted for life force with a leeching funnel prepared in one hand, they scattered and ran. I wasn't used to hunting, so I was terrible at it. The clattering buckles of my boots and my resounding heavy footsteps alerted all nearby life to my presence, and the funnel had a limited range. I hunted fruitlessly while everything was a confused blur until finally, by expending energy through time and my relentless pursuit, the urgency for power lessened. Suddenly, I realized how badly I'd lost control. Power still throbbed in my veins and I had a newfound sense of arrogance. Nonetheless, my first ever leeching high was gradually losing its influence. Having never experienced one before, I didn't know how I would feel once I was back to normal, or if I could get back to normal at all. But for now, it didn't matter. Thornwell was tantalizingly close, but in my lust for power I'd wandered farther away from it.

I turned back to the north and hastened my pace. I must have spent longer hunting than I realized, for it was over an hour before I passed the Twelve soldier dangling from the tree. Behind a shield of apathy, I inwardly recoiled at the sight. I remembered killing her, but I couldn't believe I'd had the strength to impale her. As if to agree with my bafflement, my arms ached so badly they felt like solid stone, heavy and stiff with overuse.

I didn't compare my experience with the power of leeching to what I'd read in the necromantic book. Not yet. After half a year of traveling and dealing with trauma without being able to process it, all I wanted to do was talk with someone who wouldn't fight me or push me away. I needed a sense of familiarity. Thornwell may forever have been off-limits to me now that I was a criminal, but I knew my parents would come with me wherever I needed to go.

Thornwell beckoned to the north once more, though the skies over it darkened to prepare for the storm that seemed too bashful to ever arrive. My pace quickened toward my hometown until I ran to it like it was my saving grace.

Familiar faces noticed my arrival and peered with a quiet distance. Perhaps they saw the blood stains on my clothes, or maybe the Twelve had spread the word of my crimes. I paid no mind to them, hurrying through eerily quiet roads to the tiny shack that seemed so welcoming.

The fishing boat my mother built for my father no longer hung on the rack outside, so I immediately scanned over the ocean to see if they were out together. Choppy waves harassed the shoreline, rocking small fishing and trading vessels at the docks farther east. But no one was on the water. The impending storm promised to be harsh, so everyone had rowed inland to avoid its beating.

Whispers echoed around me as I rushed to the front door of my house and grabbed the handle. It was locked, so I knocked rapidly.

"Mother! Father!" It was half shout, half hiss. Stares bored into my back like throwing knives. I leaned my forehead against the door, desperate to be inside, desperate to collapse with mental exhaustion in the company of people who loved me no matter what. My hearing was still sharpened with my fading leeching high, so I listened intently. I heard nothing inside.

I turned back toward the inner town. Most staring villagers averted nosy gazes and pretended to be busy. A growing sense of foreboding rose in my esophagus like nausea, born out of intuition rather than understanding.

"Where are my parents?" My hoarse voice nearly squeaked with desperation during the last word. The last few villagers who'd stared turned away.

I started to tremble with a mixture of panic and an unexplained onslaught of horror. I glanced back at our house, for the first time realizing that the boat wasn't the only detail missing. The boots my father left under our front steps that he only used on muddy days were gone. Layered boards of wood replaced the drapes that normally covered our windows.

"Where are my parents?" I yelled into the inner town, my hoarse voice rattling off of window panes. *"Where are my father's boots? Where's our boat?"* I hesitated, my teeth chattering with overwhelming dread. "They wouldn't leave without their boat," I reasoned incoherently to myself, my words little more than desperate rambles. "Mother spent so much time building it. He loves that boat. He wouldn't leave it. He wouldn't leave the boat."

"Cerin." My eyes snapped to the person who said it. Standing beside the southern wall of her inn and tavern was a woman I only knew as Red. She'd earned the nickname due to her head of fiery red hair. Red worked day and night at the bar of her inn. Neither of my parents frequented it, so the only time I recalled seeing her was when I'd gone with my father to deliver fresh fish to her inn's storage room.

Red was visually intimidating, standing six feet tall and seeming just as wide. Underneath layers of fat hid the muscle she often used to throw rowdy drunks out onto the streets of Thornwell at night. For now, however, a somber look held her friendly features hostage, and she gestured to me with her hand. "Come with me."

My chest heaved with frenzied breaths made even worse by the jittery excess energy of my high as I followed her without a word. The stares of other residents did not relent until Red led me into her tavern and closed the door behind me.

"Have a seat." Red motioned to a bar stool. As I dragged myself up onto it, she walked around to the other side of the counter. Her face was unreadable save for deep regret, so I avoided her eyes and looked down at the bar.

"Where are my parents?" Though it was a query, it came out like an urgent plea.

There was a hefty sigh. "Gone." Red's thick voice croaked out the word mournfully.

"Where did they go?"

"Cerin..." Red trailed off painfully.

"Tell me where they went," I pleaded, rubbing a fist impatiently on the bar as if the action could keep me from facing the inevitable. "I'll leave now to catch up with them." After a protracted silence, I asked, "Why were the Twelve here?"

"For you," Red replied delicately. "They came searching for you. Found your house as empty as you just did and only left after seeing proof they sold the property."

A fierce pain jolted my gut. "Why would they sell the house without telling me?"

Another sigh. "Gods, give me strength," Red murmured to herself.

"Even if the gods exist, they don't give a shit about our problems," I said, glowering at the bar as the motions of my hand finally broke the skin, leaving a smear of blood over rough wood.

Red noticed me bleeding onto her bar but said nothing of it. “Thornwell was attacked, Cerin. About a year and a half ago.”

I stopped scraping the bar and glanced up. “By who?”

Red met my gaze. Her eyes shone with unshed tears. “The Icilic.”

The breath left my lungs and didn't come back until lightheadedness consumed me. “Why?”

“They, too, looked for you.”

“I wasn't here.” The intense rattling of metal on wood alerted me to my shaking. The ring my parents gave me for my birthday years ago danced along the bar until I yanked my hand into my lap.

“No, you weren't,” Red agreed before looking elsewhere. “But the Icilic *thought* you were, and they were willing to slaughter everyone here until they found you. Your mother...” she trailed off and hesitated. “Your mother felt responsible. Offered to go with them to smooth things over with your grandfather in Glacia if they'd just stop killing innocents.”

I stilled. Ice grasped onto my heart. “Father wouldn't have let her go.”

“No,” Red agreed. “Lucius didn't want to let her go. Others held him back while she went with them.”

I said nothing. I blanked out the thousands of what-if scenarios that materialized and stared at my blood on the bar.

“We waited for Celena's return,” Red finally went on. “A season later, a Glacian trading vessel came to dock with a single package addressed to your father.”

I still said nothing.

"Nobody knows who murdered her, Cerin. We don't know if it was your grandfather or if—"

"How do you know she's dead?" I interrupted, the statement nearly incomprehensible.

"Because the package—they sent parts of her back."

A wave of dizziness overcame me. I almost fell backwards, so I lurched forward to crash my head into my forearm on the bar, perspiration beading over my face.

"Lucius turned to alcohol," Red went on, her words resounding in my head. The world spun around me and I swayed at its edge. "Stopped working and stayed here from open to close drinking until I kicked him out each night. He'd go back to the house and wail until it woke your neighbors. He fell behind on house payments. Spent every piece of gold meant for the house on ale. Alcohol turned your father from the friendliest person in the world to a mean-spirited man looking for a fight. One night, I had a lute player here performing for tips. Lucius bickered that he didn't want to hear a lute if it wasn't Celena's. It infuriated him until he got up and quarreled with the musician. When I came over to break it up, he fought *me*. We exchanged some punches." Red abruptly stopped after her voice hiccuped. "After one of mine, he went down and didn't get back up."

My forearm was a mess of sweat and tears beneath my face, but I remained quiet.

"I'm so, *so* sorry, Cerin," Red offered, her voice masculine as it held a collection of negative emotions.

"I need someplace to stay," I mumbled, the back of my throat stretching painfully to allow the words to pass over withheld grief.

"I can't let you—"

"Anything. Anything I have on me," I offered desperately. "It's yours. Just give me a bed for one night. *Please.* I just need one night. I haven't slept in a bed in half a year. I promise not to bother you ever again. You'll never have to see me again. I have no money, but you can have anything else. My clothes. My boots."

"I *can't,* Cerin," Red managed, remorseful. "I can't let you stay here. I'm putting the entirety of Thornwell in danger just by bringing you in here."

"The Icilic?" It was a vague request for clarification, but Red understood.

"The Icilic have already pledged to find you no matter where you are," she replied. "No—what truly puts Thornwell in peril now is Sirius Sera."

More nausea rose in my throat just at hearing the bastard's name.

"Sirius sent the Twelve here for you, as I said. Earlier this afternoon. You mentioned seeing them."

I gritted my teeth, flashbacks of my last battle running through my head. "I did."

"Then thank the gods you missed them," Red continued. "They have the order to kill you. They informed us that if you ever showed up here, we're required to report it to Sera. If we harbor you, Thornwell becomes an enemy of Sera. *All* of us could be imprisoned or killed." She hesitated her ramble to ask, *"What* happened, Cerin? What did you *do* in Sera?"

I finally raised my head, and it alarmed Red to see that my face was a mess of tears. I seldom cried, and when I did, I kept it quiet. "I made enemies," I said vaguely.

Red's eyes flicked back and forth between mine before she requested, “Confide in me.”

“The only people I'd confide in are long gone,” I replied, the words traveling over pebbles of retreating emotion. I clutched the edge of the bar, using it to help me get off my shaking bar stool without toppling over. “The Twelve won't trouble you. They are far away from Thornwell. I beg you to let me stay just one night.” The plea was monotone this time; suffering so much trauma in one day finally persuaded me to revert back to apathy to protect myself.

Red swallowed hard, but she shook her head. “I can't. I'm *sorry.”* She squatted behind her bar and reappeared with a long object swathed in canvas. “Do you have something to carry this with?”

I stared at it. “No. What is it?”

“A loaf of bread.” Red handed it to me. “I won't report your visit to Sera, but I can't promise you that someone else won't. I could lose everything if they find out I spoke with you. They'll likely spread this news to other settlements, Cerin. I don't know what trouble you got into, and maybe it's better that I *don't* know, but please...” She watched me take the bread before leaning back from her bar. “Find a way to get yourself out of it.”

Silence permeated the tavern for a few moments. My head floated away from my body and into a fog of misery. I glanced down at the bread in my hand and said, “Thank you for this.”

Being polite to Red only made her sadder, and a single tear rolled down her face as she attempted to smile. “You're welcome. I'm so sorry. It's been so painful to have to tell you all this. I'm sorry I couldn't—”

"Where are my parents buried?"

Red exhaled slowly, the breath wavering as it escaped her lips. "Lucius had your mother cremated and wore her ashes in a bottle around his neck. When he died, we didn't know what he wanted, so we buried him on the hill. The one your parents loved—"

"I know the one." I turned away and took my first step toward the door.

"There's a tombstone we made for him," Red said behind me. "That's how you'll know the spot."

"Thank you," I murmured, before gripping the door handle and leaving.

Fearful and confused chatter dulled in Thornwell's streets when I left the tavern and the surrounding villagers hushed their gossip. I shook so profusely with mourning and upset that each step I took felt unstable. I clutched the wrapped loaf of bread to my chest with an attachment unfitting of such an object. With the injustices of fate rendering me totally alone, it seemed I pathetically clung to the last symbol I had of mercy.

Thick rolling clouds so sinister and eerie they appeared blackish-purple bunched up over Thornwell like a bruise on the sky. Long yellow grasses attempted to flee the rolling ocean up the incline of a hill southwest of the home that used to be mine, pointing me to what was left of my parents. Red's warnings that all settlements might be warned of my criminal activities duly reminded me that my first visit to this grave should also be my last.

My parents loved this hill. The view from its crest was magnificent, showcasing the decline of the Seran prairies until they turned control over to the sandy coastline. Beyond, nothing but expansive ocean awaited, inhibited only by the limits of eyesight and the merging of water and open sky on the horizon. It was the perfect comfortable spot for my mother because even in the hottest season of High Star, the natural breezes coming in from the ocean would swoop up the hill and pass over her, alleviating some sweat she always combated due to her low tolerance of heat. My parents loved observing the casts of crabs that wandered the coastline looking for snacks and doing territorial dances. While my mother could build boats and tools like fishing poles just as well as most experts, my father had once managed to build her a spyglass she loved to look through here. If the skies were clear, she claimed she could see Glacia on the other side of the sea.

My parents loved cooking small meals and bringing them up here to eat while viewing the water. Sometimes we came as a family to eat together, but oftentimes they would come here alone. As much as I loved my parents, I'd always understood their need to be alone. While many kids feigned disgust at the love between their parents, I found the bond between them fascinating and did my best to encourage it. Despite their diverse personalities, viewpoints, and backgrounds, they'd been passionately in love. And I wanted them to be.

The yellowed grasses were much shorter at the top of the hill. Just where my mother would place a picnic blanket, a human-sized segment of grass struggled to grow as long as the blades surrounding it. Between this area and the ocean was a small and poorly made headstone, barely more than a simple polished stone cube.

Lucius Heliot
369-409 M.E.

How was it possible that my parents had been dead for so long without me knowing? Logically, it made sense. They'd last written in 408 to tell me they'd paid my tuition for the Seran University in full through 410, so the school had no obligation to inform me since they likely hadn't known yet, either. No one in Thornwell could afford to spend gold on a messenger. The only indication I'd ever had that something was wrong was their lack of letters during my last year in Sera.

Yet, I felt crushed with guilt simply for not knowing. For not *feeling* the death of someone close even when I was so far away. Intuition, I decided then, was just as big of an asshole as fate. It only works when convenient, and it holds monumental grudges against unfortunate people.

Red's words about my father's late-life alcoholism floated around unwelcome in my mind. Underneath overwhelming grief and despair, I simmered in muted resentment. My father had only gotten drunk once as far as I could remember, and it made him cocky and mean-spirited. He'd said some hurtful things to my mother before she locked him out of the house for the night. After waking up in the mud the next morning, he'd apologized to her profusely, promised never to drink to excess again, and cooked her a feast. After dinner, they'd asked me to leave the house to fish so they could be alone. Even before I left I knew my mother had forgiven him, for the twinkle in her eye indicated that it wasn't conversation that would fill their time.

My father was true to his word and never got drunk again, nor did he so much as sip alcohol without my mother around. This was one of the greatest reasons I looked up to him. He wasn't as talented nor as smart as my mother, but his devotion to her and the sacrifices he made to make her happy made up for his shortcomings. Knowing that he'd slipped in his resolve and it'd cost him his life made me lose a modicum of the respect I'd had for him, and that crashed with my grief and sense of self-loathing to leave only confusion in its wake.

What was it about alcohol that could so easily change and ruin people? In just a few short years, I'd seen two people I loved turn to it in their time of need just to be betrayed. It shattered Kai's confidence and will to live even though she'd otherwise had unmatched fortitude, and it turned my fun-loving father into a jerk.

It's the ability to overcome that makes a man a man.

My father hadn't taken his own advice, but as I stood over his grave and the foreboding breeze stole my long black hair out of the embrace of my dark hood, I decided to take it in his place. My family's dangerous link with tragedy would end with me. I made myself two promises that I swore to uphold forever.

I will never fall victim to the clutches of alcohol. Its sickly influence on those I loved could never affect me if I refused to partake in it.

Unlike my father, I will take my own advice: as awful as life can get, there are always ways forward. I would not bow down to the cruel vagaries of the universe and give up. I would mourn my losses, but I would grow from my misfortunes rather than flounder. If the Icilic wanted to hunt me down for my racial impurity, I'd become stronger to be ready to face them. If Sirius's ridiculous laws against necromancy forced me to be an outcast from civilized society, I would put up enough of a fight to get their attention and inconvenience the bastard every chance I got. It wasn't likely that I would ever see Sirius in person again, but I had demented hope that I'd run across Kenady Urien one day. Since he was a dual caster, he'd be an excellent choice for any mercenary parties or armies sent my way. If I ever saw Kenady again, I swore my revenge for his part in my exile would be savage. I would forever be a criminal; the least I could do was make a name for myself. Some necromancers never became strong enough to be noteworthy in history books, but I would rise to become a necromancer in the vein of Valerius the Undying.

Though I made these commitments in the back of my mind as anguish preoccupied the rest, they already influenced my train of thought. As a foreboding rumbling of thunder galloped through the clouds like a rude chuckle, my eyes searched over the surrounding landscape.

I can't always rely on magic. I need a weapon. I need armor.

My eyes caught on the northern border of the Seran Forest. I could loot supplies and weapons from the Twelve corpses, but I couldn't expect their armor to fit me, nor did the idea of brandishing a bow or a spear appeal to me. Taking their supplies would be a temporary measure. I needed to set my sights on somewhere else to go. In the far distance over the forest I could see the snow-capped peaks of the Cel Mountains. I wasn't an expert on the locations of Chairel's smaller settlements, but I knew that the dwarven town of Brognel sat in the mountain range and that it was accessible via the Cel Pass. The Cel Pass was the only direct route from central Chairel to the eastern border through the mountains, and its western end was said to be deep in the Seran Forest.

Given the Twelve had only now made it to Thornwell, I assumed they hadn't yet warned Brognel of my criminal history. I had no gold, but the dwarves were known to be overwhelmed with it since they often mined the precious metal. It was possible that by looting what I could from the Twelve and anything else, I could trade for supplies that suited me. The Seran Forest would hide half my trek before I reached the perilous winding mountain paths.

I let my eyes fall upon my father's grave one last time. "I love and miss you both," I murmured. Speaking to them finally prompted the brimming tears in my eyes to fall, leaving glistening streaks of saltwater down my cheeks. "I may not have removed us from poverty, but I will break this cycle of tragedy. I'll persevere and make you proud."

I took out the letters I'd written to my parents in Sera. After half a year of hitching a ride in my trouser pocket, they were frayed, bent, and faded. Other than the ring my parents gave me and Kai's note, they were the only things of importance I had left. I opened my hand, allowing the breezes to steal the letters from my grasp and carry them off into the air in swirling dances. I didn't believe in an afterlife, so I doubted my parents saw the gesture. But I thought it best if I left the letters in Thornwell. They belonged here.

I turned from the grave and my finicky intuition promised me it would be the last time I would ever visit it. I headed toward the Seran Forest. After a loud clap of thunder, the plains lit up with a flash of neon lavender light and tears spilled from the heavens.

Nine

Rains fell over the plains like the display of bodies I'd left close to the Seran Forest disgusted the gods until they tried to cleanse it from their view. As my clothes grew heavier with precipitation, I crouched over the Twelve spearman's corpse, searching his pockets and belongings for anything interesting or valuable.

The soldier carried a weapon's belt with a sheath for his short sword, so I removed it from him and fastened it on myself. It hung loosely from my thinner frame and lack of armor. I took the short sword from the grasses near his open hand and sheathed it on the belt. Until I found my own weapon, this would do. I didn't care for either the bow or the spear because they required two hands. I wanted something that I could wield with one while using magic with the other; due to my ability to take energy from foes and ease my fatigue, switching between magic and melee seemed like a fruitful prospect.

I left the spearman in the plains and moved closer to the Seran Forest, stopping by a griffon corpse to loot through its saddlebags, where I found an abundance of dried meat and fish. From the horn at the front of its saddle hung a dark military satchel I swiftly removed and hung from one shoulder. It would carry a good deal of supplies. I didn't yet go through its contents, though I stowed away the food I'd gotten in its wide main compartment.

The Twelve soldier who wielded the longsword was the one who'd compared my appearance to a piece of parchment, so I headed to his corpse next. The small leather pouch attached to his belt darkened with recent rainfall, so I leaned over it as I pulled out its contents, hoping to keep the rain from ruining parchment and ink.

Multiple documents were inside. I unfolded the one on the top of the pile and suddenly stared at a startlingly accurate depiction of my face as it was half a year ago before I'd lost weight. Even though the sketch held no color outside of strokes of black ink over creamy parchment, my appearance was unique. The human ears passed to me by my father were visible between locks of flowing black hair, but my sharp angular features were proof of my mother's elven blood. Using shading, perfectly placed lines, and skill, the artist called attention to my high cheekbones, full lips, longer face, and prominent Adam's apple. The drawing depicted me looking unfazed and unimpressed, and I didn't know if it was due to my stoicism or if the artist simply wanted a neutral expression.

Just under the sketch were my details:

WANTED! Cerin Heliot

Charges: Necromancy, 16 counts of murder of Seran armed forces, evading the law, practice of magic without a proper license

Known connections: Lucius Heliot (father, trades listed as a fisher and merchant), Celena I'lluminah (mother, trades listed as a fisher and ship builder). No peer acquaintances have stepped forward.

Race: Human

Age: 15. Birth date on university application is the 73rd of Red Moon, 395. Birth location is Thornwell.

Special characteristics: Cerin is abnormally pale and may suffer from nutritional deficiencies. Reports state that his skin has a slight glow in direct light. He overdresses to hide this feature. Cerin is thin but stands taller than most his age at six feet. He speaks little, but his voice is said to be rough and guttural in nature.

Notes: Permission granted to attack on sight. No arrest necessary, but if convenient his execution may be held here in Sera upon your return to serve as an example. Cerin's only known connections outside of Sera are in Thornwell. The public shall not know of his charges; do not induce panic. While Cerin's methods of obtaining death spells are unknown, it is unlikely this knowledge came from Thornwell, so interrogations are unnecessary. For now, maintaining control over the situation is paramount. Beware, for Cerin is a dual caster of life and death. Reports state he used life magic to protect and heal himself during his escape from Sera. Cerin's abrupt departure from this university cut his studies short; he did not yet learn all life spells, and he had only just started his first surgical course. While his knowledge of healing may lack, we should consider Cerin potentially more dangerous than most necromancers for his ability to protect himself from attack alone. Cerin was well-known at the university for being a loner; it is thus unlikely he will seek out any settlement other than Thornwell. If no signs of him are in Thornwell, use your best judgment. You may seek him out in the solitude of the Seran Forest, but it may be best to bring the griffons back here rather than risk them in ground battle. I have the resources necessary to send mercenary parties if need be. May you be victorious and make Sera proud.

Stamped red ink boasting the name of Sirius Sera concluded the note. I folded it back up, my mind reeling from everything I'd read. I put the stack of documents in my new satchel, keeping them safe and close to me. As the storm worsened overhead, releasing sharp rain droplets like tiny knives, I headed into the embrace of the Seran Forest.

The elaborate bow of the last Twelve soldier shone in a pile of brush near her body, and I grabbed it and secured it in the scabbard that once hung by her saddle. I only paused long enough at the hanging corpse to remove the silver rings from her fingers and check her pockets before moving on.

At some point soon, someone would discover the remnants of these soldiers and their battle against me. I didn't feel the need to hide any of it. Sirius's warrant clarified that despite my young age and newness to battle, just the prospect of my talent intimidated them. Sirius and his men knew of my rare dual casting abilities, and that I'd won battles when outnumbered proved I quickly taught myself how to use them to my advantage. Leaving the corpses of the prestigious Twelve soldiers and their mounts littered along the edge of the Seran Forest would only intimidate my pursuers more. The soldier hanging on the spear would likely bewilder whoever found her. It would force Sirius to question my true power. I wasn't normally strong enough to wield such a weapon; the powers of leeching had enabled me. However, due to the general ignorance of necromancy in Sera born out of its prohibition, it was more than possible Sirius wouldn't know that. Just the mystery of how I could kill in such a way would cause distress and bafflement.

The shadows of the Seran Forest consumed me as I made my way east. The severe storm combined with the onset of evening until it was nearly pitch-black, but I kept walking for hours, wishing to put as much distance as I could between myself and the prior battle. The leeching high faded over time and exertion until it left entirely, depleted of its fuel. Finally, I stopped to rest on a bed of pine needles beneath the lowest wide-reaching branches of a large tree. I crawled under its flimsy shelter and pulled my loot with me.

The pitter-patter of rainfall hummed through the forest, but the dense foliage kept the ground quite dry here. I wasn't comfortable, not in the slightest. Yet, as I laid there alone, overwhelmed, and with nothing but time to think, sobs rolled forth freely.

I cried for my parents. Not only for their deaths and my deep longing to confide in them, but also for their awful misfortune. All they'd wanted was a life of peace and to be left alone. My mother's explanations of the cruel realities of the Icilic bloodline came back to me then. Years ago, the idea that someone could want to murder another simply due to their racial impurity was so ridiculous that I'd barely considered such hatred could one day affect me. Glacia had always seemed so far away due to both its distance from Chairel and the fact that few of its inhabitants ever ventured out. Even once I knew they wanted me dead, I'd thought that they would find it too inconvenient to come and kill me. There were no Icilic elves in Sera. To this day, I'd been near none other than my mother. The

Icilic disdain for other races was a possible benefit to me, for it meant they were less likely to venture inland themselves.

Of course, they could always rely on the Alderi to track me down. The Alderi were also a race rarely seen in Chairel, for the dark elves were born and bred in the underground. Little was known about how an entire nation could exist out of sight and far below the surface of Arrayis, but knowledge wasn't required of the Alderi for them to be a threat. I'd heard the word *Alderi* here and there in Thornwell, but it was during my time in Sera that I learned more. Anytime someone controversial or well-known was killed by a dagger blade in the night with no trace of the culprit, they blamed the Alderi. In Chairel, Alderi were so closely associated with assassinations that the race was synonymous with the word *assassin*. Rumors stated that anyone with knowledge of how to reach the underground could hire them to remove a threat for the right price. Some gossipers claimed the Alderi were a female-only race, for all assassins ever caught were women or juveniles. Other gossipers argued that the Alderi culture was one of misandry where the women enslaved the men. I'd heard one tourist in Sera swear up and down that she'd seen a male dark elf piloting a mercenary ship while on the seas west of Nahara.

Regardless of fact or fiction, I'd never seen an Alderi, but I could expect the Icilic to rely on assassins to do their dirty work while they remained safe and comfortable in Glacia. Perhaps one day I would find a way to travel to my mother's homeland and enact vengeance for the Icilic wrongdoings against us, but the idea seemed so unrealistic and distant that I didn't allow myself to entertain it.

With my mind on my parents, I thought about the subjects I would bring up if I'd been with them now. There were so many things about the last half year that I hadn't allowed myself to think too deeply into for fear of what I would find. I knew I'd had the support of my parents no matter what, so perhaps waiting was my way of softening the blow of extreme life changes and onslaughts of uncomfortable introspection. Now, with two loved ones dead and the third on her deathbed and forever lost to me, the only opinion I could rely on was my own.

My involvement in necromancy had led to all my misfortunes other than the deaths of my parents, yet I couldn't blame myself for harmless curiosity. I hadn't delved into necromancy thinking I would never use it. I'd been all too eager to test my abilities in private, and the more I did so, the higher the risk of being caught as I was. When threatened, I'd defended myself with the only weapon I had. I couldn't fight with life magic, and I knew little about steel weapons. So I'd used necromancy to kill and stay alive, and the resulting battle forced me to confront that not only did I face danger and brutality for my interests, but I had to *become* dangerous and brutal to survive the consequences.

With some solace, I understood I wasn't alone in this regard. The Seran University's curriculum made it clear the elements were as brutal as they were deadly; if they weren't, they would keep their use in warfare to a minimum, and thousands wouldn't clamor to learn elemental magic hoping to rise in the ranks of the Chairel Army. They feared death magic for its savagery, but wasn't that hypocritical? Kai had told me bits and pieces of what she'd learned in her various elemental classes. They taught her how to spot the differences between degrees of burns on victims of fire magic. They taught strategies for when to use metal versus stone earth magic to cause cuts, mutilations, or blunt force trauma. Water magic could be used to drown, suffocate, or destroy. Air magic could cause mass casualties in seconds by virtue of electricity's tendency to spread and seek out the exposed moisture of bodies. In comparison, leeching someone's life until they died after minutes of fatigue sounded like a mercy.

Every student mage was trained to kill using the elements they were predisposed to. I was no exception. The only difference was that simply knowing the element of death criminalized me, so the people I might have once fought beside were now my foes.

The same doubts I had after taking a life would likely occur in the heads of all mages who ever saw battle. It wasn't using necromancy to kill that bothered me; it was the simple act of taking a life and doing it *well.* Yet, each kill was easier to pull off than the last as if killing the first allowed me to shift identities from a child to a merciless murderer of men. Killing a man made me feel more enlightened about things I should have already known; the dwarven trader who took me to Sera tried to convince me the world was cruel and required one to respond in kind to survive. At the time, I'd known nothing but a peaceful life with parents who loved me. Now, though? *Now* I understood what she meant.

At the Seran University library, I'd read through many books before deciding which kinds I liked best. My least favorite were fables that told fictional stories of righteous heroes who rose to fight a tyrannical and powerful villain. Even when young and naïve to how cruel the world could truly get, I'd understood such stories were bullshit. Every hero would make it through to the end despite their weaknesses and somehow slay a villain who was more powerful than them. Sometimes, their methods of success were overly convenient and relied on luck or nonsensical resurrection of the fallen. The real world was not so virginal, nor was it so dumb. No heroes or villains could exist when primal human nature drove us all. The idea that forces of good only fight forces of evil was not just false, it was dangerous to believe. The only way to survive was to be *willing* to resort to barbarous actions against those who threaten you.

And so far, I'm doing a damn good job of it.

The image of the impaled woman came back to me. My arms still felt like two heavy stones on either side of me, protesting their massive efforts. With the leeching high gone, every muscle in my body screamed for rest and healing. I tried to recall everything the necromantic book mentioned about such power. The terms *leeching high* and *leeching rage* were interchangeable. The book stated that the sudden surge of power felt comparative to the highs of some illegal and dangerous drugs, and such ecstasy could become addictive if one cannot control it. Thus, the necromancers of history had referred to their bursts of strength as leeching *highs*. But to *witness* a necromancer under the influence of a high was terrifying for foes, who were more likely to call them leeching *rages* due to their similarities to the berserker rages of orcs.

Leeching highs could only be acquired by accumulating an excess of life force in the system. The book stated the average high took the life force of six men to obtain, but when thinking back to my battle, I hadn't leeched from six. However, I remembered how the griffon's life force was stronger than that of a man, and I'd killed more than one. I had plenty of time with which to study the limits of leeching, so for now, I focused on what I knew. The book mentioned that while leeching highs were massive benefits that could change the tide of battles, they could also be dangerous. Not only because the brain could react in wildly different ways including lusting for more power after experiencing it, but also because the highs sharpened all senses but dulled pain. During battle, the inability to feel pain was a blessing *and* a curse. On one hand, I could ignore wounds for long enough to finish off a foe in time to heal myself. On the other hand, just one wound I wasn't aware of could kill me with blood loss or sudden disability.

I abruptly remembered the injuries I sustained throughout the day and went to heal them in the darkness. The cut along my temple from the Twelve archer's arrow narrowly missing my eye had scabbed over, but as I urged it to heal, flakes of dried blood fell down my skin as the life magic evicted them from their new home. Life magic was either white or clear depending on the spell, but when surrounded by blackness it glowed, lighting up my pathetic temporary home like a mini grounded moon. Next, I healed the hand I'd broken open at Red's tavern. The energy I used fatigued me only slightly, so I dug through the satchel at my side for food. I ate the bread first, for the rain had spread its fingers through the wrapped canvas. It was soggy and fell apart in my hands, but I had little food and knew that the dried meat and fish I'd found would last longer.

I ate the entire loaf, desperate to use it for sustenance before time and mold could claim it. Afterward, I rested alone in the darkness, listening to the never-ending rain that tried its best to lull me to sleep. Despite my fatigue it took me hours to fall asleep, for the most uncomfortable subjects refused to be put to bed.

Ten

Birds tweeted happily like they were oblivious to problems. I admired and envied their ignorance and inwardly thanked them for their waking song, for the rays of light that broke through the canopies angled downward, confirming the sun was overhead rather than rising. It was unlikely that anyone was currently after me; Sirius would only send more soldiers or mercenaries once someone found and reported the Twelve casualties. Still, every minute I spent walking east was another minute I could be ahead of them.

I collected my things from under the tree and brushed dead pine needles out of my hair before relieving myself. The simple act of urinating reminded me that I needed something with which to gather water. For the first time, I scrounged around through the satchel I'd looted and found a half-empty water flask. I mumbled a curse at my oversight, for I hadn't thought to look for such a thing the night before when the rainstorm offered me opportunities to refill it. I'd kept myself hydrated on the way to Thornwell by eating snow and sucking on icicles, but when the weather warmed I relied on the moisture in berries. Until I came across a water source or it rained again, I would eat berries and use the water flask as a last resort.

As I started my trek east for the day, it bothered me that I didn't outwardly mourn my parents. I'd never been the most demonstrative person; perhaps I'd found myself so attracted to Kai's outgoing nature since in many respects we were total opposites. Rather than cry or wallow in self-pity, I moved on with nothing more than a hole in my chest and a to-do list in my head. Still, moving on felt disrespectful, somehow.

It was as if I expected one of my parents to jump out from a conifer before me and ask, "Don't you *care?*"

I do care. The hole in my chest craved to be filled once more with their love and influence, and my active brain's ramblings only sought to distract me from inner torment. I'd felt enough pain in Sera when Kenady and the others treated me with nothing but cruelty. I'd felt enough pain when the friendly and confident girl I'd fallen in love with was given a death sentence by fate. When fleeing Sera, I found dwelling in denial more comfortable than facing the truth. I worried about leaving Kai alone with no friends and no methods of dealing with her horrible father other than blacking out from alcohol, and I feared she would either die young because of her talent or commit suicide before getting the chance. The what-ifs and questions that plagued me during that trip were torture. So I hid everything in a far corner of my mind where everything collected dust. I could do nothing to change some situations; all the worry in the world couldn't fix anything.

I'd felt enough pain. So I quit focusing on it and moved on. That didn't change that it was still there and hidden in a shell of protection. I may have lost everyone I loved, but I found merit in solitude. If I were destined to be forever alone, the only person I could lose was myself, and then I would feel nothing.

The Seran Forest made for a delightful companion and protector as I walked east over the next few weeks. Beds of red pine needles scattered between carpets of lush mosses so green I almost questioned their authenticity. Split trunks littered throughout the forest, some degrading with time and others deliberately cut by passersby long ago. Clusters of mushrooms poked their heads out of malformed trees, parted foliage, and rich dirt. The deeper into the forest I traveled, the more it hugged me from all angles with higher canopies and thicker brush. It also became easier to find water and possible sources for fish. Moist earth parted for trickling streams that sprung out of rock formations, and some held hands with small ponds to exchange ecosystems. I glimpsed fish in these waterways, but I had no fishing rod. My mother taught me how to make one long ago, but while there were plenty of flexible branches I could use for the rod, finding the line and metal for the hook proved more difficult.

A fishing rod or materials for one rose to be the first thing on my list to trade for. I needed a weapon and armor, yes, but such things weren't useful if I died from undernourishment. I wasn't feeble, for hauling heavy supplies and cutting my way through dense foliage was building muscle, and I still had food from the Twelve. But I wasn't yet strong enough to wield a weapon effectively without a leeching high, and my supplies dwindled. I bolstered them with what I could find from foraging, but I wasn't skilled at recognizing which plants and fungi were edible, so I stuck with gotton and twilby berries. An alchemy book wiggled its way onto my necessities list.

I lost track of time, for I didn't count the sunrises. I simply kept moving. So when I came across another traveler for the first time, all I knew for sure was that it had been a while since leaving Thornwell. The sun still conquered each day with glaring bright rays that penetrated the gaps of needled canopies, so surely the seasons hadn't yet changed.

The other traveler clearly heard my approach before I saw him, because as soon as I detected something in my peripheral vision and spun to look, I only saw a friendly smile.

"Hail," he greeted. The man was a Celdic elf with fair skin and curious brown eyes, and he had chestnut-colored hair that he pulled back in a lazy ponytail. The Celd sat alone on a fallen log. A full backpack weighed down his shoulders, and a large open bag sat at his boots. In the shadow of its flap I could see a book and some alchemy tools.

I thought twice about speaking to him at all. I could trust no one. But I desperately needed to trade, and the endless days I'd spent walking encouraged me to ask for directions.

"It's a beautiful day," the Celd went on when I'd said nothing, motioning to the rays of sunlight that reached greedily toward the mosses of the forest floor.

"Have I traveled so far I've reached the Cel Forest?" I pondered aloud.

The Celd burst into laughter until he wiped at an eye. "No, friend. You have a *long* way to go if that's where you're headed." His smile sobered as he noticed my blank stare. "Are you lost?"

"I don't know," I admitted.

"That sounds like a yes," the Celd surmised. "Where are you headed?"

Brognel. I reconsidered admitting that and only replied, "The Cel Pass."

"You're on the right track," he informed me, leaning to the side to jerk a thumb farther east. "Keep going east until you hit the mountains. If the path looks treacherous, don't take it. Head *south.* You'll recognize the pass because it has a sign marking it and you'll be able to see its various routes." He pointed above him as if to reference where I'd need to look.

"What do these routes look like?" I asked.

"Hanging bridges," the Celd replied. "Rope and wood."

"Thank you."

He nodded once. "You're welcome."

I hesitated. "Why are you out here alone?"

The Celd chuckled. "I could ask you the same thing." When I said nothing, he went on, "I like to travel every once in a while. Get out of Celendar and see the sights of the rest of Chairel." He motioned to the sprawling pines around him. "It's much different here. Celendar is marvelous, but one can only appreciate it when compared to other locales." He twisted his lips to the side. "I also carry some things travelers like you might be interested in, but you look a little young for some."

"Drugs," I surmised. If I knew anything about Celds from my time in Sera, they loved hobbies, entertainment, and smoking just about any herb.

The Celd laughed at my dry tone. "Don't sound so *enthused.*"

"I have things to trade," I said, realizing how random it sounded only when it came out.

He lifted an eyebrow. "I'm sure you do. It looks like you had yourself a spat with the orcs. Lucky you made it out alive."

Orcs. I glanced down at myself. My clothes were still bloodstained, and I carried multiple looted weapons. Perhaps he suspected I'd fought orcs since there were few other great threats in this forest. I'd let him think it.

"I'll tell you what," the Celd continued after some silence, "I won't question your choices. If you're already addicted to something at your age, nothing some stranger says will stop you." He readjusted on his seat to pull the backpack off and set it on the log beside him. He dug through it as he asked, "What's your poison?"

"Food."

The Celd glanced up, noted my serious face, and sighed with relief. "Thank the *gods.* Now I don't have to feel like a piece of shit for selling drugs to kids. Take my advice: smoke all the herbs you want, but stay *far* away from rempka."

Rempka. It was a hard drug notorious for degrading the body before leading to death unless users overdosed first. The poor district of Sera had offered glimpses of its crippling touch, for many of its people had lost teeth, hair, and fingernails. As far as I knew, the drug was a clear syrupy liquid that could either be drank or injected in the veins. As the Celd scrounged through his bags, I noticed tiny bottles of similar liquid within and connected the two.

"You advise to stay away from rempka, yet you sell it," I pointed out.

"The best part about rempka is the gold, friend," the Celd replied. "I can't make anything off it if I'm my own best customer. I have a mind for business, you see." After a few more moments of digging, he announced, "I have dried Celdic fruits. Some fungi."

"Do you have any meat or fish?"

"I apologize, friend," the Celd replied. "I'm a vegetarian."

A vegetarian drug dealer. I couldn't help but smirk with amusement, and he noticed.

"Kill an animal for food and it has no choice," he mused with a grin. "Kill yourself with drugs, and you made your choice a long time ago."

"Your logic is sound," I said, taking another step forward to glance in his bag. "I will trade you for fruits and fungi if you can spare them. All I have on me is meat."

"And gold, I presume?" he asked, eyeing the military satchel hanging over my shoulder. It was a quality made bag, so he might have thought my wealth was greater than it was.

"I have little gold," I replied. What I had was looted from the Twelve, and they'd carried little since it hadn't been necessary for their mission. Remembering that Celds were known for their ranged abilities, I offered, "I have a bow."

The Celd nodded as he eyed the bow in its scabbard on my back. "I appreciate the offer, but that bow is made of low-quality timber. I prefer the wood of the Cel Forest. It lasts generations." He nodded toward my left hand. "I'll trade you for the ring. Metal jewelry is rare in Celendar."

I glanced down at the ring my parents gave me. "This ring is sentimental. I have others."

The Celd tilted his head curiously. "All right, I respect that. Let me see them."

I walked over to the log he sat on, resting the satchel some distance away and searching through it. I didn't want to risk him seeing the official Seran warrants I still carried with my face on them. Pushing them to the side, I withdrew a small pouch that held the rings I'd looted from the Twelve. Though they hadn't used magic on that awfully hot and windless day, all three had clearly been mages. Between them all, I'd looted sixteen rings of various sizes.

"Good gods," the Celd mused, taking the bag when I offered it and fingering through the selection. "Where did you get such quality rings?"

"It is best not to ask."

He stopped and glanced up at me. Eyeing the bloodstains on my clothes in a new light, he asked, "Will someone come looking for them?"

"Not anymore."

The Celd chuckled and returned to studying the rings. "How old are you, kid?"

"I don't know. What's the date?"

"The 26th of High Star."

I marveled at that. Only twenty-three days had passed since Thornwell, but it felt like longer. "Then I'm fifteen."

"You know how to take care of yourself," he mused. "You seem like you've been alone for awhile. Since you have no one to teach you better, let me save you some frustration by telling you to understand the true value of things." He lifted one ring and squeezed its band as if to call attention to its thickness. "This is quality dwarven craftsmanship. Did you know that?"

"No."

"I could give you most of everything I have on me for this and *still* get the better end of the deal," he said. "And that bow? As much as it isn't to *my* tastes, it'll make a fine weapon for somebody. The more desperate they are, the more they'll give you for it. Regardless, that bow should fetch you a good..." he trailed off and tilted his head, "five hundred gold or so, I'd say. You almost traded it for food worth only a dozen gold pieces."

"I'm not looking to get rich. I'm looking to survive." My detached tone seemed cold to someone who'd only been genuinely helpful, so I added, "Thank you for your honesty and advice, though."

The Celd smiled at the sudden politeness and handed me back the pouch as he held a single silver ring. "You should go to Brognel if you're already headed through the pass," he said. "The dwarves pay more than anyone else."

"I'll consider it," I agreed.

The Celd pulled out small packets of dried fruit. "Is there anything else you're looking for? I'm still ending up with the better end of the deal, here."

"I assume you have no fishing supplies."

"No."

"Silk? Horsehair? Bendable metal?"

The Celd laughed abruptly. "What are you planning on doing with all *that?"*

"Building a fishing rod."

He raised an eyebrow, impressed. "You know what? I *do* have metal that would work for a hook. I have needles."

I eyed the bottles of rempka in his bag. *"Clean* ones?"

The Celd followed my gaze and burst into laughter. "Not injection needles, my friend." He grazed one finger along the lobe of his ear, where multiple looped silver piercings shone in the sunlight. "Piercing needles. And yes, they're clean."

"I'll take a few," I replied, convinced.

"I also have horsehair, but I have no silk," he said, separating a few piercing needles from his collection and wrapping them in a small strip of fabric.

"I'll take some of that as well." I watched as he dug through his things and opened a bag full of pure-white horsehair. Since the Celd had been friendly thus far, I mimicked his earlier words. "Will someone come looking for this?"

He snorted a laugh at my unexpected humor. "No. The horses are treated well and grew it back."

"That might not matter to a particularly vengeful horse."

The Celd grinned as he wrapped the long hair around his hand, creating a loop before securing the hair in another pouch. He gave me everything and watched as I put it in my satchel. "Why are you alone?" he questioned.

"Made enemies with all the wrong people and lost all the right ones."

"Well, I pray that you find your way," he offered. As I silently collected my satchel off the log, he added, "Is there anything else you need by way of advice? This ring will fetch me a good price."

I hesitated and looked around at our surroundings. "Which fungi are edible? I've been avoiding everything."

"Avoid everything with bright color on its cap or stem," he replied. "Red is most common, but if you ever venture underground by way of dwarven town or tunnel you might come across bioluminescence. Avoid mushrooms with skirts or sacks on their bases. Everything else should be safe." He nodded toward my bag. "I recommend picking up an alchemy book if you come across one. Until then, compare the mushrooms I gave you to those you see in the forest, and that'll help you learn."

"You've been most helpful," I said. "Thank you."

"And you've been entertaining," he replied with a smile. "Good luck to you."

"You as well."

I continued on my way to the east, feeling relieved after my exchange with the Celd. I had new supplies, but being able to talk and trade with someone who had no idea of my crimes was refreshing. He clearly understood I had a troubled history, but he wasn't so clean himself. It seemed secrets could be well-kept among criminals.

Just as the sun's glow gained a tinge of red with its yawn, I stopped early and used my new supplies to build a fishing rod. Though it had been years since building the last, each step came naturally to me. Crafting it was the most successful I'd been at anything in a long while, but I felt little pride.

Over the next week or so, I stopped at every stream and pond on my way to the Cel Pass, taking my time fishing, descaling, gutting, and sun-drying my catches. The Cel Mountains were now so close they cast the forest in shadow and its temperature fell considerably. With a simple glance through the canopies I could see snowy peaks and rough gray rock, but I took my time fishing nonetheless. I needed a stock of food, and I could possibly trade fish for additional gold if I needed it later.

But fishing also took me back to a nostalgic time and place when things were simpler. For the first time since losing my parents, I left the denial stage of grief and moved on to acceptance. I grieved silently while trying to relax in a manipulative cloud of familiarity, and somehow, I no longer felt alone.

Eleven

The Seran Forest thinned and relinquished its claim of the land to rockier dirt and colder climates. The trees at the easternmost woodland border allowed the Cel Mountains to make their entrance as dramatic as possible through parted branches. Slopes of gray rock rose to snow-capped peaks surrounded by dense clouds. It appeared the upper mountains were currently assaulted by a snowstorm even though the ground was dry beneath my boots.

Even after reaching the peaks, it took two days to find the Cel Pass by traveling south along the base of the range. There was an old, worn path of trampled pine needles devoid of rocks from those who came before me who'd also emerged from the forest too far north. I passed by groups of mercenaries and travelers, and most of them gave friendly greetings, oblivious to my identity. While I responded in kind, my rougher voice sounded so intimidating that I decided it was best just to nod. Sirius's warrant mentioned my unique voice. I had no reason to believe word of my crimes had spread this far east, particularly with the regent's pleas to keep the situation under control to avoid panicking the populace. Nonetheless, I didn't need to find reasons to arouse suspicion.

At the meeting of two mountains was a clearly defined wide path that sloped upward from a worn sign that simply read *Cel Pass*. Large boulders that had once fallen from the peaks littered the inside of the route, and many were cut down to leave room for walking. Far above my head and between the mountains hung the wood and rope bridges the Celd told me about, and as the snowstorm raged where I couldn't yet feel it, the bridges waved and rattled with protests.

I headed up the path, winding around rock formations and only stopping to sleep under outreaches of stone and in alcoves. The higher up I traveled, the colder it became. The snowstorms calmed within the first two days, but the path remained intimidating and treacherous. Oddly, I felt little fear or anxiety of the unknown, instead focusing only on experiencing something new.

Days after first entering the pass, the trail forked. Rather than choosing right away, I hesitated my advance to look over the land I'd left behind. The Seran Forest was an undulating green ocean hugging the near coastline of gray rock. Though the chill whistling through the mountains made it feel like Red Moon where I stood, the sun relentlessly assaulted the forest, driving the exterior canopies to glimmer reflectively for mercy. The woodland had been cool with shadow, but while looking down upon it one would think it steamed with heat. The skies were a cerulean blue that faded softly into the horizon where fluffy overlapping clouds chased their brethren.

The forest called out that it would hold my secrets and offer me shelter, and I believed it since it did such a good job thus far. After visiting Brognel and buying necessities, I would return to it. I had no desire to run all my life. It would be dangerous and take time, but eventually I would make that forest my haven. Much like Valerius the Undying had taken shelter on an island north of Chairel and goaded men to him only to collect their corpses over the centuries, I could do the same. By living in the forest and learning its every intricacy, I would always be in my element no matter who came after me. Then, their bodies would only be added to my repertoire.

Just thinking about such a thing made me look forward to the challenge, so I turned from the view and studied the fork in the path for a few moments. I had no idea which way to turn, and there was no helpful sign here like there had been on the ground. No travelers were around, so I couldn't ask for directions. Relying on luck alone, I went right.

The passage curved, narrowed, and continued around the mountain until it led over a long rope bridge that creaked even when it barely moved. I tested my weight on the first plank. When it didn't break, I walked a little too swiftly across the overpass, eager to leave it behind me.

The route evolved and became steeper and even more narrow, but I was forced to rest for the night. The next morning, I kept going uphill until the path broadened and leveled off in a crest. Blocking the skies above it was the next mountain peak over. When I finally reached the path, breathing hard with the climb and with legs so stiff my knees threatened never to bend again, my breath caught with wonder.

I'd traveled above the clouds. The path broke through rock to allow a view of the open sky to the right, where the early afternoon sun glistened off the mist of clouds so close I almost reached out to touch them. I could see no land, for under the endless blue of Arrayis's upper atmosphere, the clouds stretched out like a cotton carpet. I'd weathered no storms over the past day, and now it made sense, for I'd traveled above them. The air was still and unbelievably crisp, but somehow it felt warmer here. The sun's warmth was trapped between it and the clouds.

The path continued on the edge of the peak until it led into an open cave. From what I'd heard of Brognel, it was half above ground and half below it, so I didn't find this suspicious. I headed toward the cave, the glaring sunlight keeping me from seeing within its shadow until I stepped into it.

The temperature cooled once more, and my eyes adjusted to the sudden darkness. This was not a cave, but a tunnel. This path tunneled through the remaining mountain peak, where an absurdly long rope bridge stretched to the next.

A golden gate that encompassed the entire opening split the tunnel in half. Three humans loitered around it, which I found telling given Brognel had a dwarven populace. A woman crouched just inside, rummaging through a crate of goods that likely was dropped off recently. Two men guarded the gate, one outside and one inside. All three painted their skin a golden hue. As I approached, the woman glanced up and stood at my arrival, but the two men refused to make eye contact with me.

"Well, *well,"* the woman greeted, her eyes wandering down the length of me. Instead of seeming flirtatious, she glared down her nose like I was a piece of meat. "You're a little *pale,* but you'll do. Welcome to Whispermere, handsome."

I stopped when I was still a distance away from the gate, bewildered and uncomfortable. "You have me confused for someone else."

"You have let the name slip," one of the men protested, still not moving his gaze from the ground. "You must *never* let the name slip when a stranger arrives at the—"

"Silence," the woman hissed, and the man complied. I noticed with distaste that he shook fiercely with fear. Ignoring the panicking man, the woman glanced back up at me. "You're not a volunteer?"

I frowned and looked past her to the bridge. I couldn't see what lie beyond. "No. I thought this was Brognel—"

"I didn't ask you what you *thought,*" the woman snapped, one eyebrow raised with offense. "I asked you a yes or no question. A simple *no* would have sufficed."

Suddenly, it felt like I was back in the Seran University and surrounded by bullies so lacking in intelligence they could think of nothing but insults. I thought of how Kai would often fight back and how wonderful it felt to defend myself to Kenady. It encouraged me to reply, "Perhaps a *no* would have sufficed, but I offered you more. I don't need your permission to speak."

The woman flinched back like I'd hit her, and she spat, "I change my mind. You are *fucking* hideous."

"You're not the first to think that," I mused dryly.

The woman glared at the two men who still wouldn't give her eye contact. "Don't let him in. I don't *care* what he wants." She spun on her heel and hurried through the tunnel to the bridge.

"I apologize," said one of the guards, "but they have banned you from entering."

"And it was the easiest thing I've ever done."

"You spoke out of turn and disrespected her," the man went on.

"That woman deserves no respect from me *or* you." One of the men gasped in response to my revulsion, but I couldn't tell which one since they both stared at the ground. I glanced through the gate, noticing the woman was out of sight. "What kind of cult is this?"

"We answer no questions of this nature," came the response. "If you have things to trade, we may do so here. Otherwise, I have to ask you to leave."

"I *would* like to trade," I said, letting my satchel slip off my shoulder to the ground. As submissive as the men were in Whispermere, it seemed most of them were human. Perhaps they'd have attire in my size. "I need new clothes. I have sun-dried fish, dried fruits from Celendar, jewelry, and weapons."

Though the guards agreed to trade, when they looked me over to judge the size of the clothing I'd need, they still refused to look me in the eye. One left across the bridge and returned with two identical outfits. After judging their quality and size and finding both sufficient, I offered them what I had. The men seemed particularly impressed with the dried fish I'd prepared myself, especially when I told them the species. Perhaps their suppliers and traders normally brought ocean fish instead. After handing them enough packages of fish for the value of my new clothing, the men continued guarding the gate.

"I came looking for Brognel," I said, flicking my eyes back toward the tunnel's entrance. "Could you point me in the right direction?"

"Brognel is in the northern range," one guard replied, pointing north despite staring downward. "Where did you come from?"

"The Seran Forest."

"Then you must have come to a fork and went right," he replied, which reminded me I had. "You should have went left. If you go back the way you came, go straight. Eventually, you'll come to another fork. Stay straight to go to Brognel, turn right to head through the mountains to the eastern border."

Straight and straight, I deduced from his directions. "Thank you."

The man only bent forward in farewell. I left Whispermere perplexed and confused by its purpose. I had never heard of it before, nor did I remember seeing it on any map. Its outward beauty appeared like a cover for underlying corruption; while its mystery intrigued me, I didn't care to dig deeper and was happy to leave it behind me.

I headed back the way I'd come, going straight at the fork I saw just days earlier to head north. The path quickly widened and smoothed like it was more often used than the one to Whispermere. I promised myself that I would become better at studying my surroundings and tracking, for if I'd noticed such a thing days ago I could have avoided the detour.

Its appearance didn't lie, for no sooner did I walk up its incline when the first travelers came into view from its crest ahead. Two dwarven men pushed a wooden trading cart toward me, using a lever on its side and above the rear wheel to apply a brake that resisted the steep hill. As we neared one another, the two dwarves smiled in friendly greeting. Since I'd ditched my bloodstained clothes for the new ones I'd traded for, I assumed I gave off a better first impression.

One dwarf helped his friend control the trading cart from a handle, though his left arm hung in a sling attached to his neck. The other fared much better and used both arms, his muscles bulging from overcompensating. I eyed over their merchandise. Tarps and blankets covered some of it, but a curved blade partially hidden by a tarp caught my eye near the back of the cart.

The dwarves noticed my stare just before our paths crossed. One reached down and cranked the lever back further, and the cart came to a standstill despite the decline.

"Ya lookin' to trade?" the injured one asked, eyeing my heavy satchel.

"I want to see the curved blade," I replied, pointing to it.

"This one?" The other dwarf tugged an ax with a rounded blade from the cart.

"No," I replied. "The other one. In the back."

"Oh..." the dwarf looked over the cart's contents until he saw it. *"This?"*

One thick, grubby hand threw the blanket to the side, revealing the weapon in its entirety. It was a scythe similar in shape to those made to harvest grass, but it appeared someone built this one for battle. Its long, curved blade was broader in width to increase its durability, while steel encapsulated the end of its black handle to act as the blade's counterweight. The handle itself wasn't as long as a polearm; instead, it was forged to nearly half-size, allowing one to wield it one-handed and exert greater control of the blade.

It was a hellishly gorgeous weapon and I wanted it immediately.

"I'd advise against the scythe, friend," the dwarf said hesitantly. "It's a better weapon in theory than in practice, ya see. The guy who had me forge it said he wanted t'be a *harvester of men—"*

"I want it," I interrupted, letting my satchel strap fall down my arm as I prepared to trade.

"Ya don't know what yer gettin' into," he protested. "It's an unwieldy son of a bitch. Any fighting style yer used to? You'll have to rework it."

"Perfect," I said. "I have no fighting style. I'll make my own." I nodded toward my satchel. "I have food, jewelry, weapons." I stared back up at the duo as they frowned and exchanged glances.

"Gold," said the injured one.

"I have little," I admitted.

"Then ya ain't gettin' the scythe," he replied.

I stared at the weapon as I pondered. Finally, I nodded toward the man's broken arm and said, "I will mend your arm for it."

The dwarf frowned. "Ya have a healer's license?"

"No, but I have a healer's education."

Both men quieted and glanced around them for witnesses. Using magic without a license from the Seran University was a crime in Chairel. An unlicensed healer could not only be imprisoned for using their magic on someone in need, but after three offenses the punishment escalated to execution for life mages *and* their patients. Thus, even offering to heal him was risky, but I wanted that damn scythe.

"Mm..." the other dwarf began, motioning off the side of the path to a small camping spot that hid in an alcove behind some rocks. "Maybe this is the type'a thing to talk about in private, aye?"

I swept an arm toward the alcove in an open and silent invitation.

The two dwarves waddled around the nearby rocks, delicately pushing their cart over rougher ground and parking it. I followed, reaching in the cart and taking out the scythe to ensure I liked the way it felt in my hand. The traders watched me carefully, making sure I wouldn't run off with it.

The scythe was a masterfully crafted weapon. Despite its large curved blade, it didn't feel unbalanced as I held it in one hand. Due to the shape of the blade, regular swings and thrusts were impossible to make, and its shorter handle would require me to get close and personal with any foes. I understood how confusing the weapon would be for someone to learn if they'd wielded something simpler like a sword, but in this case, my general ignorance of weapons felt like an advantage. I could train with the scythe over time to learn its vulnerabilities and strengths and adjust accordingly. Already I'd gravitated toward berserker combat, using circumstances and even my own body to gain the advantage in battle; I'd used a spear on one foe after a split-second decision and dabbled in melee with another by kicking to stagger and break bones. If such things came naturally to me, I doubted I would have issue using the scythe. Already, ideas popped into my excited mind.

"How would I carry this?" I questioned, putting the scythe back on the cart to alleviate their suspicions.

"Don't know," the one who claimed to forge it replied. "Ya would have to get a weapon's belt specially made, I'd reckon."

"You said you made this for someone," I said. "Why is it here?"

"He couldn't get the hang of it," the dwarf replied. He nodded at my arms and added, "You'll have to build more muscle to use it effectively."

I glanced down at my arm and was quite pleased with the muscle I'd built thus far from constant travel and carrying supplies. "You should have seen me last season," I commented. I nodded toward the injured dwarf. “Do you agree to the trade or not?”

“Aye,” he agreed, coming over to me with his sling. “If ya heal it, the scythe is yers.”

“Sit down,” I requested, pointing to the ground beside an old firepit. “I need you still and stable.”

As the other dwarf helped his friend follow my order, I tried to keep my nerves at bay. This would be my first time attempting to heal someone else *and* a broken bone. The Seran University taught those in the healer's division that sometimes both magic *and* surgery were required to heal certain injuries; while magic could merge bone and tissue, it could not pull shattered pieces together or align bones before mending them. Fleeing the university when I had ensured my anatomical knowledge was also limited. I didn't know how to fully diagnose someone.

In this situation, the dwarf was already diagnosed and his bone in a stable position due to its sling. I repeated that in my head over and over in reassurance as I sat down across from him, trying not to let my expression betray my nerves. The dwarf watched me with concern as I scooted closer to him and reached into his sling to hover my hand over his flesh.

Sik la trama. Life magic escaped my fingers and traveled through his skin and muscle until it found his injury, before zipping back to my hand in the form of heat, alerting me to the location of the break without having to cut him open. I readjusted my hand over the break and switched spells.

Givara le life. This energy followed the footsteps of the last, only this time, it found breaks and tears and convinced them to rebuild. I kept the arm as still as possible as I allowed the magic to work.

"It tingles," the dwarf blurted, alarmed.

"That means it's working," I replied, not moving my eyes from his flesh.

"Yer a little young to be a healer, ain't ya?" he asked next, as if just noticing.

"He's an elf," the other said. "Elves look young for *centuries.*"

I glanced up. "I am no elf. I'm human." I couldn't know how aware these men were of the Icilic, but I didn't want them finding out about my secret origins.

"Ah, forgive me," the dwarf replied. "Ya got them perfect facial features that reminded me of elves. Thought ya were Celdic. Can't see yer ears under all that hair. What are ya doin' out here alone?"

"My business is my own."

The dwarves exchanged glances, but they said nothing else. When the life energy stopped escaping my fingers I sat back, for the wound was healed.

The dwarf pulled off his sling and stretched his arm out, slowly flexing his fingers. "Ya healed it, but I'm still sore."

"Healing tears and breaks cannot always ease the swelling or trauma they cause," I replied, standing up. "I offered to heal your bone, as I have. I cannot ease the swelling. I'd suggest finding an alchemist who can give you an anti-inflammatory or letting it rest until it calms. Any more questions?"

The two men slowly stood up and shook their heads.

"Then I'm taking the scythe," I informed them, grabbing the weapon out of the cart.

"May ya have better luck with it," one called after me. "And...kid?"

I stopped at the rock formation blocking the alcove from the road and glanced back. The dwarf motioned to his friend's mended arm and said, "Thank ya for this. But if anyone asks—"

I turned back toward the road and replied, "It never happened."

Twelve

59th of High Star, 411

The road to Brognel was far longer than I'd anticipated, though less treacherous. The dwarves kept the path clear for travelers, and they built enormous stone and gold bridges between mountain gaps. A magnificent view accompanied me while walking over these overpasses, for the enveloping mountains boasted of snowy, windy peaks that melted into the gray rock, sporadic greenery, and pools of sunlight at their bases. It was like experiencing the beauty of two seasons at once. The dwarves were phenomenal architects and proud of it; their bridges conquered the gaps at such an elevation and breadth I would have otherwise believed impossible. A glimpse beneath the bridges before crossing them revealed sturdy piers leading to wide foundations stretching out of the descending mountainsides far below. I found it hard to imagine the work and time necessary to build even one overpass, but there were several on this simple path.

This route was less steep than the one to Whispermere, but its length allowed it to gain height over time. They built the path on the edges of the mountains and only occasionally provided rope, wood, or stone barriers to block one from toppling over to their death. Once the road reached the peaks, it stayed fairly level.

This close to Brognel, it was impossible to be alone. Groups of dwarven miners leaving the town to travel to various mines along the path were commonplace, and while multiple camping sites sprang up alongside the trail, someone always occupied them. I tried to find smaller spots in which to sleep, but sometimes none existed, forcing me to sleep near groups of total strangers.

On one such a night, I settled on an overhang of rock. The only thing keeping me from tumbling over was an iron and wire barrier installed along its outer edge. Snow dust swept along the flat rock before sparkling in swirls into the abyss. The small moon of Eran hung in the sky over the northern mountains in a bright circle of white light, casting its soft curious glow over the campsite. I kept myself as covered as possible; not only did the severe chill surpass the limits of my Icilic tolerance, but the moonlight gave my skin a slight glow that could arouse suspicion as to my racial identity.

Seventeen dwarven miners gathered around a campfire on the same overhang drinking, telling dirty jokes, and causing a ruckus. I'd stayed unnoticed in my little corner of the site as I quietly ate from my packs of dried fish and kept my hood tugged over my head.

My arms ached profusely; I had to carry my scythe by hand, and I consistently practiced swinging it over my travels. Such an exercise couldn't compete with the strains of a real battle, of course, but little by little, my body strengthened. The curves of developing toned muscle were most noticeable in my upper arms, but even my hands seemed larger, and I wasn't sure how that was possible. Developing a bond with the scythe, understanding its capabilities, and becoming strong enough to wield it effectively were a good start. I'd learn the rest in battle.

As I nibbled from a slice of sun-dried river fish, I listened to the jovial conversation happening near the campfire.

"Nah, Aengus is an ass," one dwarf blurted, firelight shimmering off the ale that spilled over his beard.

"Never said he wasn't, ya daft bastard," another retorted, her eyes glassy with booze. "I just said I liked workin' for 'im, is all."

"'Cause he's one of a few who has stubble longer than yers?" the man replied, to which a few of them chortled.

"Nah, 'cause his cock's longer than he is tall," the woman retorted. The dwarf beside her snorted and lifted a mug to toast.

"He's a *dwarf,"* another pointed out. "That ain't *that* impressive."

"Do ya have a three-footer in them drawers?" the woman inquired. When the man said nothing and only drank, she badgered, "Pull it out then, aye? Let's see it, Mr. Itty-Bitty!"

"He don't need to pull it out," the next dwarf over said. "Everybody here knows what it looks like. There's a reason he got the nickname Itchy Britches."

The group roared with laughter. While it preoccupied them, I pulled out my water flask and stuck its opening under a nearby rock, where snow melted from the heat of the campfire and dripped slowly.

"Kid," one dwarf blurted, proving the move hadn't been subtle enough. I pretended not to hear, holding the flask still as it collected water. *"Kid."*

"Whatcha yappin' at?" another asked. Seconds later, she went on, "Ah, hell, I ain't even seen him there. Ya tryin' to hide in the night in that corner, kid?"

"Maybe he's deaf," one suggested.

"Or hidin' somethin'."

"Kid," the first dwarf blurted again.

I turned to glare at the group. *"What?"*

"Gods *damn,"* he snorted. "Hit a nerve."

"I haven't bothered you," I replied evenly. "Leave me be."

"Yer sittin' in our camp," he retorted.

"You're sitting in *mine,"* I said. "I was already here when you built the fire."

"Gotta admit," one woman said, "I like his sass. What's yer story, kid?"

"Not one I'm willing to tell."

"Do ya know anything about the *sun?"* another asked me, before a few of them burst into laughter.

"As much as you know about silence," I retorted.

Instead of being offended, the dwarf chortled. "Sharp mind, that. Come drink with us."

"And dull my sharp mind?" I questioned, to which he laughed again. "Thank you for the offer, but I need my sleep."

Though I laid down and turned away from the others, their rowdiness kept me awake for a while yet. Eventually, I must have dozed off, for when I awoke, the low light of the dying campfire and the surrounding silence confused me.

Did I fall asleep? I blinked heavily, but my eyes soon fluttered closed again. *What's it matter?*

Somewhere far off in the distance or my subconscious, a ghostly hiss forced my eyes back open. I stared through the nearby barrier with fatigued eyes. Nothing but dark shadows filling in the valley between this mountain and the next greeted me. I readjusted and went to hug my satchel closer to my chest to guard it just to realize it was gone.

I quickly rolled over to stare into camp. The once bright campfire was losing its fight for life, existing as little more than tiny flames and wisps of smoke rising from smoldering embers. Sixteen dwarves were passed out drunk under blankets, and the last sat right beside me with my satchel in his lap. Two grubby hands held the warrant with my face on it. While the dwarf was tipsy, he seemed to understand what he read, for his eyes flicked from the sketch to me. As soon as he realized I'd woken, he stiffened. My hand lurched forward to yank the warrant out of his grasp.

"Nec..." the dwarf trailed off, staring at me with horror as he began to tremble. *"Necromancer."*

I tugged my satchel out of his lap and shoved the warrant inside. "You should have left me be," I warned. My mind scrambled for ideas. Brognel was close. I desperately needed armor and supplies. As annoying as this group was the night before, I didn't want to kill them just to keep a secret. I could try reasoning with them, but I doubted that would go over well. While many feared and loathed necromancers, dwarves hated them the most. The dwarves loved their elaborate funeral rituals, numerous religions, and building sprawling underground libraries of sarcophagi called the Halls of the Dead. Thus, my requests for a peaceful resolution to this unfortunate incident were unlikely to be heard.

"I will forgive this intrusion of privacy if you forget what you saw," I told him, coming to a stand and grabbing my scythe. The tip of its blade scraped along the rock with a *shing.*

The dwarf's eyes widened as he struggled to stand while inebriated. He threw his gaze back to his friends and screamed, *"Necromancer!"*

A rush of warmth flowed through my extremities as my heart followed adrenaline's advice to race. As the dwarf kept hollering, his drunk and fatigued friends woke up with glazed stares and scrambled to fight. While the dwarves weren't a magical race, they were hardy melee fighters. These miners had no armor, but neither did I. I'd built up strength, but I faced severe doubts about my abilities against so many at once even if I had magical shields.

"What are ya sayin'?" one blurted irritably, grabbing a hatchet from a pile of her things.

I glared at the thief and said hoarsely, "I'm *warning* you!"

The others glanced between me and their friend. I gripped my scythe and wavered on my feet with apprehension.

The thief pointed at me and repeated, "He's a *necromancer!* There's a death warrant in his satchel!"

"The *kid* is a necromancer?" another asked in bewilderment. "Warrant from *who?"*

"Sirius Sera," the thief blurted. "Says he's a murderer of sixteen men."

"Soldiers," I corrected him, my tone tight with stress but my stare unceasing. "I bested sixteen Seran *soldiers* in one battle. There are seventeen of you and not *one* of you is as well-prepared as they were. If you go up against me, you will *die.* Forget about what you learned and I will let you go."

"He's sayin' he'll let *us* go," one dwarf mused with a huff, his gaze turning hostile as he leaned down to grab a sword. "Like one kid has a chance against us. Look around, *necromancer.* Ain't no bodies around for ya to fuck with."

I set my jaw, grasped my scythe tighter, and replied, "Not *yet."*

Kaaarrriiisss!

Our spat quieted as a chilling hiss deceptively kissed our ears. I recognized it as the same noise that woke me earlier even though I'd since thought it came from my imagination. We were so high up on the mountain while surrounded by rock and valleys that it was impossible to tell where it came from. Nonetheless, a few dwarves stared up into the skies and shuffled around in fear.

"What the hell kind of—"

"What did ya *summon,* necromancer?" one woman screeched, as another hiss echoed through the skies.

"I summoned *nothing,"* I retorted, switching my gaze between the dwarves and the skies. Panic stretched its sharp fingers around my heart.

"Stoke the fire!" a dwarf screamed, pointing desperately at the dying campfire. As his friend did just that, he continued, *"Flame can destroy them!"*

One woman backed away from the fire with an ax gripped in one hand, bewildered. As the flames roused once more, they cast our immediate surroundings in a bright orange glow. The dwarf's fear contorted her face in the new light. Just behind her, a shrunken husk of a body hanging from two corpse-colored leathery wings swooped in from the overhead darkness.

As the others panicked at the new arrival, the woman blurted, "Flame can destroy *what?"*

Two gray hands with abnormally long fingers and claws grasped around the woman's throat from behind. With the harsh whirling of flapping wings, the unknown creature carried the dwarf off into the shadows.

Clink!

Metal clanged off stone as the woman's ax fell and rattled until it stilled. Hoarse but restrained cries echoed through the darkness as the woman struggled to breathe against the creature's grip. All of us remaining on the path struggled to track her movements in the skies using only her screams as a locator. The sound ceased, and the night became eerily quiet. So quiet, in fact, that the normally subdued echo of drizzling cried out like an alarm from the road, where blood collected in an expanding puddle after falling from the stars like rain.

The shattering of multiple bones called our attention to the rock face on the opposite side of the path, where the dwarf's corpse was thrown like trash. Though the woman had been stout and hardy like any dwarf, her body was now shriveled, relieved of all its juices. Newly loose clothes gaped, revealing glimpses of withered nudity. It wrinkled formerly taut and smooth skin over knobs of bone and deflated muscles. Two deep puncture wounds oozed blood on the far right side of her shrunken face: one just below her jawline, and the other through her ear where a fang had punctured her eardrum.

WHOOSH.

The flap of wings preceded the creature's descent. It landed in the road facing us without a care, standing ten feet tall even though it appeared humanoid. Emaciated legs led to feet with long toes and sharp nails. It didn't have genitalia, only an eerie absence of it in the groin. Above dangling arms were two frayed and folded leathery wings, the forearms reaching even higher than its head before arcing down to the tips near its legs. Solid black eyes sunk deep in a skull above only a mound where a nose should have been. Its mouth was far too wide for its face.

Blood streamed down lengthy fangs to the shriveled, crusty gray flesh of its chin.

For a moment, no one said a word. The creature's hollow but perceptive black eyes peered at us with equal parts calculation and hunger before it shrieked. The high-pitched wail pierced through the chill of the night and raced over mountainsides like the warning bells of conflict. The creature lifted its face to the skies and trembled intensely as if it were amidst a seizure. In mere seconds, its crusty and dehydrated flesh filled out with new life. I noted the new moisture of its skin and the dwarven husk nearby and quickly understood.

"Vampire!" The drunken screech spurred us all into action. Despite the threat of the intimidating creature nearby, many gazes still turned to me.

"A creature of the undead," one woman rambled, pointing at me. *"You* summoned it, necromancer!"

"I summoned *nothing!"* I shouted back, preparing life protections with my free hand as I sidestepped toward the road, trying to get out of being surrounded. I nodded toward the vampire as it set its sights on another dwarf and tilted its head like a bird watching prey. *"That* is the true threat! Work *with* me to defeat it!"

The dwarves were overwhelmed, panicked, and confused. The vampire, however, was simply hungry. It lurched forward, hobbling unsteadily on spindly legs and whipping out its arms at the closest man. The dwarf clumsily swiped his blade at the creature as it grabbed his face with one hand. It twisted his head to the side abruptly, and the man went limp with the snap of his spine. Still holding the body upright, the vampire bit into the man's exposed neck. The creature's slender throat expanded. With the harsh noise of masses of siphoning liquid, it drained the man's blood and internal fluids in mere seconds. A once hardy body visibly shriveled before my eyes, turning into a husk of skin and bones. Newly refreshed with life force, the vampire shook with a frenzy, adding the second dwarf's power to its own body.

Undead. The dwarf's description of the creature stuck out like a warning. Normally, I couldn't leech from the dead. But if this creature solely subsisted on stolen life force to survive, perhaps I could defeat it by stealing it *back.*

Shing!

My internal strategies were pushed to the side as multiple dwarves attacked me. The life magic protecting me flickered as four different weapons hacked away at its strength.

"What are you *doing?"* I hissed, summoning death magic in my free hand. I didn't want to rely on my scythe until I had the extra power of a leeching high. "Let's work *together* to defeat it, or else we will *all* die here."

"Kill the summoner, defeat the summon," one woman spat back, slashing at my shield once more.

"Gods," I breathed with disappointment and perplexity, "you are *all* idiots."

I'd given enough warnings and pleas. I stretched my arm out to the woman's chest, and the crackling of her life force hissed and popped off the nearby rock. As I drained her life, the vampire finished doing the same with a third victim across the newly raging campfire. The irony of the situation wasn't lost on me. The vampire and I were alike in many respects, for not only did we defeat foes similarly, but like leeching highs strengthened me, the creature grew more powerful with each body it drained.

Its body filled out and strengthened, and its motions became more determined and quick. I hadn't just offered the dwarves mercy to keep from killing them; I also needed their help to defeat the vampire. I didn't want to be the only one left standing to face it.

As soon as the woman fell dead before me, I thrust a different necromantic spell to my feet. Four dwarven corpses picked themselves off of cold stone, and I started regenerating from another unfortunate volunteer.

The surrounding mountainside flashed with orange light when a dwarf kicked through the campfire's embers at the vampire as it drained yet another victim of its fluids. The embers spewed over the creature's right wing and flashed with light past its eyes, and it screeched in agony and stumbled back, dropping a half-drained corpse at its feet. In a pattern like blood splatter over its wing, gray flesh sizzled and degraded into ash.

"It's too strong!" one screeched across the camp, reloading a dwarven crossbow and hesitating a second to aim for the vampire's eye as it recovered from the light. "It's drained too much! Fire can't yet destroy it; we need to spill its blood!"

A dwarf fell dead from my leeching, but I didn't yet target another. My shield desperately needed regenerated. I summoned life magic in my free hand, but my defensive measures were too late. With a clatter of weapons and a collection of grunts, the surrounding dwarves weakened my guard until it shattered to nothing. It offered enough resistance to slow thrusts and swings, but two hits came through regardless. I blocked one with a quick raise of my scythe, but the other sliced through the side of my neck like an afterthought. A yelp of pain escaped my lips on a voice I didn't recognize due to its desperate panic. Rushing blood ran over my neck and shoulder like a sticky waterfall, filling the air with a metallic stench. The sudden fear of my head toppling off my neck consumed me, and I scrambled backwards while refreshing my shield.

Am I dead? My left hand clasped over my wound, trying to stop the bleeding and explore its damage all at once. Two fingers slipped past broken flesh and into the warm embrace of split muscle, and a rush of lightheadedness left me swaying.

Not yet. But I will be in minutes if I don't turn this around.

The move would have decapitated me if I hadn't had the shield. Despite its weakness, it broke the swing's momentum. My neck spurted blood from a half-inch wound across its left exterior; it would kill me quickly if left unmended. I hoped to the gods life magic would be enough to save me.

With one hand clasped over my wound and the other holding the scythe, the dwarves' pursuit forced me to the defensive. Over their shorter statures, however, two hollow black eyes zoned in hungrily on the gushing blood staining my clothes and the trail it left over the stone. My heart skipped a beat as the vampire slapped its nearest combatant to the side and hobbled past the campfire to me.

Focused on attacking me, the dwarves didn't notice the vampire's approach. Using this to my advantage, I gave them no warning. I blocked hits with my scythe and refreshed my shield once as the creature finally towered over the heads of the foes before me. Two corpse-colored hands grabbed the heads of two dwarves, throwing them to the sides to get to me. Their bodies knocked over the others beside them, and the inebriated men and women toppled to the ground in messy piles of confusion and gear.

My nostrils flared with indecision and fear as the vampire faced me alone. I reached out to its chest with summoned death magic. A black funnel connected us, and it darkened further as the crackling of life force echoed into the night.

My theory about stealing life force from vampires was right. I *could* kill it.

The vampire lurched an arm out to grab my neck, but my shield rejected the forceful move. Its head tilted in confusion. The transparent white magic of my protection reflected from its hollow gaze as it studied my defenses. An intense feeling of horror settled in me as I realized this creature possessed the highest form of strength: wit.

Still leeching from the vampire with my left hand, I swung my scythe toward its arm from the side. The tip of the blade tore through the leather of its nearby folded wing, but when the scythe hit the arm, the cut wasn't nearly as deep as I wanted it to be since I didn't yet have a high. Nonetheless, I pulled my weapon back with a grunt, taking great pride in the blood spilling from cold flesh.

The lightheadedness came back to me, this time from blood loss. I couldn't wait any longer to heal the wound. I summoned healing energy in my left hand and clasped it over my injury. The life magic glowed in the vampire's eyes for a split second before it thrust both arms at my shield in a sudden burst of anger.

Its immense strength knocked me off my feet and threw me back. Swirling snow and rock filled my vision, and only the splattering of my blood met my ears before I landed. Desperate for survival, I left my scythe on the rock beside me to keep both hands open for magic. I resumed healing with one and refreshed my weakened shield with another.

Perhaps the vampire meant to break through my defenses with its hit, but now that I was far from it, the dwarves had its attention. The corpses I'd raised had been defeated, so I recruited them once more. The ensuing chaos of sparring dwarves, corpses, and the creature finally gave me enough time to focus on my wound. As I healed it, I watched the battle and studied the vampire's movements. It bled freely from its wounds, and the blood never seemed to clot. Perhaps if I spilled enough of its stolen blood with my scythe, it would dry up to easily burn.

A wave of relief washed over me as my neck wound closed. I hadn't had enough healer's training to know whether the magic itself could correctly connect severed veins, nerves, *and* flesh. When I felt healthy enough to stand and grab my scythe again, however, I sensed nothing amiss other than a faint throbbing as my body reminded me it'd been hurt at all.

Six corpses now fought for me against the vampire and the living, and the panic of the miners was palpable in the air. I rushed to the aid of my minions when one was defeated easily from a simple swipe of the vampire's. I re-raised the corpse before protecting it and the others with shields. One dwarf noticed my strategy, and a flash of distaste crossed her features before she attacked. I stole the energy from her soul through a funnel, and she fell at my feet. Another dwarf screamed with battle lust and rushed me, but a protective minion hobbled forth, swinging a hatchet at its former friend's throat. The blade split flesh easily but lodged itself in the man's spinal cord. His eyelids twitched rapidly with neurological damage. The body fell abruptly, and the corpse let go of its weapon when it proved too difficult to retrieve. The zombie bounded away, all too happy to re-enter the battle with only its fists, but I mentally directed it to come back to my side. I held down the recent casualty's skull with the thick sole of a boot and grabbed the hatchet handle, jerking multiple times until the spine released the blade with a *crack.* As newly uninhibited blood gushed from the wound, I held out the weapon handle-first to the zombie.

"Here," I breathed.

The corpse grabbed the weapon happily, and an excessively moist gurgle escaped its cooling lips as if in gratitude. A warm feeling of camaraderie settled in my chest from the exchange. I followed the zombie as it engaged a dwarf in melee, leeching from its contenders to protect it as it once protected me.

Five, I thought as the fifth dwarf fell from my leeching alone. It was time to test the necromantic book's theory about the average leeching high requiring the life force of six men. Only two living dwarves were left. I was determined to steal their power before the vampire could. As worried as I was over how such power would affect me, I desperately needed it if I would stand a chance against the creature.

Just moments after leeching again, my senses sharpened. The dwarf fatigued, her movements becoming slow and clumsy. In direct contrast, my second leeching high suddenly triggered. It lit my brain aflame with excitement and emboldened the strength in my limbs. A hoarse cry burst through my lips and shattered through the air until the vampire hesitated from fighting and tilted its head with curiosity at my enthusiasm. Unlike my first high, I didn't lose control. I only felt...powerful. And good.

Really good.

The vampire lifted out its arm and dropped its most recent meal. Dark intelligent eyes found mine as it shook with a regenerative seizure. Somehow, it seemed to understand how alike we were. It knew I would be its greatest match tonight.

I released necromantic tendrils over the stone, and all seventeen miners were mine to command. The corpses swarmed the creature as I gripped my scythe with both hands, finally having enough strength to use it well. My eyes traveled down the curved blade as if I gazed sensually at a lover, and I trembled pleasurably with the anticipation of using it.

I raised one eyebrow at my remaining foe and taunted, “Let's get this party started.”

Thirteen

The vampire released a shrill cry into the night air as if in mockery of my earlier scream of power. Unwilling to miss an opportunity, I swung the scythe toward its left arm, determined to deepen the wound I'd started earlier. The scythe whistled charmingly in its arc, ending its song with the moist splitting of flesh and the cracking of bone. Blood splattered over my face due to my proximity to the wound, but I only spit when I tasted its metallic spice and focused on my hopeful victim. The blade hadn't cracked through the limb, so with a grunt, I kicked the vampire's chest, holding it steady with a thick boot as I violently tugged the scythe toward me repeatedly in a move to mutilate its arm once and for all. My hands tingled with the reverberations of the blade ripping through tendon and sliding by broken bone, and a tingle of pleasure traveled up my spine from being intimately acquainted with such viscera. The creature's forearm twitched with nerve damage. Before I could separate it, the vampire grabbed the boot with which I held it still, and I tumbled off balance before it threw me back at the mercy of my own leg.

Air whistled through my lips as I landed in a heap farther down the road, and my lungs protested the stolen breaths as I searched for my foe. The vampire's left forearm dangled loosely near its elbow, spraying so much blood over the stone that the cool tones of the surroundings bowed to red's majesty. It clearly wished to hunt me down, but the dwarven corpses swarmed it. Those without shields posed no threat, but the vampire seemed particularly annoyed with the corpses to whom I'd given protections. It couldn't injure them directly, so it dealt with them like it did with me by throwing them, shields and all, out of its immediate vicinity.

I stood to return to battle, but the vampire decided on a new tactic. Its wings whipped out to either side with the slap of leather, throwing multiple corpses back with such force they dispelled. It ascended into the air as my minions swarmed beneath it, hopping up while swinging weapons futilely. The vampire disappeared into the night sky, and it was my turn to be irritable.

Don't you dare leave now, I taunted internally, scanning the skies. My minions hobbled past me like they chased the creature, so I trusted their direction. The magic animating them clearly sensed what I couldn't.

Splat! Just feet before my minions, the ashen arm I'd mutilated fell to the stone after the final sliver of flesh tore and released its grip. Long fingers curled up in an eerie reflex as the stump end leaked blood. I headed over to the arm, kicking it into the nearby campfire. The overpowering stench of sulfur expelled from the limb as it burst into dark ash.

WHOOSH. WHOOSH. WHOOSH. WHOOSH.

I tried following the noise, and I finally spotted the creature. In the night sky ahead, sections of twinkling stars blacked out as the vampire swooped in from the heavens.

A curse escaped my lips as my foe was suddenly before me, its remaining arm out for my throat, fingers grasping. Its hand rammed into my shield, and an angry shriek pierced the skies before it flew back up into the darkness.

I huffed with dry amusement. Although the vampire had intelligence, it couldn't reason like a man. It had thought that by changing its own position, it could break through my guard to get to me.

Blood fell from the heavens like rain in the vampire's path as it circled the campsite a few times, calculating and planning in its own way. My minions trailed it, humorously hobbling around in ceaseless circles.

I simply stood back, waiting for the vampire's next attack. I couldn't reach it in the skies, so I goaded it to make its next move by remaining alone and vulnerable and spewing insults at it in my head.

Finally, it acted in a way I hadn't foreseen. It landed amid my eager corpses and grabbed one as if to feed. This dwarf had died from leeching alone, so she wasn't drained of her fluids. The vampire tugged it close, biting the corpse's face. One fang easily shattered the thin temple bone as the other sunk into an eye socket, rupturing the organ within. The vampire held the corpse so tight as it harvested its fluids that the skull collapsed as the brain inside shriveled rapidly. The body fell to the stone seconds later in much worse condition than before.

As the vampire shook with another seizure, I took advantage of the distraction and targeted its wing. The curved blade clashed into the flesh covering its metacarpal bone, but despite shedding blood, the wing didn't break. Its flimsy and movable nature ensured it caved to the hit's pressure rather than putting up the resistance necessary to snap bone. I grimaced at my novice mistake and mentally directed my closest minions to grab the wing and hold it in place. When they complied, I pulled the scythe back with a grunt of effort and brought it down over the limb.

Crrk! With it held taut, the metacarpal bone snapped. I reached out to grab the edge of the wing with my left hand as I tore my scythe through the break with the other. Leathery gray flesh ripped apart like parchment. This time when the vampire swatted me away like a pesky fly, my firm grip on its wing ensured I took a piece of it with me. The creature's shrill screams of annoyance and agony pierced the night as I picked myself up off the rock again, a section of mutilated wing in one hand. I carried it over to the campfire as the vampire fought off my minions, and we glared at one another as I tossed the limb to its demise like a non-verbal threat. The resulting cloud of ash rose from the embers as the creature defeated two of my minions. I sent death magic through the area to rebuild my small army. The fallen corpses rose, but the energy required for the spell depleted my leeching high. A sudden onslaught of agonizing soreness assaulted my overworked arms, and the weight of my scythe felt like an undue burden. The weapon hung heavily from my grip as I summoned death magic in my free hand, desperate to regain my strength.

I leeched from the vampire relentlessly, only hesitating to refresh my protection when I needed to. The sudden ecstasy of a new high excited my brain in dozens of static flashes, and the battle fatigue left my limbs like it'd been just a facade.

At ten feet in height, the vampire proved too tall to decapitate. But disabling it one limb at a time wore it down and removed much of the threat it posed, and it now bled freely from dozens of cuts made by my minions. Nonetheless, it didn't fall. While the vampire sucked the life out of multiple people in a matter of minutes earlier, it proved to take much longer to die. So much blood escaped its wounds that my boots splashed through puddles, and as I formed a plan to take it down once and for all, I continually leeched enough energy from it to kill many men. Its power was immense.

I backed toward the campfire, and the black funnel stretching from the vampire's chest to my hand lengthened until it dispelled once my distance was too far. The vampire refused to follow me. It wanted me dead, and my minions parted between us when I directed them to, leaving me tantalizingly vulnerable. However, the creature's black eyes reflected the orange glow of the fire whenever it dared to glance up. Connecting puzzle pieces in my head, I realized that while fire was particularly deadly to vampires, they also avoided looking at its light.

The vampire was intelligent enough to know why I tried leading it back to camp. It refused to flee since it hungered for my blood, but it also refused to follow me into an obvious trap.

"Fine," I muttered, lifting an arm to wipe at my forehead when it itched. The blood that splattered over my face earlier had dried, but perspiration from a long fight now trickled from my pores despite the frigid weather. I stalked back over to the vampire, gripping my scythe with both hands and directing my minions to scatter from the foe's right side. "Don't like the fire?" I asked as I neared, and it tilted its head like it could understand me. "I'll fucking *drag* you to it."

Silver reflected starlight and firelight in streaks of orange and white as my scythe flew into the vampire's upper leg. While my sharpened hearing picked up on the fracture of its femur, the leg stayed stable as the creature's heightened cries sliced painfully into my eardrums until it felt like they'd shatter. I jerked on the weapon repeatedly, hoping to break through the bone. Without keeping my foe still with a boot I couldn't put enough force on the break, however. I certainly wouldn't kick the vampire again when it used my leg to throw me earlier. I tugged the handle of the scythe outward, and the curved blade rolled out of the wound's embrace. I backed up a few steps, using the strength of my high combined with the momentum of a running start to swing the weapon at the break a second time.

Crack!

The vampire tumbled forward. I skirted its fall and jerked my scythe from its disabling break. I was so close to my foe that its remaining arm was within my life shield, rendering the protection useless. The creature grabbed my right boot, and when it tugged, I crashed to the ground beside it. Though the fall rattled me, my need for survival sharpened my focus. As the vampire reached out futilely for the tender flesh of my neck like it could smell the blood pumping through it, I stomped the heel of my boot into its skull. Once, twice, three times. Finally, the bone shattered, sinking in just above the brow. I expected the injury to disable the creature, but it only hissed and glared at me with hatred. Blood escaped its right eye like a tear, proof of internal trauma, but it acted no worse for wear.

I muttered a frustrated curse and backed away from the vampire as my minions swarmed it, desperate to protect me. I glanced at the near campfire when I stood. I couldn't drag the vampire into it easily without lighting myself on fire, but the gurgles and hisses of my minions reminded me that I always had eager volunteers.

I turned back to the vampire. It swiped this way and that at my corpses as they broke open new wounds in its flesh until it was as holey as wire mesh. An obscene amount of blood covered the entire mountain path like an entire army had fallen in the area. I nearly questioned my methods of fighting the vampire until I realized that wearing it down had worked.

Over its entire body, moist gray flesh finally dulled and wrinkled with the loss of blood and energy. Its skin crusted from dehydration, loose flakes separating and floating in puddles of blood. The vampire reached out desperately toward the only corpse left that it hadn't drained, but its movements were fatigued.

Blood slowly dripped off the tip of my scythe from the mess of torn tissue that caked near the blade's tang. I took a step back from the vampire and mentally willed my minions to drag it to its demise.

The corpses complied, ignoring the vampire's angered wailing protests. Crusted skin flakes and shredded chunks of gray tissue sloughed off over stone as it neared the fire. My minions backed into the flames first, and the overwhelming stench of charring flesh dominated the air, reminiscent of roasting pork. As dwarven bodies bubbled and melted from the heat, the corpses invited the vampire to their flaming destructive party.

Hollowed screams distorted as the vampire's flesh darkened and cracked like dehydrated earth before the sounds ceased altogether. Smoke billowed out from the area, followed promptly by an explosion of ash. The odor of sulfur rose to prominence just as my burning minions collapsed in the pile of their victim's ash. All around the blaze, corpses fell in piles of loose bones in withering skin as I dispelled them.

A cloud of ash floated over the path's barrier, carrying all evidence of the vampire off the mountain and dispersing it in windy bursts over the valley far below. Across the valley, a soft pink glow was visible over the next shadowed peak over, proving that my battle with the vampire had lasted through most of the night.

A leeching high still coursed through my veins, giving me the energy I surely hadn't obtained from a full night's rest. A chilly breeze whistled over the path, teasing the flames of the campfire and picking up some body heat that hitched rides with my sweat. Before me, the dwarven corpses set the scene for a horrific murder. I could only imagine how it would look to an outsider who didn't know a vampire and necromancer were present for this fight.

I wouldn't be there for their discovery. I'd kept my identity and crimes a secret, for all witnesses were dead. But my clothes were now bathed in blood, and I couldn't expect to enter Brognel looking like this. Eavesdropping on the conversations of travelers over the past weeks taught me that the Cel Mountains were spotted with hot springs. Before finishing the trek to Brognel, I'd find one to bathe in and clean all my gear.

I looted the miner corpses, grabbed my satchel, and left the campsite and road behind me before the rising sun could bring the earliest travelers with it. I couldn't help but feel a surge of loneliness throughout the morning as I traveled. Over the course of one battle, I'd bested an immensely strong and fearsome creature and honed my skills with the scythe, but I had no one with which to share these accomplishments. I succeeded at pushing the depressing thoughts from my mind and finally found a hot spring to bathe in. As time wore on and my high faded, the pain from battle exertion settled in; the spring's embrace not only washed all blood from my body and gear, but the heat calmed the protests of my muscles. The hot spring was so overwhelmingly soothing that I spent most the day soaking in it. Because why not? I had no one to answer to, and waiting to return to the path where the bloody campsite likely crawled with investigators would keep suspicion further from me.

Spending the day at the springs gave me time to think, however, and my mind went back to loneliness. It was an emotion I hadn't felt often until entering Sera, and I'd dwelled in it ever since. Perhaps it was a simple case of not knowing what I had until it was gone. I thought of Kai. I wondered how she was and how much she knew about my crimes. I would have given anything just to know what she thought of me now. It wasn't like it mattered; Kai's opinion couldn't change my situation even if she remained open-minded to it. Yet, somehow, the idea of having her support—even silently—gave me a surge of hope and motivation. I pulled her note out of my satchel sitting on the border of the spring and read it with longing. Somehow, even though it was old and irrelevant to my life now, reading it gave me a certain calmness I could get nowhere else.

Stay realistic. Pessimism overrode hope to settle me back into reality, and I folded the note back up and put it away in its protective pocket. It was childish to think I would ever see Kai again, let alone that she would support me now. Necromancy was only one of my crimes; at this point, I'd also killed dwarven miners and members of the prestigious Twelve. Not only did the Twelve report to Kai's father, but Bjorn was responsible for training them. And if Kai loved anyone, she adored Bjorn. I'd never learned the full extent of their relationship, but I realized in Sera that they meant the world to each other. By killing soldiers who worked closely with Bjorn, I'd secured my place as Kai's enemy.

Kai's enemy. Just the thought of being against her clenched my heart and soured my stomach. But realistically, it was likely that I would one day have to fight her. After all, Sirius called her the greatest asset of war that existed, and the Chairel Army was the mightiest in the world; he would no doubt use her in his army. It was possible that he'd send Kai to hunt me down in the future. With skill superior to most mages and willpower that put most to shame, Kai would not only be a fantastic pick to kill me if other pursuers failed, she would likely give me my greatest challenge. Just the tinges of fear pricked my heart at the thought of fighting her. If it came to that, would I be able to kill her?

I set my jaw and forced my mind to clear. When it stubbornly refused to stay quiet, I grabbed my recently washed clothes from the satchel sitting on the rock nearby and set about washing them again. I'd cleaned them so well the first time that the bloodstains were barely visible as tints of rust in creamy fabric, but I scrubbed them all over again anyway. As my body soaked in the heat of the springs, my mind took solace in the comfort of denial.

Fourteen

Two days and nights passed before I left the hot springs behind me and retraced my steps back to the road. The campsite was within view when I re-entered the path, but no evidence of the fight remained. Two dwarves chattered nearby, but I couldn't ascertain their conversation. I feigned disinterest in the scene and headed north.

Only three days after reaching the path again, dark clouds collected overhead, and a blizzard assaulted the peaks. It felt absurd to experience such weather in late-High Star, but I pulled my hood up over my head and didn't complain. Rapidly swirling snowflakes cut into my exposed skin like tiny knives, and my pace slowed to a crawl as I was forced to walk into the winds. I watched my boots, one step at a time, trying to keep from looking into the storm. Only when I heard a muted murmuring did I glance up just in time to see Brognel.

Brognel's placement in the northern range of the Cel Mountains kept it secluded and far out of the way of passersby. Thus, it was rarely spoken about other than in passing from those who visited it, which tended to be traders going by Thornwell or mercenaries in Sera. Perhaps this was why I had expected little of the settlement other than a place to rest and trade. Though Brognel was not one of Chairel's major cities, it impressed me with its size and extravagant greeting.

The final bridge to Brognel was a magnificent structure of stone and iron that stretched from the mountainside path of one peak to the face of another. Snow flurries danced across paved stone and twirled in puffs of temporary clouds over and through ornately designed iron railings that allowed glimpses to the depths of the valley below. A trader cart pushed by a few bundled dwarves creaked ahead, its wheels leaving thin impressions in the gathered snow until the winds swept away the evidence. The traders nodded at me in greeting, and we passed each other without words.

At the far end of the bridge, falling snow melted in the heat of rising billows of smoke from multiple chimneys that created tiny clouds above clusters of dwarven architecture. The peak of the mountain was a pyramid above businesses and homes stacked like blocks around both sides of a massive tunnel likely leading to Brognel's underground neighborhoods. Covered outdoor stone staircases and bridges offered avenues of travel for people looking to shop and move between buildings without getting caught in finicky weather.

Despite the ongoing blizzard, dwarves congregated in the town square settled between the outermost shops. At first, I took this as a sign that the town was on high alert for danger, possibly connected to me or the bloody campsite. However, as I neared it became obvious that harsh weather simply didn't faze the dwarves. Conversations filtered through falling snow and howling winds about the mines, mercenary work, and two particularly jovial dwarves exchanged pleasantries and asked about each other's kids. It was as if the heavens attempted to punish Brognel with a beating and the dwarves didn't notice.

My greatest concern in Brognel was ensuring word hadn't made it here of my crimes, and I saw no evidence that it had. I'd witnessed no griffons in the skies ever since fighting the Twelve near Thornwell, and I hoped Sirius's admission that my necromancy was to be kept under wraps meant no messages would make it here at all. Nonetheless, I kept an eye out for posted signs with my face or name and regarded each civilian with a healthy dose of suspicion.

The citizens regarded my presence in Brognel with little more than a passing curiosity. I was not the only non-dwarf in the town, for human and Celdic mercenaries intermingled with dwarven comrades and supervisors, looking far more affected by the frigid weather than the locals. These mercenaries were bundled in thick cloaks, coats, and heavy hoods while the dwarves collected lost snowflakes in unruly beards and eyebrows. Though my pale face hid within the shadows of a hood, my clothes were thin and I didn't have enough layers to protect me properly from the weather. If anyone stared at me at all, it was because I was under-dressed.

One store caught my interest along the edge of the town square. *Maude's Fittings,* it boasted from a stone plaque beside its door. A large window to the right of the entrance showcased a variety of clothing on carved wooden mannequins. Some mannequins were short and stocky, while others were in the taller, more limber shapes of humans and elves. I headed there, convinced they'd have something in my size.

A warm blast of air assaulted my face as I walked through the door with the sound of a jingling bell. A dwarven woman with a head full of frizzy copper hair glanced up from behind a counter. The counter was set up to be level for humans and elves to trade, so the employee's height confused me. Most dwarves stood between three and five feet tall, but this woman seemed to be the height of a human since she could lean on the taller counter.

"Hail," she greeted, her hazel eyes moving over my satchel and weapons until they stuck on the scythe in my hand. I felt a pang of panic wondering if she'd connected the weapon with the deaths at the campsite. “Welcome to Maude's Fittins,” she went on in her heavy accent, still staring at my weapon. “Yer here to buy? Not cause any trouble, I hope?”

I stopped in the entryway of her shop with hesitation. “I need clothing. I can leave my weapon at the door.”

“Which one?” she asked with an uncertain laugh. “Ya carry at least three, from what I see.”

“The scythe is my own.”

“And ya openly carry it like that in the middle'a town?”

My eyes widened as I realized my mistake. “I don't mean to. That's part of why I'm here in Brognel. I just traded for this weapon from some traders on my way here, but I have no sheath for it.”

“If ya think you'll find a sheath for a scythe, ya shouldn't be wielding it,” she commented, raising an eyebrow.

“I understand I'll have to get something specially made,” I replied. “If you could recommend someone, I'd be grateful.”

The dwarf finally met my gaze and sighed. “Aye, I'd recommend Beshil at *Rock Hard Weapons and Gear* underground.”

It was my turn to stare at her. Some silence went by before she asked abruptly, “What?”

“I'd prefer it if you gave me a recommendation for a *real* location.”

She snorted in amusement. “Nah, that's the name of it. Beshil's pervy, but he knows what he's doin'.” She glanced off to the side with a twinkle in her eye and murmured, “In more ways than *one.*”

A smirk raised my lips, and I asked, "Are you Maude?"

"Aye," she replied, looking back to me and motioning to the rest of her store. "And these are my fittins."

"I'm beginning to learn that dwarves don't bullshit with the names of their businesses."

Maude grinned. "Aye. Ya here to buy?"

"If you take trade rather than coin."

"That ain't no problem," Maude agreed. "Find what ya want and we'll sort it out. Most of the stuff that might fit ya is near the front."

"Thank you," I offered. I wandered over to the section with taller clothing. Movement in my peripheral vision caused me to glance up just to see Maude disappear. I frowned for a moment before all three feet of her reappeared at the end of the counter as she walked out to the main floor. I looked away to hide my inner amusement; Maude *wasn't* as tall as a human. She'd simply been sitting on a high stool.

Maude feigned interest in refolding clothing on shelves near the entryway of her shop, though I knew she likely kept an eye on me to ensure I wouldn't steal. I wondered how often she dealt with thieves and felt distaste at the idea that someone would steal from a place so willing to trade. Then I thought of the various lives I'd taken and realized I couldn't judge the morals of others.

"Are ya here alone?" Maude asked as I fingered the thick black fabric of a long cloak.

"Temporarily, yes," I replied vaguely.

"Tourism? Work?"

"A bit of both. Work calls me elsewhere, but I need supplies and had time to kill. I figured I'd visit Brognel since I never have before and I've heard the traders are reasonable." There was quite a bit of truth in that statement, but what surprised me most was how talkative I was with a total stranger. I reminded myself to be cautious, but I thirsted for social interaction.

"I promise to be reasonable, then," Maude replied with a chuckle. "I'm glad ya stopped by my store, don't get me wrong, but I don't know how ya lasted this long without proper clothes."

"Well, that's why I'm here," I mused lightheartedly, and Maude smiled with agreement.

I set my gear on the floor to try on the black cloak that caught my eye, and Maude watched from across the store. "I was hopin' ya'd pick that up," she mused as I checked its fit.

"Because it's the most expensive item here?" I questioned, and she laughed.

"Nah, because I made it so long ago and nobody's ever bought it. It's just takin' up space. Few are tall enough to wear it. Are ya elven?" Maude tried to glance at my ears even though they hid in my hood.

"No," I lied. "Human."

"Ah. Looks good on ya," Maude complimented. "Black suits ya."

"Thank you." I pulled the cloak off and folded it lengthwise before draping it over my arm.

Less than an hour later, a pile of clothing sat on the counter, all of it black. Maude sat on her stool so she could see the belongings I'd put up for trade. She twisted her lips to the side as she compared the clothing I wanted to the things I offered. I kept the Celd's trading advice from the Seran Forest at the forefront of my mind, prepared to haggle.

"I gotta be honest," Maude began, "I got a thing for jewelry, and these are some fine pieces." One stubby finger moved a few rings around but lingered on one in particular that had an arcanic design. "But I can't give ya as much for 'em as the jeweler down the street could. If ya trade 'em there and come back with gold, that'd be the better deal for ya."

"This ring alone is worth a great deal," I commented, pointing at the one she seemed to like most. It was the same ring the Celd told me was dwarven.

"Aye," Maude agreed. "Worth more than everythin' yer wantin', if I'm honest. You'd be better off tradin' it to Beshil for the sheath yer wantin' to commission. I'd reckon that'd cover most yer expense there."

Remembering Maude's earlier admittance that she'd been intimate with the armorer, I asked, "If I do that, is there a chance it could make it back to you?"

Maude raised an eyebrow. "...Aye."

"We could trade for other things now, and when I see Beshil I can casually mention you loved this ring but couldn't give me enough for it," I suggested.

A mischievous grin brightened her features. "What are ya, a messenger of Amora?" she questioned, speaking of the goddess of love.

"No, just someone who appreciates the power love holds over people," I commented, thinking of the relationship between my parents before the echo of one of Kai's husky laughs rose from a favored memory. I rolled my head to the side until a sharp crack sounded from my neck, trying to urge such thoughts from my mind. "It's a rare phenomenon that often ends in tragedy. You are lucky."

Maude's smile faded as she sensed the pain behind my words, but she said nothing of it. "Well, if ya would do that, not only would I appreciate it, I'll give ya a deal." She tapped on her favorite ring. "Trade this to Beshil. Tell 'im I got teary eyed over seein' it go and tug on his heartstrings a bit. Make him think it's his idea, like." She pulled two other rings toward her. "I'll take these two for the trade. It's a deal for ya, but I'm happy to see that cloak go to somebody who'll use it."

After settling the details and gathering all my belongings, I thanked Maude again and turned to the door.

"Wait," she called out just as my hand grabbed the door knob to leave. I glanced back. Thousands of thoughts flashed through Maude's hazel eyes before she said, "Good luck to ya if I don't see ya again. And be wary of travelin' alone. A group of miners was just murdered up the path a ways. People are arguin' over whether it was the work of a man or a beast."

Both, I mused to myself. I thanked Maude for her concern and left the shop in a cloud of sad introspection. As wonderful as socializing was, our conversation had been truly meaningless. It was amazing how two people could speak like friends and yet not know each other well at all. I was a criminal necromancer and murderer of Seran soldiers, but such a reality never crossed Maude's mind. She'd only seen me as a hard-working teenager who spoke of love like it was an unobtainable tragic concept. Similarly, the friendly shopkeeper could have been any number of awful things and I would never know.

There was a tragic side to having such secrets. Kai came to mind a second time in too short of a period, and I didn't bother pushing her from my thoughts again. It was futile. I was still in love with her, and I could only hope that feeling would dull with time and take this pain with it. Even back when I'd seen her often, our growing friendship was one-sided. Kai hadn't known who I truly was. I hadn't *allowed* her to.

Secrets were a necessity of life for me now. Not revealing my true identity to Maude allowed her to think I was a decent person, and that proved beneficial to me. I just had to stop thinking I could grow close to people without consequences. I often treated my corpses like friends I could protect in battle, and they were always loyal, carried no secrets, and had no underlying intentions. I *needed* no one else. I could raise an army of dedicated followers in mere seconds with a single spell.

...But how attractive was loyalty, really, when one isn't given a choice? Corpses were loyal because they *had* to be. My mastery of the magic that reanimated them demanded it. My parents had been loyal to me due to their love and our relation. Kai had relentlessly sought out my friendship because despite all reason, she'd found something in me she liked and could relate to.

"Who died?" a coarse voice barged into my thoughts as I entered Brognel's tunnel connecting its upper district to the underground. Only when I realized the dwarf who'd spoken glared at me did I understand my depressing thoughts came through my expression. I almost replied to the callous question with a proper sarcastic retort but decided against it and kept walking. The less attention I drew, the better.

Brognel's tunnel was about a city block wide and multiple stories tall, yet the temperature considerably warmed within seconds of walking within its shadow as the wind surrendered. Glistening swirls of snow dust danced over the stone floor before collecting in crevasses and against the walls. Sconces perched on either side of the wide tunnel, flickering flames rising from a black alchemical sludge. I assumed the concoction was a flame accelerant, for even the most persistent blizzard winds couldn't dull the fires.

The tunnel didn't wait long to reveal Brognel's underground secrets. It opened to a massive cavern overlooking layers of neighborhoods and elaborate architecture that descended ever farther beneath the mountain. An uncharacteristic feeling of excitement and discovery rose in my chest as I realized just how large Brognel was despite its seclusion. I glimpsed signs for inns and taverns and felt elated. Even if it could only be a temporary pleasure, I might sleep in a bed for the first time in over half a year if I gained enough gold through trading.

Exploring Brognel would have to wait, however. Just to my left and a block away was *Rock Hard Weapons and Gear*, settled at the crest of the path leading down into the depths. I crossed over the road, getting to the shop just in time to take the door from a human mercenary leaving with a new sword.

The building was far wider than it was deep, stretching far to my left as I entered. Weapons of many varieties hung on racks along the exterior wall, while a long counter ran down the center of the entire building. Mannequins displayed complete armor sets behind it, steel and leather glowing in the firelight of oil lamps and chandeliers. The shop smelled of leather, oil, ale, and body odor. Six dwarven employees scrambled around behind the counter, and given their heights and that of the furniture surrounding them, I assumed they elevated the employee area. Sympathy flowed through me as I tried to imagine having to alter architecture just to be tall enough to face potential customers. Such alterations hadn't been common in Sera; the shortest dwarves were simply out of luck when it came to utilizing human furniture and buildings. Though Brognel had a mostly dwarven populace, they seemed to cater to other races by building their architecture to support humans and adding features of convenience for themselves.

Two customers were being helped farther down the counter, so I wandered up to an empty spot. As I waited for an employee to approach me, my gaze fell to the glassy countertop. Beneath the glass, small weapons shone in the chandelier's light. Throwing stars, blades small enough to hide in boots, and even an odd weapon I'd never seen before with four holes beside a folded paper sign that read *brass knuckles*.

A breeze of bitter body odor pulled my attention up to the dwarf who stopped before me on the other side of the counter. She tilted her head, glanced at my human ears, and said, "Ya waitin' for a parent?"

"No," I said, trying my best not to be annoyed by her dismissive tone. "I'm waiting to trade and put in a special order."

"For toys?" she retorted with a snort.

"Brunhild," snapped a man who'd been conversing with the next customer down. He glared at the woman before me and gave a quick disapproving shake of his head, causing the brown and gray strands of his long beard to swish across his broad chest.

"I need to speak with Beshil," I went on, and Brunhild lifted an eyebrow and glanced back at the man who'd scolded her.

"Boss?" she mused. "The kid wants *you.* I told ya to always wrap it before ya tap it, and *this* is what ya get for not listenin' to me."

"I should fire ya," Beshil replied with a sigh, scribbling some words on a bill before him as the customer waited patiently.

Brunhild ignored the comment and looked me over. "'Course, he's too *pretty* to be yer kid. I expected fields'a body hair. Lotsa fat, like. More expressions of scorn."

"I can't help the first two," I began dryly, "but keep talking and the scorn will come naturally."

Beshil burst into laughter at my jest, and the customer he dealt with and Brunhild both grinned despite themselves. "Kid," Beshil began, "ya just became my favorite customer, and I don't even know yet why yer here."

"To kill ya," a male employee piped up as he dusted a set of steel armor. "Then he'll be *our* favorite customer as we all fight each other for the deed to this gods forsaken place so we never have to work another day of our lives."

"I *got* the deed," Beshil retorted playfully, tearing the bill before handing one half of it to the customer. "And here I am, workin'."

"Ya call that *workin'?"* another called over.

Beshil sighed with faux exasperation and said a friendly goodbye to his customer before waddling over to me. "All right, kid. Who sent ya?"

"Maude."

Two employees chuckled and exchanged lowered whispers. I glanced over at the noise to see one of them quickly flick up their pointer finger as if mimicking a sudden erection.

Beshil snorted in response and ignored his employees as he asked, "Recommendation?"

"Yes," I replied. "I need something specially made to carry a unique weapon."

Beshil lifted his bushy eyebrows with intrigue. "Let's see it, then."

I hefted the scythe up onto the counter and the dwarves went quiet. Finally, Brunhild chortled. "What the hell are ya gonna do with *that* thing?"

"Evidently, he's already done a lot with it," Beshil answered for me, lifting the blade and eyeing its edge. "This is a beautiful weapon, kid, and if yer lucky enough to know how to use it, ya gotta take care of it. How often do ya sharpen the blade?"

"I haven't," I replied. "I recently acquired this. I know little about taking care of a weapon and could use some advice."

Beshil nodded slowly and seemed to appreciate my honesty. "Have ya fought with it yet?"

"Yes," I replied hesitantly, hoping my answer couldn't connect me to the campsite.

"If it were any of my business, I'd ask what ya fought," Beshil mused. "Yer not that built, but I can tell this scythe has done some damage." He glanced up to look at my ears. "If ya were elven, it'd make sense. Pretty bastards can get twice the strength outta a single muscle, I've always said."

"I need something with which to carry this," I replied, uncomfortable with his prodding ponderings.

"Aye, I'd imagine so," Beshil agreed, wrinkling up his nose as he thought. "Yer best bet would be a weapon's belt." He lifted up the scythe and held the handle just below the tang. "It'd hang from here on yer waist. I'll have to take some measurements. Of *you* so I could get the belt size right, and of the blade so I could make ya a sheath."

"A separate sheath?" I asked for clarification.

"Aye," Beshil said. "Ain't no way yer gonna hang this from the blade without making things inconvenient for yerself. Now..." he trailed off and glanced at the bow behind my back and the satchel strap over my shoulder. "An order like this is gonna take some time, and it ain't gonna be cheap."

"Then I'd like to make more requests before I show you what I have to trade," I replied. When Beshil appeared open to hear them, I went on, "I like the idea for the weapon's belt, but I'd like to be able to carry multiple weapons. I need the holder for the scythe first and foremost, but I come across other weapons from time to time and need a way to carry them." As if to prove it, I pulled the bow out of its scabbard to put it on the counter between us and put the other side weapons I'd looted from the Twelve beside it.

"That'll be a heavy duty belt," Beshil warned me. "What kinda armor do ya wear?"

"None. Not yet." As a few of the employees murmured to one another, I pulled out the various rings I'd collected and put them in a line on the countertop. "I need to be fitted for armor, too, and I need it specially made. I carry everything I own on me and need extra compartments, rings for hanging, and buckles for readjustment. I'd also like someone to teach me how to take care of my gear when it's inevitably damaged and I need all corresponding supplies."

"That's a big order," Beshil mused softly, though he eyed my trade offer on the counter before him.

"I have a quality-made dwarven ring here that should make up a good deal of our trade," I commented nonchalantly, lifting the ring Maude had been fond of. "Offered it to Maude for all the clothing I picked up there, but the deal was just too far out of my favor. She was teary-eyed over seeing it leave, but I knew this would be a hell of an order. I can't be too careful." Beshil's face sobered as he stared at the ring in question. I pretended not to notice and added, "Of course, I have plenty here to barter with and I have more in my bag—"

"Wait." Beshil's eyes flicked up to mine. "Did ya say Maude was in tears?"

"Oh, she tried to hide them," I mused, waving him off. "She said she had a thing for jewelry. Something about this ring caught her eye."

"Aye," Beshil murmured, fingering it. "How'd ya get it?"

"By beautifully random circumstance," I replied vaguely.

Beshil stood back from the counter and pulled offerings to one side. He then grabbed parchment and itemized my things with the values he placed on them. When he wrote *400* next to the bow, I remembered the Celd's words on its value and commented, "This bow is worth at least five."

Beshil hesitated, looked over the bow again, and nodded. "Aye, I'll give ya that." As if my bartering impressed him, he moved his quill to a previously listed item, crossed out the number, and put a higher value beside it.

Before long, everything I offered other than two final rings and a short sword were to one side, but considering what I'd asked of him I felt it was a good deal. Beshil stood back, exhaled heavily, and said, "I'll accept your order if ya trade me all a'this. Ya might wanna think about it before ya answer me for sure. I'm takin' near everythin' ya own."

"Why don't you help me out by taking this as well?" I asked, tapping the handle of the short sword. "I'm assuming you take trade *and* offer gold for quality goods."

"That's the last weapon you'll have other than yer scythe," Beshil commented.

"Yes, and it's a pain to carry," I replied.

Beshil chuckled and moved the sword over with the other items. "All right, then. We'll get ya outfitted and you'll even get a handful a'gold." He reached a hand over the counter to seal the deal, and I took it for a brief shake.

Beshil motioned for me to follow him and said, "Now, let's get yer measurements."

Fifteen

The scythe hung heavily at my side as I descended the central road into underground Brognel, causing a few passersby to stare. Beshil took all measurements and garnered more detail about what materials and colors I preferred for my armor before giving me an estimation of a fortnight for the order's completion. After stopping by a jewelry store to trade my last two rings for gold, I had nothing else to sell. I ignored all manner of jewels, baubles, and dwarven inventions, determined to secure lodging with what little I had left.

Ridding myself of the weight of extra weapons and loot made me realize just how much stronger I'd gotten over my travels because walking suddenly felt like floating. When Beshil measured me he commented that I had an elven build more than once, for he found hardy muscle in my upper back, arms, and legs in particular. Elves could be weak or strong like any other race, but even the most muscular among them looked deceptively lean. Battling the vampire left me sore and stiff for days, but the aftermath wasn't nearly as bad as it was after fighting the Twelve a season ago. It seemed I'd grown stronger than it looked, and the power from leeching helped wonders with my training. Because I masqueraded as only human and had been surrounded by humans my whole life, this aspect of my elven half came as a welcome surprise to me.

Beshil offered to train me himself in caring for my gear, but he told me to come in the mornings and after he completed my armor so we could get it done all at once and during his shop's calmest hours. For now, I had nothing but time, and Brognel pleaded for me to explore it.

Brognel was set-up like a city on the side of a mountain, but its location within the landmark instead meant that the main road only angled farther underground. The high cavern walls ensured the town didn't feel cramped. Despite being underground Brognel appeared like any other settlement, with spacious roads meeting side streets through descending neighborhoods of stone multi-story businesses and homes. Signs for mine entrances stood on street corners with higher traffic than normal, proving that mining was a lucrative business here.

Firelight and non-dwarven mercenaries were rarer in the mid-tier of Brognel. As the temperature grew cooler with depth, the caverns became damper and alight with the cool tones of bioluminescent fungi. Between shadows, dark stone glowed turquoise and lavender from clusters of mushrooms that grew out of cracks and thrived in the new humidity. A bright turquoise glow glimmered like a halo over buildings in the deepest neighborhoods, but I couldn't yet see what emitted it.

It was in Brognel's lowest depths that I noticed their guard force grew greater. Chairel soldiers clad in green and black traveled in packs toward the left wall of the giant cavern; others loitered on street corners or headed to pubs and brothels on their breaks. Non-dwarven mercenaries were suddenly commonplace as well; it was like humans and Celds didn't exist in the middle tier of the city, only at either end. Such a force would only be here for a good reason; curious about the threat to Brognel's lower district, I decided to spend time there first.

In the presence of armed mercenaries, openly carrying a scythe no longer called attention to me. I headed past the corner of an enormous marketplace to finally find the source of the vast blue glow radiating over the buildings and onto the cavern walls. Flowing south from a deep breach in the northern cavern wall was an underground river. Like the fungi, the river glowed a bright neon turquoise, acting like the lower city's beacon. The water etched a path in the rock from north to southwest and disappeared beneath the western wall. Nearby its exit was a tunnel leading farther underground, but Chairel soldiers blocked it off. A large group of mercenaries sauntered up to these guards before unfolding parchment and handing it over. After considering its contents, the guards let the mercenaries through, and they disappeared into the tunnel's shadow.

Just across the street was a combination inn and tavern that appeared to be a popular spot for mercenaries looking to face whatever was in that tunnel, so I headed there. The business took up most of a city block, but its entrance held back from the street corner to allow for an extended patio. Mercenaries lounged while eating or drinking at tables and chairs, and a few showed sloppy affections for one another as onlookers leered. Though the patio was outside the tavern, it was shrouded in shadow like everything else in these depths, only lit up in splotches of cool fluorescent glows of patches of fungi and flickering orange from lamps that aided them. The combination of shadow and rainbow glows was oddly beautiful for being so simple.

Harsh heavy drum beats resounded through the inn's walls even before I opened its door, releasing a scent wave of roasting venison and ale that intermingled with jovial arguments and conversations. Immediately, I was bathed in the orange light of fire from sconces, lamps, and a giant fireplace that took up the right wall. A few dwarven musicians rested to the side of the fireplace, creating music far harsher than anything I'd heard in Sera, for it relied on the bass of drum beats and the rough strikes of percussion instruments rather than the lutes and flutes dominant in most of Chairel. Despite the music's harshness, multiple people danced together before the fire, many of them seeming to find the rougher flow of the music sensual given their movements.

The rest of the floor was set-up like a full-service restaurant and bar. In the shadowed back and left corners of the far walls were two staircases leading up to the higher floors, presumably where the lodging rooms were located. Between the stairwells stretched a long bar and open kitchen where a handful of overworked employees scrambled around. One dwarf tore into roasted venison with a butcher knife and arranged the resulting slices on a decorative bed of greens. Excess saliva escaped my glands and drenched my tongue before I swallowed hard. I hadn't eaten a hot meal since fleeing Sera.

I made my way around tables and patrons to the right end of the bar. The dwarf behind it hastily shifted through orders on parchment before my taller form placed a shadow over them.

She glanced up. Thankfully, my youthful appearance didn't seem to faze her. “Aye, how can I help ya?”

“I need lodging,” I replied, getting straight to the point. My eyes wandered to the venison on a counter behind her. “And a hot meal if I can afford both.”

“Small one bedroom?” After I affirmed, she said, “That'll be ten gold a night. If ya stay at least five nights and pay in advance, all yer meals are free.”

"What?" I blurted in sudden elation, and the woman chuckled in response.

"Aye. Within reason," she explained. "We keep our mercenaries well-fed for up to three meals a day. Any more than that, ya have to pay like the rest. Ain't no free ale or room service. Ya have to boil yer bath water yerself and request to change yer linens."

After so long with no amenities at all, this sounded like a dream come true. "I'll take your smallest room for a fortnight."

She lifted an eyebrow, happy with the promise of a good sale, and grabbed a book from beneath the counter. "Aye, then. Here for work?"

"Yes."

The dwarf opened the book to the latest page of listed patrons. I noticed the names and signatures and mentally merged my mother and father's first names to come up with an alias. "If ya have the time, take a look at our contract board," she suggested, dipping a quill in an inkwell as she nodded toward the front door. I glanced back to see a giant pegboard on the wall absolutely covered in overlapping parchment. The sketched faces of wanted criminals stood out to me most. I hoped to the gods my warrant wasn't among them.

"Name?"

I turned back to her and replied, "Cerin Luna."

"Beautiful name," she complimented.

"Thank you." I watched as she wrote the rest of my lodging details down and spun the book to face me.

"That'll be one hundred forty gold," she declared. After I counted it out to her, I went to sign my name. I realized with gratefulness that she misspelled Cerin as *Searin,* perhaps due to its pronunciation and her familiarity with searing meat. I allowed the mistake to flourish, further protecting my identity by signing it that way without a word.

"Ya look hungry," the employee went on as she gave me my half of the bill. "I can put in an order of venison for ya. We also have a menu, but orderin' off that costs extra."

"Venison is fine," I replied. "Thank you."

"Aye. Any spirits?"

"No." I thought of the mercenaries outside and asked, "I can eat outside?"

"Aye. Give me a few minutes to get ya a plate. Bring it back in with ya or else we'll have to charge."

I wandered over to the mercenary contract pegboard as I waited for my meal. Sheets of parchment overlapped from ceiling to floor, and before them all stood a single dwarf looking for work. She nursed a mug of ale in one hand and kept walking up to the board to lift up contracts and read the ones beneath.

I stood two steps behind her and to the side, not wishing to call attention to myself as I searched through the papers for my warrant. It surprised me to see so many non-combat contracts in the mix.

Strong arms wanted to move furniture. I am elderly and can no longer afford my home. Need to move by 1st of Red Moon. Lost all children to the tunnels. Will pay 10 gold per day and am more than willing to trade.

I wondered if the tunnels mentioned were the same ones guarded by Chairel soldiers outside. Skimming over the text contracts, I focused only on the warrants with sketches. One warrant set up like mine had the drawing of a young human woman on it.

WANTED: Lisha Foyer.

Charges: Practice of magic without a proper license, evading the law, seven counts of civilian murder, seven counts of torture.

Notes: Lisha is an illusionist with access to illegal spells such as invisibility, charm, and fear. While her origins are in Dagmar, Lisha has been sighted in Comercio and may be moving east. Lisha's first victim was her lover of seven years. Claims of prior domestic violence were investigated but never confirmed. Witness accounts state she offers to kill for a fee and only takes hits on men. Lisha uses illusion magic to aid in her entry and escape, but she kills with a blade. Victims are always male and found gutted and castrated. Cause of victim deaths is blood loss.

REWARD: 3,000 gold offered for proof of death. 1,500 gold offered for her capture. 100 gold offered for substantiated tips.

"There are rumors that she charms the men with her magic so they don't run when she castrates 'em," the dwarf nearby spoke up after noticing my presence and stare.

"Lovely," I said dryly, and she laughed.

"Aye. Ya gotta love it, too." She strode up to the contract and pointed at the charges. "They listed her illegal magic use first and her worst crimes last, like usin' magic is more offensive than castratin' a man until he bleeds out."

I frowned as I realized she was right. "Maybe it is to them," I commented. "Perhaps they care more about controlling the masses than caring for their well-being."

"Perhaps?" The dwarf laughed. "Nah, that's just how it *is*. Get used to it now. Good thing yer already workin' on yer own. Learn to take care of yerself, and you'll never have to worry about political bullshit."

I said nothing for the moment, only scanning over the rest of the contracts and feeling overwhelming relief that my warrant wasn't among them.

"Yer a quiet type," the dwarf mused after a moment.

"I'm just glad you didn't call me *kid,"* I replied, and she chortled.

"Aye, well, ya *look* like one, but callin' ya that seems disrespectful. Ya got that *look* in yer eyes."

"What look?" I inquired, glancing over.

The dwarf shrugged and huffed. "Ya've seen some shit."

I didn't argue. We looked over the pegboard together in silence until she spoke again. "Ya lookin' for anything in particular for work?"

"No. I'm just curious about the lack of warrants for necromancers," I said nonchalantly, motioning to the giant board. "Everyone fears them, but *why?* They must be rare."

The dwarf laughed nervously, as if just the mention of death magic bothered her. "Ya gotta have a lotta pull with the government if yer wantin' to hunt down necromancers. They keep all that under wraps, like."

"Why?"

"Don't know, truly," she admitted. "Guess it's a combination of things. They don't want the commonfolk to panic or get any naughty ideas, maybe. It's like they just want us to forget necromancy's a thing at all. But it don't work. Not when rumors run amok because they're such good fighters."

"How do you know that?"

"I had a friend who came across a necromancer right in these mountains," she reminisced. "They fought for a bit. My friend's group was almost wiped out. The necromancer claimed she didn't wanna kill anyone, but that's kinda hard to say when surrounded by bodies, innit?" The dwarf sniffled as I marveled at the similarities between this necromancer and me. "The necromancer eventually fled, and my friend made it out with a few injuries. Ya wanna know the scariest part of it?"

"Sure."

"My friend said he got a few hits in on the necromancer, and that the blade barely hurt her. He said it was like her skin was made of wood. She barely bled. Now, what manner of sorcery is *that?"*

"That's what makes necromancers so powerful," I replied. "Valerius the Undying was much the same. Years and years of harvesting life force grew his strength until even his flesh seemed impenetrable."

The dwarf shivered with fear beside me. "I heard Valerius was over four hundred years old when he was killed. And he was *human*. It ain't natural."

"No," I agreed. "Many things aren't."

An employee came up to me then to deliver my meal, and I took it gratefully outside after saying a friendly goodbye to the dwarven mercenary. I headed over to a small two-seater table beside the barrier fence separating the patio from the road. The aroma of venison teased my nostrils until I swallowed down excess saliva. When I finally took the first bite and the perfect mixture of oil, salt, and savory meat settled on my tongue in a rush of warmth, I closed my eyes with pleasure and promised myself I'd find fire-making materials while in Brognel. My gold reserves from trading were almost out, but surely I could find some way to trade for matches or flint and steel.

As I ate, I watched the tunnel across the street. Groups of soldiers and mercenaries loitered around outside, but none of them seemed keen on venturing in. Thankfully, I wasn't the only one who noticed. A diverse party of mercenaries one table over was a wealth of information about the mysterious tunnel.

"Fuckin' tunnel rats, man," a human mused, leaning back with both boots on the table as he picked bits of food out of his teeth with a dirty fingernail. At first, I wondered if Brognel's troubles really centered on underground rodents. "If they weren't so gods damn sneaky and lethal, there'd be so many I'd want to fuck."

Now I *really* hoped he wasn't talking about rodents.

"Bein' sneaky and lethal is part of the appeal for me," a dwarven comrade replied. "But not when they're attackin' like this is their land. The gall of these women enrages me."

"Brognel is the aggressor here," a Celd spoke up, his voice calmer than the others. "The Alderi might simply believe they're protecting what is theirs. We have no idea how large the underground truly is—"

"Oh, *please,*" the dwarf retorted. "Our miners didn't know they'd break through to that tunnel. They tested the rock beforehand. That excavation was as harmless as any other."

"Evidently not," the Celd replied. The dwarf snorted in response.

A female human next to the Celd nodded to the dwarf and asked, "When you went there, what did you see? Is it true the Alderi have no males?"

"I don't know if it's true or not," the dwarf replied. "But all I saw was dark-skinned women. All the shades of a bruise. Blues, purples, blacks, grays. Shapely, too. Like Mikael said, they would'a been beautiful if it weren't for the bloodlust in their eyes."

"That was the fight that lost you your ear," the Celd surmised, motioning to the dwarf's mutilated left ear.

"Aye," he replied. "Pissed me right off, it did. There I was, my big hammer in my hands, and the bitch sidesteps me so quick she was barely a blur. Next thing I know, my ear's on the ground and Peggy's intestines are leakin' out of her gut. Them tunnel rats are fast and *brutal.* They bested me, and that ain't an easy thing to do."

"Pretty sure it only makes you harder, though," Mikael jested, and the dwarf flipped him off.

"I think Alderi men exist," the woman interjected, a whimsical tilt to her tone.

"Oh?" Mikael huffed. "Why?"

"Bridget told me that during her stay in Hammerton, she heard rumors about two Alderi men who came to Olympia by ship years earlier. Escapees of the underground, apparently."

"Why in the world is that newsworthy enough to keep being talked about for *years?"* Mikael asked, unconvinced.

A gleam lit up the woman's eyes, and she replied, "Because the Alderi are rumored to be magnificent lovers. These men had *a lot* to work with in their drawers and their drives were so high they didn't even charge the women for a good time. The sex was *that* memorable."

"I don't recall such rumors being said about *you,* Mikael," the Celd teased the male human, and the woman laughed.

"And that's all they are," Mikael retorted. *"Rumors.* According to the story, Bridget didn't even *see* these mysterious men. She only heard rumors. The women in Olympia must be starved."

"They *are* starved," the dwarf commented. "Ya know how dwarven women are. They could have a line of men takin' turns and they'd still never be satisfied."

"Sounds like the Alderi and dwarves would get along famously if they weren't always bickering over land," the Celd pointed out.

"Aye, but bicker is what we do," the dwarf replied. He took a sloppy bite of meat and nodded toward the tunnel. "All I know is that when ya dare to attack my hometown en masse, I ain't takin' it easy. Tunnel rats are gettin' serious about startin' a little war with all these damn attacks, and I'll be on the frontlines to meet 'em."

I finished my meal while watching the tunnel, trying to file away as much information as I could about the Alderi. At some point, between Sirius and the Icilic wanting me dead, I would face assassins. It was only a matter of time. Oddly, such a prospect wasn't as intimidating to me as it had been just a season ago. After all, I'd managed to slay a vampire wearing no armor, and I would be even more prepared to face any pursuers by the time I left Brognel.

I felt grateful for that, for I knew that by the time I re-entered the Seran Forest, enough time would have passed for any pursuers to be hot on my trail.

Sixteen

I left Brognel looking like a new man. Instead of shivering perpetually in double layers of cream-colored clothing acquired from Whispermere, I now wore multiple layers of black. All the undershirts I'd bought from Maude had hoods, ensuring I could always hide my face in shadow even when the weather didn't require wearing the heavy cloak. Over my underclothes was the armor Beshil made and taught me to care for. It was a sharp mixture of dark-stained leather and silver buckles and rings with which to help me store and carry excess supplies or belongings. Such accoutrements meant that I jingled as I walked, but I'd never been one for stealth and didn't plan on doing much hiding.

Beshil gave me supplies with which to take care of my equipment as part of my order: oil and sealing to care for the soft leather armor, filler with which to repair it, and a file to sharpen my scythe. I'd spent most my remaining time in Brognel trading my healing abilities for gold and supplies from those desperate enough to risk the illegal exchange. With the gold I made from healing I was able to buy fire-making tools, books including those to expand my knowledge in anatomy and alchemy, and camping supplies like blankets and waterproof tarps. I also bought a chain necklace on which to hang the sentimental ring from my parents, for my growth the past year ensured it no longer fit and I wanted to keep it close to me forever. Official life mages were so rare in Brognel that I could have stayed there to make a decent living by illicitly healing the populace, but my past would catch up with me eventually. Besides, I'd already set my mind on building defenses in the Seran Forest.

I caught glimpses of the woodland as I descended the same mountain I climbed weeks ago. The fields of pines and conifers lightened since I last saw them, for the hot season of High Star handed off its reins to Red Moon. Once deep green needles shone gold and copper in the overhead sun, and in the mornings a fine mist often rose from the trees after rains that became more common with each passing day.

As I traveled back to the forest, I wondered if it would be my final resting place. I felt peace knowing that it likely would be, for at least it was a beautiful place to die. I wouldn't allow myself to be defeated easily, of course, but there came a day when every necromancer met their end. Surviving alone and in the wild was already a hard life, and adding to that the fact that many wanted me dead made the idea that I'd survive more than a handful of years laughable. For as much as I took inspiration from Valerius the Undying, he *did* in fact die. Even the most legendary necromancers hadn't lasted forever. But just as I sought to learn from his successes, I could do my best to learn from his failures so I wouldn't recreate them.

Valerius the Undying was born in 5592 G.E., just one hundred and ninety years before the Golden Era morphed into the current Mortal Era. The Golden Era was known as an age of discovery; books I'd read on the subject said it was a time when gods walked among mortals, the countries of the world formed after ancient wars for power and land, and magic was as misunderstood as it was fought over. Arturian Kilgor had not yet discovered the Kilgorian Law, so mages learned and used spells without understanding the sources or limits of energy reserves. Thus, magic was even more dangerous to wield at the time and rarer. Magic was the most powerful weapon of all, but few risked even learning it due to high mage mortality rates. In the current Mortal Era, necromancy was so taboo partially because it was common knowledge that its wielders could expand their lifespans by stealing life force. In the Golden Era, however, *all* magic was so rare that necromancy was even rarer; it took a catalyst to jump-start the common fear of necromancy by exposing its ugly truths. That catalyst was Valerius.

Much of what was known about Valerius was rumor or myth up until his defensive position on the island just north of Chairel was discovered. He possibly involved himself in wars or spats for land in Chairel to grow his power over the first two hundred years of his life. Some rumors stated he was the most prolific serial killer in the country and responsible for thousands of unsolved homicides. Other more ridiculous rumors claimed he had broods of children just to harvest their life force upon their birth. Whether one or more of those stories were true, Valerius eventually ended up on the island named after him just between southern Glacia and northern Chairel.

An old dilapidated watchtower remained on the island that Chairel commissioned centuries earlier during a war with Glacia. Chairel attempted to force the Icilic to adhere to their magical monopoly, and Glacia hit back with such force the war ended in a stalemate. The watchtower was reportedly a sturdy and excessively tall monument built to give the Chairel Army advance notice of Glacia's sea movements, but due to its odd location they abandoned it after the war. Though the island was said to be uninhabitable for the long-term due to its lack of wildlife and good soil, Valerius made it his home despite all the odds.

The Island of Valerius was large enough that he lived there undetected for many years. To the right of the island existed the only trade route between Glacia and Chairel that ended in Thornwell. Trading vessels belonging to both countries went missing until trade between the two came to a full stop. Because Glacia's isolationism prevented it from reaching out to Chairel diplomatically, Chairel investigated the seas. They found a family of krakens just east of the island that relentlessly attacked trading ships, dragged their loot to the depths of the ocean, and ate their fill of sailors. Because Valerius's island was so close, the shipwreck survivors would swim to its shores, where the necromancer was free to harvest their lives.

By the time Chairel declared war on the lone necromancer in 64 M.E., he had thousands of skeletons stowed away on his island, all equipped with weapons and supplies from missing trading ships. Valerius could call these corpses to his aid repeatedly while staying safe near his tower. Over the span of two hundred years, the Chairel Navy delivered thousands of men at a time in waves of attacks to Valerius, and he'd only overwhelm them and add the corpses to his army. Reports at the time stated that neither magic nor blade could puncture Valerius's flesh. The fear that grew of necromancy's power due to Valerius's seemingly never-ending lifespan and his growing undead army only worsened Chairel's morale, adding to their troubles.

Eventually, Chairel outsmarted Valerius by utilizing different tactics. Rather than surround the entire island, they blockaded most of Valerius's undead army on the western side of it and used mages to set fire to the tower after bathing its lower floors in flammable alchemical solutions. Then, they waited, doing nothing but watching the exits and keeping the flames stoked. Soldiers who witnessed the battle told scribes at the time that Valerius's screams of agony lasted hours even though bodies normally took minutes to burn alive. Valerius's skin not only rejected most blade hits, his lungs put up abnormal resistance to the damage of smoke inhalation. Only when all remaining skeletons on the island dispelled at once did the soldiers realize Valerius died, for he no longer controlled them. They found his body on the top floor of the tower, leaning over an open windowsill as if gasping for breaths. The last remnants of parchment were in his right hand as if he held a letter dear to him to his last breath, but due to its damage, its significance was never discovered. It was said that Valerius's body was in spectacular condition for one who'd burned alive. Even his eyes weren't destroyed, for his iris color was noted in the autopsy report: gray.

I found Valerius's story incredibly sad and intriguing. Unlike most, I didn't automatically believe Valerius was an awful person. Morality was such a subjective concept, and Valerius was birthed in an age when civilization still developed and formed laws due to varied biases. It was possible Valerius and I were alike in more ways than wielding necromancy. Perhaps he'd discovered death magic and figured out its life expanding powers simply by using it in standard warfare. Witnesses might have seen the magic in action and feared it, thus establishing his place in infamy before he had any say. Gods knew that had happened to me—I'd had no plans to use necromancy for ill until I needed it for self-defense. By harboring such irrational hatred for necromancy, the Seran soldiers had unwittingly turned me into the very thing they feared.

The laws of Chairel decided my fate. I chose not to accept it. Mercenaries, soldiers, and assassins alike were welcome to hunt me down. I'd do my best to be ready to face them and take as many out as I could before my inevitable demise. If nothing else, my name would go down in history with the other necromancers who refused to surrender, and word would spread of death magic's power. Eventually, necromancy might be so desired by the commoners of Chairel that they'd be forced to legalize it or risk rebellion.

This may have been a far-fetched dream, but it was the only one left available to me. That didn't mean I couldn't be excited about it. As I re-entered the Seran Forest in early Red Moon, nothing but determination filled me.

I decided to set up a base in the northwestern area of the forest, for it would be nearest to Sera while allowing me shelter from the worst weather and the eyes of the Twelve. The location along the woodland's border would make me an easy target, but if I planned on harvesting as much life force as possible and building a stash of bodies, the least I could do was cut down on the time and inconvenience for my foes. I *wanted* them to find me. I needed their energies, and their deaths would only lead to unorthodox recruitment opportunities.

I'd bought a tent in Brognel with which to guard me from immediate scrutiny and the harshest weather. During the weeks of traveling through the forest to find a good spot to live, I only used it during the worst storms. I tried to train myself to sleep in uncomfortable temperatures; I would never have a proper home again, so I needed to learn how to catch sleep anywhere. Still, I longed for the plush soft bed of Brognel's inn, but it seemed so far behind me now. During the worst storms of finicky Red Moon, I cursed myself for deciding not to stay in Brognel and venturing out into the wilderness. But for the first time in my life, I felt determined to make something of myself, and that was reason enough to fight through the worst inconveniences.

On the 73rd of Red Moon, I celebrated my sixteenth birthday by taking a break from searching for the perfect location in the forest. I fished for most of the day, adding as much food to my stores for the upcoming harsh weather as I could. Dark Star would approach in seventeen days. Its close presence marked the forest floor with a glimmering sheen of ice crystals instead of dew in the mornings, and the birds stopped their constant song in protest of the rapidly cooling weather. It wasn't the weather that made me uncomfortable, however. I needed to settle down somewhere soon, or the thinning foliage and upcoming snowfall would inconvenience me in terms of survival *and* defense. I'd been searching for denser growth in which to pitch my tent; as much as I wanted to goad my pursuers to me, allowing myself to be surrounded or openly vulnerable would be ludicrous.

I continued on my search, trying my best not to be picky. Just a week before the seasons changed, something unique quite literally stuck out from the detritus ahead, giving me a sign. From a thick layer of dead pine needles, fallen gotton bush leaves, and twigs rose the right forearm of a human. The limb was stiff with rigor mortis. While the hand was in good shape and still wore a few rings, a wild animal looking for a nice cut of meat had ripped the brachioradialis muscle off the bone. The arm clearly still attached to the rest of a body given its upward angle, but forest debris hid the rest of it. The hand curled, but the pointer finger stuck out as if urging me to follow its direction.

I glanced to the right to heed the corpse's unintended advice. A thicket of dense pines and bountiful gotton berry bushes drew my attention like a beacon. I wandered over to the area, walking around the underbrush and looking it over with a judgmental eye. The thicket was set up in a U-shape that opened facing south, the brush so dense around its curve I could barely see through it. There was enough room to pitch my tent with space left over, and the family of gotton bushes dotted throughout ensured I would have a source of food nearby.

The thicket was the perfect location to set up camp. I dropped my gear within the protective hug of the plant-life and walked back over to the corpse, seeking information. This thicket was possibly an attractive prospect for more reasons than I could see; maybe others who lived in this wilderness fought over it. Of course, it was probable that others simply found it a convenient location to camp in.

Corpa te risa a multipla.

I released the area-of-effect magic. A dense black fog misted over the surrounding detritus until it separated into a dozen tendrils. One buried itself in the corpse with the exposed hand while the others slithered off and wiggled between scattered pine needles in the general vicinity.

Twelve corpses rose from the forest floor. Plant debris flaked off them and fluttered to the ground like red and green snowfall. All the corpses were human, and given their relatively good conditions had died recently. As they gathered around me to abide by my orders, I felt a smidgen of relief, for the loneliness burrowed into the thick walls of my soul dissipated just a bit.

The corpses were fully-armored, but they had seen battle. One woman's head was so bashed in by a spiked mace that only half her cranium remained, and it was hollowed out by hungry wildlife. Two corpses were decapitated. One had all four limbs amputated like he'd been brutally tortured. Whoever these people were, they'd died traumatically.

"Why were you out here?" I murmured, trying to understand what had happened. The corpses watched me with blank gazes, unable to respond. I walked up to the woman with the missing cranium, taking her right hand in mine and lifting it. She wore multiple rings, and I studied their designs. They were all arcanic, but none of them seemed to *mean* anything.

I went up to each corpse, looking for something that would tell me who these people were. A man who had died by a severe cut of the abdomen had the most answers. His thumb ring had a thick band of steel that showcased a skull. I held his hand still as I worked the ring off him and put it on my own thumb. Most mages wore jewelry, but many chose designs that meant something to them. The skull made sense for a necromancer to wear, but this man had been a mercenary. I wondered if he fancied himself, then, on being a *killer* of necromancers.

The corpse stared at me with indifference as I went through its pockets. Only when I scrounged through a bag hanging at its waist did I find my answer. Folded up amongst maps and bills of sale from Seran merchants was a death warrant with my face on it. It'd been updated since the last one I found on the Twelve.

WANTED: Cerin Heliot.

Charges: Necromancy, 19 counts of murder of Seran armed forces, evading the law, practice of magic without a proper license

Notes: Cerin has access to necromancy and life magic. BEWARE, for he has now claimed the lives of three Twelve veterans. Investigators of this latest battle report evidence of excessive strength with melee weapons unusual for a juvenile with no known prior battle experience. Criminal profiling of the aftermath suggests Cerin openly invites conflict, so he may be aggressive on sight. Given the site of the Twelve battle, Cerin may be scouting out his hometown of Thornwell and wishing to return. Interrogations of its populace revealed that Cerin has no living family and has not yet returned, though the fallen Twelve members visited the town before their deaths. No witnesses have come forward since Cerin's escape from Sera, and his plans are unknown.

REWARD: 5,000 gold offered for death. Body required. 500 gold offered for substantiated tips.

Satisfaction washed over me as I realized my bounty surpassed the highest posted in Brognel of Lisha the castrating serial killer. I doubted that meant I was Chairel's most-wanted criminal already, but I'd gotten their attention.

It fascinated me to see how parts of the warrant were true and some notes were completely off. Red and the people of Thornwell evidently hadn't admitted to my return, but I couldn't allow that to flatter me. Sirius's threats of them becoming enemies of their mother city if they saw me without reporting in likely kept them quiet. I hoped they would leave Thornwell alone from now on; they were the last people I wanted to inconvenience with my personal rebellion.

I added the updated warrant to my satchel with the older one, and then I pointed to the defensive thicket. The corpses followed my direction, filing into the thicker brush before I dispelled them. I would focus on burying them in debris later for safe-keeping. For now, I scattered loose detritus into the body-sized gaps the rising corpses left, removing any evidence of a necromancer being here at all. Though I searched for more information about the fight that took place here, I found nothing and could only wonder. The most likely explanation was that the mercenaries hunted me but came across an orcish war party. That would help describe the brutality enacted against them. With no nearby orc corpses, however, it was only a guess.

I buried the mercenary corpses at various locations within the thicket, covering them with loose dirt and debris. Then I set up my tent in the center of it all and took a much needed break. I would spend as much time as I could building a firepit and learning the intricacies of the surrounding forest in the upcoming weeks, finding sources of fish and water and berries.

For now, I only rested. I stared at the canvas of the tent peak, my mind at peace. Sera's willingness to set its most trusted mercenary parties loose to find me meant that Sirius likely also hired Alderi assassins. I wondered just how many people currently hunted or searched for me throughout northeastern Chairel. Living forever as a criminal could mean nothing but death, but this only felt like a challenge. I wanted to see how long I could last.

Thoughts of my potentially short lifespan caused my mind to wander back to Kai. I scrounged around in my satchel and pulled out her note, reading and rereading it for comfort.

I'll miss you, she'd written. Those words were always where my eyes lingered. The sentiment wasn't true. Not anymore. But perhaps I could always cling to denial. For as long as I was alone, I would hold on to this note and pretend I could one day resume having a normal life. There were plenty of war stories I'd read in Sera about men and women who went to battle and found solace in letters from loved ones, and I understood why now. Just the knowledge that Kai had once cared for me was enough. It didn't *have* to be true anymore.

I put the letter away and tugged out a book I'd traded for in Brognel. It was an anatomy book for alchemists, which was the closest thing I'd been able to find to a healer's guide. Healing books didn't exist in Brognel, for any mages there were migrants or visitors from Sera. Additionally, Chairel required spell book vendors to check for a Seran magic license upon any purchase, and I didn't have one.

The book I had was helpful despite its limitations, however. It described the uses of various plants in alchemical solutions and how to spot these plants in the wild. Many only grew in the mountains, not the forest, but there were plenty of plants listed that I'd become familiar with as I learned the forest in and out. Some alchemical solutions would allow me to replace the oil and sealing I'd traded Beshil for once I ran out. Others were salves, potions, or mending solutions for injuries. In the descriptions of how to apply these was an abundance of information about anatomy and various ails that I studied over and over again, trying to supplement my Seran education. I expected to get injured no matter how well I fought and living in the wilderness could expose me to sickness. I needed to prepare for anything; mercenaries weren't the only threat to me in this forest.

But they *were* the closest one.

Seventeen

31st of Dark Star, 411

I peeked out of the flap of my tent, and a world of white greeted me with a sparkling wink. The two arms of the thicket surrounded me in a protective hug, but the gap between allowed for a view beyond. Inches of snow stretched out like a field over the forest floor, thinner beneath pines and the thickest brush. Snow and icicles weighed down tree branches until the plants themselves looked forlorn; some wooden limbs had snapped with the pressure and laid on the covered ground below. I'd never seen this much snow in the forest; even now, chunky snowflakes fell through the canopies, eager to join their kin on plants and ground. Last year after fleeing Sera I'd seen snow and ice farther west in the woodland, but last Dark Star hadn't been nearly as harsh.

I was prepared for it this year, however. My breaths expelled whirls of smoke and the tip of my nose felt like ice, but I didn't even shiver. My mother's Icilic blood offered me a natural buffer, but the black cloak I'd bought in Brognel aided by keeping my body heat close. I let the flap of the tent fall back into place, and then I pulled out a journal I'd traded for. I didn't log my experiences and trials since doing so would give any foes a gold mine of information if I were ever captured or killed. Instead, I'd marked its pages with dates during my stay in Brognel. There were three hundred and sixty days in a year, and the book was four hundred pages long and had a ribbon of a bookmark attached to its spine. I'd marked one side of the ribbon with ink, and now I used the journal to track the passage of time. It started out with the new year on the 1st of New Moon. It then cataloged each of the season's ninety days, moved on to

High Star, then to Red Moon, and finally to Dark Star where it ended on the 90th. Each morning I'd move the bookmark, either turning it to face a different page or turning the page completely. So far, this method worked. I had missed no days yet; with no companions or anything else occupying my time, changing the date in the book was the one thing I looked forward to. At least it meant I'd survived another day.

I scrounged around my supplies, counting out packets of dried fish and pouches of berries. Gotton berries grew at all times of the year, but the bushes in the neighboring thicket grew thin with my constant foraging. Over the weeks of living in the thicket I scouted out the surrounding area. I learned the land well enough, but the sources of fresh fish were scarce this far north in the forest. There were a few tiny streams, but nothing big enough to hold its own ecosystem. So while I'd found the perfect defensive location to pitch the tent, there weren't enough food sources nearby. I couldn't rely only on berries, and I couldn't hunt deer or fowl worth a damn.

Today, I decided, I'd search for somewhere to relocate. I had enough dried fish to last me a while yet, but it couldn't hurt to plan ahead. With this plan in mind, I slipped off the cloak, folding it tightly so it would retain some of its heat while I pulled on my armor.

Crrk!

I stilled at the snapping of a twig, finding its location in the northwest telling. Only once since camping here had travelers passed by, and they came and went without incident. Even still, as they'd passed adrenaline filled me. I didn't only expect a fight, I was revved for one. Like a masochist, I'd grown a fondness for the physical strains and aches of battle, if only because it meant I grew stronger.

The twig possibly snapped with the natural weight of snow and ice, but I took no chances and kept dressing in my armor. My heartbeat picked up its pace as other sounds reached my ears: the crunching of packed snow under heavy boots, the murmuring of casual conversation, the jingling of gear.

With my armor on, I put the cloak on over it and tugged its hood up over my head, pulling out my long hair on either side to keep the coldest breezes from reaching my neck. I grabbed my scythe from beside my bed mat and exited the tent into the brisk morning. I hung the weapon from my belt and stared out into the open forest through the thicket's gap. Then I waited, my fingers playing subconsciously with the strap of the blade's sheath that wrapped around its upper handle.

"...Audri's group came back with no luck," a woman's voice filtered through the brush, amid an ongoing discussion. "Orval's didn't. *That's* what concerns me."

"Audri's one hell of a fighter," a man replied.

"Yeah," the woman agreed, "but she can't track to save her life. That's why she always brings Faendal, but he's doing a little stint in Sera's dungeon for his debts so he wasn't with her. I didn't *expect* she'd find him. Orval can track *and* fight, and his group's missing. That leads me to only one conclusion, and it isn't good."

The group went silent, but their footsteps came closer. I tried tracking them through the holes of the foliage to my right to no avail. I could see little other than reflections of snow on the opposite side.

"I don't get it," another male voice spoke up, this one sounding younger than the last. "He's a *kid.* This should've been a one and done kind of deal."

"Sirius thought it *would* be," the woman replied. "Hence why he sent the Twelve. We saw where *that* led."

My fingers that picked subconsciously at the scythe's sheath finally unbuttoned the strap and slipped the protection off the blade. I refastened it to one of the many loops of metal on my armor for safe-keeping. It took a couple of tries, for I trembled with the anticipation of battle.

"That looks like a good camping point," the younger man said as the group's footsteps came ever closer.

"Yep," said the woman. "We'll check it."

I stood in the clear opening of the thicket, the blade of my scythe glimmering with the reflection of snow. My hood shadowed my face so well that it would possibly keep them from recognizing it, but my long black hair slipped out of its embrace and flowed along the breezes, brightening up in spots from melting snowflakes.

The group of mercenaries finally wandered into view while checking out the thicket. There were only nine, comprising seven humans, one Celd, and a dwarf. I felt sorry for them at first since I'd wiped out far larger groups, but then I remembered not to grow too prideful. These men and women were all well-armored and likely skilled.

The mercenaries slowed to a stop. They seemed to compare what little they saw of my features to the warrant likely in their pockets. A human woman stepped before the others, placing herself as the leader of the group. I noted the rings on her fingers and the sword in her hand, anticipating her fighting style. I further noted her fiery red hair and green eyes, anticipating her possible elements. Other than the hair color, she looked absolutely nothing like Kai. I was grateful for that, for even the hair resemblance had me on edge.

The leader opened her mouth to speak, but I interrupted her by reaching up to the flap of my hood and pulling it out to the side, giving the group a glimpse of my face. "Looking for me?"

That spurred them into action. They dropped bags of supplies and unsheathed weapons. The Celd went about stringing her pearl-white bow in the back. I summoned an area-of-effect death spell in my left hand, but I didn't yet cast it.

"I'll offer this only once," I began. "Leave me be, and no harm will come to you."

My warning changed nothing. The first few mercenaries who prepared first ran toward the thicket, their boots kicking up splashes of snow.

Fine. I released the magic. As black tendrils slithered off to raise the mercenaries I'd buried last season, I prepared a life shield and ward and stalked forth to meet my hunters.

"Do *not* lose your heads!" the leader shouted, building fire in a palm as she watched her dwarven ally parry a sideways slash of my scythe with his ax. *"Torsten! Move!"*

The dwarf abruptly retreated a few steps to the side. The surrounding snow-kissed trees lit up in flashes of orange as the leader unleashed multiple fireballs. The first two hit my ward, sizzling out into smoke and leaving the protection flickering. I averted my eyes from the bright light and sidestepped to avoid the rest. They hissed past, following on their path to the thicket I'd left behind. A disgruntled growl sounded out from one of the mercenary corpses that hobbled out of the brush to support me. After weeks of decomposing, they were a sight for sore eyes; their skin was gray, wrinkled, and leaked a variety of fluids. Insects invaded them, eating eyes and burrowing deep into skulls and fleshy crevasses. A centipede made its home in the broken cranium of one, slithering between the woman's once buoyant lips to take refuge under her fading tongue.

Retching echoed through the forest as one mercenary's tolerance for the macabre was tested to his limits. I paid little attention to it; the leader's last few fireballs missed me, but the corpse I'd looted the skull ring from was now on fire, gurgling with distaste until it fell back into my tent. The flames burning his hair slowly spread to the canvas.

Shit. Everything I owned was either on me or in that tent. I turned to protect my belongings, but the dwarf and three humans surrounded me like scavenger animals. I focused on blocking hits with the scythe and leeching, seeking strength.

"That was Orval!" a mercenary only a few years older than me screeched, pointing at the burning corpse. By his voice, I could tell he was the younger man who'd spoken earlier. "You lit Orval on *fire,* Fia!"

The leader shook her head authoritatively, though she seemed just as perturbed by this realization as her comrade. "That is no longer Orval, friend." Redirecting her focus to me, Fia added, "You will pay for your crimes committed against good people, *necromancer."*

I didn't explain that something else had killed these mercenaries. The innate fear most had for necromancy already played to my advantage; the morale of even the oldest mercenaries here was affected by fighting in the presence of undead peers. I'd allow them to think I'd killed every one of them myself.

The fight was soon contained like a layered circle with me at its center, for the mercenaries surrounded me and I directed my minions to surround them. Previously smooth, bright white snow became disturbed with frantic steps and splashes of blood and decomposing acids as mercenaries and corpses exchanged blows. My arms ached profusely from blocking and parrying between bouts of leeching; I hadn't yet used the scythe for an offensive hit because being outnumbered kept me on the defensive. That changed as my loyal corpses cut down a few foes and I drained a life, but now there were only five mercenaries left.

A leeching high requires six lives. Even if I leeched from everyone else, my high would only trigger once I had no enemies left. I thought this over as I refreshed my guards and slipped between two fighting corpses to get out of the chaos now that mercenaries no longer overwhelmed me. Then I raised the most recent casualties. Excess energy pumped through my veins, but only enough to keep fatigue away and make me jittery. I couldn't rely on a high for strength, but that was okay. I needed to learn to fight without it.

As my corpses swarmed three humans and the dwarf, I checked on my tent. The fire scorched and frayed the front canvas but had since petered out on its own. Feeling safe with the knowledge my belongings were intact, I paved a new path through the snow around the skirmish to get to the Celdic archer. She squeaked with fear as she noticed she had my undivided and hostile attention. After one of her pearl-white arrows bounced off my shield and rolled over on the snow, she hesitated to reload. Instead, she held her right hand out, assembling two magical protections. Throughout the battle I'd noticed that life magic protected some foes, but I hadn't found who summoned it. Now the Celd interested me even more; if I killed her, I removed their healer *and* protector from the equation.

"Fia!" the Celd nocked another arrow and fired. It whizzed into my shield, weakening its energy. I regenerated it.

"I see him!" the leader called out behind me. Given the fatigue and panic on Fia's voice, she seemed preoccupied with fighting corpses. I picked up my pace, determined to best the archer before Fia could aid her, sweat from adrenaline and exertion running down my brow.

The Celd exhaled with a shudder as I closed in. Her arrows harmlessly littered the snow beside my tracks, but she continued firing them. Life protections were temporary and could normally only be refreshed with new energy, but this poor woman seemed oblivious to the fact that my energy reserves wouldn't run out soon since the life force of her peers fueled them. The ignorance of necromancy would forever be to my benefit.

"No, no no no no," she rambled desperately, her eyes catching on the scythe's blade as I swung it in from the side, two hands on the shortened handle. Steel ricocheted violently off the magical force field, my bones aching intensely from the sturdy resistance to my efforts. Even still, I'd clearly grown stronger even without relying on leeching's power, for the Celd's guard dulled from the damage and the force of my hit sent her stumbling until she fell back into the snow. The curve of her life shield made a perfect oval impression in the snow around her as she scrambled to stand.

I took two steps to make up the distance between us and kicked her so hard I heard the *whoosh* of my boot in the air. Her shield prevented the hit from reaching her gut, but now it flickered, and the force knocked her back again.

The Celd's eyes teared up with a mixture of fear and panic as I stood over her and raised my scythe. *"For gods' sake, Fia!"* she screamed hoarsely, her voice unrecognizable from earlier.

I ripped my scythe down from the skies, using gravity to aid my strength. The blade clashed into the healer's weakened guard until it shattered, and the blow still had enough momentum to finish the arc. The scythe's tip cracked into the Celd's skull just at the center part of her hair, casting a magnificent pattern of red over the surrounding snow. The last of the shield's resistance kept the hit from splitting her head. A dull nausea permeated my gut as I watched the capillaries in her eyes burst from the sudden pressure on her brain. She twitched sporadically as her neurological system assessed its damages. Although her eyes went blank, she blinked once almost like her body fought death by mimicking the familiar.

"Bastard!"

The song of steel whistling through the air preceded my own tumble into the snow as Fia finally caught up to me, her strength emboldened by a need for vengeance. I struggled to stand, but Fia brought her sword down over my shield repeatedly, using my last tactic against me to keep me grounded. My hands patted frantically around on the snow, searching for my scythe but coming up empty. I rolled onto my back, lashing out a leg to knock Fia off her feet.

It didn't work. My boot connected with her ankle, but without a high the awkward hit did nothing but unbalance and irritate her. I sent a ball of death magic across the disturbed snow at the fallen Celd to call her to my aid. When I heard the spell fizzle out, I lifted on my elbows to see the archer's tan boots still shaking in place.

Dear gods. She's still alive.

No wonder I couldn't raise her from the dead. She was in a state of traumatized limbo before death. Despite its injury, her brain refused to die.

I mentally willed my corpses back to me between curses of frustration from losing track of my scythe. I reached out to Fia with leeching funnels in both hands to double my efforts and quicken her defeat. She felt the spell's fatiguing effect but lifted her sword high, determined to break through my shield at last.

My shield. Throughout the evolving chaos, I'd forgotten to refresh it. My heart jumped in my throat as I prepared the spell, but I was too late.

The life magic broke, and the sword finished its arc toward my gut. I scrambled back on my elbows, trying to avoid the hit entirely by forcing the arc to end in the snow between my parted knees.

Then, splashes of bright lights filled my vision, and a feverish wave overcame me as my body reacted to severe trauma before I even knew what it was. Vomit spewed from my lips just before my vision cleared. I still held the prepared life shield spell in my hand, so I subconsciously cast it, then stared stupidly down between my legs. I'd been a mere *inch* away from avoiding the hit; blood spurted from a break in my armor where it was thinnest under my groin. Normally, the thinner material allowed me to move freely in the leather. *Now,* however, it'd allowed Fia's sword easier access to the parts of a man no one wants to lose.

My breaths grew hoarser, panicked. I frantically felt around my armor, trying to ensure all parts of me were attached. The tip of Fia's blade broke through leather and sliced open my right testicle. Dizziness overwhelmed me at the mere realization, but I screamed orders at myself to stay cognizant. I reached out to Fia, harvesting energy as my head spun so fiercely with trauma and panic that everything was a blur. When my corpses finally caught up to us, their footfalls vibrated in my head like a stampede. Fia spun to face my minions since they were currently the largest threat. As they kept her busy, I turned over to my stomach as best as I could and stood, an embarrassingly high-pitched noise escaping my lips when the movement put pressure on my injury.

Blood drained down my right leg as I hobbled over to the Celd's still-shaking body. Only now did I realize that my scythe was still in her skull, so embedded that it remained upright from where I'd let go. I leeched from the shuddering woman with both hands, finally putting her out of her misery. I tugged at my scythe next, but the blade refused to budge. I held the body down with a boot and tried again, jerking multiple times before the skull finally released it. A rush of fluids chased the blade, still so hot with life they smoked in the air.

Corpses surrounded Fia when I turned back to the fight. A trail of undead and recent mercenary casualties littered the forest between her and the fight's starting location at the thicket. Splashes of blood melted the snow in red-streaked impressions. Only five minions remained standing after I'd had sixteen fighting at once earlier, but I raised no more. I needed energy for healing, and Fia was the only enemy left standing.

I'd planned to fight with melee a lot more in this battle, but I was already exhausted and leaking freely from my injury. When I joined my minions, I only leeched from Fia until she became overwhelmed and fell dead in a lump. I collapsed in just as pathetic of a lump beside her body, alarm bells ringing in my head.

Passing out will kill you, I warned myself as if there were two people in my head. *You can't pass out. Heal first.*

My injury disoriented me so badly that I didn't think to dispel the remaining corpses. They watched me with blank gazes as I tore off my armor piece by piece in the middle of blood-drenched snow and tugged down my trousers. Another wave of lightheadedness flooded through me as I assessed the wound. I'd studied anatomy and injuries as best as I could, but *nothing* could have prepared me for seeing my own lacerated testicle.

I awoke with a shivering start sometime later, but I hadn't remembered passing out. Confused, I sat up and searched myself. I'd managed to heal the wound and pull up my trousers, but I had no memory of it. Perhaps I'd slipped in and out of consciousness, or maybe my brain simply blanked out the traumatic things it didn't want to remember. My trousers were a ripped mess of matted blood.

But at least I was *alive,* and I'd managed to keep my manhood.

I laid back in the snow, too exhausted to move for the moment. The corpses I'd left animated still stood around me like ardent stalkers. I didn't want to dispel them yet; as I laid there exhausted, achy with battle fatigue, and overwhelmed by the prospect of already having to find a new place to camp, the last thing I wanted to feel was *alone*. My rough exasperated laughter echoed into the air and off the surrounding tree trunks as I let out a rush of emotion in the only way that felt relevant at the moment.

And to think I'd almost pitied these mercenaries for having a smaller group. One thing was for damn sure: I would *never* pity a foe again.

Eighteen

The Seran Forest evolved from a tranquil environment into a hot spot over the course of only two seasons, for after I bested the first mercenary party, many more followed in their place. They came in all sizes; the smallest party I defeated had only three members while the largest had twenty-five. From overhearing their conversations and looting their bodies, I learned as much as I could from them and the contracts they accepted from Sirius. For example, now I knew Sera reserved so much of its budget for mercenary advances. While the current reward for my head was 5,000 gold, Sirius also gave the mercenaries a smaller advance if they agreed to take on the contract. The gold was for travel and supply expenses, but it also ensured that mercenaries did not speak of their targets. The word *necromancer* was not to be uttered outside of parties sworn to secrecy and the pretentious walls of the Seran University. Instead, I was to be referred to as a simple *ruffian*.

I couldn't pretend this all didn't greatly amuse me. The government's handling of the situation was rudimentary and crossed the line from ineffective to counter-productive. Sirius didn't wish to risk his soldiers, so he threw some of his endless gold at mercenaries looking to make an honest living and called it a day. And as I bested each group of them and added their corpses to my own army, my strength only grew. It seemed we fed each other. Sirius supplied me with new minions and battles to look forward to, and I delivered a nice gift of endless frustration back to the bastard's doorstep by being a problem he couldn't easily fix. Even though Kai was far removed from my life, being a thorn in her father's side felt like getting a tiny bit of justice for the emotional abuse he put her through.

I searched for a place to relocate in the forest for the better part of half a year, taking my growing horde of corpses with me. I hid them every night under plant debris and in the thickest brush to keep my secret safe from anyone other than my pursuers. Only once did I have a close call when a group of dwarven friends from Hammerton wandered through the forest on their way to Sera after crossing over the eastern Chairel border. The dwarves camped near to the burial site of a dozen corpses beneath a broad pine, their existence only covered up by a thin layer of red needles. I overheard one dwarf comment about a stench, but they otherwise thought nothing of it. They also took a break from traveling for a day, so I couldn't move on since I couldn't raise the corpses in their presence. I spent that day fishing, but as soon as the dwarves moved on, so did I.

If I learned anything at all during the first half of the year 412, it was that the human body is a disgusting and fascinating invention of nature. I grew a special understanding and appreciation for anatomy since I was constantly surrounded by decomposition and brutal battle. Even reading the whimsical fables and historical accounts of warfare at the Seran University hadn't prepared me for the harsh realities of true bloodshed. One such reality is how bodily waste is such a common product of conflict. Men urinate unintentionally from fear even in mid-parry, and many defecate at the exact moment the soul leaves the body through the eyes. Another reality is how one simple injury can send the entire body into a death spiral. Once, I killed a man by attempting and failing to sever his arm at the arm pit. All it took was a single cut to the axillary artery, and he'd bled out in mere minutes while calling desperately for a healer. Such things were always glossed over and fancied up for retellings, and details given sparingly. I found this did a grave injustice to the bleak beauty of viscera and the tragedies interwoven in the savagery of conflict. When two people are at the point where they're ripping each other's bodies apart, there's a story there that deserves telling, and the details aren't always pretty. Because they *can't* be if the story is to remain honest.

It was one thing to take a life. But as the days went on and I faced more and more foes, I grew physically stronger, and with the strength came the savagery. Gore had once turned my stomach and blanked out my mind, but as I became accustomed to it, it no longer fazed me. I saved my most savage acts for the foes who were troublemakers: those who mocked me, injured me during battle, or were the hardest to kill. Gods only knew what Sirius or Kenady would look like when I was done with them if I ever had the chance to see them again. Pain isn't hard to inflict if one feels the target deserves it, after all. Internally I wondered what this change in me meant for my humanity, but part of me didn't care. The grimy side of human nature already wronged me in every way it knew how, so I returned the gesture with equal disrespect. Still, I tried to hang on to a shred of common decency. Every time I fought mercenaries, I gave them a chance to withdraw before I showed deadly force. Each time I sensed a foe's intense fear or felt someone had talked them into this mission against me, I'd kill them painlessly through leeching if possible. Once, I even let a man go after he begged for his life. I told him to drop his weapon, and he did. Then I told him to run, and he did that, too; I kept his weapon for my corpses and didn't bother chasing him. Even if he was a blabbermouth and gave away my location to all of Sera, it made no difference.

By late-High Star of 412, my search for a new camping site had long ago turned half-hearted, so when I stumbled upon the perfect solution I was more surprised than relieved. A mere hour after fishing at a well-stocked stream, a solid splotch of brown filled in the gaps of needled foliage like a structure sat just across a line of pines waiting to be discovered. I hadn't come across any buildings in the forest yet save for a shoddy lean-to some campers had put together haphazardly and then left without a care. My tent was already scorched and frayed from that first mercenary fight half a year ago, so the idea of living in a solid structure enticed me.

I willed my small army of corpses to gather together before dispelling them in a clearing at the center of four trees. They collapsed together, the resulting scented breeze a juxtaposition of decomposition and pine. I didn't bother burying or hiding them for now. I wandered through the forest toward the structure as nonchalantly as possible in case someone still occupied it. I found it ironic that despite my lengthy and severe criminal record, I worried about being perceived as a simple thief. Perhaps because I *wasn't* one. Contrarily, people could call me a murderer or necromancer all they wanted, and it wouldn't bother me in the slightest because I couldn't argue.

Sometimes the mind makes the dumbest arguments when it has all the time in the world to think.

As I closed in on the structure, its form became clearer through the fuzzy green branches of conifers. It was a small log cabin that appeared barely half the size of the one I'd grown up in. It couldn't have been larger than ten by ten feet. Its simple walls were layered unshaved pine trunks that laced together at each corner. It had a peaked roof with tiny windows at the tops of the western and eastern walls that seemed built for ventilation, for they were far too high to see through and the cabin only had one floor. On either side of a centered front door were single-pane windows, but they were closed, and hunter green drapes blocked my view of the inside. Along the cabin's left wall was a small herb garden that bowed to the authority of wild forest overgrowth as it stretched its greedy green fingers over and under the tiny enclosed fence. Clusters of brown mushrooms sprouted along the inside edge of the garden barrier. Given the knowledge passed along to me from the drug dealing Celd last year, I knew the fungi was edible. What wasn't clear was whether it grew here naturally or by intelligent encouragement.

I circled the cottage a few times, eyeing it and considering claiming it for my own. I heard nothing inside the home, so I walked up to the front and tried the door. It was locked, so I backed away. If this home belonged to someone, they were innocent to my situation. I had no qualms with killing those who hunted me down, but I still took issue with committing atrocities against people who were no threat to me. I was a criminal out of unfortunate circumstance, not because I'd started out my life hurting people. I didn't want that to change today. Maybe I'd become more of a monster over the years of surviving in such a state of loneliness; perhaps one day I would devolve to resemble the myth of the insane necromancer that everyone believed was inevitable.

But not today.

I walked back to where my corpses waited for me in a pile of mismatched limbs and wrinkled, parched skin. I raised them just to direct them to various hiding places and dispelled them again. As I covered them up with forest debris and conveniently placed branches and logs, I formed a plan.

A week.

That was how long I'd give the owner of this cabin to come home. If I saw no activity for that long, I'd break in and make it my own. The owner possibly went out fishing or hunting and would be home as soon as tonight. After all, the cabin was in a convenient location for both, which was why it was so attractive to me. If I broke in after a week and the owner still ended up coming home to the cabin just to find me in it, I would apologize and offer trade or work as recompense.

This justification seemed reasonable. I camped out near the cabin for seven days, watching and listening for any signs of life. None came. Finally, I approached the home, testing each of its windows for an easy entry. None of them budged. I returned to the front door, kicking at it relentlessly until it finally burst inward on its hinges, trailing a cloud of wood splinters.

I immediately recognized the stench of advanced decomposition that billowed out in the door's wake, and I was so used to it that I didn't hesitate walking in. I left the door open behind me to allow the home to air out. As I'd surmised, the entire cabin was one room. A tiny wooden cabinet and counter sat in the immediate left corner. Someone left a ceramic mug on it beside a tea kettle. Dried herbs hung from a rack above another shaded window. A table for two but with only one chair sat against the wall next to the counter. In the right corner were a pair of shoes below a small coat rack that held a collection of clothes. I brushed through them as I passed; they were men's clothes, but for a much shorter man than me.

A small fireplace took up the center back wall with a place to hang a pot to cook food or boil water. A pot hung there now, clean but with the slight residue of good use. The stone surrounding the tinder led up the center wall and to a chimney. Just to the right of the fireplace and along the far right wall was a single bed with a thin mattress and wool blanket. Both were crusted with a thick film of fluids from a single corpse that was so decayed that it looked just like a skeleton wearing skin to be fashionable.

A bed. It was a simple thought, but it was my main focus for the moment. I never imagined I'd be lucky enough to come across a bed with a mattress again. I'd struck gold.

I pulled the blanket down. Maggots had long ago infested the body. The luckiest among them evolved into flies and moved on, but a few dead insects rolled out from the creases in wool after failing to escape its maze. I could safely assume no one would come back to claim the cabin. They'd had long enough to do so.

Immediately, I set to work cleaning up the cabin and making it my own. I relocated all my corpses to the area and moved the previous owner out to a shallow grave to join them. I buried a sword with him that another corpse had as a side weapon, ensuring he could protect his home even in death. After covering the corpses with debris as usual, I broke brittle twigs off the nearby trees and scattered them in a circle barrier around the cabin. It was an additional layer of defense I'd started using last season; the twigs didn't look out of place in a forest, but they offered an alarm to alert me of near pursuers. When hunkered down in one location that had only one door—a door I'd just broken to get into the house—I needed every defense I could get.

I dragged the thin mattress and wool blanket to the stream and washed them as best as I could, though I double and triple-washed them using boiling water back at the cabin and a pathetic soap I made myself following the directions of the alchemical anatomy book. The soap did little to clean the stains, but at least the smell was gone. As well as I could stand the stench of death, I didn't prefer it.

If I'd thought that staying in one place would attract a sudden onslaught of mercenaries, I was sorely disappointed. The first few weeks living in the cabin were relatively peaceful. I spent the days fishing and the nights reading. I'd bought only a few books in Brognel, and by this point I'd read them all. But I had nothing else to do save for laundry and gear upkeep, and I certainly didn't want to spend all my time reading Kai's letter in one hand while holding onto the sentimental ring at my neck with the other. I was lonelier than I'd ever been, but if I didn't acknowledge the people I lost I could pretend otherwise.

This inescapable black hole of loneliness was perhaps why I was so vulnerable to the companionship offered to me by happenstance in early Red Moon. I awoke to the snap of a twig and late morning sunlight prodding through the cabin's windows and underneath the green drapes. As I reacted to a possible threat and pulled on my armor, I cursed inwardly at myself for sleeping so late. I'd always been a heavy sleeper and a natural night owl; such things often worked against me considering most mercenaries did their traveling during daylight.

I grabbed the scythe from where I kept it beneath the bed and hung it from my belt. The sheath lie nearby; I didn't bother slipping it on the blade. I tugged the chair out from under the broken door handle and exited the cabin, prepared for a fight.

A surprised masculine yelp sounded out, followed by a scurry of frantic footsteps. Standing against the rusted backdrop of the cooling forest was a single man clad in brown leather. He wore light armor, though it was mismatched and missing pieces like he'd created his own suit out of nothing but spares. He reached up, tugging a dark hood back to reveal his face. Human ears popped out between strands of greasy brown hair. He would have been handsome if it weren't for his gaunt features and the bags under his eyes. I assumed he was a rempka user, for it appeared the drug already took a toll on his otherwise youthful body. Despite his physical wear and tear, he appeared to be only a few years older than me. I estimated his age to be twenty-one, twenty-two at most.

I said nothing to him, but my right hand found the handle of my scythe like a warning.

The man ducked low in a crouch and held out both hands to me in surrender. "I don't want no trouble, man," he protested, his dialect indicating he'd likely lived in squalor during a rough childhood. It was a common dialect that developed in humans who either grew up in a family of agriculture in Chairel's rural areas or the roughest slums of its major cities. It made sense, for it appeared this man never escaped poverty; a knapsack was slung over one shoulder, but he otherwise carried nothing but himself.

"What do you want?" I asked. I had the inkling he wasn't a mercenary.

The man exhaled shakily, still holding his hands up like a weak defense. "I wanted food, sir. I saw this garden here. The place look abandoned. I swear to the gods, I didn't know someone lived here. I took nothing." As if willing to prove it, he pulled the knapsack from his shoulder and tossed it toward me. It landed in a spray of pine needles between us.

Sir, he'd called me. It was a step up from *kid,* at least. I had no way of looking at myself save for my reflection in the water while fishing. Perhaps my growth over the last year and a half was more substantial than I thought and I looked older. Either that, or he feared me for reasons he wasn't telling.

"Why are you here?" I inquired, scanning the surrounding forest for signs of others. I found nothing suspicious, so my eyes returned to the man.

"I...just told you," he protested, confused.

"You told me you wanted food from my garden. You haven't said why you're traveling through the forest."

He hesitated, searching for the right words behind his eyes. "I'm on my way to Sera."

My grip tightened on my scythe. The other man noticed and winced. "Why?"

"To...trade," he replied nervously.

"Bull*shit,*" I spat, fed up with his clear dishonesty. I tugged the scythe from my belt and stalked forward. The stranger scrambled backward so fast he fell back into a bed of pine needles. He grabbed no weapons, only holding his hands before his face defensively as I lifted my scythe.

"I'm a criminal! Okay? I'm a criminal," he blurted.

I lowered my weapon and glared. Between two spread fingers, his fearful eyes found mine, but he said nothing.

"Then why are you going to *Sera,* of all places?" I demanded. "Sirius does not grant leniency to criminals."

"No, but Sirius can't be everywhere at once, and many Serans are rich," the stranger breathed in another ramble. "The rich pay good money for drugs. I gyp them and they barely notice. As soon as they raise an eyebrow, I can leave and go elsewhere."

"You use rempka," I stated.

"Yes," he admitted easily. Pulling his hands away from his face to return my gaze openly, he added, "I have some in that knapsack. I'll share it with you if you let me live."

I glared at him silently until he cowered back, and then I grabbed his knapsack. Opening its flap, I looked over its contents without digging through. Sure enough, there were small bottles of rempka, needles, and tourniquets. I found no evidence of a warrant, but I wasn't about to risk sticking myself with used needles to be certain. I tossed the knapsack back to the ground.

"I have no need of rempka." I secured the scythe on my belt again.

"Then..." he trailed off, noting my fading hostility with relief. "What do you want?"

I stared off into the forest. I didn't even know this criminal's name, but my chest felt congested with an attachment to him I couldn't explain. He was the first person I'd come across in so long who didn't want to kill me, and what little I knew of him were things we had in common. The void in my gut caused by loneliness pleaded with me to fill it with this sudden stroke of luck.

"You are hungry and alone," I stated. "Have you no skill to feed yourself?"

"I'm not much of a hunter."

"I'm a fisher."

"You're more than that." He stared wearily at my scythe.

"That's none of your concern."

"No," he agreed quickly, eager to stay on my good side. "It's not."

"I will feed you," I offered.

He frowned. "Why?"

"Because you're hungry."

"That's none of your concern," he said, repeating my own words back to me.

"Don't decide that for me." I spun to walk back into the cabin.

"Okay," he agreed eagerly behind me. "What are you doing?"

I didn't reply, but when I re-emerged with a fishing rod, he relaxed. He looked absolutely ridiculous still lying on the ground from where he'd fallen earlier in defense, but I said nothing of it and only stopped nearby to hold out a hand to him. He took it while noting the many rings on my fingers, all of which I'd looted from my hunters.

"Are you a mage?" he asked, grunting as he stood with my help.

I started off toward the nearest stream, listening to him grab his knapsack off the forest floor and hurry to join me. "Perhaps."

"You must be unlicensed," he surmised.

I glanced over with a neutral expression, though it concerned me that he'd so easily figured that out. "Why would you conclude that?"

"Because mages make good money," he said. "If you were licensed, you'd be working somewhere. But here you are, alone in the forest, avoiding civilization and dare I say *discovery.*"

"You say all this like you have me figured out, but I never said I was a mage."

"Do you have to?" He motioned toward my hands. "The rings are a dead giveaway."

"I love jewelry."

He laughed at my dry tone. "Yes," he said with an edge of sarcasm, "you certainly seem the type."

I said nothing, but a smirk lit up the side of my face opposite the stranger. We walked for some minutes in silence before he spoke again.

"Why do mages *wear* jewelry, anyway?"

"They believe it increases the accuracy and potency of spells," I replied. "Mages harness energy out of the environment. Metal is extremely conductive."

"Have you noticed a difference?" he asked. "Between casting spells with jewelry and without it?"

I judged the question to be one of curiosity rather than prodding, so I decided to answer it. "Not a difference in casting, but harnessing. Collecting energy for spells seems to be quicker."

"How do you know? You can't *see* energy."

"No," I agreed. "I can feel it."

"Like...*tangibly?*"

It surprised me he was well-educated enough to know that word. "I don't reach out and *touch* energy. It's something I feel regardless of whether I look for it or not."

"I don't understand."

I stopped, pine needles skipping outward from the abrupt kick of my boots. The stranger stiffened like he thought I'd suddenly changed my mind about fighting him, but I made no hostile move. I peered around at the surrounding trees. A cool Red Moon breeze whistled through the branches, creating a song of rustling and creaking.

"Do you feel the breeze?" I asked.

He frowned. "Yes, of course."

"That is energy. You aren't reaching out and touching the breeze, but you feel it all the same." I started walking again, and he fell in by my side.

"There isn't always a breeze," he pointed out.

"You exude body heat," I said. *"That* is energy. The animals of the forest do the same. The residual energies that exist after conflict or intense emotion last far longer than people would believe. There are many sources of energy."

"But mages can't harvest energy from people. Only necromancers can."

"Necromancers *are* mages," I corrected him, though I clarified, "but no, mages can't take energy from the living. The living give it freely through their own anatomical processes. Body heat exudes naturally. It is not taken."

"This is all very complicated."

"It's actually not hard to learn at all," I argued lightly.

"It takes some mages a decade or more to graduate from the Seran University," he pointed out as an argument.

"How could you know that?"

"I was born in Sera. Lived in the lowest district, but I knew enough." He noted my confusion and explained, "I'm on my way back to Sera from Celendar. Barely got halfway through that elven forest before a Celdic hunting party spotted me and forced me back out since I'm human. Thought Celendar might be a reprieve from Sera's bullshit, but no, they got problems like everyone else."

The more we talked, the more I found I had in common with this man. I felt a strange comfort take root in my chest, and I clung to it.

"The problem is *Chairel,"* I mused. "It has always been domineering, and that mentality trickles down from the queen to her regents. Magic is fairly easy to learn, but as you said, it takes some mages a good portion of their lives to learn it in Sera, and it puts thousands into debt. Put two and two together, and one begins to realize that the discrepancy isn't due to simple *mistake."*

The stranger smirked, though his gaze softened with a bit of sympathy. "You talk like you know all about Sera's nonsense, but you don't speak like a guy from the lower districts and you're not rich."

"I'm not originally from Sera," I said, coming to a stop at the stream that was my destination. The fish were plentiful this morning, fighting the current in tiny schools. The chill of the early hour invigorated them. As I prepared my fishing rod, I told my companion, "I *do* know all about its nonsense."

Nineteen

Under a cascade of late morning sunlight that danced through the canopies, my new companion and I worked in silence. He built a small cooking campfire in the clearing between the cabin and its protective barrier of snapping twigs. He unknowingly used many of them to build the fire since they were dried out and nearby, but I didn't complain. I could replace them easily. As I descaled and gutted my recent catches for our meal together, I watched the other man situate two large rocks on either side of the fire. His method intrigued me; I'd never seen such a way to prepare a cooking fire, so I noted it for later use.

"What is your name?" I asked. He glanced up at the broken silence, and his eyes caught on the fish entrails I threw off to the side like they were an inconvenience.

"John," he said. I could tell it was a lie. John was a simple human name, perhaps belonging to his father or some other man he'd been close to in the past. But it was not his name. Somehow, the lie didn't matter to me. While we were cordial to each other thus far, we'd held back certain details and admissions during our conversations. We both had things to hide, but that seemed like a relief rather than a concern since it was something we shared. I likely had a worse track record than he did.

"What's yours?" John asked when I didn't call him out for his lie.

"Give me one."

"Give you a name?"

"Yes. Make one up. You are good at it."

John wasn't perturbed that I called him out. "Bob," he finally decided.

I huffed with amusement as I scooped out more organs and threw them to the side. "That's a name for an old farmer."

"Yes," John agreed. "It makes no sense for you. That's why I chose it."

"How would you know it makes no sense for me? I have a garden." I motioned toward it with a bloodied hand.

"We *both* know that hasn't always been your garden."

John's perception impressed me. I said nothing.

"What are your crimes?" John asked.

I chuckled low and shook my head. "If I won't tell you my name, what makes you think I'd tell you that?"

"You could tell me because without a name, I'd have no way to connect your crimes to it," he reasoned.

I gave him nothing but silence.

"Okay," John breathed at the edge of a sigh. "Can I at least know if your crimes are a danger to me?"

"They aren't."

John nodded with relief.

"I am not a danger to you," I continued, "but it's only fair to warn you that I have many enemies. If mercenaries approach us, it's best for you to run."

I felt John's eyes on me even though I still worked on preparing the fish. *"Mercenaries?* What are you, a murderer?"

I didn't deny it.

"So you really *would* have killed me earlier," John went on, taking my silence as an answer. "And here I thought after all this time talking to you that you must've been bluffing." Another hesitation. "Why *didn't* you just kill me, then?"

"Because you didn't deserve it," I replied. "You've done nothing to me. If you wronged me, I wouldn't hesitate."

"I get the feeling there are quite a few people out there who've wronged you."

I instantly thought of Kenady. "Yes."

"And you would kill them?" John snapped his fingers. "Just like that?"

"In a heartbeat, and I might even enjoy it." I tried to get the fantasy of killing Kenady out of my head since it was unlikely to happen. "You seem surprised by this."

"I am," John admitted. "You speak as if death doesn't faze you."

"It doesn't anymore. When something is a common occurrence in your life, is it *possible* for it to faze you?"

It was John's turn to be silent. He watched as I deboned the fish and threw the tiny bones into a small container. I normally took them back to the stream so other fish could pick them over; the last thing I wanted was to keep them at the cabin and waste energy raising useless fish corpses when the next inevitable attack came.

"Do you mind if I use some of your water for tea?" John pointed toward the buckets of water I kept next to the exterior cabin wall, where I collected rainwater for reserves.

Excitement laced my voice as I blurted, "You have tea?"

An exceedingly amused smile broke out on John's face. He looked over my expression like it was the funniest thing he'd ever seen and said, "Yes. Hell, you'd think you were a kid who was just promised sweets."

"What kind of tea do you have?"

"Gods, I don't know. I'm not a tea connoisseur. Just got it off some Celd on my way here." John dragged his knapsack over and dug through it. He took out an enclosed packet and threw it over to me.

I wiped off my bloody hands with a small towel and opened the packet. I took a quick whiff of its scent, sighed heavily with contentment, and then stared at the dried leaves, noting their shape. "Black tea," I murmured. "I figured it would be fruity since you said you got it from a Celd."

John shrugged with indifference. "I don't know. Like I said, I'm not a tea connoisseur. Apparently, *you* are."

I huffed but shook my head. "It's easy to tell it's black tea. Black tea is only one type out of several. Depending on how or where it's grown, tea develops completely different tastes. They make most teas—white, green, black—from the same plant. The oxidation of the leaves after harvesting turns them this dark color. That's how I know it's black tea. But as for what it tastes like, I'll have no idea until I try it."

John blinked at me a moment. "First of all, I have no idea why anyone would need to know that much about tea. *Second* of all, that was the most you've spoken at once since I got here, and the subject was, again, *tea. Third* of all, I'm pretty sure you just invited yourself to *take* some of my tea."

"I'll trade you for it," I offered.

"No—that's not my issue," John protested, though he laughed like he thought this was all ridiculous. "I mean, *look* at you. All undone over some fucking *tea."*

"I love tea."

He snorted another laugh. "Yeah. Yeah, I guess you do." He stood up and swiped at the front and back of his legs to rid himself of debris. "Don't worry, *Bob*. I'll make enough tea for both of us."

The sun crept past the center of the sky by the time we sat across from each other at the campfire. John set a thin, flat rock over the two he propped up over the fire. On one side, the fish sizzled in its natural oils on the bare rock. On the other side, water boiled in a pot for our tea. John and I spoke no words for now, but just having him there felt like a relief. Sometimes respectable silence with someone is a comfort all on its own.

The forest looked beautiful. It was a sunny but cloudy Red Moon day, so a bright yellow glow spilled over the edges of cotton in the sky, creating a pattern of light and shadows throughout the wood that brought it to life with shades of color. The chill in the air invigorated the wildlife; animals sang, scurried, and foraged for food and warm homes to nestle in.

John seemed to feel as peaceful as I did. I couldn't know if he was running from something or not, but his willingness to so readily agree to share a meal with me indicated he was also lonely. Otherwise, he could have asked to trade for food rather than stay for it, and he wouldn't be so curious about me.

John prepared the tea using my ceramic mug and a cup seemingly made of tin that he pulled out of his knapsack. After I turned the fish over to cook the other side, he handed my mug over to me and watched as I took a sip.

The robust, slightly roasted caramel flavor of a high-quality tea settled on my tongue. I closed my eyes, holding it there as I ducked my head forward to reminisce. Memories of my father surprising me with a box of variety high-quality teas flooded through my mind. He'd been *so* excited that day; such quality tea was expensive and rare, but he'd claimed to have gotten a good deal on it. My father's simple-mindedness had been just another reason to love him. Once I told him I had a fondness for tea, he'd never forgotten it to the point of becoming obsessive. He had been so insistent on searching for good deals on teas from neighbors and traders at the docks that others teased him for it; traders from other towns started bringing larger shipments under the belief that Thornwell had a high demand for tea.

And it did. But only because of one boy's love for it and the desperation of a father to keep his son happy.

I swallowed hard, and the tea slipped down my throat, massaging the esophagus with warmth on the way down. My eyes burned with emotion I held back by necessity.

John cleared his throat across the fire, but I didn't meet his eyes. The packet of remaining tea leaves landed by my side a moment later after he tossed it.

"You steeped it well," I told him, my voice slightly hoarser than normal as I tossed the packet back. "I need no more leaves."

"I know," John conceded, throwing it back. "I'm letting you have it. Tea means nothing to me."

I rolled my neck to remove a crick, disturbed that he sensed my emotion. But I took the packet of tea and put it safely in a pocket. "Thank you."

John nodded politely and watched the smoke escape the underside of the cooking fish. "You have lots of regrets," he stated.

"No," I argued, poking at the fish with a stick. "I have lots of memories. Only one regret."

"What is it?"

"That I didn't appreciate what I had until it was gone," I replied, staring into the fire and thinking of my parents. "And I wasn't fully honest with the people who would've understood the most." I thought of Kai.

"Why weren't you honest?"

"Because I couldn't be," I replied. "Being honest could've gotten me killed."

"Then you shouldn't regret it."

"Easier said than done."

"Yeah, but isn't it always that way with regrets?" John pondered aloud. "They don't make sense half the damn time. I regret a lot of things even though they were necessary. Couldn't have done things any other way, but here I sit wishing I had."

His words mirrored the way I felt about how I'd gotten into this whole mess to begin with. As much as I'd accepted living life as a criminal, I would've never chosen it. It was simply the only option left. I would've killed to go back to learning how to make a decent living at the university and cherishing what I'd had with Kai. Times were so *innocent* then. Back before I knew how to rip a man apart and do it *well.* Before I knew the stench of stomach bile by heart and how a person's voice changes when they face the reality of a brutal death.

I served the fish on two plates, and John took his happily. We ate in silence for a few minutes, though John was halfway through his second fish before I'd had time to finish my first.

"This is delicious," he complimented, glancing up with gratitude. "It's fresh. Cooked well. Good herbs." He smiled while chewing his next bite and nodded toward the garden. "That *is* your garden."

"I know just enough about herbs to get by," I replied. "But you were right earlier. That wasn't always my garden."

"Did you kill the guy who lived here?" John asked this like it wouldn't surprise or bother him if I had.

"No. He died naturally. I came across the place and it looked abandoned, so I removed his body and took it for myself."

"Lucky," John commented. "I'd have done the same thing."

"I thought you were on your way to Sera."

"I am," he replied quickly. "But my life doesn't depend on it. I make shit up as I go along. See what opportunities arise. I have no love for Sera. I'll steal from the rich when I go back, but I'm not gonna skip on the way in."

I opened my mouth but quickly closed it. I frowned with distaste at the thoughts running through my head; I'd nearly asked John if he wanted to stay here with me since his plans weren't certain. What the hell was wrong with me? I barely knew this man. I likely couldn't trust him. Was I so desperate for companionship that I'd lost my mind?

"Will you ever go back to Sera?" John asked, sitting back from the fire when he finished his second fish. He picked at his teeth with a fingernail as I replied.

"The only way I'd go back to Sera is if I had the manpower to burn it down."

John burst into laughter and slapped his knee. "Good *gods,* Bob! That's a story I need to hear if you're *that* upset with it."

I smirked, but mostly because it felt so awkward to be called *Bob*. "You'll be going there next."

"Yeah, and I won't say a damn thing about whatever vendetta it is you have against it," he replied. "I've gotten into so much trouble in Sera that I can't use the front gate no more 'cause the guards will either turn me away or attempt arrest."

I sighed, unconvinced. I decided to settle on a vague story because I truly wanted to share it with someone who might understand. "Let's just say I was in the middle of getting a great education in Sera when I stumbled across something illegal. Instead of turning away, I gave in to curiosity. A walking waste of space eavesdropped on said curiosity and reported me to authorities. I fled, a criminal but a harmless one, and when Sirius's men came after me I used deadly force. That's the day I became a murderer."

"That's not murder," John retorted lightly. "That's self-defense."

I shrugged. "Self-defense *is* murder by another name. Arguing semantics to Sirius would get me nowhere."

"No." John tilted his head with curiosity. "You speak of Sirius like your hatred of him is personal."

"I've met him."

His eyebrows raised. "Truly? Is he as ugly as they say?"

I huffed. "Yes."

"Is Sirius one of those people you'd kill if you could?"

"Painfully, yes."

"Is there such a thing as a painless death?" John smirked.

"Yes," I repeated, thinking of leeching.

John shrugged and chuckled. "Ah, it don't matter. If you were wanting to go on some crazy quest to kill Sirius, you'd have my support."

I raised an eyebrow. "Like I said before, I'd have to be dragged kicking and screaming back to Sera unless I had some way of swarming it with force. Otherwise, I'd have no chance." I took a sip of my tea. "Besides, I'm not looking to start a band of criminals. I do fine alone."

"I can't disagree since you're still alive considering the troubles following you," John agreed, "but there's strength in numbers. No matter what crimes you've committed, there will always be like-minded people who would join you, if only for common survival."

I stared at John across the fire for a moment. "Is that advice or a suggestion?"

"I don't know," he replied. "Maybe both."

"I'll stay in the forest for a while. Build my strength. Remove any threats thrown my way. Hope to the undeserving gods that one day the walking waste of space I talked about earlier will be one of them so I can spill his blood."

"Do tell," John said excitedly, and I huffed with amusement.

"Not much to say other than he treated me like shit for years. Humiliated me and someone I love time and time again. He's the reason I was exiled and had the troubles I did. Worst part of all?" I thought back to Kenady's rich background and dual casting abilities. "He's *talented."*

"Ugh," John blurted sympathetically. "Like fate itself is pissing on justice."

That mental image amused me greatly. "Exactly."

Afternoon evolved into evening until nightfall came to beat all daylight into submission. John told me about many things: delving into drugs, the majesty of the Cel Forest, and he hinted at being a runaway from a childhood of abuse. We could somehow empathize with each other despite not telling whole stories. After listening to his stories of abuse, I mentioned Kai and the emotional abuse Sirius put her through, hinting to John that I'd fancied her. We bonded over that. John hadn't lambasted me for my admittance that I'd killed many pursuers, but he openly accepted when I expressed a hatred for undeserved mistreatment. Our moral compasses differed from most, but that warmed us up to one another.

By the time I stood up to head into the house for bed, I seriously considered asking John to stay. I felt rejuvenated from a long day of socializing, no matter how meaningless most of it was. Such an idea would require immense trust; I'd have to come clean about my necromancy before the next attack forced me to use it in front of him, and John would need to be honest with me in turn. I wasn't ready for that yet, but John seemed reluctant to leave.

John watched me carry things into the cabin, still stoking the fire. Over the course of the night he'd started twitching and showing signs of anxiety, but I said nothing of it.

“Where have you been sleeping?” I asked, nodding at his knapsack as I carried my dishware to the cabin. “You have no tent.”

“No. I've been sleeping under trees and using the bag as a pillow.” He stared at it and wrinkled up his nose twice in a row like a tic.

“That's dangerous to do considering all those needles you have.”

“I secure them as best as I can.” He twitched again.

"I have a tent and a sleeping roll you can use," I offered. "You can stay here tonight, but you'll have to sleep outside."

Relief washed over his face. "Oh, thanks, man. I appreciate it." He stood and rolled his neck to the side. Once, twice.

"Are you okay?" I asked, motioning to his tics.

"Yeah." John squinted his eyes shut and opened them again. "Just having rempka withdrawals. You don't mind if I shoot up out here, do you?"

I frowned and glanced at his bag. "As long as it doesn't affect me, you can do whatever you want."

A shaky grin brightened his face. "Out of all the Bobs I've met, you're the best one."

I huffed and turned away, feeling conflicted. I didn't know much about rempka, but rumors stated it was the worst drug of all. Few tried it once; its destructive and addictive nature killed thousands every year. As I prepared to go to bed, I pondered over whether any life magic existed that could cure addiction. I doubted it. There were so many psychological aspects to addiction, and life magic couldn't affect the mind. If there had been such a spell and I'd known it, I would have offered it to John for free in a heartbeat to help him.

I situated the chair beneath the broken door knob like I did every night. It didn't offer much protection, but I didn't know the first thing about fixing hardware and couldn't lock the door. I tugged the blankets down on the bed, but before I crawled in I brushed the near drape from the corner of the window to check on John. He hadn't touched the tent supplies I'd left outside for him. John still sat by the fading fire, resting one arm on a raised knee and tightening a tourniquet around it with his teeth. A prepared injection needle sat on a rock nearby, and he grabbed it like a saving grace.

John put the needle just outside a deep purple bruise on his inner elbow, and he grimaced as it punctured the sore skin. He emptied the clear drug into his veins. He'd told me earlier that while one could drink or inject rempka, putting it directly into the veins caused a more potent high. I believed him, for he abruptly stopped twitching and went limp, dropping his supplies and falling back into the bed of pine needles like a weighty lump. At first, I was concerned he'd overdosed, but then his stomach rose and fell with breaths.

I turned away from the depressing scene and went to bed.

*

Crrk! Crrk! Crrk!

I awoke with a start and scrambled out of bed. My hand instinctively swept under my bed and grabbed my scythe.

"Open up!" John screamed hoarsely on the other side of the door. It rattled in its frame. The chair keeping it closed scraped into the wooden floor, leaving scars and sprinkled wood chips.

"What do you want?" I shouted, my heart racing as I tried to figure out if he'd become hostile or was simply under the influence. I shoved my feet into my boots, but I didn't tie them.

"I want that blade, man," he called through the door like a whine, beating on it again.

I glanced down at my scythe. "You're not getting it."

"But I want it," John argued childishly, hitting the door again. His words slurred, but they weren't sluggish. Still, that told me he wasn't of mind.

"I have many more weapons you can go through," I reasoned, thinking of all the looted weapons I'd buried with my corpses. "You can't have my scythe."

"Open up," he repeated.

"You're high," I retorted. "You don't know what you're doing. Go sleep it off."

"Oh, *trust* me. I know what I'm doing," John argued through the door. "That scythe'll fetch me a nice chunk of gold in Sera. Beautiful weapon. Unique, too."

I froze. Somehow, John admitting that hurt worse than the last time someone stabbed me. "You planned on *robbing* me?" I yelled, my voice heavy with sorrow. "After everything I gave to you *freely?"*

John chortled outside the door like he found my shock hilarious. "How do you think I pay for my habit, genius? Rempka ain't cheap. No hard feelings. I like you better than most. I definitely reconsidered doing this at all, but..." he trailed off and laughed again. "Well, then I got high. It makes me loopy!"

I stood in the middle of my cabin in a cloud of befuddled misery as John beat at the door. All the conversations we'd had throughout the day flooded back, along with the contentment, relief, and camaraderie I'd felt from having someone near. Now, a sick betrayal took their place.

I stared at the soft moonlight that leaked under the door as it danced with John's kicks. *I helped you. I confided in you.* I'd only confided in four people in my entire life. John was the only one I'd done so out of desperation, but I'd started to trust him nonetheless. Because it felt safer to do with a fellow criminal.

I would stop giving people the benefit of the doubt from this day forward. None of them *ever* deserved it.

"John," I called out. "Just *leave.* I don't want to kill you, but I *swear to the gods,* if you kick at the door one more time—"

Crrk!

Anger took over, triggered by John's betrayal and his refusal to listen to me. I jerked the chair out from its place beneath the door handle. Before I could open the door John did so by kicking it again, tumbling into the cabin at the mercy of a sudden lack of resistance. I stepped to the side, watching him fall flat on his inebriated face before standing over him to block his exit, one boot on either side of his shoulders. John grunted as he spun between my boots to stare up at me. A squeak of a noise escaped his lips as he noticed the gleam of the scythe's blade in the moonlight streaming through the windows.

"Wait, man," John blurted, hitting my left boot and trying to scoot out from under me. I moved the boot, but only to stamp it on his chest and hold him still. I held the scythe handle with both hands and ensured I could make the swing without hitting nearby furniture.

"Wait," John pleaded again, though he still slurred with bewilderment from the rempka in his veins. "Keep the scythe. I don't fuckin' want it."

"There was a line," I retorted, my heart roaring so loudly in my ears I couldn't hear the curses John rambled that matched up with his moving mouth. "You already crossed it."

The sharp whipping of metal cracked through the cabin as I swung the scythe in a downward arc. The tip of the blade sunk into the back of John's neck, curved in toward the spine. A metallic stench immediately engulfed the room as the wound bled, but the awkward angle kept it from killing him. As he coughed up blood and shook with sudden trauma, I jerked the blade further into his throat one tug at a time, ripping stubborn tendon to work metal through to the spine. Steel hit bone, sending reverberations of resistance through the handle to massage my arms. With his spine punctured, John finally ceased moving, and eyes widely dilated with a drug-induced stupor dulled.

With the quick confrontation over, the rage fled my head and left only misery. I stared at the body of a man I'd only hours ago considered befriending, and a profound sense of loss overcame me. I swayed on my feet until I collapsed on the side of my bed. Blood leaked out of John's wound in a constant stream, puddling over my hardwood floor and spreading to my belongings.

I grabbed my head with both hands and shook profusely. *"Fuck."*

I'd been wrong to think death no longer fazed me. Death of *foes* didn't bother me at all. But as John's neck audibly emptied his body of all its blood onto my floor, I kept repeating everything he'd ever said to me in my head. It was possible he told me nothing but lies. Maybe he hadn't been born in Sera or traveled to the Cel Forest. Perhaps he'd had a lovely childhood. None of that mattered; I'd started to *trust* him. And here he was, dead by my blade after manipulating my only vulnerability: desperation for companionship.

I shed silent tears as blood pooled to all four corners of my cabin. It wasn't like I had anyone to hide it from. Once again, I was rendered utterly alone.

Twenty

I buried John in a shallow grave within view of the campfire where we'd eaten our shared meal. I found two hidden daggers in his boots and carved initials on the underside of multiple pieces of his armor. None of the initials were the same; his thievery had known few limits.

I dumped John's rempka and needles in with him, but I kept the knapsack. After some cleaning, it would serve me well. I found nothing to indicate John's true identity or whether anything he'd told me was true. As I shoveled dirt over his corpse until it disappeared, my eyes burned with unshed tears of panic because I second-guessed myself.

Conversations and happenings repeated in my head. Everything about the night before happened so quickly it was a blur, but a nagging question refused to leave me be.

Which was the true betrayer: John or rempka?

I didn't understand how rempka affected a man; I'd never knowingly seen someone abuse it before John. Anger from feeling betrayed and threatened was the final straw leading me to kill him, but what if he hadn't meant to betray me at all? What if the drug affected his decisions? John's daggers were still in his boots after death. When sober he was well-aware of my willingness to kill to survive; he'd have to be ignorant to think he could barge in to steal from me without a weapon in hand and win.

These reflections after killing John haunted me similarly to how I'd felt after taking the first man's life in Sera. There was no going back to re-evaluate situations to handle them correctly, if there were correct reactions at all. I could only move forward and learn from it. Beating myself up over decisions made during chaos meant I still possessed a shred of humanity, at least.

Even after scrubbing the cabin floors multiple times the blood stains in the hardwood refused to leave, like my own home would never let me forget tragic memories. It didn't matter whether I handled the situation with John well or not; every time I walked across the floor stained with his blood, I questioned it. The worst forms of torture are self-inflicted and psychological.

Mercifully, mercenaries took that time to show up again, which took my mind off of over-thinking my morality and put it back on battle. Once one group found my new location in the forest others followed, attracted there from pursuing the tracks of their predecessors and signs of recent conflict. I buried the corpses after each fight as usual, but I couldn't always find or remove other evidence such as bloodstains on tree bark or dropped supplies.

My seventeenth birthday passed in late-Red Moon without me realizing it until I changed the date in my journal the day after. I noted this birthday in particular for one important reason: it meant that soon I might face mercenaries who had once been my peers at the Seran University. Many mages began fieldwork at eighteen, and I'd been a good year younger than most my peers due to a late start. They allowed mages still enrolled in classes to take up work with university approved mercenary parties or the official Seran Army as a form of internship. Kids I'd once shared classes with could end up hunting me. This excited *and* terrified me. I would jump at the chance to kill Kenady and his pretentious sidekicks, but the prospect of facing Kai in battle was too much to bear. Even if I managed to kill her, doing so would likely cause me to become deranged from despair and guilt.

Perhaps the myths about necromancers *were* right. They probably all went insane from lives of turmoil and loneliness. After all, Valerius died with a letter clutched protectively in his hand. He likely loved just as deeply as anyone else.

Similarly, I found solace in Kai's letter and the ring that hung from my neck. As more time passed, however, their nostalgic value changed. I still clung to them like lifelines connecting me to a normalcy I desperately wanted and could no longer have, but the memories I had involving both objects no longer felt like my own. My life had become so dramatically different in the course of a few years that it felt split into a *before* and *after*. The boy who once hoped for a good future wasn't just gone; I convinced myself he never existed. I read Kai's letter like I was a third party to it all, because surely I'd never had a friend. How had I ever trusted someone enough to make one? I held the ring from my parents and realized that if they were still alive, they wouldn't recognize me. I no longer resembled the son they'd loved and encouraged.

The seasons changed three times, and I barely noticed. I fell into a pattern.

Fish. Listen for attack. Raise corpses and defend cabin. Loot new corpses. Bury corpses. Rebuild defenses. Rinse and repeat.

The dates didn't matter when I had nothing but time, so the ones I ended up remembering most were particularly special for better or worse.

The 17th of High Star, 413 was the worst of them all.

Scorching sunlight rampaged through the forest canopy and became trapped in a fog of strangling humidity. After waking from a restless night of sweat-soaked tossing and turning, I grabbed my fishing rod and set out for the water. I wore my armor as usual, but mercenaries never found me at the stream since it arced south of the cabin and they came from the northwest. As I neared the cool water, I allowed this sense of security and the awful heat to guide my decisions. I set the fishing rod up against a dead pine and hung my satchel from a knob of wood. I started tugging off my armor, but I hesitated to pile it below my other things since recent rainfall turned the dirt into sopping mud. Eyeing the bank of the stream, I spotted a rock large and flat enough to hold my clothes, so I headed there and stripped.

I wore nothing but the ring around my neck as I submerged myself in the water, its coolness an immediate relief from High Star's unrelenting heat. Usually I bathed with the water at my cabin by combining it and soap on a wash rag, but today I soaked and scrubbed freely in the stream. Sticky perspiration and grime floated away, leaving me feeling both cleaner and lighter. I felt more relaxed than I'd been in years.

Perhaps I should've taken that as a sign. It was impossible for me to enjoy anything without a double dosage of tragedy and inconvenience tagging along.

The first sign of trouble came in the form of snapping twigs and the dull murmur of conversation. I reacted quickly, eyes darting through the forest as I hurried nude out of the water and to the rock with my clothes and scythe. I tugged on my clothes and then my cuirass to protect my vital organs first and foremost. Mere moments later, mercenaries trickled out of the deeper forest, immediately spotting my hanging satchel farther up the bank and swarming it.

No, no, no...

My most important belongings were in there, including both death warrants and Kai's letter. I could only watch helplessly as they tugged the satchel off its knob and into their group. I estimated at least twenty mercenaries were here. Normally that wouldn't faze me, but I was an hour's walk away from my cabin and its strategically placed army of corpses.

I pulled on more armor pieces as silently as I could, for it took the group an embarrassingly long time to notice me dressing by the stream. When one of them spotted me, she pointed in my direction and blurted, “He's here! At the stream!”

I tightened the next strap of gear so quickly that I grimaced from the sudden pressure. A few mercenaries reacted to spotting me by preparing their weapons. I shoved my feet into my boots, leaving both gauntlets on the rock. I'd have to do without.

“Wait!”

A chill rolled down my spine at the voice that echoed out amid the crowd and stopped the other mercenaries from rushing to attack. That voice was prevalent in most memories I had and didn't want to keep. Every time I had self-doubts, I heard his taunts. His mockery. His hatred. Agreeing with the doubt and adding to its destructive power.

For three years I'd anticipated coming across this bastard again. I'd fantasized about how I would kill him and cause just a smidgen of the pain and inconvenience he'd introduced into my life. I looked *forward* to violently spilling his blood. The last thing I expected to feel when hearing his voice, then, was panic.

But that's what I felt.

"Cerin," Kenady called out of the crowd, framing it like a mockery. I couldn't even *see* him yet and I already recognized his cruel smirk. "Meet me in the library come nightfall on the eve of the new year if you have no other plans."

I froze with dread at the familiar wording, glaring at the mercenaries with a stare that could kill until they made way, directing my attention to the man who stood beside my hanging satchel and held Kai's letter. Kenady's cold gray eyes returned my stare with smugness and hatred. He was three years older but just as ugly, though he adorned himself in a costly set of armor his parents no doubt purchased. His face glistened with sweat from the ceaseless heat, but he otherwise seemed calm and collected.

Because *of course* he was. Kenady lived a wonderful life of luxury in Sera despite doing everything necessary to ruin what little I'd ever had. I shook with anger as I pulled on my gauntlets, taking advantage of the group's hesitation to finish dressing.

"I apologize for being so busy with all my classes, but I'd like to make it up to you," Kenady continued reading in a mocking, sing-song voice. "The stars are *most beautiful* while viewing them from the northeastern wall. I want to celebrate the new year with you and take you out for a night on the town." He hesitated and laughed as another mercenary made an exaggerated wolf whistle. "Most shops and restaurants are open all night for the holiday. We'll stay out as late as possible if you can keep awake for it. I hope to see you there. If you don't show,

I'll understand. But I'll miss you." Kenady smiled coldly at me and finished, "Signed *Kai.*"

"Kai who?" another mercenary asked.

"Kai Sera, of course," Kenady replied, though he still stared at me. As the others murmured with gossip behind him, he called out, "How was your nice night out with Kai, *necromancer?* Did she buy your poor ass everything you needed? Did you manage to *finally* get your dick wet?" He tilted his head dramatically and glanced back down at the note. *"Wait.* This letter's from the 79th of Dark Star, 410. That date rings a bell. Why? *Hmm..."* He grinned with pride. *"Oh,* that's right! That's the night me and a buddy of mine found out about your sick secret and you ran from the university like a *bitch.* I guess this fun little night never happened. Guess we don't need the note, then."

Kenady lifted the note, one hand on either side of its center crease.

"Leave it be." The hoarse words escaped my lips in frantic trembles of rage and panic.

Kenady hesitated before he laughed shortly. *"Wow,* how pathetic. You've still got a hard-on for royalty after all this time. Carrying her note with you when it's no longer relevant."

"Not only that," another mercenary sneered, "but that woman's a mess."

"Who, Kai Sera?" a younger woman asked.

"Yeah."

I felt a dull tug at my heart. *Kai's still alive.*

Kenady gave me a cruelly amused look and said, "Yeah, that's *true.* You're pining away for a broad who isn't even worth it. Kai forgot all about you, you know. She's got some Celd by her side at all times now, probably warming her bed."

"Silas Galan," the younger mercenary said dreamily. "Handsome guy. Celdic royalty, too."

"Royalty attracts royalty," Kenady mused, looking me over as I tugged on my weapon's belt. "It's *almost* cute how you thought you ever had a chance." He lifted the note again. "And that's *twice* as sad because Kai's still a pathetic fucking drunk."

As the tearing of the note reverberated harshly through the forest, I snapped.

"Leave the fucking note!" I screamed, pulling the scythe up from the rock with a *shing*.

Kenady glared at me as the others grabbed their weapons. Overlapping the two torn pieces of the note, he said nothing as he tore it again. Red tinged my vision as he handed the pieces to a fire mage nearby.

"Burn it," Kenady demanded, tugging a flail from his belt.

"Don't!" It was a warning, a plea, a desperate cry. Kenady ripped the note, but I could still put the pieces back together to read it. Just as long as I *had it*. I released death magic to raise any corpses this forest could offer me, my eyes stuck on the fire mage as he summoned fire in one hand and held the ripped note with the other. *"Leave it! It's all I have left!"*

Raw pain shredded my heart as Kai's note curled in the flames, an inescapable charred blackness crawling over her words of interest and hope. Her unique handwriting distorted and disappeared, removing the last connection I had to the only person I loved who still lived. As the fire worked through the parchment and degraded it into nothing but rolling gray smoke,

I felt such mourning that they might as well have told me Kai committed suicide.

The earth trembled almost as badly as I did, handing nearby corpses over to my care as I rushed to meet the mercenaries in battle with more gusto than they had. Kenady stood near the back of the group, using his life magic to give the others shields. It reminded me that I hadn't yet protected myself, so I generated both a shield and ward, zoning in on the younger woman in the front since she had no magical guards.

The mercenary held a small buckler with her left hand and a short sword in the right. Her eyes widened as I reached her, intimidated by the rage I exuded. I pulled my scythe to the side, and she prepared to parry the hit with her buckler. I swung my weapon wide, arcing it around the exterior of the buckler and jerking the handle back, rolling the curved blade over her guard like a hook. I violently tugged my scythe toward me, and its grasp over her buckler encouraged it to come along.

Crack!

The woman squealed in pain as two of her fingers holding the guard broke from the sudden blow. She swung her sword at my shield frantically in defense, but I paid it no mind since the magic held strong. I regained control of my scythe and launched it at the woman's neck from the side. The curved blade passed over her left shoulder and sliced through the flesh at the back of her neck in one smooth movement. Fear overwhelmed her eyes as she shook in place, too shocked to move as blood and cut locks of her hair fell to the forest floor behind her. Keeping the scythe in the flesh wound, I kicked a boot into her stomach, keeping her standing against the pressure as I ripped the blade toward me until it punctured the spine. She went still with death. I stepped aside to avoid her body as it fell.

"Fucking hell," another mercenary breathed, watching his comrade bleed out over the pine needles. His shock over the brutal kill turned to fear as the still-bleeding corpse rose to meet my demands.

"Focus on Cerin!" Kenady screamed, which made me realize that other mercenaries battled corpses. There weren't nearly as many here as there were back at my cabin, but there were enough to keep me from being surrounded.

I leeched from one man while parrying the weapon swings of another, seeking a leeching high. By the time I killed Kenady, I wanted to be strong enough to turn him into mush.

One life leeched. Two. Three. I raised their corpses as soon as they fell, adding to my numbers and to the panic of my foes. As the fourth mercenary fatigued before me, the ground under my boots suddenly gave way.

I fell backwards, landing in a heap of adrenaline within a crater of magically lowered earth. The mercenary I'd been fighting followed to finish me off, but the corpse of a comrade hobbled up behind him. The minion's mace met the mercenary's skull with a sickly crunch, and an arc of shattered bone and bloodied hairy scalp flesh spewed forth over me. I sent black magic into the corpse, and he rose just as quickly as he'd fallen. I protected my new soldier with a shield as soon as I stood.

Then, I tumbled back again as a new crater indented beneath my feet. I cursed with frustration and scanned the area for the culprit. Kenady laughed at my misfortune as he generated a new shield for a mercenary who lost the last one to my minions.

"Lose your *step?"* he taunted, protecting another comrade before focusing on me as I stood to meet him.

It took everything I had not to respond with equal mockery, for Kenady's strategies in battle left a lot to be desired. He wasted precious energy toying with me with his earth magic when he should have conserved it. Mocking him for that would only make him realize it, so I said nothing. Kenady had no way of regenerating like I did. I could eventually win this just by wearing him down.

Kenady shoved his left hand toward the ground at my boots, and I braced myself to avoid falling back again. This time, however, a sturdy pillar of stone jolted up beneath my feet, knocking me up in the air until gravity coaxed me with its flirtations. My lungs deflated from the sudden landing, expelling air from my nostrils in a violent burst.

"It's quite sad that you get this sentimental over a stupid *note,"* Kenady mused, his voice coming closer as I tried to regain my bearings. My eyesight shook with a mixture of rage and aftershock from my landing, but I saw my scythe some feet away from where it fell out of my grip. Kenady kicked it farther from my reach. "Of course, if nothing but corpses always surrounded me, I guess just the *thought* of a warm body could become a fetish."

I scrambled to stand again, reaching out to leech from Kenady's chest with both hands. The black funnels connected to his magical ward, chipping away at its strength. I stepped to the side, trying to retrieve my scythe. Kenady sidestepped to block me. He summoned no magic, but he held a flail in his right hand. The weapon had a thick chain connecting the handle to its cylindrical head, which boasted multiple nail-like protrusions.

Facing a weapon with the ability to both puncture *and* bash was intimidating all on its own.

"How *is* necrophilia working out for you, Cerin?" Kenady asked viciously, preparing to swing his flail as he eyed my face, imagining the two meeting in an explosion of blood. "Do you even get to come before it goes limp from the cold?"

The rage that bubbled over in my chest from his taunts almost killed me, for I barely noticed I had no magical protections. After they broke from the battery of Kenady's stone wall, his insults distracted me so badly I hadn't regenerated them. I had no time to now, and I didn't have my scythe to parry with. As the head of Kenady's flail flew at the side of my skull, I vertically lifted my arm to protect it as a last resort.

The flail's head flew past the limb before the chain wrapped around my forearm just beside the elbow in a death grip. A flash of annoyance passed over Kenady's features before he smiled with a new idea. Keeping the flail wrapped around my arm, he tugged it back. The chain tightened, sinking the nails of the weapon's head through my armor until they impaled my arm, their sharp points scraping off the radius and ulna bones beneath.

"Fuck!" The pained curse escaped my lips against my will. I glanced past Kenady, scanning over mercenaries fighting minions. The young woman who'd been my first victim ganged up on a mercenary with an orc skeleton. I mentally willed her back to me. Sensing my direction, the corpse spun and hurried past ally and foe without a care, her focus on Kenady.

Kenady grinned with the satisfaction that he'd started to best me. His eyes rolled over my fatigued face before catching on something around my neck. A jolt of panic clenched my gut as I realized what he found.

Kenady reached up to my throat, tugging the necklace from my neck with the *snap* of a broken clasp. He dangled the ring my parents gave me between us from the broken chain. "Did Kai give you this, too?"

"No," I growled. "My parents."

"Ah," he huffed, jamming the jewelry through an open flap of a pouch on his belt when I tried to grab it with my free hand. "The dead ones, I assume." He noted the renewed pain in my gaze with a look of satisfaction.

The points of Kenady's weapon were stuck in my arm, and blood drizzled from multiple wounds and ran down to my fingertips like rain. For as long as Kenady held his weapon like this he couldn't use it, and I couldn't get away to use mine. But we were close enough to each other that I was within his life shield, rendering it useless. So I did what I'd wanted to do to Kenady ever since he'd first humiliated me at the university five years ago.

I rolled my right hand into a fist and threw everything I had into punching his face. The steel of multiple rings shone from my knuckles before clashing into the protrusion of his left upper cheekbone. The same curse I'd uttered only moments ago repeated in Kenady's voice as his head caved to the hit. Spittle sprayed off to the side after loosing from gritted teeth. My hand immediately felt inflamed from the brutal punch, but I ignored its protests, instead focusing on worsening the purple bruise sprouting on Kenady's face. I cranked my arm back and punched him a second time, a rush of ecstasy flowing through me when his flesh split from the prodding of a ring band, releasing hot blood to trickle down to his jaw.

Kenady's rage rose to meet my own, and he grabbed the handle of his flail with a second hand, jerking the weapon away from me. With the flail's protrusions still embedded in my arm, the weapon didn't budge from its nestling place. Instead, it convinced my forearm to flee the rest of my body, and my elbow snapped out of socket.

A rush of nausea flooded through me at the added trauma, and bright lights flashed around the edges of my vision. Panic overcame me as I tried to figure a way out of this.

Shing!

Kenady coughed and jerked forward, glaring down at his gut in surprise. The tip of a sword dripped with blood after traveling through his torso from the back. The corpse I'd willed over earlier tugged the weapon back, releasing a fresh stream of blood tinged with yellowed digestive acids.

Kenady let go of his flail, and I stumbled back from the sudden lack of resistance. I immediately tugged the weapon's nails out of my flesh with a grunt and unraveled the chain from my arm. I dropped the flail to the ground before hurrying to grab my scythe. Meanwhile, Kenady released a barrage of metal blades at my minion. It fell when one zipped through the skull at the nasal bone, partially decapitating it.

The forest suddenly seemed so quiet. As I retrieved my scythe off the ground, I scanned the area. Only two mercenaries other than Kenady were left, and they both battled corpses. I released more death magic to raise bodies new and old to overwhelm them, and then I refocused on Kenady.

The bastard was *running.* Kenady jogged northwest with an injured, wobbling gait, life magic spreading over his stab wound from one hand as he used the other to push off trees and rocks for support. My left elbow was still out of socket, but I endured the throbbing pain as I pursued Kenady with a furious pace, hopping over fallen logs and dodging tree branches. He glanced back as he heard the rustling foliage, and immense satisfaction filled me when I recognized fear in his eyes.

"All that *talk,* and now it's *you* running like a bitch," I called hoarsely, shaking with the anticipation of killing him.

Kenady glanced back again with alarm as he realized my pace was much quicker than his. He looked around frantically for some saving grace. As I neared him, I assumed he hadn't found one.

I was wrong.

Kenady thrust one hand toward me as I prepared to swing my scythe. The sharp whirling noise of metal met my ears just before a scalding pain punched me in the side. I flew backward, slamming into a tree trunk. My skull snapped back abruptly with whiplash, hitting bark with a *thunk.*

Everything went black.

*

A chorus of chirps from tens of thousands of insects echoed through the dark forest. I blinked heavily, fighting a combination of fatigue and deep aching pain. When a dozen shadowy humanoid forms creepily appeared in my clearing vision, I snapped to attention and tried to figure out my surroundings.

I remembered chasing after Kenady as he ran from me like a coward. It'd been daylight then. Night had fallen, and the pale moonlight illuminated the surrounding greenery with a silvery glow. I breathed shallowly with anxiety as I tried to figure out why twelve people watched me sleep in the darkness. Then I realized that I stood against a tree, and even more confusion settled in.

Piecing events together, I tried willing the bodies before me to back away. The shadows stepped back in unison, and I breathed a sigh of relief. These were the corpses that had made it through the battle. With no foes remaining, they simply returned to me for further instructions. I left them there for the moment; I desired company while out in complete darkness in a section of the woods I didn't know well.

I tried to take a step away from the tree, but a piercing pain shattered through my left side. I gasped for breath with sudden agony. When I gathered my bearings, I slowly felt around the area with a hand.

Dear gods. No wonder I'd passed out while standing; Kenady shot a metal shard through my side until it impaled me to the trunk.

Stay calm. Assess. Deal. Overcome. I forced my breaths to regulate. I reached for my satchel to grab a match so I could see the wound, but it wasn't there. I remembered I'd left it hanging on a tree near the stream.

While enduring a lot of pain and fear, I somehow managed to figure out my wound using nothing but softly prodding fingers and my knowledge of anatomy. The metal shard lodged in a groove of my lowest rib. The bone took the brunt of the damage, leaving all my internal organs safe. It was still a severe wound, but it didn't have to be fatal.

I shimmied as slowly as I could off the metal shard, biting my lip until it bled to keep from screaming with the intensity of the resulting pain. When the blade released me, I fell abruptly in a lump on the forest floor, shaking profusely while listening to the trickle of my own blood.

I undressed as best as I could with only one good arm, and then I healed. I started with the rib first, using life magic to rebuild the compact bone until it felt smooth to the touch. I worked my way out of the wound, mending muscle and flesh. Because it had been injured for sometime, I would be swollen and sore for a while yet, but at least I would live.

I healed the puncture wounds in my arm from Kenady's flail next, but I waited to pop my elbow back in socket. I'd gone through enough pain healing thus far and couldn't stomach more, and I also wasn't certain what angle was best for mending it. Most of the alchemical anatomy book's knowledge was now my own from memorization and use, but I couldn't memorize sketches as well as words.

By the time I headed back to the location of the initial battle, the forest glowed pink and yellow-orange from the rising sun. I used it as a guide, keeping the light on my left since I needed to head south. The battlefield was an interesting juxtaposition of a colorful early morning woodland and a bloody murder scene. Mutilated bodies cooled in puddles of blood so thick it appeared gelatinous over soft beds of pine needles and rich green mosses. Birds tweeted happily, their shadows fluttering over dropped weapons crusted with fluids. Bright yellow flowers sprouted out of moist soil near the descending stream bank, shattered bone sprinkled around their roots like an unhelpful fertilizer.

I passed the scene and headed straight for my hanging satchel, grabbing the anatomy book and rereading the section on dislocations. Since the book focused on alchemy, it wasn't the most thorough, but it would have to do. I laid on the ground to try to relax, and when I realigned the bone, I muffled my pained protests behind closed lips.

I looted the mercenaries, using one man's extra shirt as a makeshift sling for my recovering arm by strategically tearing it and hanging it over my neck. I found all the usual goods: jewelry, toiletries, some pieces of gold, dried food, a few labeled potions, and supplies like blade files and leather oil. Most interestingly, I found an updated warrant:

WANTED: Cerin Heliot.

Charges: Necromancy, 19 counts of murder of Seran armed forces, evading the law, practice of magic without a proper license

Notes: Cerin has access to necromancy and life magic. Survivors claim he wields a shortened scythe in melee (both one and two-handed). BEWARE: Cerin's listed counts of murder only include official forces. Including officially commissioned mercenaries, we believe Cerin is responsible for the deaths of nearly five hundred men. Cerin openly invites conflict. Earlier reports of him possibly returning to Thornwell are outdated; Cerin has been sighted camping in every known section of the Seran Forest, though most notably in the northwest and central locations. No bodies have ever been recovered; we believe Cerin collects them for his horde.

Official Acknowledgments: In response to the collective rising concern of this necromancer, Sirius Sera has moved Cerin from a level 2 threat to a level 1. Queen Edrys has been informed, and Sera has requested approval to consider a military response. We have told civilians that the central Seran Forest is restricted, but under NO circumstance is the nature of the threat to spread. Nevertheless, we have doubled the reward. If any mercenaries want a place in the Seran Army, fulfillment of this contract guarantees acceptance, and Sirius will also seriously consider further military awards and promotions.

REWARD: 10,000 gold offered for death. Body required. 500 gold offered for substantiated tips.

"No bodies have ever been recovered," I mocked in an exaggerated *official*-sounding voice, folding up the warrant and adding it to the rest in my collection. "We *believe* Cerin collects them for his *horde.*" I turned to face the dozens of corpses splayed out in the forest and threw death magic at the ground, waiting as the tendrils slithered off and recruited new minions. *"Obviously.* Fucking *idiots."*

I waited patiently as corpses new and old gathered before me. I glanced at the nearest mercenary and asked, "What do they think I *am?"*

He didn't respond, only glaring back at me with a blank expression on his severed head. I pretended that meant he was just as unimpressed and spun to lead my small army north.

I had seriously injured Kenady last I saw him, and now that I hadn't found his body, I worried he'd made it out alive. The corpses that gathered around me while I was pinned to the tree should have killed him if they sensed him.

Of course, it was possible they *didn't*. Most corpses were fighting the other mercenaries when I fought Kenady. He'd defeated the only one I called over to me to help. By the time the others were dead and the remaining minions came to find me, Kenady might have been long gone.

Panic rose in my throat, but I swallowed hard to keep it at bay. I couldn't have had the chance to kill the bastard just to squander it, especially now that he'd destroyed the last two things most important to me. I'd fought well. Other than forgetting to refresh my defenses, I made good strategic choices. Kenady had simply been my match.

And I hated that fact more than I'd hated anything in a long while.

I refused to think of anything other than catching up to Kenady and finishing him off. Allowing the new information about Kai and Sirius's escalating plans for my demise to distract me was not an option.

The dozen corpses I'd dispelled by the tree and metal shard were still in a pile of gear and flesh, so I raised them and continued north, scanning the foliage for clues. The air still smelled faintly of Kenady's digestive acids. Only a few meters north of where he impaled me, I found a few dried droplets of blood sprinkled over a bed of moss. I followed the zigzagged blood trail north until the heavy stench of urine replaced the acidity in the air. Glancing around, I noticed blood on a tree trunk only a few feet up from the ground. It appeared Kenady stopped to lean against it and heal. His wound had punctured all the way through his torso, after all; it likely bled out onto the tree from the back as he mended the front. Moisture darkened the bark at the base of the same trunk where he'd relieved himself, and in a pile nearby were the unmistakable stems of gotton berries.

It appeared Kenady fully healed himself before urinating, refueling with food, and moving on to Sera. Just to confirm this theory, I searched the forest just north of Kenady's resting point for an hour, looking for more blood or signs of trouble. When I found none, I laughed humorlessly with overwhelming disappointment.

The one man I wanted dead most in the world managed to re-enter my life, destroy the last two things important to me in a fury of hatred, and escape unscathed. My whole body trembled with anger and mourning, but I didn't have my nemesis here to take it out on. I remembered the fear in Kenady's eyes when he realized I pursued him and wondered if I'd scared him off forever. Gods, I *hoped* not. I couldn't just waltz in to Sera any time I wanted to; killing Kenady required him to pursue *me*.

That was likely, I decided. After all, he'd left me alive. Considering the whole situation, I realized Kenady mistakenly believed he'd killed me. The last thing he saw was me getting impaled to a tree trunk and going limp. Perhaps he thought that by bringing something of mine back to Sirius, he'd have proof of my death without my body. But showing my ring to Sirius wouldn't satiate him no matter how prestigious of a position Kenady's family had in Sera. Even if Kenady wasn't reprimanded for not following protocol, he would likely try to vindicate himself by agreeing to hunt me down and finish the job. Maybe he would come back just to restore his everlasting pride after learning I made it out alive.

I would be ready for him, and I would show him *no* mercy.

Twenty-one

13th of Red Moon, 413

In the season following my spat with Kenady, I went through my final metamorphosis leading into adulthood. All the events of the worst years of my life formed my personal perspective. Rather than be bothered by the brutality I displayed to my pursuers, I accepted it as a fact of life. Rising to become as cruel as the rest of the world seemed to be the only thing I'd truly succeeded at. I no longer trusted anyone because of John's betrayal and Kenady's everlasting sadism. When a stray civilian wandered through the forest, I did not spark conversation or even offer to trade. I didn't kill them unless they hunted me, but I wanted nothing to do with them. No longer did I wish for companionship; as lonely as I was, I could only trust myself.

With Kai's note destroyed and my childhood ring stolen, I had nothing from my old life with which to comfort me. I looked at my past not with hope, but with bitterness; my good memories were surely egregious lies. Kenady's cruel words about how Kai forgot about me and moved on with another royal didn't even anger me because I expected it. At one time my world revolved around my attraction to Kai like I was some type of lovestruck idiot. I felt dumb for it now. People had proved to only show compassion to others if it could selfishly serve them, and as a poor outcast child I could offer Kai nothing. Nothing developed between us because it couldn't. She'd only befriended me to quell her own profound loneliness.

I couldn't blame her. Loneliness was a mind-breaking and painful thing to endure. But when Kai inevitably hunted me down like all the rest, I would show her no mercy. I expected the worst out of people now; I predicted that Kai would try to use the friendship we'd shared to taunt me or weaken my morale in battle. Even if I committed suicide from the guilt after killing her, at least I would die knowing I hadn't shown weakness in the face of another cruel manipulation.

Despite Sirius escalating my threat level, little changed. Civilians passed through from time to time, either ignoring the forest restrictions or having not heard of them yet. Mercenary parties grew larger and more varied, like the high-reward contract on my life now attracted seasoned warriors from outside Chairel. Dwarves from Hammerton with accents heavier than most accepted the hit with glee, eager to hunt a necromancer. Dark-complected humans from Nahara tested their might against me with all kinds of foreign weapons, from curved swords to varieties of whips, chains, and arbalests. I hated killing the Naharans the most. The dwarves harbored a special hatred for necromancers, so they mocked and cursed me in battle. By the time I killed them, I enjoyed it. Contrarily, it seemed most Naharan warriors simply desperately needed gold, for they wore little to no armor and owned nothing of value when I looted their corpses.

My army of the dead grew ever larger. Hundreds of corpses littered the forest surrounding the cabin, all in strategically placed mass graves. No matter which direction attacks came from, I had a defense force. It would take swarming numbers or a new strategy to surprise me.

Just a fortnight into Red Moon, I spent the morning fending off a particularly proficient mercenary party before going through the motions of the aftermath: looting corpses, healing wounds, mending my armor. Despite the excess energy of battle exertions lingering in the air, the forest seemed peaceful. The stench of blood and displaced organs existed like a lie alongside tweeting birds and rustling trees. A cool breeze whistled through the forest, picking up my long black hair and carrying it across my face until I had to finger-comb it back to see. Though the corpses in the mass grave before me were only partially covered by soil, I struck my shovel in the ground so I could lean on it and scan my surroundings.

An eerie tingle pricked the back of my neck as my gaze swept through the trees. I'd lived in this cabin for a year, so I could tell when something was out of place. Mercenaries sometimes attempted to take the stealthy approach and catch me off guard, but I knew this forest by heart. Few details got by me unnoticed.

That made this intuition that someone watched me all the scarier. Nothing was out of place. No logs had been strategically placed to allow for easy cover for archers, as had happened before. No noises alerted me to whispered orders. I took special notice of the tweeting birds. Once, I'd anticipated a stealthy attack simply because the birds quieted their singing. Wildlife was a terrific indicator of trouble.

Today, however, intuition was all the proof I had that something was wrong.

I jammed the shovel further in the soil with a boot so it could stand alone. Then I stalked off through the trees, following my gut. I passed by puddles of blood still soaking into the detritus until I crossed over the border of twigs I used as an extra alarm. At one point when passing a notably wide pine, my chest ached like my body anticipated sudden trouble, so I spun around.

Nothing was there.

I stood still for a moment, listening to the sounds of the forest and searching my surroundings. Buzzing flies directed my attention west. With my hands on my scythe, I followed the noise until I stumbled upon something odd.

A pile of scat sat just beside a tree trunk, serving as a feast for flies. The excrement couldn't have been more than a few hours old, for it still glistened with moisture and gave off a potent smell. I looked for footprints or signs of someone nearby but came up empty.

As amusing as I found the thought, it was unlikely that one of the mercenaries I'd bested today had taken the time to relieve themselves behind a tree before returning to battle. A random traveler may have passed by and left this, but I doubted it. Who would stop to defecate while a battle between mercenaries and the undead raged within viewing distance?

No—someone followed me. Spied on me. Whether to wait for the opportune moment to attack or gather information, I couldn't know. I still felt eyes on me as I walked back to the cabin to finish burying the dead, but with no evidence of the culprit, I could do nothing but wait.

I finished burying the corpses with barely an effort. It amazed me just how easy battling and physical labor became after building significant muscle from doing both all the time. By the time evening fell, all evidence of the morning's fight disappeared.

The last remnants of a leeching high pumped alongside the blood in my veins when I crawled into bed to sleep, keeping me energized. While I could stay awake due to the excess energy, I didn't want to get into the bad habit of sleeping in late each morning. Such decisions could mean death.

My head sunk into the pathetically flat pillow to the thin mattress beneath. Behind closed eyes, I imagined Thornwell and its view of the ocean. Smelling the salt of its water. The tense muscles in my upper back relaxed just a bit. It didn't matter how separated I felt from early memories of Thornwell, my parents, and Kai; against my better judgment, they were always what I used to lull my brain to sleep.

The memories progressed in order to Kai. Her smile, her laugh, the way her golden eyes would linger on my upper neck and long fingers when she thought I wouldn't notice. The intense eye contact she'd given me whenever I spoke, like she respected me enough to listen intently to everything I said.

A dull ache spread through my heart, an irritating reminder that despite everything, I still loved her. I didn't want to, but I couldn't help it.

I shoved thoughts of Kai from my mind and settled on something related but simpler: the view of the ocean from Sera's northeastern wall the night I'd fallen in love with her. The soft yellow sunlight evolved to an orange-pink that announced the setting sun as Kai and I talked for hours, replacing the day's warmth with the ardor of friendship. My contented mind finally slipped into the state of welcome grogginess just before slumber.

Crrr...

My eyes snapped open. Blood rushed through my veins with adrenaline, encouraged by a racing heart. Still lying down, I lifted my head slightly to stare at the door where a soft scraping noise sounded out from its broken lock.

Quietly, I summoned a leeching funnel in both hands, deciding not to risk going for my scythe.

When the perpetrator realized the door was unlocked, they tried the handle. It squeaked softly as it spun and then pressure applied to the door. The chair holding it upright jerked, but it refused them access.

The door settled back in its frame without tension, and all went quiet. I listened intently for sounds of movement outside but heard nothing. Whoever it was must have been alone, and they worked so silently I wondered if some form of magic I couldn't understand aided them.

Swwff!

The chair leaning against the door flew back legs first, wood scraping against wood until the long angle forced the furniture's back to unlock from beneath the handle and fall on the floor, useless. I jumped to my feet with extreme bewilderment as the chair clattered noisily over wood. I'd heard no gusts of wind, or else I might have believed the perpetrator sent air magic under the door.

The door swung open, and I immediately held a hand out to leech. The black funnel connected to a living being, for it crackled and siphoned life force.

But there was *nothing* there. My pursuer was invisible.

A bright purple ball of magic summoned in thin air in the doorway, and I reacted by building a ward to protect me from magic. The perpetrator acted first, and the purple energy zipped into my chest.

Skin-crawling terror overcame me as the spell took over my mind and manipulated my emotions. My chest seized with horror; nothing mattered but *getting out of here.* I dispelled all magic and jumped over the fallen chair, rushing out the open door.

I collided with an invisible body. A female grunt pierced the air before she collapsed on the ground, and I fell on top of her. I saw nothing but leaves and pine needles beneath me, but a woman squirmed between my arms. Metal zipped out of a protective sheath. As I scrambled to stand, an invisible short blade stabbed my left bicep. A frustrated huff sounded out below me; the assassin meant to hit my heart.

Terror still affected my decisions, so I bolted, seeking the solace of the shadowed woods. The scattering of debris echoed behind me as the assassin leapt off the ground and gave chase.

The foreign magic released hold of my mind just as I rushed through a moonlit clearing. With the unexplained fear gone, I thought quickly and summoned a ward to avoid further magic and a shield to fend off the assassin's blades. Newly protected from both types of attacks, I scanned the area and grabbed the first weapon I saw: a fallen tree branch.

Pine needles sprayed toward me as the invisible assassin skidded to a stop in the clearing. I swung the tree branch at the location, surprised when I missed her entirely. Two footfalls landed a second later like she dodged the hit.

Shing-shing-shing-shing!

A flurry of dual blade hits to my left weakened my shield. I spun, swinging the branch through the air. Footsteps scrambled back, dodging the swing easily. I threw the branch to the ground; it was too slow.

I summoned two leeching funnels and spread my arms out, spinning in a slow circle until one of them connected. Crackling echoed into the night for a few seconds until the assassin summoned a transparent but glowing egg-shaped magical shield. The crackling stopped, but the black energy connected with her guard until the magic vibrated, almost as if it absorbed the energy of the spell.

I stopped directing the magic, unwilling to feed her reserves. I didn't know what the hell kinds of spells these were, but logically, a shield to absorb magic likely couldn't combat physical force. Death energy still swirled above both my palms, but only to make my foe think I would use magic so she'd be vulnerable to a physical hit. The assassin unleashed another flurry of attacks on my shield, and I took that moment to strike.

I kicked her gut so hard my boot likely left an impression, and she flew back until her invisible body cracked through the lowest branches of a fir tree. The glimmering of metal pulled my attention to the ground where a black dagger clattered over debris after loosing from her grasp. I reached down on the way to her to grab it.

The broken branches of the fir trembled as the invisible assassin used them to help her stand. I slashed at her with her own weapon, using the glowing magic of her shield as a guide for her location. She returned the gesture with her remaining dagger; given her familiarity with the weapon, she was better at it.

Shing! Shing!

The protective life magic surrounding me broke. I lifted my left arm defensively to guard my throat and heart. A sharp prick of pain jabbed the knob of my ulna bone in a stab meant for my jugular. I dropped the assassin's dagger from my right hand so I could grab her arm now that I knew where it was.

My hand felt slick leather armor. I could still see nothing, but I didn't need to. Still holding her forearm with my right hand, I grazed up her arm with my left, finding her elbow and then her bicep. She struggled in my grasp, but I overpowered her.

With her elbow bent between my hands, I snapped the limb backwards. The creaking protests of leather armor preceded a crack of bone. The assassin inhaled sharply with pain, and her second dagger dropped. When it hit the forest floor it became visible, no longer affected by her magic.

As disorienting as it was fighting an invisible assassin, I found one way to use it to my advantage. While staring through her, I noticed the sharp lower branches of a dying fir tree. One in particular looked sturdy enough to hold her weight.

The assassin released a bright emerald spell at me, but it hit my ward and fizzled out. With one hand on her throat in a stranglehold and the other on her waist, I forced her back into the tree.

A yelp echoed out. Some branches broke with weakness as she hit them, but the sturdiest one stabbed her in the back. Blood drizzled over the debris below, the only visible clue as to my success. Still holding her with both hands, I shoved forward with all my might, further impaling her. Though she stayed invisible, the sharpened point of the branch inside her darkened with blood.

I heard a moist cough. I finally released her body just to back up and kick her. Only when her blood dripped off the tip of the branch did I relent the force since that meant it fully impaled her. She couldn't escape.

“Are you Alderi?” I demanded.

“Wait a few minutes and find out,” she retorted, her voice wheezy and trembling with trauma.

"Dispel your illusion and I'll give you a quick and painless death."

A sarcastic laugh. "Too late for that, isn't it?"

"I could leave you to bleed out on this tree to serve as a warning to others. Considering what I smell, that would be quite the humiliation for you."

"Fuck you," she wheezed. The argument worked, however; she dispelled her invisibility.

Hanging on the tree before me was an Alderi woman. The Alderi were sometimes casually referred to as *dark elves,* but I'd never expected them to be *this* dark. She was quite short, only standing midway between five feet and six, and she wore black leather armor with a sheen to it which suggested someone made it from the hide of an unfamiliar underground creature. Somehow, her skin seemed almost as dark, a mixture of deep purple and charcoal gray. Her eyes were completely black with no discernible separation of iris and sclera. If it weren't for the moonlight, the shadows would claim her as their own.

"You were hired," I surmised.

"No shit," she spat back. Blood dribbled down her chin from internal trauma, and a wheeze joined her next inhale.

"By who? Sirius?"

"I don't know *who,"* the assassin retorted. "We aren't told *who.* I'm in this for the gold, not the *politics."*

"How'd you find me?"

"Are you serious?" She laughed sarcastically before wincing when it hurt. "This forest is crawling with mercenaries. Nearly *all* of them are after you. *Finding* you was the easy part. Even the *orcs* are searching for you."

"Why are *orcs* after me?"

"I don't fucking know," she rambled. "You got their attention, somehow. Maybe you pissed them off by collecting bodies since you're taking away their main source of food."

I raised an eyebrow. I hadn't known the orcs were cannibals. "So that's how you knew I was the right target," I deduced. "You knew about my necromancy and witnessed my fight today."

"No," the Alderi shook her head. "I didn't know about your necromancy *until* I witnessed the fight today. That's why I waited to try to kill you where your corpses couldn't help you. All I knew was that you're half-Icilic. None of us could find you in Sera for the past few years. We put two and two together once we found one of your old warrants. Followed the paper trail, and here you are, one of Chairel's most-wanted criminals. I don't get paid enough for this shit." She spit to the side when blood overflowed her tongue. "That's all I know. You promised me a painless death. Follow through before the numbness beats you to it."

"Thank you for your information," I said. Using two leeching spells to double their effect, I siphoned the life force from her chest. It took only seconds for her dying body to give up its fight.

No wonder I'd had no assassins after me yet. Sirius hadn't hired them. The racist bastards in Glacia had, and their intel was dated given they listed my location as Sera. The assassin hadn't known who paid for the hit, but she hadn't needed to; she correctly stated I was a half-breed. No one had ever discovered the secret of my impure Icilic bloodline outside of Thornwell. I'd never told Kai, and Sirius's warrants only listed me as human.

I raised the assassin from the dead and marched back to the cabin while healing my defensive wounds. I didn't bother burying her with the others tonight; I just wanted to sleep.

Mercenaries were after me. Before long, the Seran Army might be as well. Little had I known that the Icilic supremacists had been after me for years. Now that the first assassin found me, I knew others would be close behind.

Who's next? I wondered as I drifted off to sleep. The world was all too happy to prepare its answer.

Twenty-two

31st of New Moon, 414

"Smell blood! Bodies here."

The wood ceiling of my cabin appeared in my vision as the guttural voice woke me from a late slumber. Expecting a fight, I dragged myself out of bed to pull on my armor. Behind the green drape hanging from the cabin's east-facing window, multiple shadowed forms loomed from the deeper forest.

"Smell blood," a female croaked, using the same simple dialect. "Smell acid, too. These bodies are old."

Snatching my cloak from the bedside table, I pulled it on and threw the hood up over my head.

"Makes no difference," a male replied. "Just a little bitter."

I grabbed my scythe from under the bed. As it dragged over the floor, the scraping of steel on wood reverberated off the cabin's walls.

"House!" Someone roared it like a directive. The ceramic tea mug wobbled over the counter as the vibrations of a sudden stampede rattled the cabin, and then it tipped off and shattered on the floor.

I summoned protections against melee and magic, and then I tugged the chair out from under the doorknob. The door bashed open, and I barely had time to register the green bulky body just outside before a giant ax blade swung up at me in an uppercut. The immense strength of the hit sent me flying through the tiny house, and my shield broke when I slammed into the fireplace and collapsed in a lump on the floor. The scythe clattered over hardwood in the corner.

As I stood wearily and regenerated my shield, I realized my rising power had caught the attention of an entirely new kind of foe.

Orcs. As skeletons, orcs were among my best minions. When alive they were far more intimidating, for broad bones were wrapped with broader muscles that filled them out to look twice the size. The orc who hit me was so gargantuan that he ducked dramatically to come through the cabin's seven-foot doorway. Greenish-gray flesh stretched over bulging muscles and pronounced veins. Other than worn leather leggings, boots, and a belt to hold loot and his ax, he wore nothing at all, seemingly unconcerned about being injured. Battle scars crisscrossed over his torso, some hiding beneath fields of black hair. He grinned with the anticipation of a good kill, showcasing a mouth full of missing and rotten teeth. Most frighteningly, his nose was shaved down to the bone, only a shadow where cartilage should have been.

I reached out toward his chest. Sizzles and pops echoed off the walls as his life force siphoned to me. He glared down at the funnel with solid black eyes and croaked, "Magic is *weak.*"

He swung his ax again, but this time I stepped back. The weapon still collided with my shield, but not as hard; it flickered as he pursued me into the back corner.

Fwoosh!

The unmistakable sound of ignition rattled through the cabin, followed by the crackling of fire overhead. The whoops and hollers of bloodthirsty orcs outside came next. A thick heat radiated through the windows and upper vents. Panic cluttered my chest, but there was no room to avoid the orc to leave, and he didn't seem to care that the place was in flames.

Corpa te risa a multipla.

Black magic fogged out over the hardwood. As the energy collected into thin tendrils and slithered out the door to the forest like an army of snakes, a green fist clashed into my shield, shattering it. Before I could regenerate it, the orc grabbed me by the throat and lifted me until my head hit the ceiling with a *thunk*. Heat filled my head from the sudden pressure. The orc cranked his ax back to cut me in half horizontally. Hanging by my throat and with a prepared shield spell in one hand while stealing his life force with the other, I had one choice to avoid mutilation.

As the ax cut toward my side, I reached out and shielded it. A tiny white guard bubbled over the weapon. When it clashed into my side, it only knocked the breath out of me, for the shield hit me rather than the blade. The orc glared at his weapon, appearing overwhelmingly confused. I took advantage of his hesitation and my higher position to kick him in the genitals.

"Aggh!" He threw me down onto the counter, and my head snapped back against the wood. Stars danced before my vision over a backdrop of rolling smoke that collected in the ceiling. Sounds of battle echoed in the doorway from outside, where corpses heeded my call and swarmed the other orcs. I sent a desperate mental plea for them to aid me as I rolled off the counter to avoid another punch. After hitting the floor with a thud I stood, only for a boot in my back to send me face-first into the door frame. More stars joined the first set, and dizziness settled in.

I refreshed my shield and stumbled out the door, passing three corpses that hobbled to the cabin from my request.

As they clashed with the orc in the doorway, I realized I left my scythe in the home. Spinning, I leeched from the orc with both hands as I directed a minion to fetch my weapon. The zombie hobbled into the smoking cabin. Moments later, it reappeared with my scythe in its hand, watching me with empty sockets as I took it.

"Thank you," I said, and the zombie waddled away.

Three dozen orcs surrounded the cabin, all in conflict with undead soldiers. The orcs were brutal battle veterans and had already defeated many of my minions easily, collapsing skeletons and bursting swollen decomposing flesh with hooked axes and maces with sharp flanges that appeared more like torture devices. The undead already outnumbered them, but I hurried back from the flaming cabin to another mass grave, calling more to my aid.

As an army of nearly one hundred corpses swarmed the orcs, I focused on leeching. I needed as much energy as possible if I wanted to keep the dead rising and protected with shields.

Surprisingly, only four orcs dropped dead from leeching before their life force surged to my head and threw my brain into the orgasmic vat of a high. My eyelids fluttered with the welcome feeling, and a pleasurable shiver worked out from my core to my extremities. The closest orc noticed my sudden trance-like state and turned from my minions to face me. I jerked my head to both sides to work out a few kinks before I ran to face him.

The orc pointed at me and announced, "You get power from magic? I get power from *blood.*" He rolled his free hand into a fist and pounded his chest. "Spill my blood."

If you insist. I held my scythe out to the side as I ran, trying to determine if I could hit his throat. At eight feet tall, he would be hard to decapitate. The orc noticed my glare on his throat. I allowed him to think I'd hit him there as I angled the scythe instead for his unarmored waist.

The orc lifted his weapon to deflect an attack for his throat. I ran past him, using my momentum instead to rip my scythe through his gut just below the lowest right rib, tip facing his spine. I felt the resistance of his inner viscera before the overbearing stench of half-digested food spiced the air. The scythe blade swept through his gut to the other side, ending its arc with globs of maroon marring its silver sheen.

I shook my weapon by its handle, flicking harvested gore to the ground. The orc turned to face me, and I stilled with confusion. I'd severed his colon and likely part of his small intestine. At the *very* least, he should have doubled over with pain.

Sheets of blood oozed out of the cut, draining down his hip and leg. The metallic stench of it wafted up to the orc's flared nostrils, where it sunk through to his brain. His gaze sharpened. Muscles bulged. Fingers clenched. Incisors bared.

A guttural roar shattered through the forest, spittle spraying from greenish lips. Ax in hand, he rampaged toward me with a bloodlust like my leeching high.

Berserker rage.

The orcs were known for them. Rumors stated that such rages boosted their strength and their resistance to bleeding out. The only way to end a berserker rage was for the orc to run out of energy or its foe to die.

And I didn't plan on dying today.

The life shield still bubbled around me, but I didn't trust it as my only defense. As the orc closed in, I dodged his trajectory before reaching out to leech from him as he flew by.

He skidded to a stop just feet away and spun, throwing his ax toward my shield. The move was so quick and unexpected that even with the quicker reflexes of my high, I couldn't totally dodge it. I flinched away, watching the ax scrape along the magical barrier before skidding backwards from the force. I leeched with my left hand and parried his next hit by raising my scythe.

Shing!

Steel skidded along steel as we locked ourselves in a deadly embrace. Just behind the orc, one skeleton and two fleshy zombies hobbled to our fight, eager to aid me. The orc gritted his teeth until his incisors broke open his lip, doubling down on his weapon. I dispelled the death magic so I could focus on doing the same with both hands on my scythe, buying time.

A mercenary corpse was first to defend me, hacking into the orc's torso wound and trying to deepen it. The orc roared and broke our embrace so suddenly I nearly fell into him. As he spun and grabbed the corpse's head with his free hand, I screamed hoarsely with effort and sliced my scythe through the air at his right arm. The curved blade hooked around his inner elbow. The wound sprayed blood even before I jerked my weapon back, splitting tendon and cutting through veins until the orc dropped his ax.

The orc paid little attention to his wounded arm, his mind already set on ridding himself of the zombie defender. He lifted the corpse up in the air by its cranium before slamming it into the forest floor headfirst. The skull exploded like a grape, unleashing a geyser of corroding brains. Bits of bone ricocheted off the surrounding trees like pebbles of marrow.

Weaponless, the orc spun to me and threw a punch. I managed to hold my ground as it shattered my shield. I situated my scythe on my belt and summoned magic in both palms. Using the excess life force running through my veins, I refreshed protections for me and the nearest minions. Then, since this orc had been such a nuisance, I raised the corpse he'd just defeated to piss him off.

Tendrils slithered over moist mosses to do my bidding, finding the bits of shattered skull and encapsulating them in a cool hug. Pieces of bone rolled over blood splattered plant-life to reunite. The mercenary corpse rose, leaving its unnecessary brain matter on the forest floor and shambling forth with a skull that now appeared made of as much black magic as it was bone.

An angered huff burst from the orc's nostrils as he saw his victory was short-lived. I smirked in response.

The orc flew at me with a flurry of punches. I continually backed away, leeching from him with both hands, satisfaction filling me as I watched his movements slow. Minions chased after him like scavenger animals, drawing blood from multiple new wounds. I directed the dead to target his legs, and they loyally complied. With one dramatic sweep of a scimitar, a Naharan corpse dealt the incapacitating blow across the back of the orc's knee, just between shredded leather armor. The brute fell face-first to the forest floor, still heaving enraged breaths.

I dispelled my magic and grabbed my scythe once more. I walked up to the orc's right side, avoiding his only good arm as he tried to snatch my boot with it. With a cry of adrenaline and effort, I brought the scythe down in a curved arc, swinging the blade between his vulnerable throat and the ground. Blood audibly drained with the cut, but he only gurgled on it. I put a boot to his upper back and jerked the blade upward, cutting through the trachea. Wheezing joined the bubbling blood until the orc finally went still.

Still jittery with a high, I scanned my surroundings. At this point, the cabin was utterly destroyed. Scorching flames reached toward the canopies like lost souls surrounded by the black smoke of hellish misery. Blackened logs glowed with neon embers, pieces flaking off like burnt snowfall. A cloud of smoke so dense it appeared tangible rolled out of the door and windows, much of it getting trapped under the canopies and billowing out like smog.

The cabin was beyond repair, but if I finished the orcs off I could at least save the remnants of my army. While the corpses I raised outnumbered the orcs three to one, the brutes proved stronger. Some orcs lie dead or dying, but many more defeated minions surrounded them. This didn't concern me; as long as I had foes, I had power. I released a new bout of necromantic tendrils at my boots and defeated corpses and recent orc casualties rose to fight together. As the living orcs noticed their kin rising as foes, some went into berserker rages. It seemed different orcs had different triggers for it.

Only one orc remained an hour later. His blood-red irises scanned over me and my approaching minions. As willing as he was to fight despite impossible odds, he seemed to consider retreat.

"You *think* you win," he barked, pointing at the walking corpses of his kin. "But this just pittance. You think forest yours?" He laughed. "We bring army. And *friends.*" He pointed east. “Friends from mountain, friends from cave. We squash you like *bug.”*

I huffed. “So why *didn't* you?”

The orc snorted and backed away another few steps. “We not prepared. When we prepared, you lose. You not respect orc strength? We make you.”

I raised an eyebrow. “If retreating from battle deserves respect, consider me your greatest admirer.”

An absolutely bewildered look distorted his features like he hadn't understood the logic of the insult. Clearly, intelligence was uncommon among orcs.

I watched the orc run off through the forest, noting his eastern direction before turning to the cabin. The home that had been mine for a year and a half was in shambles. The timber of its roof caved in, making the structure look more like a gigantic campfire. I collapsed lazily on the forest floor with a huff and dug into my satchel for dried fish. With one hundred corpses gathered behind me, we watched the cabin burn together while I ate a meal. Morning turned to afternoon, then afternoon turned to an evening cloudy with smoke. The cabin burned throughout all of it until it was little more than a smear of char.

“Well,” I announced, standing up and wiping my hands together to clear them of crumbs, “having a house was nice while it lasted, I guess.”

The corpses turned their hollowed gazes to me, waiting for orders. Many of them were barely held together by black magic; the brutality of the orcs tore them apart.

“You've seen better days,” I commented. The ruined corpses didn't look amused at my awful jest. “Guess we'll clean up here and relocate.”

We. Who am I kidding? I'll be the only one working. I chuckled dryly at my internal musings and dispelled the corpses. They returned to their eternal rest as I sifted through the ashes of everything I once owned.

Twenty-three

79th of Red Moon, 415

The whole world was against me, and my only response was to survive.

The assassins seemed limitless, like the underground placed little value on the lives of its people. I killed many assassins per season, and sometimes they came one right after the other within the span of a fortnight. Did this mean multiple people hired them? Perhaps many Icilic hired the Alderi to come after me because a lethal combination of overwhelming gold and racism were common in their people. Maybe Sirius or even Kenady turned to the Alderi since other options weren't working, just to find the assassins weren't working either.

Not that the Alderi were a weak threat—quite the opposite. Mercenaries were predictable, and because Sera officially commissioned them they only used legal options of warfare. Contrarily, the Alderi were unpredictable, utilized the mysterious lesser magics at ease, and each assassin had her own method of assassinating that differed from the last. Some attacked during the day, but most at night. Some could turn invisible—others couldn't. Some didn't use magic at all.

The assassin who came closest to killing me wielded a small black crossbow and shot me in the temporal bone of my skull. She meant to shoot my eye socket and would have succeeded if it weren't for me turning my head unknowingly. Still, the wound nearly killed me simply because it was *distracting.* With the bone cracked, I had to fight her with an ear-shattering headache while worrying my brain would swell. While I stumbled around drunkenly, I'd managed to surround her with corpses. Though the bone healed fine, the injury stayed swollen for a fortnight, and I had an unexplained bout of fever. In further battles, the undead assassin wielded her crossbow like a melee weapon. All archers did upon death; it seemed necromancy did not allow the dead enough intelligence to aim and shoot.

Because assassins constantly pursued me, my sleep suffered. No time was safe to rest, especially now that I had no home. The cabin fire destroyed all the belongings I hadn't kept on my person, so I lost even my tent and bed. I became accustomed to scattering noisy debris around myself in the hopes I would wake from a snapping twig, but the Alderi were extraordinarily stealthy. As an extra precaution, I left two corpses reanimated while I slept. Twice I jolted awake because the corpses sensed a pursuer and made enough noise. The Alderi made the best minions for such a job; their natural agility during life carried over in death.

The mercenary threat lessened at the same time the orc menace grew heavier. Now that orcs swarmed out of the woodwork due to their random declaration of war against me, the two groups likely clashed unwittingly throughout the forest while searching for the same target. I noted this fact for one reason in particular: if I ever needed more corpses to collect, I would head northwest. Since the mercenaries came from Sera, I'd likely find their bodies in that direction. The orcs didn't tend to leave survivors, after all, and some didn't even leave bodies. One orcish war party I bested had been dragging mercenary bodies east to their tribe to butcher for meat.

The orcs loathed me simply for being powerful and existing in a forest they considered theirs. During our battles I heard them mention their "war" with me that they'd evidently declared after I had the gall to survive their first attack. If they wanted to treat our spat like a war, so would I. I figured the orcs came from *somewhere* with a resemblance to society. Like in a true war, I could stop staying on the defensive and prepare an assault. I could attack *and* seize the location of an orcish tribe if I found it. With an undead army that always teetered around five hundred strong considering destroyed skeletons and new 'recruits,' I had the resources to succeed. I wanted a sturdy location to defend that was already built since I knew little about construction.

Just four years in to my pledge to rise as a powerful necromancer, I'd already made myself a force to be reckoned with. Once more I looked to my inspiration of Valerius the Undying, and I realized how in some respects I'd surpassed him. Though I stayed in the forest, it certainly wasn't as safe from attack as the Island of Valerius had been. The attacks came in waves for both of us, but Valerius likely had advance notice from his tower. Given how slow navies traveled he surely didn't face foes as often as I had to. That I'd survived even *this* long on my own and against ever-evolving odds was impressive.

The day a regiment of the Seran Army launched an assault on me would be the day I considered myself a success whether or *not* I lived through the battle. Though I wished for nothing more than to see Kenady Urien dead before my own demise, I hadn't seen the coward since he fled after mistakenly thinking he'd killed me two years earlier. I evolved past the sentimentalism of youth due to his incessant cruelty, for his destruction of everything I once held dear caused me to lose faith in humanity. If my ever-pondering mind stopped to think about it, I hated those changes about myself. The bitterness and distrust I held toward people that subsequently corroded otherwise wonderful memories of my parents and Kai was not only a heavy burden to bear, it felt like an awful flaw. A *necessary* one since it was birthed from deep scars left by the cuts of experience and cruelty, but a flaw nonetheless.

Thus, denial became my favorite companion. Denial felt like a luxurious and familiar bed; I'd visited it often and it was always so comfortable to dwell in, but my greatest fear was having to *wake up*.

Staying focused on one goal at a time helped to keep my mind off such philosophical musings. For now, that goal was just ahead in the form of an orcish fort.

It'd taken long enough to find. The cabin collapsed a year and a half ago, yet the orc stronghold was the first structure I'd come across since. Finding it was hard enough; the orcs didn't seem to rely on fortifications to live. Following them through the forest often got me nowhere, for they could smell the meat of my corpses from a distance. Even if I *did* successfully trail them, they never seemed to have a destination picked out. Orcish war parties would often roam just looking for a fight. By this point, I'd killed countless orcs simply because I'd followed them in meandering circles until finally growing impatient enough to instigate a fight. Then I'd have to start from scratch, searching the forest for signs of an orc settlement while taking the time to bring my corpses with me. The only positive out of the ordeal was that far fewer civilians wandered the forest compared to two years ago, so I didn't have to be as careful when traveling with my minions.

In either case, finding this fort was happenstance. I'd started coming across multiple orcish war parties per *day,* which seemed a lot even considering their agitated state. As I surmised, there was a reason for it. In the darkness of nightfall, I studied the fort with the intention on seizing it while crouched in the shadow of a large pine.

Moonlight spilled over the needled canopy, glowing over the orc stronghold like a beacon. The sharpened points of a wooden palisade were a collection of incisors around the open mouth of the fort, where grunts and segmented sentences echoed roughly. The shadows of raised, haphazardly built guard towers rose above the wall in four places, where human and goblin slaves watched over the fort with bows, their heavy collars connected to chains that secured them to their posts. Firelight flickered off the smoke haze that rose over the palisade from a cooking spit. A deep grumble sounded out to the right before a rumbling expulsion of gas.

"He need horse!" shouted an orc through the wall.

"No horse here!" another yelled back, just as angry. The simple-minded natures of the orcs would have amused me if they weren't such magnificently challenging foes in battle.

"Smell bad," one barked.

"He fart," another replied. "He need horse. Human meat stale."

"Maybe he sick. Smells *really* bad."

I wasn't sure whether to smile or mourn my dying brain cells.

"You smell bad and you not sick."

There was a hesitation. "Maybe I'm sick and not know it."

"Oh," the other replied, impressed, as if he'd never thought of a second option.

Another rumbling expulsion of gas echoed through the fort. It sounded like it came from a giant creature, so concern filled me. Every time I fought them, the orcs were either alone or handled human, Celdic, and goblin slaves. I'd never fought something larger than the orcs themselves.

After a third gaseous release rumbled from over the wall, one orc asked, “How we *get* horse?”

“City.”

“We far from city.”

“That's why we have no horse.”

“Sometimes horses come through forest,” another explained. “Traveler. Not soldier. Soldiers don't use horse in forest.”

“How about boar?”

“Boar comes from east. Far east, with the little people.”

“Dwarves,” another clarified.

“You been there?”

“Yes. Boar is delicious. So is dwarf. Meat the same, just as hairy.”

Another gaseous rumble. Then, “Why don't we get *boar?”*

Silence. Then came a crack in the air like someone was punched. *“I said they were in east! Are we east?”*

“Yes!” came the shouted retort. “The sun rises in east, and it rise *every morning!”*

A lengthy exhale blew through my nostrils as I listened to the resulting fistfight. When the unknown creature released gas so loud it overrode the violent fight, one orc announced, “I leave for fresh air. Don't like smell.”

Finally. The orc's reasoning for leaving the area didn't make much sense since the fort wasn't enclosed, but I had waited hours for someone to pass through the gate so I could see inside. I wouldn't complain about his illogic.

The gate had a smooth top and bottom unlike the rest of the palisade, so it was easily discernible even at night. A bright orange vertical light shone through the crack between it and the wall. Wood scraping wood echoed out like the gate had a primitive door bar. Finally, the gate shoved forth and the orc wandered out alone, just a bulky shadow against the fort's well-lit interior.

I stayed quiet in a crouch beside the tree. I couldn't kill silently so I had no plans to take the lone brute out as much as I wanted to. I simply developed a plan from what little I could see.

A large fire served as the centerpiece of the fort, surrounded by a disorderly mishmash of orcs and supplies. Weapons piled with little rhyme or reason beneath the roof of a lean-to left of the gate. Instead of sturdy structures, the orcs relied on tents and other easily assembled forms of domicile. The most complex buildings in the entire fort were the guard towers that allowed the slaves to keep watch over the wall, but even those were unimpressive. The towers were made entirely out of wood crisscrossed in a rudimentary pattern, and their most redeeming quality was that they had a wrapping staircase leading up to their tops rather than ladders. I assumed that was a necessity given the slaves had to be led to their posts.

Though the palisade surrounded everything the orcs owned, trees still grew within its grasp, many relieved of their branches. Tall pines stretched toward the skies, adorned with macabre decorations. Meat hooks hung from low branches and metal rings were installed in trunks. Suspended from them were decomposing nude mercenary corpses. The orcs hung the corpses by inserting the hook up under the lower mandible, allowing the bodies to hang for days while the brutes cut the most delectable pieces of meat off them. Many of the corpses were old and surrounded by clouds of buzzing insects attracted to the messy butchery.

Human meat stale, I mused, thinking back to the orc's words. It was little wonder the brutes could live at *all* on such offerings. I still couldn't see the creature with the gastrointestinal problem, but knowing what it was wouldn't affect my plan.

Times like these were when I longed to have access to Kai's strategic intelligence. Many times she'd gushed about particular military leaders and how they outsmarted a foe despite seemingly impossible odds to win a battle or seize land. While I had always listened to her, my interest in the subject at the time was solely due to finding her obsession endearing. I didn't have a mind for strategy like Kai did, but I recalled some of her words to me on the subject.

"Strategy is *simple,* Cerin," she'd told me amid a ramble while tapping on battle plans she recreated on parchment revolving around a war event long ago. "Use your army's strengths, limit weaknesses. Do the opposite with the enemy. The tricky part is identifying your weaknesses. Do *that,* and you can anticipate the moves of your foe because they will mean to exploit them."

"You say this like you think I would ever be a general of an army," I had replied with a smirk. "Not many people *like* me to agree to follow me to begin with. Certainly not enough of them to make *army* a correct definition."

Kai had smiled that beautiful smile and looked away, somewhat embarrassed by her passion for war. "I meant *general* you, not *you*-you."

"No," I'd commented, finding the courage to hold her gaze once she gave it back to me. "I think you meant *you.*"

Kai had changed the subject. While she'd never outright said it, her passion for war and strategy spoke wonders of her dream of leadership, particularly of leading men in battle. Perhaps she wanted it so badly because she'd grown up in a royal warmongering family. Regardless, her combination of intelligence and ambition convinced me she would have been perfect for such courageous feats if only fate were so kind to offer her the lifespan for it. Hence why the idea of coming across her in battle was so intimidating.

I purged the latter thoughts from my mind and focused on Kai's unintended advice: *use my strengths and limit weaknesses.*

I can't sneak worth a damn. I'm alone. I have nothing with which to get through that gate. I'll need the orcs to open it for me. Only then can I swarm them with corpses. But how will I get them to open the gate? Are they ignorant enough to do it if I goad them to?

My mind chewed on these thoughts for a long while as I tried to imagine scenarios in my mind and come up with a plan. The lone orc in the forest eventually wandered back into the fort, unaware of my hiding spot behind the tree but also blocking my view by closing the gate behind him.

I turned and slowly traveled back the way I'd come, returning to the army of corpses I left buried beneath the trees. If I went about this the wrong way, I could end up hanging from a meat hook rather than having a dry place to sleep.

Undeterred, I rose my corpses from their rest, preparing to lead them as close to the stronghold as possible without being discovered. With the rustling of hundreds of minions in the brush behind me, it was sometimes hard to remember that I was truly attacking an orcish fort alone.

We attack in the morning.

Twenty-four

A pink and gold glow kissed the forest as the sun yawned with a new day. A soft mist hung low over the ground, obscuring most twigs and fallen foliage. Five hundred corpses gathered in the fog, their armor creaking as their chests rose and fell with the mimicking of breaths. Otherwise, they were silent. Expectant. Staring.

I mentally willed them to stay as they were. Then, I walked alone to the fort.

The morning was brisk, energetic, and perfectly tailored to the needs of a mage. This whole tribe of orcs had not one magical bone between them, so every bit of environmental fuel was mine to play with. The rest would come later when I convinced the orcs to meet me face-to-face in battle so I could harvest their life force. By sunset, this fort would be mine.

It is inevitable.

An ocean of copper and red foliage parted to reveal the wooden palisade I'd scouted the night before. The wooden towers were all manned with slave archers. Two humans, two goblins. They would likely be a nuisance. Ranged foes were often challenging for me to defeat because I had no long-range spells, and corpses could become confused when tracking the trajectory of arrows. Additionally, the slaves of orcs tended to fight to the death. Rather than be easily convinced to turn against their captors, they believed from experience that orcs would always be victorious. Why rebel when failure would mean a brutal death and cannibalization?

I glimpsed something else concerning in the fort just before turning and leaning my back against a tree near to the gate. As I mentally prepared to go on the offensive, I tried to understand what I'd seen.

It's taller than the walls, but the walls are at least twenty feet high. All I'd seen was a massive head that rose about ten feet higher than that. The only detail I could ascertain was that its flesh was the same muted green color of the pus of an infected wound. Clearly it was the creature that couldn't contain its gas the night before, and I hadn't seen it because the size of its shadow rivaled that of the trees and guard towers.

I have an army I can call to attention many times. That creature is big, but not impervious.

I took a deep breath, then two. I thought of how wonderful it would be to have a wall surround me while I slept. Most things worth having are worth the challenge, after all.

With my palms parallel to the ground, I harnessed the energy out of the air's chill, feeling its vibration through the magical barrier as it collected and turned black. Only when my hands trembled with the power of the spells did I release them. Black magic clouded out around my boots, mixing with the fog and searching for bodies.

Sss...

Hundreds of tendrils darted around the trunk I stood behind and slithered toward the fort. I turned against the tree, allowing myself a look past the edge of its bark. The cirri did exactly what I wanted them to; they found open crevasses and raised timber in the palisade, slithering into the stronghold like sneaky little snakes.

I waited silently. Through the wooden wall came muffled grunts of confusion, then gurgling hisses as all the corpses in the fort's food supply awakened.

"Meat is alive!" came a shout that echoed over the wall.

Pandemonium ensued. I kept hidden behind the trunk as the sounds of chaos kissed my ears. Blades mutilating already dead corpses. Body parts falling to the ground. Orcs scrambling for weapons. Bones collapsing in piles. The latter made me realize the orcs kept skeletons in their camp I hadn't seen while scouting. Perhaps they used bones to craft, or they might have only kept a large garbage pile. Regardless, that was in my favor.

The sounds of battle ceased, and only heavy breaths reverberated through the cracks of the palisade. Finally, *"Why* meat come alive?"

"Maybe enemy come to us," another suggested. I assumed he meant me.

"If enemy come, where is he?" A silence. "Slaves see nothing."

A heavy snort. "Now meat is tainted with dirt," an orc complained. "Camp a mess. Slaves clean."

"Slaves watch for necromancer," came the reply, confirming my suspicions.

"Necromancer not here."

I repeated the necromantic spell I last summoned and released it at my feet. Within seconds, black tendrils raced toward the stronghold a second time.

"Magic!" an orc roared. "Necromancer *is* here! *Find him!"*

"Unchain the ogre!" another ordered.

Ah. So that's what it is.

The sounds of yet another fort battle broke out as the corpses within rose, and this time my minions seemed to put up a better fight. Many of them must have been cut down from hanging on meat hooks, and I remembered the pile of weapons the orcs kept in the fort openly available for them to use. The ear-splitting roars of orcs going berserk as minions shed their blood shattered through the air. Then, wood scraped against wood as they opened the gate.

In the western forest, the ground trembled as my waiting corpses marched forth, following my mental direction. I waited against the tree until a few orcs ran past me in their search.

Zwip.

The life shield bubbled around me, robust and glimmering white. With my scythe still on my belt, I stalked toward the orcs as they turned after hearing my spell, and two black funnels zoomed in and attached to them like leeches.

Orcs snapped with anger and clashed weapons into my protection as I harvested their energy, seeking a leeching high. At first, they massively outnumbered me, for the corpses in the fort were defeated fairly quickly. The orcs looked to surround me, so I backed toward the west, getting out of range of their slave archers and goading them out of their camp. It wasn't long before my undead army broke through the brush behind me. As soon as my minions came within range of the orcs, they hissed and gurgled with unbridled hostility, charging forth with hobbling gaits to support me in battle.

BWAAAMMM!

Coarse orcish war horns blew in the fort as the brutes called all their comrades to battle. Adrenaline roared through my veins as the trembles in the earth grew more violent. Orcs spewed forth out of the gate like a rush of vomit. A breeze of sweet decomposition blew by as my minions clashed into the orcs like a malleable battering ram of flesh and bone.

I leeched just enough to get a high, and then I recycled that energy into providing shields for my decomposing loyalists. When protected, the corpses lasted much longer against the brutes. As usual, the orcs were stronger than my minions, but the numbers of undead were overwhelming.

BOOM. BOOM.

Amid leeching, I glanced up. The orc at the other end of my funnels finally dropped, depleted of her life force. Over the heads of corpses and brutes alike, the ogre loomed. Large black eyes scanned over the battle as two orcs beside it pointed at me and screamed orders.

I harvested a life in my left hand and formed a new spell with my right. Seconds later, death magic claimed the dead. Mercenary and recent orc corpses pulled themselves up for another battle. Berserk roars echoed through the forest as orcs previously unaffected snapped upon fighting their kin.

The ogre's eyes followed the magic's path back to me. For a few moments that became stuck in molasses, we stared at one another. The beast was at least thirty feet tall, bulky with both fat and muscle. Its massive head seemed uneven in bone structure, and its black hair was so sparse and wiry it would have better served in a pubic region. A quick glance down between its legs affirmed this, for it wore no clothes at all. Though it had dangling male genitalia, wide breasts settled along the top roll of its gut with nipples as wide as saucers.

The ogre was clearly strong, but it was nude and carried no weapons. What kind of danger could it possibly pose? Then again, I thought of its gas problems from the night before and figured that with a simple lifted leg and some determination, it could convince *all* of us here to evacuate the forest.

I smirked despite myself.

The beast grumbled like it'd only been wakened from a nice nap, then waddled over to the side, avoiding the battle entirely. It threw a muscular arm vertically through the outstretched branches of a fir tree, and they broke in quick succession. With one side of the tree bare, the ogre grabbed the trunk with both hands and pushed.

Crrk!

The tree broke near its base with an explosion of splinters. The ogre tugged it in the other direction, and another crack echoed out. With a grunt and some effort, it tore the tree from the ground, leaving only a stump so rough it appeared to be growing wooden blades.

The ogre turned to glare at me again, an entire tree in its hands like a club. Then it revealed mushy yellow and brown teeth and roared, raining grimy spittle over its orc allies.

Well, that's new. Sarcasm laced the words even though they never left my lips.

BOOM. BOOM. BOOM. BOOM.

Orcs and corpses alike flew out of the ogre's way like shrapnel as it charged. Pine needles loosened from the trees and fell through the area like fluttering green and copper rain. I refreshed as many protections as I could for nearby minions as the ogre ran to me. Then I scrambled back, using another tree as cover once the brute came so close the vibrations of its feet threatened to dislodge my bones.

Whoosh! CRACK!

I tumbled forward when the tree I used for cover started to fall with one persistent hit of the ogre's favored trunk. Wood chips sprinkled to the detritus as I hurried to stand and face the brute. I fed my sharpened senses with its life force as my free hand pulled the scythe from my belt.

The ogre cranked its arm back for another swipe of the tree. I dodged to the right, avoiding the hit and running past the brute all at once. As the tree flew behind me I pivoted, tearing my scythe through the air, using the momentum of my charge as its force.

My vision blurred with movement, but my eyes caught on glimmering silver, then green, and then everything turned red as the blade clashed with the flesh of the ogre's left calf. Metal permeated my taste buds as I kept my scythe in the wound and jerked it deeper. I relied on my ears, for I could see nothing. So much blood erupted from the ogre's wound that it drenched me, obscuring my vision and weighing down my hair and hood. As I gritted my teeth, my gums tickled with excess moisture as its blood overwhelmed even my mouth. I spit to rid myself of the flavor and prepared to tear my scythe from the wound. Before I could, the ogre punted me out of its way.

I relaxed my mouth so I didn't crack teeth in the fall; instead, the lower flexible branches of a tree cushioned me, and I ended up still standing once I came to a stop, though my magical guard was one hit away from dispelling. It felt like something gnawed at both my eyes, for blood still overflowed them.

The ogre cried out with a mixture of pain and anger, and by judging the volume of its distant voice, I had a few seconds to recuperate. I released necromantic tendrils from one hand as I stumbled away from the tree's embrace, waking fallen minions from their sleep to keep the orcs occupied. Then I flipped my head back. My long hair unstuck from my face and flew back in an arc. The blood it had collected splattered over the forest debris in a line behind me with a sound reminiscent of a sudden downpour. Pinching my nose with my thumb and forefinger, I swiped at both eyes from the tear ducts out. Though red still tinged my vision, at least I could now *see*.

The ogre limped toward me, blood erupting from its left calf from a particularly angry severed artery. The wound still claimed my scythe, which was buried so deep its blade wasn't visible. Its black handle stuck by the ogre's leg just where I'd left it when the bastard flung me away like a pesky fly.

I glanced at the nearby battle. Though many orcs remained, my army had grown with their losses. The corpses on the frontlines looked the worst since they were the first subjects of ire. Many were mutilated, crushed, and missing limbs since the orcs shattered them beyond repair. The flanks of the undead were relatively unmarred, however; because my minions swarmed the orcs, many went unnoticed and thus unblemished.

I called a few of them to me, if only to serve as a distraction. Multiple minions turned away from clamoring to get to the orcs and made a beeline for the ogre. With its attention on me, it didn't notice them until a mace crashed into its right kneecap. With a confused wail, it stopped its pursuit of me to face its new contenders.

I broke out into a run, forest debris spraying away from my boots as I skidded to a stop beside the ogre's still-bleeding calf. I tugged my weapon free of the wound as the tree-club swept through my minions like they were merely granules of bony dust. It flung one corpse into a tree so hard its previously decapitated head separated once more from the body and flew through the canopies. It possibly found a new home there, for I did not hear it fall.

More necromantic tendrils released at my boots. As the ogre grunted with frustration and spun in a slow circle, I ran past it to give the rising corpses shields. The next time the beast tried bashing them with its tree-club, they stumbled but were otherwise safe.

The battle raged on. I fell into a pattern like I often did. *Leech. Shield. Raise dead. Slice. Defend. Shield. Leech. Raise dead.* I absorbed life force just to recycle it into spells or bursts of physical adrenaline. The morning crawled into early afternoon. Though my army grew with orc casualties, the ogre stubbornly refused to fall. For the first time in my life, I considered using the plague.

I'd wanted to avoid it. The Seran necromancy book had warned about the dangers of the spell, for the onset of a contagious disease could quickly get out of hand. It might even evolve to be a threat to *me.* Life spells existed to boost one's immunity to disease and infection, but I didn't know them because of my shortened education.

Using the plague was a risk, but one I would take to finish this battle.

Enflic le plague.

The air in the vicinity was stale and void of energy, but I allowed the spell to take from my life. After all, my blood hummed with excess from a long battle of harvesting. Magic the color of pestilence collected over my palm, brownish-gray and swirling with wisps of sickly green and vomit-yellow. I swore the energy even gave off a stench before I thrust it at the ogre.

The ugly spell hit the brute at the center of its chest and fanned out until the energy absorbed into its skin. As I waited to see it work, I focused on ironically protecting the dead with the element of life.

A deep gurgle rumbled in the ogre's gut. For the first time during the battle, it released a gust of gas that was followed by a spray of steaming waste. I switched to breathing through my mouth, unwilling to let the smell affect my prowess. My corpses continued fighting it, undeterred due to their lack of senses. Then, pus flowed freely from all the ogre's bleeding wounds, so clear and thin it appeared like water.

Green skin blackened in some places and distorted into open sores in others, bubbling and popping before my eyes just to leak infected fluids. I stayed back, refreshing the shields of my minions as they opened new wounds in the ogre like it was merely a pin cushion. Lethargy cursed the beast's movements until it became unsteady on its feet. An open sore erupted just below its left eye, splitting the skin of the lower eyelid until the organ protruded from its socket and dulled.

The ogre abruptly fell forward. The bloodied tree loosed from its grasp, severing an unprotected corpse in half with its crushing landing. When the brute landed in a cloud of disturbed dirt and debris, it forced such an aftershock through the area that the fighting orcs noticed. Their battle cries grew panicked.

When I raised the dead next, the ogre answered the call. Unwilling to fight in its near vicinity due to its festering disease, I simply shielded it and sent it to my army's right flank as I joined the left.

The longer we fought, the easier the battle became. The minions that turned to mush from repeated defeat crawled over the ground uselessly, but the new orc corpses more than made up for it. I found myself emboldened once my corpses flooded through the fort's gate at last. By protecting my minions and fighting by their side, I'd actually launched a successful assault. An overwhelming feeling of accomplishment washed over me as I entered the stronghold, clashing with orcs until leaving them in bloodied, mutilated piles. All my life, I'd been taught orcs were beasts to fear, yet here I was, slaughtering them.

Now, *I* was the one to fear. This intoxicating realization almost overrode the deep pit of isolation that consistently threatened to implode my chest.

Almost.

My minions swarmed the camp like ants around a fallen dessert, surrounding orcs and hobbling up tower staircases to get to the archer slaves. Three of the four slaves refused to stop attacking and were quickly cut down by the undead. I set my sights on the fourth.

The background noise of battle fell silent with victory behind me as I reached the covered floor of the watchtower. A goblin huddled in the corner, holding shaking green arms before its face and rambling nonsensically in its stilted native tongue. Wide-set floppy ears stuck out behind its hidden gaze. As I neared it, black eyes peered at me through spread knobbed fingers before it whimpered.

I took the bow from the floor by its bare feet and threw the weapon over the wooden plank that served as a low wall. With the orcs demolished, my corpses gathered around the tower, and the bow clunked one in the head in its descent. The zombie gurgled with distaste and crumpled to the ground, dispelled. I huffed with amusement at the scene before turning my attention back to the goblin.

"Where is your key?" I asked. When it lowered its hands to meet my gaze, a look of confusion snagged its ugly features.

"Your *key,"* I repeated, squatting to point at the slave collar around its thin throat.

The goblin said nothing, only ducking away from my nearness. I sighed and went back to ground level. After some searching, I found a crudely fashioned key ring hanging on the tip of a meat hook. When I took it back up to the goblin, it huddled and shook again. The third key opened its collar, and the iron ring fell to the wooden floor with a clank.

The goblin stared at me, confused. I stared right back. Despite my limited knowledge of goblins, I knew from fighting them as orcish slaves that they spoke in clicks and grunts, not words. Still, they did *speak.* Perhaps this one would understand words even if it didn't speak them.

"Free," I said, backing up toward the staircase and pointing at the fort's open gate. "You. Free."

The goblin kept its stare for a moment before it trusted the situation enough to stand. It wandered tentatively over to the staircase. To help convince it, I trotted down to the ground. With a sweep of my arm, I convinced my minions to move to the other side of the camp where I dispelled them.

With the dead back to their rest and me far away from the gate, the goblin finally ran for freedom like it still expected me to kill it. I watched it rush through bloodied foliage to the west until it disappeared and silence fell over the forest. I assumed the goblin would try its best to go home to its tribe of like-minded peers. Perhaps it would reunite with other goblins it once knew and cared for. Did goblins shed tears? Maybe there would be an emotional homecoming.

Or perhaps I was projecting my own underlying self-conscious desires.

It will do you no good to be envious of goblins.

Disgusted by my sudden sentimentalism, I blanked out my mind and focused only on preparing my newly claimed land for inevitable attack. If I'd learned anything from surviving on my own for years, it was to trust my intuition.

And my intuition promised a storm was brewing.

Twenty-five

In the seasons following the camp's takeover, my mind slowly crumbled and melted into a realm of insanity. I was *aware* of this. I understood it. I just could do nothing to stop it.

The last semblance of friendly companionship I'd had was with John, and his corpse had long ago been destroyed after repeated use in battle. How long *had* it been since I killed John? My memories were blurs. I remembered the weather had been cool and the forest had a red tint, so it must have been Red Moon. I also remembered that I was sixteen at the time. Gods, had it really been *four* years? *Four years* since I'd last had a cordial conversation where the other person spoke back?

I definitely believed the rumors that necromancers were insane now. They lost their minds because they had no choice; lives of isolation were precursors to insanity. I'd become a statistic.

The assassins and orcs were undeterred by my claiming the fort. If anything, it encouraged them to hunt me down prepared and fight particularly cruelly. The orcs always brought ogres now, and their brute strength was evident in the many places of the palisade that were worn, dented, and outright broken. I assumed ogres came from the mountains based on what little I heard about it from the orcs, so the fact that sightings of them ramped up over time told me the orcs searched far and wide for aid to help root me out of their forest once and for all.

One enemy stopped coming altogether: mercenaries. And *that* spoke wonders.

On one late-High Star evening in 416, I tugged a shoddy wooden chair up the steps of the northwestern guard tower. The tap of its wooden legs on each step overrode the footsteps behind me, albeit barely. When I reached the square floor, I set the chair down next to another more familiar seat. I claimed my usual chair and pointed to the new one. The Alderi corpse following me plopped down in it, facing me with a blank stare in her solid black eyes.

This assassin was far lighter than most. Her skin was an even mix of blue and gray, and it was free of imperfection. She seemed young enough to be a juvenile, but then again, it was hard to tell age with elves. Her shoulder-length black hair was pulled up in a ponytail, but many frizzy locks escaped and hung by her face, proof of her efforts in battle the night before when she tried to assassinate me. I knew nothing about this woman. Her name, her story, her hometown, her skills, her hopes and dreams—all of this would forever be unknown to me. I'd only picked her to follow me here because she was the freshest corpse I had in this fort. I could pretend, even for a short time, that she listened and cared about what I said.

"I apologize," I began, my voice wavering with a combination of embarrassment and disbelief of my current state, "but I desperately need someone to talk to."

The assassin didn't move or blink.

"If you were alive, I would ask you for your name," I went on, spinning the skull ring around my thumb and staring at it. "I would ask you more questions than I would answer. I never used to feel comfortable talking about myself. What was there to say? Most people judge others by their preconceived biases. I never felt convincing enough to change their minds. I didn't want to, anyway. Few people impressed me enough to inspire the effort." I thought of Kai. "Those worth the effort were determined to learn more about me as it was. That's why I'm apologizing. I'm better at listening than I am at expressing myself, but I cannot listen to you. That leaves you in the awful position of having to listen to *me,* and even before I resorted to talking to corpses I couldn't find the right words to say."

I sighed with frustration and glared off into the forest. Tree branches overlapped until the canopies were one big collective blur of green.

"I'm slowly going insane," I murmured. "And there's nothing I can do but let it happen and pray to the nonexistent gods that I'm *of* mind when I kill Kenady and *out of* my mind when I kill Kai."

The corpse readjusted in her seat. A low, raspy gurgle rose in her throat before it cut short at her tongue. I imagined her saying, *And both are coming.*

"I know," I agreed. "I feel it in my gut. I wait for it every day. After the mercenaries ceased coming, I knew Sera was preparing an army. Too many have come to this forest just to die. Sirius is sick of wasting gold on contract killers. He's the type who wouldn't blink at throwing his men at the situation instead. I expect them any day now."

The assassin tilted her head. *Both of them? Kenady and Kai? Together?*

"Gods, I hope not." I frowned and met her hollow gaze. "I will tear Kenady apart for many things, but most of the reasons revolve around Kai. Tormenting her like he tormented me, forcing me away from her and into this isolated life, destroying the note she gave me. He has destroyed my life and all the good things in it and left nothing but cruelty and despair. Yet, when Kai hunts me down, I'll have to kill her, too. Who really wins in all this?" I glanced down at my rings again. *"Sirius.* He is nothing but a puppeteer pulling strings in Sera, directing his minions to solve problems for him as he watches from his high tower. Killing Kenady will allow *me* vengeance and relief, but Sirius won't sweat the loss. Kai will likely hunt me down just to win her father's favor, but *nothing* will breathe life into a heart that's already black. I will kill the one person left in the world who ever meant anything to me, and the reasons we are enemies at *all* stem from her father who won't shed a tear when she breathes her last."

Then vow to kill Sirius. The assassin blinked once, stiff eyelids slipping over drying eyeballs.

"I can't." I reached down to clean a piece of debris from my boot. When the hard object didn't budge from the tread groove, I kept picking at it as I spoke. "I don't make vows I cannot keep. Sirius is well-protected in Sera. I would need tens of thousands of corpses to make a dent in that city. Even if I thought I could lead that many alone, I would need centuries to build an army that size. I'd need some way to get through the wall. I can direct a corpse to open a door. I can't direct thousands of them to lift a locked gate." The object finally loosened from my boot, and I studied it between two fingers. It was a piece of shattered bone. I flicked it over the half-wall before continuing, "Even Valerius didn't last that long." I hesitated and laughed dryly. *"How* did Valerius last as long as he did? Despite all my success, here I am at twenty, pretending I'm having a conversation with a corpse."

The assassin only stared.

I huffed. "Exactly." I stretched my arms out wide, and my muscles ached at just the right note between pleasure and pain. "I used to think I would forge a life for myself like this. And I *have.* But my only avenue of success isn't much of a success at all. After killing Kenady and Kai, will I have the motivation left to go on? What will be *left?* I've already proven my point. I've shown enough resistance to Chairel's necromancy ban to leave my mark on its history. The only thing keeping me going now is the intense urge to see Kenady's brains come out of his ears."

Creative. The corpse gurgled again.

"There is nothing more savagely passionate than one man ripping another apart one layer at a time," I mused as an excuse. "That is, in its own way, a form of beauty." I laced my fingers behind my head. "Might as well remove something ugly from Arrayis and replace it with beauty before my inevitable demise, right?"

The assassin turned her head in reaction to a tweeting bird on the other side of camp. *Such dark wit you have.*

I frowned and said nothing, overcome with nostalgia. Those words too closely resembled those said by a particular fiery-haired girl so long ago.

If you could have anything in the world, what would you want? The assassin blinked at me expectantly.

"A sense of belonging," I told her without hesitation. "No one has ever accepted me for the way I am. My mixed racial heritage is enough for the Icilic to hire assassins like you to kill me. My family's poverty made me an outcast in Sera as much as my appearance did. Learning necromancy has the world after me. Just owning *land* in this gods damn forest is enough for the orcs to declare war. Only three people have ever accepted me, and my parents were bound by blood. The other..." I trailed off and shoved Kai from my mind for the millionth time. Finally, I summarized, "I want to *belong* somewhere. With someone."

You belong here with us, she seemed to reply, facing the inner camp. All throughout its dirt and debris were mass graves filled with bodies. How quickly such uncivilized and macabre things became my normal.

"Yes," I agreed, "but I am the only one here." Though I'd always known that, saying the words aloud made them real. A sick feeling of despair clenched my gut.

She turned to face me again. *Yet you speak to me.*

"Yes," I murmured. I averted my eyes as I went on, "John suggested finding a band of criminals to be a part of all those years ago. The idea seemed so far-fetched, yet so attractive. Maybe one day..." I cut that thought short.

You do not trust, she reminded me.

"No," I agreed. With memories of various betrayals and cruelties flashing through my mind, I laughed low and asked, "Would *you?*"

The corpse only stared.

"I cannot trust those I can't control," I murmured, looking off over the camp's mass graves again. "And how sad of a concept that is."

But you control us, she said. *You can trust us. And there are hundreds of us here.*

I stood up from my chair, unwilling to hear it. "This is why I don't like talking about myself and my struggles," I proclaimed. "I learn new things all the time and none of them are hopeful. *Yes,* there are hundreds of you here."

I waved my hand through the air, dispelling the assassin. She slumped in her chair until she fell to the tower floor. “I am surrounded by *hundreds* of bodies, but I've never felt so fucking alone.”

*

42nd of Red Moon, 416

Even before I felt the forest's tremble, I knew today was the day.

I awoke feeling an intense lust for carnage. It started as a tremor in my bones that traveled out to my fingertips. I shook as I pulled on my armor, full of adrenaline I didn't yet have a reason to expend. Thoughts of Kenady's face flooded my mind before splashes of red overcame them.

Intuition is its own form of magic.

When I stepped outside my tent, I heard scrambling footsteps just outside the worn palisade. I stilled and listened as best as I could, but without excess life force, my hearing was normal. When all noises faded, I tentatively climbed the northwestern watchtower to scan the area outside the wall.

The trees closest to the fort were wounded or torn from the dirt by virtue of all the previous battles here. Over time, ogres gained armor and packs of war supplies as the orcs outfitted them, but they always insisted on using trees as clubs and they harvested them mid-battle. Thus, the immediate area around the palisade was soft dirt and rotting tree trunks. I could oversee it easily from this tower, and right away I knew someone would attack me today. For in the rich soil just outside the wall, multiple decomposing limbs announced their buried presence like wayward weeds. Nearby were boot prints of the person who uncovered the stash and ran northwest after hearing me stir.

At first, I loathed my decision to keep corpses both in *and* out of the fort since those outside its protective wall were so easily discovered. But such decisions were strategically made; in my previous battles with the orcs here, having corpses rise both in the fort and out of it allowed me to encircle my foes when they tried bashing their way through to me. What had Kai called this strategy?

Ah, yes. A *pincer* attack.

In either case, I didn't regret being found today. Based on the mixture of foreboding and anticipation that swelled in my gut, someone was here that I'd looked forward to killing for years. And because my foes were smart enough to scout out the area, it seemed I would deal with mercenaries rather than orcs or assassins. Unless, of course, Sirius finally deemed me enough of a threat to require sending an army.

I chuckled dryly to myself as I waited for the inevitable, staring toward Sera as the sun assaulted the forest from the east. What had bloated my ego to where I thought the Seran Army was after me? Sure, I'd grown to be the largest necromancer threat Chairel had seen in generations, but Sirius coveted his precious army. He wouldn't send it unless it was a last resort. Having official armies coming after me would mean my notoriety had reached levels I once only dreamed of. It would mean *success*. While alone and surviving in the wilderness, success was the furthest thing from my mind.

Besides, my gut promised that Kenady was here. And he'd been a mercenary just three years ago. Given his cowardly abandonment and failure to kill me, there was no way Sirius allowed the bastard into the Seran Army.

All these thoughts came to a screeching halt once the vibrations of an approaching force traveled from the boots of my enemies to mine. Breaths filtered evenly through my nostrils as I waited for them to walk into view. When they finally did, I went through a variety of emotions: shock. Disbelief. Accomplishment. Determination. Shock again. Confusion. Anger. Rage. Homicidal furor.

A regiment of the Seran Army broke through the dense brush and into the close war-torn section just outside my fort. Hundreds of men and women prepared to annihilate me while dressed in the prestigious green and black Chairel armor I hadn't come across since fighting the Twelve five years ago. Many held melee weapons. Some held bows. Most wore jewelry, and their bodies betrayed their magical predispositions. Fiery hair called out the fire mages. Strong bone structure and dark features alerted me to earth mages. Pale eyes and flesh hinted at air or life mages. Blue eyes of all shades belonged to water mages. Mages were the most challenging foes to face, and there were so many here. They were, after all, a specialty of the famous city of magic.

Then, the shock of seeing the Seran Army here faded into the aforementioned homicidal furor. Front and center of this army unit stood its general, who even now pointed to either side of my fort and directed men to surround it. The prestigious armor gifted to him by Sirius shone a sharp black in the rising sun, though its details were etched in green. Bulky, expensive rings on each of his fingers indicated great wealth and an affinity for magic use. A chain flail rested at his right hip. Beneath brown hair that he'd cut shorter since our last encounter, the homicidal furor I felt reflected back to me in cruel cold gray eyes.

Fate was a merciless and unjust bastard. I'd been forced into a life of solitude and insanity after a harmless childhood curiosity. I never wanted to hurt anyone. Yet, here I stood six years later as a broken and bitter man who had to do ugly and brutal things to survive. Contrarily, the cruel boy who wanted nothing *but* to hurt and humiliate me and force me into exile was rewarded for it. Throughout every struggle and hardship I suffered, Kenady only prospered. Though I had successes, my isolated existence kept me from celebrating them. Though Kenady had failures, they rewarded him.

Fuck fate, I decided, my vision darkening to red as I gave into rage. *Its influence on me ends today. This day ends in blood.*

Twenty-six

Kenady swept his arms out to the sides dramatically as his men surrounded my fort. "Looks like we've *both* been promoted since we saw each other last, *necromancer!*"

"I *worked* for this!" I shouted down at him, building two necromantic spells in my hands. "What the *hell* did *you* do to deserve a promotion to general?"

"I defeated you!" Kenady screamed, his voice tinged with rage. The soldiers surrounding him seemed taken aback by their general's personal vendetta and sudden outburst, but they didn't question it.

"You *abandoned* your men and *ran* like a *coward!"* I released the black magic. A dark fog rose on the watchtower floor before splitting off into tendrils. As the cirri darted through the air to the corpses in the nearest caches on either side of the palisade, the soldiers reacted and prepared for battle.

"Burn it!" Kenady ordered, his voice so hoarse with hostility it caught. *"The whole fucking place! Burn it down!"*

Whoosh!

Seemingly at once, the entire northern palisade burst into flames as multiple fire mages lit the vulnerable wood from its base. Intense heat radiated from the wall as I hurried down from the tower, recasting the death spell from both hands repeatedly as I went. As the first bout of dead rose on the exterior of the flaming wall, hundreds more magical recruiters slithered across the camp and sunk into the dirt. Only when I cast the spell again and no tendrils formed did I stop, for that meant *all* my corpses answered the call.

The earth quaked. Dirt sprayed upward in mini explosions across the fort as bodies pulled themselves out of a lazy slumber. Screams and shouts echoed from outside the wall as the army came to contend with the dead. More flames sprouted over the wall as fire mages spread the element around the barrier. Perhaps Kenady found inspiration in Valerius's historical defeat and wanted to trap me until I burned alive.

I stalked toward the gate, summoning shields and wards for my minions like they were the only spells I knew. The corpses hissed and spat with excitement for battle as they glared at the inside palisade like they could see their foes through it. I tugged the door bar out of place and generated protections for myself. Finally, I unsnapped the sheath from my scythe and hung it on my belt before gripping the readied weapon in a hand.

I kicked the gate open, and it slammed into a fire mage on its outward trek as he prepared to light it on fire. The man tumbled to the ground on his hands and knees. A gasp of fear escaped his lips when he saw my shadow rise above his own in the flickering light of the nearby fire. He tried to stand, but I stomped my left boot in his lower back, forcing him back down. With a grunt, I ripped my scythe toward his raised neck like I chopped wood. Though I had no leeching high, the curved blade sliced clean through his throat, vibrating with resistance only when cracking through the spine. Blood spurted out of the decapitation like a fountain, and his head fell to the forest floor. Pure crazed rage would clearly be a benefit to both me *and* Kenady today.

Another fire mage prepared a spell farther down the wall, but as my minions flooded northwest into the forest, she was the first foe to target. The mage lit a few corpses on fire before crumpling to the ground from a blade to the heart. I raised the mages from the dead as I followed the charge of my corpses to the northwest, my eyes biased for the armor of a general.

"Aggh!" The scream of adrenaline preceded a harsh crackling not too unlike that of a leeching funnel. I didn't have to search hard to find the culprit. An air mage spread her arms toward my onslaught of corpses, releasing bursts of flashy chain lightning into the crowd. Veins of white-hot blue and purple electricity darted from her fingertips, seeking out the moisture of blood and decomposition fluids and convincing my minions to fall into violent seizures. Dozens of corpses fell at her boots, smoking from degrading eyelids. For a few moments, she and I played a game of back-and-forth. She'd overwhelm the corpses with electricity just for me to call them to attention once again. Only when other Seran soldiers joined her in the frontlines did the mage cease her spell, for its spreading nature risked friendly fire.

BOOM!

The world blinked white and forced stars in my vision as the air mage summoned lightning from the sky. I stumbled back, my ward sizzling with a warning it would die soon. I refreshed it and sent my minions to the air mage from our distance, for her persistence annoyed me and I couldn't reach her from here. They swarmed her, finally besting her with a sword in the spine.

Over the heads of sparring living and dead, I glimpsed a flash of black. Kenady protected his men with life magic while brutalizing corpses with his flail. I put my scythe on my belt and leeched lives with both hands as I worked my way through soldiers to him. Some warriors almost impressed me with the challenge they posed and the acts of valor they committed to try to best me, but I dispatched of them carelessly. None of them mattered. They were merely hurdles to hop over. I needed to enact vengeance on the man whose hatred and wrongdoings had haunted me for six years of exile.

The Seran soldiers were challenging foes. Their armor was of a higher quality than most mercenaries and didn't split so easily. I relied on magic to fell them, using my scythe only as a backup. The black magic could slip through the tiniest vulnerabilities like gaps beneath helmets or simple tears in leather and pull lives from fleshy husks. Sometimes men would die unblemished after dying painlessly through leeching, and then they would make fantastic minions, for the same high-quality armor and weapons were now on my side.

At one point, I met Kenady's cold gray eyes from over the battle between us and thought, *It is inevitable.* I hoped the words came through my glare and settled into his mind. Necromancy was the only magic to grow in strength over time; with every minute that passed, more life force collected in my veins and more Serans rose from the dead.

Perhaps Kenady *did* hear my thoughts, for his orders to his men grew more desperate and creative. By Kenady's request, an earth and water dual caster siphoned the last of the Red Moon breeze into a challenging combination spell of mud. The thick sludge arced over my horde like a heavy stream of sewage, and dozens of my minions crumpled under its weight. Though I avoided the muck by circling around the frontlines, my corpses were far less intelligent. A few hobbled into the mud willingly, their focus on the enemies on the other side. Mud latched on to decomposing bare feet and worn boots, rendering my minions still. As I redirected the rest of the horde around the obstruction, I sent death magic through the area. Though the corpses suddenly jerked awake with new life, they were still stuck. The blanket of mud expanded and trembled as the undead writhed in its clutches, but the black magic struggled to overcome its heavy grasp.

The mud obstruction was Kenady's greatest strategy against me, for it pulled many of my minions out of the fight entirely. Unfortunately for him, I'd already made up those numbers lost with his own men. And now that his mages depleted most of the breeze from the air, environmental energy reserves were low.

Kenady stood amid the clearing just north of my flaming camp, his chest heaving with adrenaline and eyes searching for a saving grace. Blood dripped from the points of his flail, extra thick with the chill of the undead. During the battle he'd pulled on a protective helmet that showed little other than his cold eyes and a few gritted teeth. Since it was mid-Red Moon, my twenty-first birthday was just weeks away. That would have made Kenady twenty-one or twenty-two given my late start in Sera. As a child, Kenady's eyes glimmered not only with cruelty but also with a sadistic desire to hurt others. He hadn't just taunted and humiliated and ridiculed; he'd *enjoyed* it. He'd likely gone out of his way to catch me doing something wrong in Sera, if only to make my life a living hell.

As an adult, little had changed. Kenady suffered no consequences to his actions, which angered me almost as much as all of his wrongdoings against me. I *recognized* this man by looking into his eyes because he never had to change. Contrarily, I barely recognized *myself* whenever I glimpsed my reflection.

The humble kid I'd been was dead. Kenady had ruthlessly murdered him with cruelty, and he was never coming back. By treating me with the utmost disdain, Kenady forced me to metamorphose until I resembled *him*. The tormented devolved into a tormentor.

I hated him for that most of all.

"You're looking a little *pale,* Cerin," Kenady breathed, flicking his flail to clear it of some blood. It was only further proof that he refused to grow; his insults were still juvenile and petty. "Have you been eating?"

As Kenady's men clashed with my minions all around us, I strode toward him like a hunter, stepping over elemental debris and fallen weapons. An intense leeching high roared through my veins. As I grabbed my scythe from my belt, Kenady lashed out a hand, sending a spell toward the ground at my boots.

I quickly sidestepped. A pillar of rock jolted through the soil just where I'd been. I didn't taunt Kenady for missing me. I didn't need to. His face set with a look of irritation that was its own reward.

I raised the scythe over my right shoulder as I neared him, wasting no time in throwing every bit of strength and rage into its swing. Kenady scrambled back, deciding to let his magical guard take the hit.

Shing!

The white magic dulled and flickered. Kenady stumbled back a few more steps from the pressure of the hit. A flash of confused fear lit up his eyes as he realized just how strong I was. It reminded me that I'd never fought him while under the influence of a high.

"Fucking *hell,"* Kenady breathed, quickly regenerating his guard.

"That's *it?"* I provoked him, lashing out a leg to kick his shield. It dulled just a bit. "A *curse?* Where are your *taunts?* Or did you run out of them when you ran from me like a bitch years ago?"

"Fuck you," Kenady hissed, swinging his flail with sudden rage. It clashed into my shield, but the magic stayed strong. Further enraged by this, Kenady hacked at my guard with a vengeance, whittling down its strength. "I *begged* Sirius to put me in charge of this army so I could kill you like the scum you are."

"Bullshit," I retorted, refreshing my guard. "Sirius gave you this mission to prove yourself since you failed so badly the last time. Did you *really* think giving him a ring on a chain would be the proof he needed?"

A flash of self-reflection and anger crossed his eyes. It appeared I'd correctly called out his failures. "Sirius didn't end up with the ring," Kenady rambled. "I *sold* the fuckin' thing. Might as well have given it away. It was worth *nothing.* You said your *parents* gave it to you?" He hesitated just to spit. Hot saliva sprayed over the lower half of my face, tickling my jawline as it rolled toward the embrace of gravity. "Then they didn't love you, either."

Shing!

My scythe broke through Kenady's shield, the curved blade clashing into the armor just above his hip. The leather split but didn't break through. I kicked him in the gut to keep him still as I tugged my weapon toward me, trying to work it through the armor. The leather's resistance softened as the blade met the flesh beneath. Blood seeped out of the break. Because I held him still to gut him, my leg was outside of my protective guard.

Wind whistled through the chain links of Kenady's flail as he threw the weapon at my leg. I had two choices: risk my leg to try to gut him, or retreat to save my leg. With my scythe drawing Kenady's blood, I decided I would die if it meant taking him with me.

Clink!

The flail clashed into my left knee, just on the underside of my kneecap. Its nails tore new holes in my armor and punctured the soft flesh at the crease of my leg. The pressure echoed sharp pain through my knee and down my shin, and I used the agony as fuel for my next tug on the scythe. Kenady yelped as it tore through more muscle. As recompense, he ripped the flail back. Its nails tore out of new wounds, and a spray of blood and chunks of ripped flesh chased its arc. I barely felt the injury with my high, and Kenady seemed to notice this detachment with another wave of fear.

I pulled my leg back into my shield. Kenady retreated from me as he turned toward the rest of the battle and shouted, *"Men! I need aid!"*

Mentally, I willed some corpses back to me. Verbally, I said nothing. I limped in pursuit of Kenady, my hands still on my scythe as it remained stuck in his wound. I wiggled the weapon, burying it deeper in his side as he gasped in pain. When he heaved his flail back, I abruptly stopped and tore the scythe toward me, slicing the entire blade through the wound to retrieve it.

A desperate wail escaped Kenady's lips unintentionally from intense pain as the cut spurted blood and leaked digestive fluids. Hearing such weakness in the same voice that had always been nothing but self-assured and cruel worked me into a crazed fervor. I prepared the scythe for another violent swing, so focused on ending Kenady that I didn't notice his call for aid had worked.

Crrk! Crrk! Crrk!

A blur of whitish-blue flew through my peripheral vision, and with the shrill echo of ice against metal, my scythe flipped out of my grasp. I spun to face my new pursuers just to see two more ice shards shatter into pieces against my ward. Once the ice cubes fell out my vision, soldiers came into view. Minions that answered my earlier call tailed them. The battlefield behind them all was a mess of body parts and blood that glowed orange by the firelight of the burning fort; the palisade was little more than heaps of charred and fallen wood. Some of Kenady's soldiers had got inside the camp and set most of the tents and supplies on fire.

Only a few dozen soldiers were left, but my corpses also dwindled. I set hundreds of tendrils free, not bothering to repeat the spell to reach all the dead in the vicinity. It wasn't necessary. We would swarm them nonetheless.

It is inevitable. The familiar words would have brought a smile to my lips if I weren't so frustrated with being distracted from finally killing Kenady.

My corpse reinforcements caught up to Kenady's allies at the same time I retrieved my scythe from a soft blanket of detritus. One soldier decapitated a minion, taking advantage of its weakened husk to fell it in a clean sweep. A legless corpse grabbed the soldier's boot, pulling itself closer just to gnaw at his lower calf. He screeched in pain and kicked the zombie away, only to fall from a different corpse stabbing him through the knee. As he laid on the ground screaming, zombies swarmed him.

"Kenady!" the water mage who protected her general earlier by disarming me shouted, switching to a sword to help her companions fight off the dead. *"We need shields!"*

"I'm *healing!"* Kenady protested selfishly from far behind me.

The mage thrust her sword through the center of a zombie's gut before jerking it out to the side, disemboweling it. Maggot-infested intestines spilled from the wound through flaps of skin before it dispelled. Taking advantage of her distracted state, I circled the woman and kicked her in the back of the knee with my good leg.

A pained squeal escaped her lips as she fell forward to her knees. With a hoarse scream of effort, I swung my scythe in an arc meant to decapitate. I misjudged her kneeling height, so the curved blade instead crashed through her mouth. The tip exploded out the back of her skull with such force that the gore it collected on the way through came with, spraying pine needles with blood and broken teeth.

I cracked the scythe out of the side of her head at cheek level, and she fell dead with a loose lower mandible. I somewhat expected to hear words of horror from my foes, but these were Seran soldiers. They were used to such savagery because they dealt it, and they would do the same to me in a heartbeat.

I didn't waste more time on Kenady's reinforcements. As my minions surrounded them, I turned back to my target.

Kenady leaned back against a tree, life magic spreading out from his fingertips to the wound over his left hip. He glanced up as he heard me near, and his eyes fell upon the gory scene I left behind.

"Like I told you years ago," I began, my voice labored with adrenaline, "my face will be the last thing you see before I rid this world of your filth."

"I'm shaking in my *fucking* boots," Kenady spat back, his voice trembling.

"Yes," I taunted, gripping the handle of my weapon with both hands and preparing to swing, "*yes,* you are."

Shing!

Wood chips rained over brush like confetti at a party of bloodshed as my scythe crashed into the tree when Kenady dodged it. Mocking laughter burst through his lips as he retaliated. His flail shattered through my remaining shield and knocked the air from my chest, though the force wasn't strong enough to break my armor. When I refreshed the magical protection, my senses dulled; my leeching high had depleted. Normally, I took that as a cue to start leeching again to build my energy reserves, but dying from leeching was painless. I wanted to see Kenady *bleed.*

Kenady backed away from the burning fort like he thought to flee again. I pursued him into the denser forest, still trailing blood from my injured knee. Without a high, the pain was biting as open wounds chafed against armor. Kenady was tiring; rage could no longer fuel him. We broke through each other's life shields at the same time. He had no energy left to refresh his. I had energy but chose not to use it, goading him to make a brutal swing.

As the flail arced toward my face, I lifted my scythe to meet it. The clash of metal shattered through the air. Just as I'd anticipated, the head of his flail flipped around the scythe's sideways blade at the mercy of its chain. Panic flashed through Kenady's cold gray eyes as he tried to tug his weapon free.

I jerked the scythe back, pulling the flail with. Kenady let go of it, unwilling to pop his elbow out of socket like he'd done with me years ago.

"That's the difference between you and me," I announced, unraveling the flail from its grip on my scythe. "Because of everything I've gone through after you snitched and forced me to flee that gods-forsaken university, I've *grown.* I've had to survive and adapt. You've stayed the *exact same.* And because of that, you're *predictable."*

Kenady stumbled backwards and stammered, "Do you have *any idea* what they'll do to you if you kill me? Do you *know* how well they regard my family in Sera?"

Holding my scythe in one hand and Kenady's flail in the other, I pursued him as he shook in fear. "Of course I know how *well-regarded* your family is in Sera," I spat irritably. "I'd be daft to think you earned this promotion based on your own merits."

Kenady's face devolved into an angry mess. "Like you'll ever do *anything* noteworthy," he hissed. "What the fuck are you going to *do* while out here alone? Your name will just be added to the list of all the other necromancers who thought they ever were *anything.* You are *nothing.* You started as *nothing* and you will forever be *nothing.* Stay out here in the forest fucking corpses and stomping your feet down like a pitiful *child* who refuses to give in to the law. Do you think *anyone* cares? No one even knows your fucking *name.* You will *forever* be *just another necromancer."*

Rage took over. I put all my might into swinging Kenady's own flail at the helmet still protecting his head. The weapon crashed into the side of the armor with a *thud.* Kenady fell back like a dead weight, dazed. I threw his flail into the forest brush like trash and collapsed on top of him in a straddle position. As he squirmed beneath me, I grabbed his helmet and tugged. Kenady grunted with panic and adrenaline as his hands grasped at mine, fighting me as I tried to remove the headgear.

"I'll be picking your fucking brains out of my boots by nightfall," I promised him through gritted teeth. When his struggles proved too strong, I abruptly stood, grabbing my scythe from the nearby debris on my way up. Kenady scrambled on the ground, trying to follow. I stomped on his torso with my left boot. The sharp crack of a rib bone pierced the air, and Kenady's gasps muffled with sobs. Holding him still, I ignored the pain in my knee and brought my scythe down from the skies with a vengeance, targeting the break in his armor just over his left hip.

Shink!

The recently healed wound reopened. Kenady squirmed beneath my boot, rambling off a string of terrified curses as I jerked the blade through his gut until I recognized the stench of his acid. Before the blade could end his suffering by hitting the spine, I tossed it aside and straddled him again. I grabbed his helmet. He fought me, but his immense pain and failing body made him weak. The headgear slipped off his head through slick sweat, and I threw it into the brush to join his flail in irrelevancy.

Then I stood. Remembering my earlier taunt to him, I circled my face with a finger, making sure he took a good look at it. The emotion in Kenady's eyes devolved from panic to resignation.

"It's hideous," he wheezed, throwing one last insult at me.

"I could say the same of yours," I replied, raising a boot. "Thank the undeserving *gods* I have the power to do something about it."

With every insult Kenady had ever spat at me and Kai resounding through my head like a taunt, I stomped my boot straight into the center of his face. I felt his nose shatter beneath the pressure, but his skull put up resistance. I lifted the boot again.

...destitute Cerin...

Another stomp.

...snooty bitch...

Another.

...filthy fucking peasant with a hard-on for royalty...

My screams shattered through the forest, overriding the echoes of crushing bone.

...you'll be stuck all alone...

I lost count. Static memories raced through my head. Kenady's pretentious smirk when my necromancy was discovered at the university, when he knew he'd just resigned me to a life of solitude and death. His glare of pleasure when he pushed me into the pits of despair by ordering Kai's note to go up in flames. Kenady's last rant about me being nothing earned him the most stomps of all, for deep inside a thick blanket of denial I worried they were true.

Finally, I stumbled back from Kenady's corpse, my breaths wheezing with exertion. Everything was a bloody mess. Kenady's head was utterly crushed. A stew of bone, brain, and teeth settled into the bed of pine needles, the blood so thick it puddled outward rather than into the ground. Maybe at one time the sight would have appalled me. But not anymore. I found it beautiful. I looked over the gruesome scene of utter savagery and felt only immense relief. I'd killed hundreds over the years to survive and rise in power, but killing Kenady was the first time I felt pride when taking a life. It truly felt as if I'd scraped a bit of scum off the edge of Arrayis.

The ground trembled. I turned from the brutalized corpse. One Seran soldier ran through the forest, followed by my army of undead. As soon as he saw me standing over Kenady's mutilated body, he squeaked with fear and skidded to a stop.

"On your knees," I demanded, grabbing my scythe from a pool of Kenady's blood and stalking toward the soldier. When he only shook with fear, I shouted, *"On your fucking knees!"*

"Okay!" He fell abruptly to his knees. The corpses slowed to a stop in a half-circle behind him by my order, watching the man with hollow stares. The soldier noticed and glanced back, only to yelp when he recognized undead former comrades.

"Are you the last?" I asked.

"What?" The soldier looked back at me and cowered as I neared. "Y—yes. The last of this army. *Please,* dear gods...I have children. I have children in Sera. *Please* don't kill me."

I came to a stop just feet away, my bloody scythe in both hands. *"Everyone* is someone's child. You believe your ability to procreate makes you more worthy to live than anyone else?"

"No," he blurted, shaking so badly he fell forward a bit, catching himself with his hands. "I just...have a life I want to go back to. I have a wife. A home. Three children." He realized his repetition and rambled, *"Not* that this makes me more worthy, but I swear to you, if you let me go I will never serve another day in this army. I won't come after you again. I won't give Sirius information about this battle or our defeat. My family is too important. I swear on their lives, I will never fight another day."

"You love your wife," I prodded. I thought of Kai, and how my father used to look with adoration at my mother.

He glanced up at me, confused by how I zoned in on that fact in particular. "...Yes. Very much."

"Are you loyal to her?"

He frowned. "Yes. It is she who could do better, but I thank Amora she is blind to my faults."

"If I let you go, I want you to promise me three things."

He nodded frantically. "Yes. *Gods*. Anything."

"Cherish your wife. *Always* be honest with her even if the truth could hurt her feelings or your reputation. *Cherish* what you have with her because there are people who would love to have such a connection and cannot."

"Of...of course," he stammered.

"Secondly: make sure your children know of this love between you. That they *see* it and *appreciate* it."

He nodded again, still perplexed by my commands. "I will."

"Give me information, and then I will tell you the third thing I want you to do."

"Okay."

"What do you know of Kai Sera?"

A shaky exhale blew through his lips. "Not much. I know *of* her. Rumors."

"She's still alive?"

"Yes. As far as I know. There was a huge controversy some years back. An attempted assassination on her life. It confused civilians because they made no attempt on Terran, only Kai. That's when word got out that she wields all six elements. Hammerton and Nahara sent diplomats to request her skills."

"Where is she now?"

"Sera, last I heard." The soldier shrugged. "Kai has unparalleled skill, so they say, but Sirius doesn't use her."

I frowned. *"Why?"*

"I don't know. Because her power means her life will be short, it's rumored among the soldiers that Sirius uses her as a bargaining chip, knowing that he can only use her in battle so many times before her inevitable death."

I believed such rumors were true; I remembered how Sirius showed no love for his daughter.

"How does Sirius regard me?" I asked next. "I have seen no new warrants since 413."

"You're his most-wanted criminal," he informed me, averting his gaze as if just admitting it made him fear me. "Most necromancers stay on the move to avoid detection, and we defeat most eventually since they cannot heal. *You,* on the other hand..." he trailed off and swallowed so hard I heard it. "Chairel has not faced such resistance from a necromancer since Valerius the Undying. They have hosted talks about how to handle you. I don't know what the next step is after us. Kenady Urien's intel from the last battle stated that you only had dozens of corpses. Sirius thought an army of two hundred would wipe you out. We had no idea you'd grown so much so quickly. And you..." he glanced toward the crackling fire in the distance, where the fort I'd claimed awaited in smoldering ash. "You've claimed land. Again, not since Valerius has a necromancer been so driven."

"What is my bounty?"

"Twenty grand." That meant it had doubled since last I heard.

"If there is still a bounty on my head, why don't mercenaries flood this forest?"

"They don't want to," he replied. "The risk isn't worth the reward. When hundreds upon hundreds of mercenaries are killed in duty, people *notice.* News of your prowess could get out of hand. The common populace isn't supposed to know you exist, but at a certain point, word *will* get out. The government decided to handle it. Like I said, I don't know what the next step is. After today," he clarified.

"Is it possible he will send his daughter after me?"

"Kai?" he asked, before nodding. "Oh, absolutely. Rumors have it that Chairel prepares its armies for a possible war with Eteri. They don't want to waste men on a necromancer they didn't account for. Sirius might send Kai instead if he thinks she could defeat you, but then again, he seems reluctant to use her at all."

"When you go back to Sera," I began, standing up straighter and putting my scythe in its belt loop, "I want you to deliver a message."

"A...message?" he questioned. "Is this your third request?"

"Yes. Deliver a message to Sirius. I don't care whether it is in person or written if you decide to abandon the army and don't want to risk punishment. I just want Sirius to get a message, and I want him to know it's from me."

"Okay. What is your message?"

"Tell him I said to *try harder."*

I turned away from the soldier and started walking back to my ruined camp. When the man stood up and ran northwest, I didn't flinch, letting him go. The forest trembled as my remaining corpses turned and followed me. I left Kenady's corpse out to rot and get torn up by wild animals. His body was the first I'd ever rejected for recruitment to my army out of principle. After a lifetime of getting everything he wanted and all that he didn't deserve, I didn't even want his body for fertilizer.

On paper, it seemed that I had just accomplished everything I'd ever set out to do. I stayed true to every vow I'd ever made. I enacted vengeance against Kenady and served to be a persistent thorn in Sirius's side. I managed to beat all the odds and survive trauma, hardships, heartbreak, betrayal, and cruelty. I'd risen to be the most powerful necromancer since Valerius the Undying. Years ago, I recognized having only one option for my future, and I conquered every step of it.

So why didn't I *feel* victorious?

When I reached the ruined camp, I searched through the rubble for anything I could save. I went about the motions of life I'd become so used to. Part of me wished to relocate if only to avoid killing Kai, but intuition kept me from agreeing to the plan.

Why?

Perhaps like killing Kenady offered me a great relief, killing Kai would do the same. Maybe she always haunted my thoughts because she was a loose end. Like the corpses that I called to rise time and time again, perhaps I was a victim of necromancy; by dispelling the magic Kai held over my mind, maybe I could finally *rest*.

Twenty-seven

20th of High Star, 417

Green. So much fucking green.

All shades of green blurred my vision as I backed through the Seran Forest to the north. The ever present pine needles and leafy brush, the gray-green of muscular orcs, the muted green of ogres. In the seasons following the Seran Army's defeat and Kenady's beautifully gory demise, I fought nothing but the brutes. Each day I waited for this intuition to calm my soul, but each day it disappointed. In the meantime, the war with the orcs raged on.

Life force crackled off the surrounding trees, and another orc fell. A leeching high already assaulted my brain with pleasure after a long morning of battle. The orcs brought multiple ogres with them today, and now most of the corpses I'd recruited over the past moons were smushed into a fine paste near the tent the greenskins so kindly destroyed. Now, I had *nothing.* While Sirius took his damn time in Sera, the orcs had nearly done his job for him. I had no tent to put over my head tonight. The only belongings I had left were my scythe and the military satchel I'd looted from the Twelve years ago. Somehow, I'd managed to keep ahold of that. What few corpses I had left sparred with the orcs who chased me north, but they were quickly defeated.

My plan? Move north and recruit the corpses that had collected in the forest since I'd last covered the ground. Less than two years ago when the mercenaries and orcs clashed during their mutual search for me I'd made the plan to move northwest if I ever needed more bodies. After all, most mercenaries came from Sera, and they likely moved through that section of the forest first. If the orcs killed them there, that's where they'd be.

Dozens of orcs chased me. I reached out to leech from the nearest, rapidly backing over forest debris. The orc retaliated by slicing his sword at my shield, finally breaking it. Then he fell, depleted of his life force. I hesitated only to pry the sword from his grasp before adding it to my belt for the future use of a minion. Behind the approaching army of orcs, the last remaining ogre charged, its heavy footsteps sending quakes through the forest.

BWAAAMMM!

The orcish war horn shattered through the forest as if they were too stupid to keep their attention on me when I was mere minutes away from their grasp.

I glanced behind me when I realized the sunshine was brighter in this part of the woodland. Instead of more forest, the grasslands between it and the Servis Ocean appeared for the first time in years. I marveled at how beautiful they looked; after so long of seeing nothing but trees, even *grass* can be lovely.

Out of room, I told myself as my boots backed out of the foliage and into waving grasses. As the lone ogre stopped in its charge just to roar, its head quaking with the effort, a second thought added, *Time to recruit.*

I put my scythe back on my belt and recited a familiar spell. Magical barriers vibrated against my palms as black energy collected. I thrust the energy to the ground, and the fog blanketed over the grasses before hundreds of tendrils raced out from my boots. Most of the cirri headed into the forest's border where I assumed most corpses would be.

The earth trembled. A few orcs clumsily tripped over fallen branches in the woodland ahead, but I was used to this. I tugged the scythe from my belt just as my corpses heeded the call.

As I'd surmised, most of the dead here were little more than skeletons, having decomposed for the better part of two years. Some were more recent and leaked decomposing sludge as they shambled loyally to me. One orc skeleton that hobbled up to my left had no weapon. I reached behind me, grabbing the orcish blade I'd looted earlier and handing it to the minion. It took it gratefully before turning to face the oncoming horde.

My newfound allies hissed and gurgled as they met the orcs in battle, and I happily joined them. For a while, I didn't leech at all; I only fought with my scythe, chopping through limbs and tender flesh. When my senses started to fade with the depletion of my high due to battle fatigue, I leeched again with one hand while using my weapon in the other.

Like always, it became a pattern. I switched between magic and melee, only changing it up when I needed to pull defeated minions back to battle or shield them. The ogre finally waddled out of the woods and roared so loud the nearby trees quivered.

Didn't intimidate me the first time, I mused internally, standing still as I prepared to call fallen undead back to the fight. *Won't intimidate me now.*

The ogre was similarly unfazed, using its tree-club to bash my minions. I kept them shielded and focused on harvesting its life force. After all its orc comrades fell dead around it and the ogre became our only foe, its frustration turned to fatigue. Its movements slowed, its former energy rushing through my veins as additional power.

Then came something I hadn't anticipated. The ogre abruptly stilled like it was paralyzed, and it wavered like it would fall. I frowned and scrambled back, directing my minions to do the same to avoid its trajectory. The beast fell into the hot, dry grasses, the vibration rattling the bones of my skeletons. Dirt clouded around its body, coating the undead in a thin layer of brown dust.

I stared at the ogre for a moment. I'd fought many of them, so as far as I knew this one hadn't yet been ready to die. But my corpses made no move to hit it, so it was dead.

That's when I noticed the arrow.

A single pearl-white Celdic arrow stuck out of the ogre's spine just between two vertebrae. With my face protected in the shadow of my hood, my eyes followed the direction of the arrow back to the edge of the forest until they fell upon four people.

Suddenly, I couldn't move.

Three of them stood just within the forest's shadow. A Celd holding a pearl-white bow to match the arrow watched me with a conflicted and worried expression on his youthful face. He appeared my age, but I didn't trust the ages of elves. Locks of sienna hair swept over his pale pointed ears and a forehead free from imperfection. The archer was likely my height, maybe an inch or two taller, and he wore silver and green armor with a shield emblem over the heart. The emblem said something, but I couldn't read it from here. Regardless, the armor looked expensive. *Royal,* even.

A human stood just to the Celd's right, watching me with an open but unreadable expression. Though he was likely five to six inches shorter than the Celd, he had muscular arms and an intimidating disposition. His rough leather armor indicated he was a mercenary not unlike the hundreds I bested over the years. Shoulder-length dark brown hair was segmented with excess grease from sweat and travels without bathing. His skin was tanned with outdoor labor or travel and creased across the forehead in the way that only time creates. I estimated his age to be forty or so, but he was lucky to have made it that far, for a long, thick scar protruded from over his right eye and continued down his cheek. He carried two identical swords, a bow and scabbard, and a satchel larger than most for supplies. Stubble shadowed his jaw, and a maroon cloak hung through a loop on his belt.

Most surprisingly, an Alderi woman darker than most sent to assassinate me stood beside the human. They shared the same height. Her skin was a deep mixture of warm purple and black. She wore dark armor like that of the assassins who often hunted me down; it was lightweight and meant for quickness and flexibility. As if to further prove she was an assassin, two black dagger handles stuck out of sheaths on her belt. The Alderi was thin but also shapely with a figure like an hourglass. She hid most of her skin, however, like it would curse her to allow any of it to see sunlight. A black hood was tugged up over her head, almost hiding chin-length black hair and an androgynous face. Solid black eyes holding a mixture of mischievous curiosity and intrigue lingered in their stare and rolled over me from head to toe, like she either found me attractive or sized me up for a fight.

These three people were interesting and mysterious enough without considering the fourth who had me paralyzed with shock and walked toward me with all the confidence in the world. I felt light-headed, for I stopped breathing once the inhale refused to slip past the lump in my throat.

Kai Sera strode across the long grasses like she owned them and could make them bow to her will. Her pace was slow, methodical. Calculating. Her fiery hair glimmered gold in the unrelenting High Star sun until it flickered like flames. Despite the heat she wore it down, and it swished across her mid-back as she walked. She wore a nice lightweight set of armor, but it wasn't as prestigious as I remembered Terran's being, nor did it have the standard Chairel green. It was only black. In the six years since I saw her last, Kai had grown from a juvenile into a woman. Her svelte body blatantly lied about her inner strength. A modest chest aided her perfect confident posture, but she had a natural sway to her gait by virtue of shapely hips. Bulky silver rings adorned most of her fingers. Other than a military satchel, she carried nothing. Golden eyes bored right through me with a hesitant but curious expression.

Just like that, I've become undone. The walls I'd so carefully erected around my heart cracked like spiderwebs at their bases. All the bravado I'd convinced myself I had when it came to facing her dissipated until I felt like a pathetic juvenile. My heart thudded so hard against my ribs I heard it. I wanted to recoil into my hood, if only that meant I could avoid the inevitable and slip by her unnoticed.

Kai stopped just meters away from me. For the moment, she said nothing, only looking over the skeletons that stood beside me like loyal guardians. There was no fear in her golden eyes. Only curiosity. As the skeletons met her stare, I took the time of distraction to tilt my face further down in my hood and sharply inhale as quietly as I could. As new oxygen fed my greedy lungs, the lightheadedness dissipated in a flush of warmth.

Those intelligent metallic golden eyes flicked to me. Wandered over my chin and upper neck to linger like they did years ago. Back then, I hoped her stare to be one of attraction. Now, I simply didn't know what the hell to think, so I thought nothing. I only stood deathly still as Kai looked over my armor, noting its silver adornments, the scythe still dripping with blood, and then my rings. She seemed most interested in the skull ring on my thumb. I wondered if she somehow connected it to the mercenary I looted it from years ago.

I swallowed hard and finally spoke, repeating the same words to her I offered to every mercenary group that had ever come to kill me. “Leave me at peace, and no harm will come to you.”

Kai seemed surprised at hearing my voice. Perhaps she'd forgotten it. She hesitated a moment, and her shoulders quivered back a bit like she shivered. She replied, “I promise you, I mean you no harm. I witnessed the—”

“Serans mean me *nothing* but harm,” I interrupted with irritation as I realized she meant to manipulate me. It was as I always feared. My words to the sole Seran survivor from the fight seasons ago came back to haunt me. I taunted Sirius to try harder. Despite his absence and distance to Kai throughout our friendship, he must have found out later on how close we'd been. What an *ingenious* idea it was to manipulate my emotions to make it easier to capture and kill me. Sending mercenaries and armies after me hadn't worked, so he sent the only person left alive I loved.

Ingenious, I mused again, mentally hearing her words repeat on her husky voice and becoming frustrated with how it affected me even still. *Cruel.*

I blurted impatiently, “Just admit you are here for the bounty your father put upon my head and be done with it.”

Kai stilled. Blinked. Once, twice. Her golden eyes flicked to the forest and then back to the pale skin of my upper neck. Thoughts fought for prominence behind her gaze before she breathed, “Cerin.” It was an exhale of relief and a bewildered statement all in one.

“You could be an actress, Kai. You sound surprised.” I tilted my head slightly with challenge. Kai had always been intelligent, but she had to know that I wasn't stupid.

“I am surprised,” she replied, her eyes rolling over me again. “I'm shocked, actually.” Kai hesitated, and her eyes widened with sudden realization. “By the gods, it all makes sense now.”

I said nothing.

“You must have practiced necromancy at the university,” Kai prodded. “They caught you, didn't they?”

I huffed dryly and allowed my impatience to form my next words. “I have no time for your act,” I insisted. “Get it out of your head that you're going to capture me, or prepare to die. I have no plans to return to Sera.”

A guarded expression took over the curiosity on her features, and she quickly replied, “Neither do I.”

I glanced over Kai's shoulder without moving my head as I realized her companions slowly approached us from where they had stayed back in the forest. They seemed concerned for her welfare, like they hadn't counted on my threats. That confused me since Sirius sent them here to kill me.

"Like hell," I retorted, calling out Kai's lie. "They welcome you there."

Kai's eyes flashed with offense. She straightened and replied, "They used to welcome me there before I refused my duty and escaped. Don't pretend you understand who I am today, Cerin, when you haven't seen me in years."

That felt like a punch in the gut. In a cloud of silence, I repeated her words in my head, trying to understand them. *Refused her duty? What duty?* My mind stuck to one word in particular: *escaped.* If Kai told the truth, what had she escaped from?

"You're right," I finally agreed. "I don't know who you are, and you don't know who I am." Though I stood still, my heart roared in my ears in a desperate request to ask Kai for more. My brain cursed my heart's stupidity and warned me against getting involved.

My heart won.

"Humor me, then," I said. "Why are you here, if not for my bounty?"

"Not for you," Kai answered bluntly, before glancing east toward the Cel Mountains. "I'm headed to Whispermere. I have reason to believe I have biological family there."

Whispermere. I remembered the mysterious cult village I visited by accident before going to Brognel, with its submissive men and domineering women. I also remembered just how interested Kai was in finding out her origins since she felt unloved and unwanted in Sera.

A pang of sympathy sliced through my chest. I remembered proposing she find her birth parents so she could understand her magic skill. Perhaps find a cure for her short lifespan. I had also suggested using necromancy to reverse magic's draining effects on her health. And here Kai was, still speaking to me as skeletons surrounded me like she barely noticed them. Was it possible my friendship and advice had affected her more than she let on? Was it possible that Kai was truly as open-minded as she seemed all those years ago? Was it possible...

I cut those thoughts short and finally replied, "I have been to Whispermere. If you have family there, you may not like what you find."

Kai frowned. "You were there? Why?"

"I move around," I replied vaguely, unwilling to give away more than necessary. "I was there. They wouldn't let me in, but they didn't banish me like most. They allowed me to trade with them outside the gate and sent me on my way." I paused, frustrated with how much I babbled on in her presence. "It's neither here nor there. The fact remains that you are on this personal mission, and yet you stopped to speak to me. Why?"

Kai huffed like her answer should be obvious. "Because I just witnessed one man single-handedly demolish an army of orcs and come out of it no worse for wear." It was as if seeing me use illegal magic wasn't even a consideration to her. In six years of using necromancy I hadn't met someone so fearless and openly accepting. "I like to surround myself with capable people. I wanted to ask you to join us."

I had little time to feel the genuine shock from that statement before the Celd archer abruptly stepped forward and grabbed Kai's arm. "Kai, you must be jesting," he protested. "Former friend or not, he is a necromancer. You would doom us all."

There it was. *That* was the response I expected from any normal person. Not acceptance. Expectation of isolation and banishment.

"You forget that I am a necromancer as well," Kai retorted, giving the Celd an even stare.

"In name *only,"* the Celd argued. "You do not practice."

"As I'm sure Cerin wouldn't if he would ever be discovered," Kai reasoned. I had flashbacks to being a juvenile when she defended me from ridicule. "And besides, I am already on the run from my father. It is not like I'm still on the good side of the law."

On the run from my father. Those words swirled around my head, followed up by the just-as-important admission that Kai considered herself a criminal. Could it be that my intuition guided me to salvation rather than utter ruin? What if our paths crossed just to join?

My brain overrode my heart to remind me pointedly, *It is a ploy! This is all said to manipulate you!*

The Celd broke through my thoughts to argue with Kai. "You are on the run from him because you disobeyed his orders and fled recruitment to his army. A much lesser charge than harboring a necromancer!"

I could believe Kai disobeyed Sirius's orders. That amused me. It seemed Kai had grown more rebellious over the years. It was a welcome development. Sirius deserved every bit of resistance she gave him. What I couldn't believe was that Kai refused to join the Seran Army. Years ago, that had been *all* she talked about. Her only future, she once told me, was in warfare.

"I told you weeks ago, Silas, that you were no longer under my father's rule," Kai said authoritatively. *Silas.* The name repeated in my thoughts a few times before I remembered where I had heard it before. *Silas Galan,* I mused, connecting his fancy armor emblem to the memory of Kenady taunting me that royalty attracts royalty. *Kai's lover.* It made sense. The concern in the Celd's eyes was intimate, personal. Kai continued, "If you disagree with my decisions, feel free to cut your ties with me and go."

The two stared at one another. Silas's gaze was concerned, panicked, worried. Kai's was defiant, unrelenting. A flash of crippling attraction rolled through me from her audacity before I quickly dismissed it.

It is a ploy, my brain warned.

Kai is just as you left her, my heart argued like a desperate plea.

Finally, Silas broke away from Kai's stare. "Do what you must," he murmured, conflicted, dropping his hand and standing back more guarded than before.

Kai turned to face me. For the first time, I met her gaze directly, no longer hiding within my hood's protective embrace. Warm sunlight hit my lower face. We stared at one another for a moment. Those golden eyes burrowed straight into me, finding the tragedies and dark secrets I'd collected over the years. She visibly swallowed, and emotion clouded her eyes. Was it sympathy? I didn't know. I wasn't good at reading expressions. Corpses often had none.

"Join us," Kai requested. On her courageous, husky voice, it sounded like a command.

"What do you offer?" I asked, stalling to have time to think.

"A cut of the money we make, all loot we acquire." She blinked and added hesitantly, "Work. Adventure. Friendship." A slight tinge pinched her cheeks as if she found the last word embarrassing.

I smirked, finding her sudden vulnerability endearing despite my best efforts not to. "You must think I am so quick to trust."

"No, I can see you're not," Kai admitted. "That hurts me, given our past."

Our past. She said it like our innocent friendship and flirtations left as much of an impact on her as they did on me. A desperate longing cluttered my chest. Kai offered me everything I lost and so vehemently wanted.

I am no longer that innocent and humble child. I am a broken man.

How much did Kai know about what I'd been through? After seeing me wield necromancy, she knew I was a criminal. But her distance from Sirius indicated she wasn't privy to all his dealings. Of course, she had never been close to him years ago. Had she any idea how wanted I was? Had she any clue all the things I'd had to do, all the people I'd killed to survive?

Even if you accept my necromancy, you may not accept my crimes.

If this was all a ploy to capture me and take me back to Sera, it worked flawlessly. All it took was Kai hinting that she accepted me despite my sins and offered me everything I sorely missed. In her presence, my mind that teetered on the edge of insanity took a step back into safer territory like I had some hope of reclaiming a life of normalcy. She was my greatest weakness.

"I do accept it, though," Kai went on, as decisive as ever. "I will earn your trust. In the meantime, if you ever suspect anything in the slightest, you are free to leave."

Then, I made either the greatest mistake or the best decision of my life. While staring directly in Kai's eyes to judge her expression, I waved my hand casually in the air, and the skeletons dispelled. A mixture of emotions passed through her golden orbs as the bones clattered to the ground. *Relief. Happiness.* And one particular emotion I'd once been so acquainted with but hadn't felt in years, the same emotion that desperately crawled on broken knees toward my blackened heart and begged me to reconsider banning it from my life.

Hope.

Deciding to join Kai when I couldn't trust her intentions could get me killed, but I wouldn't be able to live with myself if I let her go. I told Kai years ago that no matter what she decided to do, she had the drive and skill to do it well. If she told me the truth about rebelling against Sirius, our goals aligned far more than I ever could have hoped for. With Chairel's most-wanted criminal necromancer and the mage of the six elements teaming up, there would be no limits to what we could do.

"Very well," I agreed, noting that it was relief and excitement, not anxiety, that flooded through me once I said it.

Kai smiled that beautiful smile, though this time uncertainty tinged it. My hostility had caught her off guard, but courage kept her trudging forth regardless. Why did she insist I join her? To finally gain Sirius's favor by helping him defeat me, or because she honestly wanted to befriend me again after all these years? For now, there was only one thing I knew for sure.

This could get interesting.

Thank you for reading Cerin Heliot's origin story! If you already read the completed *Six Elements* series, I hope his criminal uprising was just as savage and interesting as you imagined. If you haven't read the *Six Elements* series, Cerin's story continues in *Fire,* Book 1. *The Six Elements* is a military epic fantasy series that follows the War of Necromancers through Kai Sera's eyes, from the events that serve as its catalyst (*Fire*, Book 1) to its bloody and world-altering conclusion fifteen years later (*Death*, Book 6). A teaser of *Fire* is included after the timeline!

Coming up next in *Fire* (The Six Elements Book 1)...

Kai Sera is the greatest asset of war that exists. In a world where most mages only have the ability to wield one element, she wields them all: fire, earth, water, air, life, and death. Though she is raised as royalty by an adoptive father at the prestigious Seran University of Magic, he refuses to put her skills to use in his army, so Kai breaks free of her bonds to go on a quest of adventure and self-discovery.

One simple quest will turn into a life-changing phenomenon for Kai and her companions. Beliefs are challenged. Old secrets are unearthed. Legal lines are crossed. Loyalties are divided. The seeds of rebellion are planted. When it comes time for Kai to face the truth, a legend will be born.

Rise of a Necromancer Timeline

407 - *Rise of a Necromancer* begins (14th of New Moon)

410 - Cerin Heliot and Kai Sera become friends (23rd of New Moon)

410 - Kai discovers she can wield six elements. (New Moon)

410 - Kenady Urien reports Cerin to authorities. Cerin flees Sera (79th of Dark Star)

411 - Cerin makes it to Thornwell. Cerin's first leeching high triggers during the battle with the Twelve. Learns the fate of his parents (3rd of High Star)

411 - Cerin visits Whispermere (39th of High Star)

411 - Cerin acquires his scythe (45th of High Star)

411 - Cerin's battle with vampire (59th of High Star)

411 - Cerin visits Brognel for supplies (61st of High Star)

411 - First mercenary group finds and fights Cerin. Cerin's bounty is 5,000 gold (31st of Dark Star)

412 - John's arrival and betrayal (early Red Moon)

413 - Battle with Kenady Urien and mercenaries. Kenady destroys Kai's letter and steals Cerin's sentimental ring. Cerin's bounty is 10,000 gold (17th of High Star)

413 - First attempted assassination by Alderi, hired by Icilic supremacists (13th of Red Moon)

414 - Orc war party attempts to loot Cerin's cabin and burns it down. Orcs declare war (31st of New Moon)

415 - Cerin scouts out orc stronghold and seizes it by swarming it with corpses (79-80th of Red Moon)

416 - Battle with Seran Army. Army destroys Cerin's fort. Kenady Urien is finally defeated. Cerin learns his bounty is 20,000 gold and that he has risen to be Chairel's most-wanted necromancer. Cerin taunts Sirius with a message to *try harder* (42nd of Red Moon)

417 - *Fire (The Six Elements Book 1)* begins (34th of New Moon)

417 - Cerin agrees to join Kai north of Seran Forest (20th of High Star)

Teaser of *Fire*...

The mysterious man stood in the same place he'd been in, his head tilted down beneath his black hood. His right hand reached for his scythe, pulling it off his belt as the ground near his boots broke.

Crack! Dirt erupted from the broken earth, before a single, bony hand rose from the ground, followed by a forearm, then a humerus. Dark energy connected the bones in the place of muscle and tendon. The arm bent at its elbow, the hand falling to the ground to help push the rest of the skeleton out of the earth.

It was only when I felt light-headed that I realized I'd stopped breathing. Before us, in dozens of places in the field and along the outer edge of the forest, the dead were rising. Skeletons of humans, orcs, and animals alike rose from their slumber to heed a necromancer's call. Partially decomposed corpses gathered around their master, leaking a sludge of brownish-yellow fluids as they shambled into place. One particularly bloated zombie was missing its entire right leg, but was still determined to heed the request and crawled slowly toward the man in black, leaving a trail of decomposition from the stump at its hip.

My eyes were glued to the sight. This was the type of thing I'd been fascinated with reading about my entire life. Here necromancy was, just before me. Somehow even more intriguing and gruesome than I could have ever imagined. In seconds, one man had raised an army willing to fight blindly against all the odds against an ordinarily unstoppable force.

The necromancer reached behind him, pulling a long, orcish sword from his belt, possibly looted from an earlier enemy. Moving his head to his left and away from us, he held the blade out to the nearby skeleton of an orc. As if the orc could read its master's thoughts, the skeleton reached out, taking the sword and readying itself for battle.

Then, the horde of orcs broke through the border of the forest, spreading out over the field like a green plague. The sickly hisses and gurgles of the undead rose as a collective battle cry to meet the roars of the orcs as the two small armies collided.

The necromancer fought among his minions, clashing his scythe with orcish metal, switching from one-handed to two-handed as he utilized magic and melee. All around him, the dead fought with limitless energy and no fear. Though the dead were plentiful, they weren't nearly as strong as the heavily muscled orcs. The skeletons could shatter in an explosion of bones with one heavy strike of a club, and it happened numerous times, leaving the ground scattered with bones from various bodies. A few orcs were deceased, fresh blood staining the grasses below. The undead, however, were much fewer in number. Those that had lasted this long would loot weapons off of the dead orcs, equipping themselves with better weapons as they became available as if they had the brains to plan.

The *clang* of metal called my attention back to the necromancer himself as he held his own against a hulking beast of an orc with a two-handed ax. The hooded figure switched from using his scythe with both hands to just the right hand before he thrust his left arm out. The crackling noise from earlier popped and sizzled in the air as a fog of black energy siphoned through the air from the orc to the man.

He's leeching. It was a sight to behold. The man had raised an army, fought alongside it, and now regenerated the energy he'd lost with the enemy's own life. As the energy rapidly seeped from the orc's chest, the brute became slower, clumsier. Finally, with no wound on his body from an enemy weapon, the orc fell, dead, its life harvested from its very soul.

More orcs fell, and even more undead. It was now the necromancer and just a handful of undead against a dozen or so orcs, though more enemies piled out of the forest. The shambling footsteps from earlier shook the ground until a giant monstrosity of a creature exited the woods and let out a deafening roar.

I stared at the creature, stiff from shock. The word *ogre* came to mind, but I wasn't sure why. Perhaps I had seen a drawing of the creature. Either way, it was one of the ugliest things I'd ever seen. Its head rivaled the trees at the edge of the forest, so the creature was at least thirty feet high. Its skin was also green, though it was a lighter, milkier color than its smaller orc allies. It was muscular and fat all at once, its eyes spread far apart on either side of its massive head and uneven in both shape and size. It suffered from such a hunchback that the ribbing of its spine stuck through the skin of its upper back, the bone brown with exposure. It wielded a club that was simply three meters of a tree trunk, the bark still attached. Thick leather straps over its shoulders and around its waist led to a backpack of sorts built out of wood where it carried war supplies and extra weapons. It also wore a pathetic excuse for a waist cloth, the short pieces of fur and leather not doing enough to hide the creature's dangling genitalia.

The necromancer barely moved as the ogre roared again, so loud and brutally that it shook the trees nearby and sprayed the creature's brownish saliva in multiple directions. Without flinching, the man lowered both arms toward the ground. The same black energy from earlier formed and released in tendrils, though this time, they stayed above ground, attracted to the fresh corpses. The bodies of the orcs rose again. Living orcs nearby were either enraged or afraid at witnessing brother and kin rise against them, and their battle cries became desperate and angry.

The rattling of bones called my attention back to the ground, where black tendrils dragged the bones of the original army back together over the distances that they'd been separated. All the skeletons that had their pieces scattered were put back together and rose for a second battle. The decomposed zombies, some of which had been splattered in multiple chunks of flesh and acid, spliced back together via the dark magic.

Just like that, the undead army was not only put back together again, it was doubled, and the intimidating act of using their own against them worked in the necromancer's favor. Orcs were distracted by having to fight their own and made mistakes that quickly got them killed. The ogre, however, remained unfazed. He shambled forward, swiping his trunk-sized club across his path, scattering a handful of the dead, exploding boils of zombies and scattering bones. The giant's attention was on the man, and his undead minions understood this. As they slaughtered orc after orc, the dead moved in to protect their master, rushing the ogre in such a way that any creature with a brain would know was suicide. Skeletons hacked away at the ogre's shins with orc weapons, and even the zombie with no leg from earlier had a hold on the giant's foot, gnawing with gusto at his heel.

The ogre paid no mind to this. With his eye on the collection of undead before him, he raised his club for another swipe. Then, the necromancer pulled another surprise out of his hat.

He thrust his hands toward the group of undead, just as the club was in its downward arc toward scattering them all. One by one, a glowing, clearish-white orb surrounded each of them before the impact of the club. This time, the club hit but was met with such resistance that it might as well have hit a stone wall. The skeletons and zombies stumbled back a few feet from the impact but were otherwise unharmed and continued to fight.

He's shielding them. I was outrageously confused. That was impossible. Wasn't it? Shielding was a life spell. The necromancer had clearly used death magic, and now he used the element of life.

In all my studies at the Seran University, I'd never heard of such a thing. Life and death were the rarest elements. It was unusual enough for someone to have access to one, and I'd never heard of a mage who could wield both. Of course, I supposed that even if they could, they wouldn't. Given that necromancy was banned, if a healer could also use death magic, he or she may never know it.

Either way, now that I knew this mage was a dual caster capable of both life and death magic, I was both intrigued and terrified. He just may as well have been unstoppable. Now, I almost felt sorry for the ogre. It had no chance.

The necromancer ensured he kept his minions shielded with an outstretched left hand, before holding his right out toward the ogre and leeching from its life. The creature swiped at the undead again and again with its club but became frustrated as it got nowhere. For each swipe was mostly negated by the shields, and its own life energy was being used against it, being sucked away from its body just to fuel its enemy's defense.

The minutes dragged on as the giant refused to give into its fate, despite becoming fatigued. By this point, the fight had lasted the better part of an hour, and one would have never have figured it given the energy of the man clad in black. The necromancer hadn't lost a thing. He'd regained everything he had lost through the smart use of his magic.

He would be an amazing ally. Despite knowing I shouldn't feel such a way given the law of the land, I did. And as the ogre swayed, light-headed and weakened, I stood up in the forest, my legs screaming with aches from maintaining the same crouched position for so long.

"Silas," I said, watching the fight before me come to a close. "Loose an arrow."

Silas stood up just in front of me. "At which one?"

The question amused me. I understood why he'd asked it. "The giant."

Silas took a step toward the edge of the forest so his arrow would be free of any obstruction. He pulled an arrow from his quiver, raised his bow, and nocked his ammunition. Eyeing the ogre in the field ahead, he tilted the bow upward.

The arrow flew, barely making a sound as it arced toward the giant. Silas's aim was true; the arrow pierced the skin between two vertebrae of the ogre's spinal cord, paralyzing him. The giant stiffened and began to fall. The necromancer and his army scattered around the corpse's trajectory. When the ogre hit the ground, the earth shook and dirt clouded upward from the edges of its body, coating the nearby skeletons in brown dust.

The necromancer stared at the ogre's back and noted the pearl-white arrow that stuck out from it. He glanced toward us, his face cast in shadow. A wisp of pure black hair waved out of the bottom of his hood. The minions still nearby turned their attention to us, but they made no move to attack. None of them made any movement at all.

I walked forward on aching legs, emerging from the forest to show myself and try to establish trust. I heard the others behind me warning me and cursing me in hushed tones, but I paid no mind. I took a chance on this man not being as insane as some of the necromancers of legend. I was all too aware that despite being unable to see his face, he could see me. He knew what I looked like. If he didn't kill me here, he could find or follow me, and I wouldn't have been able to pick him out of a crowd.

But it was a chance I felt I needed to take, regardless.

Made in the USA
Las Vegas, NV
27 December 2020

14877778R00240